BROOMSTICKS

'PERFECTLY MUTE AND STILL'

BROOMSTICKS
& OTHER TALES
By WALTER DE LA MARE
WITH · DESIGNS · BY · BOLD

CONSTABLE & COMPANY LTD.
LONDON ℰ ℰ MCMXXV

PRINTED IN GREAT BRITAIN BY ROBERT MACLEHOSE AND CO. LTD.
THE UNIVERSITY PRESS, GLASGOW.

THE author makes his grateful acknowledgments to the editors of *The Atlantic Monthly, The Flying Carpet, G.K.'s Weekly, Number One—and Number Two—Joy Street, The London Mercury, The Virginia Quarterly* and *The Yale Review*, in which certain of the stories contained in this volume first appeared.

THE Cat sat in front of her looking-glass;
   A-whispering was she—
" If I *told* a tale as long as that,
   How tiresome I should be!"

CONTENTS

A

PIGTAILS, LTD.

 HOW such a very peculiar notion had ever come into Miss Rawlings's mind, even she herself could not possibly have said. When had it come? She could not answer that question, either. It had simply stolen in little by little like a beam of sunshine into a large room. Not, of course, into an empty room, for Miss Rawlings had many, many things to think about. She was by far the most important person in the Parish, and everyone—from Archdeacon Tomlington and his two curates, Mr. Moffatt and Mr. Timbs, down to little old Mrs. Ort, the humpbacked charwoman who lived in the top attic of a cottage down by Clopbourne (or, as they called it, Clobburne) Bridge—everyone knew how *practical* she was.

But once that sunny beam had begun to steal into Miss Rawlings's mind and into her life, it had lightened up with its dangerous gold everything that was there. It was nevertheless an extremely fantastic notion, because it could not possibly be true. How *could* Miss Rawlings ever have lost a little girl if there had never been any little girl to lose? Yet that exactly was Miss Rawlings's idea. It had flitted into her imagination like a nimble, bright-

3

feathered bird. And once it was really there, she never hesitated to talk about it ; not at all. ' My little girl, you know,' she'd say, with an emphatic nod and a pleasant smile on her broad face. Or rather, ' My little gal '—for she always pronounced the word as if it rhymed with Sal, the short for Sarah. This too was an odd thing ; for Miss Rawlings had been brought up by her parents with the very best education, and seldom mispronounced even such words as ' Chloe ' or ' Psyche ' or ' epitome ' or ' misled.' And so far as I know—though that is not very far—there is hardly a word of one syllable in our enormous language (except shall and pal) that is pronounced like Sal ; for Pall Mall, of course, is pronounced Pell Mell. Still, Miss Rawlings did talk about her little girl, and she called her her little gal.

It never occurred to anybody in the Parish—not even to Mr. Timbs—to compare the Little Gal to a gay little bird or to a beam of sunshine. Mrs. Tomlington said, indeed,—and many other persons in the Parish agreed with her,—it was nothing but a bee in Miss Rawlings's bonnet. But whether or not, partly because she delighted in bright colours, and partly because, in fashion or out, she had entirely her own taste in dress, there could not be a larger or brighter or flowerier bonnet for any bee to be *in*. Apart from puce silk and maroon velvet and heliotrope feathers and ribbons, and pompons and rosettes, Miss Rawlings's bonnets always consisted of handsome, spreading flowers,—blue-red roses, purple pansies, mauve cineraria,—a dizzying little garden for any bee's amusement. And this bee sang rather than buzzed in it the whole day long.

You might almost say it had made a new woman of her. Miss Rawlings had always been active and positive and good-humoured and kind. But now her spirits were so much more animated. She went bobbing and floating through the Parish like a balloon. Her *interest* in everything seemed to have first been multiplied by nine, and then by nine again. And eighty-one times anything is a pretty large quantity. Beggars, blind men, gypsies, hawkers, crossing-sweepers positively smacked their lips when they saw Miss Rawlings come sailing down the street. Her heart was like the Atlantic, and they like rowboats on the deep—especially the blind men. As for her donations to the parochial Funds, they were first doubled, then trebled, then quadrupled.

There was first, for example, the Fund for giving all the little parish girls and boys not only a bun and an orange and a Tree at Christmas and a picnic with Veal and Ham Pie and Ice Pudding in June, but a Jack-in-the-green on May-day and a huge Guy on November the fifth, with squibs and Roman candles and Chinese crackers and so on. There was not only the Fund for the Delight of Infants of Every Conceivable Description ; there was also the Wooden-Legged Orphans' Fund. There was the Home for Manx and Tabby Cats ; and the Garden by the River with the Willows for Widowed Gentlewomen. There was the Threepenny-Bit-with-a-Hole-in-It Society ; and the Organ Grinders' Sick Monkey and Blanket Fund; and there was the oak-beamed Supper Room in the 'Three Wild Geese' for the use of Ancient Mariners —haggis and toad-in-the-hole, and plum-duff and jam roly-poly—that kind of thing. And there were many others. If Miss Rawlings had been in another parish, it would have been a sad thing indeed for the cats and widows and orphans and organ monkeys in her own.

With such a power and quantity of money, of course, writing cheques was very much like writing in birthday books. Still, it is not easy to give too much to a Fund ; and few people make the attempt. Miss Rawlings, too, was a practical woman. She knew perfectly well that (wheresoever it may end) charity must begin at home, so all this time she was keeping what the Ancient Mariners at the ' Three Wild Geese ' called a ' weather eye ' wide open for her lost Little Gal. But how, it may be asked, could she keep any kind of eye open for a lost Little Gal, when she didn't know what the lost Little Gal was like ? And the answer to that is that Miss Rawlings knew perfectly well.

She may not have known where the absurd notion came from, or when, or why ; but she knew that. She knew what the Little Gal looked like as well as a mother thrush knows what an egg looks like ; or Sir Christopher Wren knew what a cathedral looks like ; or Mr. Peace a gold watch. But as with the Thrush and Sir Christopher, a good many little things had happened to Miss Rawlings first. And this quite apart from the old wooden doll she used to lug about when she was seven, called Quatta.

One morning, for example, Miss Rawlings had been out in her carriage and was thinking of nothing in particular, nothing whatsoever, when not very far from the little stone Bridge at Clobburne she happened to glance up at a window in the upper part

of a small old house. And at that window there
seemed to show a face with dark bright eyes watching
her. Just a glimpse. I say ' seemed,' for when in
the carriage Miss Rawlings rapidly twisted her head
to get a better view, she discovered either that there
had been nobody there at all, or that the somebody
had swiftly drawn back, or that the bright dark eyes
were just two close-together flaws in the diamond-
shaped bits of glass. In the last case what Miss
Rawlings had seen was mainly ' out of her mind.'
But, if so, it went back again and stayed there ! It
was excessively odd, indeed, how clear a remembrance that glimpse left behind it.

Then again Miss Rawlings, like her renowned aunt
Felicia, had always enjoyed a weakness for taking
naps in the train, the flowers and plumes and bows
in her bonnet nodding the while above her head.
The sound of the wheels on the iron lines was like a
lullaby, the fields trailing softly away beyond the
window drowsed her eyes. Whether asleep or not,
she would generally close her eyes and *appear* to be
napping. And not once, or twice, but three separate
times, owing to a scritch of the whistle or a sudden
jolt of the train, she had rapidly opened them again
to find herself staring out—rather like a large animal
in a small field—at a little girl sitting on the opposite
seat, who, in turn, had already fixed *her* eyes on Miss
Rawlings's countenance. In every case there had
been a look of intense, patient interest on the little
girl's face.

Perhaps Miss Rawlings's was a countenance that
all little girls are apt to look at with extreme interest
—especially when the owner of it is asleep in a

train.   It was a broad countenance with a small but powerful nose with a round tip.   There was a good deal of fresh colour in the flat cheeks beneath the treacle-coloured eyes ; and the hair stood like a wig beneath the huge bonnet.   Miss Rawlings, too, had a habit of folding her kid-gloved hands upon her lap as if she were an image.   None the less, you could hardly call it only a ' coincidence ' that these little girls were so much alike, and so much like the face at the window.   And so very much like the real lost Little Gal that had always, it seemed, been at the back of Miss Rawlings's mind.

I don't mean at all that there was any kind of ghost in Miss Rawlings's family.   Her family was far too practical for that ; and her mansion was most richly furnished.   All I mean is that all these little girls happened to have a rather narrow face, a brown pigtail, rather small dark-brown bright eyes and narrow hands, and, except for the one at the window, they wore round beaver hats and buttoned coats. No ; there was no ghost *there*.   What Miss Rawlings was after was an absolutely real Little Gal.   And her name was Barbara Allan.

This sounds utterly absurd.   But so it had come about.   For a long time—having talked about her Little Gal again and again to the Archdeacon and Mrs. Tomlington and Mr. Moffatt and other ladies and gentlemen in the Parish—Miss Rawlings had had no name at all for her small friend.   But one still, summery evening, there being a faint red in the sky, while she was wandering gently about her im- mense drawing-room, she had happened to open a book lying on an ' occasional ' table.   It was a book

of poetry—crimson and gilt-edged, with a brass clasp
—and on the very page under her nose she had read
this line :

Fell in love with Barbara Allan.

The words ran through her mind like wildfire.
Barbara Allan—it was *the* name !   Or how very like
it !   An echo ?   Certainly some words and names
are echoes of one another—sisters or brothers once
removed, so to speak.   Tomlington and Pockling-
ham, for example ;   or quince and shrimp ;   or
angelica and cyclamen.   All I mean is that the very
instant Miss Rawlings saw that printed ' Barbara
Allan ' it ran through her heart like an old tune in
a nursery.   It *was* her Little Gal, or ever so near it ;
as near, that is, as any name can be to a thing—
viz., crocus, or comfit, or shuttlecock, or mistletoe, or pantry.

Now if Miss Rawlings had been of royal blood and
had lived in a fairy-tale—if, that is, she had been a
Queen in Grimm—it would have been a quite
ordinary thing that she should be seeking a lost
Princess, or badly in need of one.   But, except that
her paternal grandfather was a Sir Samuel Rawlings,
she was but very remotely connected with royalty.
And yet, if you think about it, seeing that once upon
a time there were only marvellous Adam and beautiful Eve in the Garden,—that is, in the whole wide
world,—and seeing that all of Us as well as all of the
earth's Kings and Queens must have descended from
them, *therefore* all of Us must have descended from
Kings and Queens.   So too with bold Miss Rawlings.
But—unlike Mrs. Tomlington—she had not come
down by the grand staircase.

Since, then, Miss Rawlings did not live in a fairy-tale or in Grimm, but was a very real person in a truly real Parish, her friends and acquaintances were all inclined in private to agree with Mrs. Tomlington that her Little Gal was nothing but a bee in her bonnet. And that the longer it stayed there the louder it buzzed. Indeed, Miss Rawlings almost began to think of nothing else. She became absent-minded, quite forgetting her soup and fish and chicken and French roll when she sat at dinner. She left on the gas. She signed blank cheques for the Funds. She pointed out Sunsets to blind beggars, and asked after deaf ones' children. She gave brand-new mantles and dolmans away to the Rum-magers ; ordered coals from her fishmonger ; rode third-class with a first-class ticket ; addressed a post-card to Mrs. Tomfoolington—almost every kind of absent-minded thing imaginable.

And now she was always searching—even in the house sometimes ; even in the kitchen-quarters. And her plump country maids would gladly help too. ' No, m'm, she ain't here,' ' No, m'm, we ain't a-seed her yet.' ' Lor, yes'm, the Room's all ready.'

Whenever Miss Rawlings rose from her chair she would at once peer sharply out of the window to see if any small creature were passing in the street beyond the drive. When she went awalking she was frequently all but run over by cabs and vans and phaetons and gigs, because she was looking the other way after a vanishing pigtail. Not a picture-shop, not a photographer's could she pass without examining every single face exhibited in the window. And she never met a friend, or the friend of a friend, or conversed with a stranger, without, sure enough, beginning to talk about Young Things. Puppies or kittens or lambs, perhaps, first, and then gradually on to little boys. And then, with a sudden whisk of her bonnet, to Little Girls.

Long, long ago, now, she had learned by heart the whole of ' Barbara Allan ' :

> She had not gane a mile but twa,
> When she heard the dead-bell ringing,
> And every jow that the dead-bell gied,
> It cryed, *Woe to Barbara Allan!*

> ' O mother, mother, make my bed !
> O make it saft and narrow !
> Since my love died for me to-day,
> I'll die for him to-morrow.'

Oh, dear, how sad it was ; and you never knew ! Could it be, could it be, she cried one day to herself, that the dead lovely Barbara Allan of the poem had got by some means muddled up in Time, and was in actual fact *her* Little Gal ? Could it be that the maiden-name of the wife of Miss Allan's father had been Rawlings !

Miss Rawlings was far too sensible merely to wonder about things. She at once inquired of Mr. Moffatt—who had been once engaged to her dearest friend, Miss Simon, now no more—whether he knew anything about Barbara Allan's family. ' The family, Felicia ? ' Mr. Moffatt had replied, his bristling eyebrows high in his head. But when, after a visit to the British Museum, Mr. Moffatt returned with only two or three pages of foolscap closely written over with full particulars of the

ballad and with ' biographical details ' of Bishop
Percy and of Allan Ramsay and of Oliver Goldsmith
and of the gentleman who had found the oldest
manuscript copy of it in Glamis Castle, or some such
ancient edifice, and of how enchantingly Samuel
Pepys's friend Mrs. Knipp used to sing him that air—
but nothing else, Miss Rawlings very reluctantly
gave up all certainty of this. ' It still might be my
Little Gal's family,' she said, ' and on the other hand
it might not.' And she continued to say over to
herself, with infinite sorrow in her deep rich voice,
that tragic stanza :

> She had not gane a mile but twa,
>   When she heard the dead-bell ringing,
> And every jow that the dead-bell gied,
>   It cryed, *Woe to Barbara Allan !*

And ' Oh, no !   Not Woe,' she would say in her
heart.

Soon after this Miss Rawlings fell ill.   A day or
two before she took to her bed she had been walking
along Combermere Avenue, and had happened to see
the pupils of the Miss Miffinses' Young Ladies' Semin-
ary taking the air.   Now the two last and smallest
of these pupils—of the Crocodile, as rude little boys
call it—were walking arm in arm with the nice
English mistress, chattering away like birds in a
bush.   Both of them were rather narrow little
creatures, both wore beaver hats beneath which
dangled brown pigtails.   It was yet one more
astonishing moment, and Miss Rawlings had almost
broken into a run—as much of a run, that is,
as, being of so stout and ample a presence, she

was capable of—in order to get a glimpse of their faces.

But, alas and alack, the wrought-iron gates of the School were just round the corner of Combermere Avenue, and the whole Crocodile had completely disappeared into the great stone porch beyond by the time she had come in sight of the two Monkey-Puzzles (or auricarias) on the lawn, and the brass curtain-bands to the windows.

Miss Rawlings stood and gazed at these, for the moment completely forgetting polite manners. The hurry and excitement had made her hot and breathless—and the wind was in the East. It dispirited her, and, instead of ringing the bell and asking for the Miss Miffinses, she had returned home and had at once written an invitation to the whole school to come to tea the following Sunday afternoon. In a moment of absent-mindedness, however, she had left the note on her little rosewood secrétaire beside the silver inkstand that had belonged to Sir Samuel. And two days afterward,—on the Friday, that is, the month being February,—she had been seized with Bronchitis.

It was a rather more severe attack than was usual for Miss Rawlings, even in foggy November, and it made Miss Rawlings's family physician a little anxious. There was no immediate danger, he explained to Nurse Murphy ; still care is care, oh yes. And, Miss Rawlings being so rich and so important to the Parish, he at once decided to invite an eminent Consultant to visit his patient—a Sir James Jolliboy Geoghehan, who lived in Harley Street and knew more about Bronchitis (Harley Street being also in a

foggy parish) than any other medical man in Europe
or in the United States of America (which are *not*
usually foggy places).

Fortunately Sir James took quite as bright and
sanguine a view of his patient as did Miss Rawlings's
family physician. There Miss Rawlings lay, propped
up against her beautiful down-pillows with the frills
all round, and a fine large pale-blue-ribboned Bed
Cap stood up on her large head. She was breathing
pretty fast and her temperature, according to both
the gentlemen's thermometers, was 102·6. As for
her pulse, Sir James fastened his eyes so close upon
the Bed Cap that he forgot to count it; and he
laid down her wrist without a word.

A large copper kettle was ejecting clouds of
steam from the vast cheerful fire in the vast brass
and steel grate, with the Cupids in the chimneypiece.
There were medicine bottles on the little table, and
not only Nurse Murphy stood on the other side of
the bed, but Nurse O'Brien also. And the more
solemn *she* looked the more her face appeared to be
creased up in a gentle grin.

Miss Rawlings panted as she looked at them all.
Her eye was a little absent, but she too was smiling.
For if there was one thing Miss Rawlings was certain
to be, it was to be cheerful when most other people
would be inclined to be depressed. As she knew
she was ill she felt bound to be smiling. She even
continued to smile when Sir James murmured, ' *And*
the tongue?' And she assured Sir James that,
though it was exceedingly kind of him to call, it
wasn't in the least necessary. ' I frequently have
bronchitis,' she explained, ' but I never die.'

When Sir James and the family physician had gone downstairs and were closeted together in the gilded library, Sir James at once asked this question: 'What, my dear sir, was our excellent patient remarking about a Miss Barbara Allan? Has she a relative of the name?'

At this Miss Rawlings's family physician looked a little confused. 'No, no; oh dear, no!' he exclaimed. 'It's merely a little fancy, a caprice. Miss Rawlings has a notion there is a little girl belonging to her somewhere—probably of that name, you know. Quite harmless. An aberration. In fact, I indulge it; I indulge it. Miss Rawlings is a most able, sagacious, energetic, philanthropic, practical, generous, and—and—humorous lady. The fancy, you see, has somehow attached itself to the *name* "Barbara Allan"—a heroine, I believe, in one of Sir Walter Scott's admirable fictions. Only that. Nothing more.'

Sir James, a tall man, peered down at Miss Rawlings's family physician over his gold pince-nez. 'I once had a patient, my dear Dr. Sheppard,' he replied solemnly, in a voice a good deal deeper but not so rich as Miss Rawlings's, 'who had the amiable notion that she was the Queen of Sheba and that I was King Solomon. A *most* practical woman. She left me three hundred guineas in her will for a mourning ring.' He thereupon explained—in words that his patient could not possibly have understood, but that Dr. Sheppard understood perfectly—that Miss Rawlings was in no immediate danger and that she was indeed quite a comfortable little distance from Death's Door. Still, bronchitis *is* bronchitis;

so let the dear lady be humoured as much as possible.
' Let her have the very best nurses, excellent creatures ; and all the comforts ! ' He smiled as he
said these words, as if Dr. Sheppard were a long-lost
brother. And he entirely approved, not only of the
nice sago-puddings, the grapes, the bee-ootiful
beef-juice (with toast *or* a rusk), the barley water
and the physic, but of as many Barbara Allans as
Miss Rawlings could possibly desire. And all that
he said sounded so much like the chorus of some such
old sea-song as ' Yeo-ho-ho,' or ' Away to Rio,' or
' The Anchor's Weighed,' that one almost expected
Dr. Sheppard to join in.

Both gentlemen then took their leave and, Dr.
Sheppard having escorted Sir James to his brougham,
for this was before the days of machine carriages,
the two nurses retired from the window and Miss
Rawlings sank into a profound nap.

In a few days Miss Rawlings was much, much,
much better. Her temperature was 97·4, her
breathing no more than twenty-four or -five to the
minute. The flush had left her cheeks, and she had
finished three whole bottles of medicine. She devoured a slice from the breast of a chicken and even
enjoyed her sago pudding. The nurses *were* pleased.

But, if anything, Miss Rawlings's illness seemed
to have increased her anxiety to find Barbara Allan
as quickly as ever she could. After all, you see, we
all of us have only a certain number of years to live,
and a year lasts only twelve calendar months, and
the shortest month is only twenty-eight days,
excluding Leap Year. So if you want to do anything
badly it is better to begin at once, and go straight on.

The very first day she was out in Mr. Dubbins's invalid chair she met her dear friend Mr. Moffatt in Combermere Grove, and he stood conversing with her for a while under the boughs of almost as wide a spreading chestnut-tree as the village blacksmith's in the poem. Mr. Moffatt always looked as if he ought to have the comfort of a sleek bushy beard. If he had, it is quite certain it would have wagged a good deal as he listened to Miss Rawlings. ' What I am about to do, my dear Mr. Moffatt, is advertise,' she cried, and in such a powerful voice that the lowest fronds of the leafing chestnut-tree over her head slightly trembled as they hung a little listlessly on their stalks in the Spring sunshine.

' Advertise, my dear Felicia ? ' cried Mr. Moffatt. ' And what for ? '

' Why, my dear old friend,' replied Miss Rawlings, ' for Barbara Allan, to be sure.'

Mr. Moffatt blinked very rapidly, and the invisible beard wagged more than ever. And he looked hard at Miss Rawlings's immense bonnet as if he actually expected to see that busy bee ; as if he even feared it might be a Queen Bee and would produce a complete hive.

But after bidding him good-bye with yet another wag of the bonnet and a ' Yes, thank you, Dubbins,' Miss Rawlings was as good as her word. She always was. Three days afterwards there appeared in the *Times* and in the *Morning Post* and in the *Daily Telegraph*, and five days later in the *Spectator*, the following :

WANTED as soon as possible, by a lady who has lost her as long as she can remember, a little girl of the name (probably) of Barbara Allan, or of a name that *sounds* like Barbara Allan. The little girl is about ten years old. She has a rather three-cornered-shaped face, with narrow cheek-bones, and bright brown eyes. She is slim, with long fingers, and wears a pigtail and probably a round beaver hat. She shall have an *exceedingly* happy home and Every Comfort, and her friends (or relatives) will be amply rewarded for all the care and kindness they have bestowed upon her, for the first nine years or more of her life.

You should have seen Miss Rawlings reading that advertisement over and over. Her *Times* that morning had a perfume as of the spices of Ambrosia. But even Miss Rawlings could not have hoped that her advertisement would be so rapidly and spontaneously and abundantly answered. The whole day of every day of the following week her beautiful wrought-iron gates were opening and shutting and admitting all kinds and sorts and shapes and sizes of little girls with brown eyes, long fingers, pigtails, and beaver hats, *about* ten years of age. And usually an Aunt or a Stepmother or the Matron of an Orphanage or a Female Friend accompanied each candidate.

There were three genuine Barbara Allans. But one had reddish hair and freckles ; the second, curly flaxen hair that refused to keep to the pigtail-ribbon into which it had been tied ; and the third, though her hair was brown, had grey speckled eyes, and looked to be at least eleven. Apart from these three, there were numbers and numbers of little girls whose Christian name was Barbara, but whose surname was Allison, or Angus, or Anson, or Mallings, or Bulling, or Dalling, or Spalding, or Bellingham, or Allingham,

and so on and so forth.   Then there were Marjories
and Marcias and Margarets, Norahs and Doras and
Rhodas and Marthas, all of the name of Allen, or
Allan, or Alleyne, or Alyn, and so on.   And there
was one little saffron-haired creature who came with
a very large Matron, and whose name was Dulcibella
Dobbs.

Miss Rawlings, with her broad bright face and
bright little eyes, smiled at them all from her chair,
questioned their Aunts and their Stepmothers and
their Female Friends, and coveted every single one
of them, including Dulcibella Dobbs.   But you *must*
draw the line somewhere, as Euclid said to his little
Greek pupils when he sat by the sparkling waves of
the Ægean Sea and drew triangles on the sand.   And
Miss Rawlings felt in her heart that it was kinder
and wiser and more prudent and proper to keep
strictly to those little girls with the three-cornered
faces, high cheek-bones, ' really ' brown eyes, and
truly appropriate pigtails.   With these she fell in
love again and again and again.

There was no doubt in the world that she had an
exceedingly motherly heart, but very few mothers
could so nicely afford to *give it rein*.   Indeed, Miss
Rawlings would have drawn the line nowhere if it
had not been for the fact that she had only Ten
Thousand Pounds or so a year.

There were tears in her eyes when she bade the
others Good-bye.   And to everyone she gave, not
one bun, not one orange, but a *bag* of oranges and a
bag of buns.   And not merely a bag of ordinary
Denia oranges and ordinary currant buns, but a bag
of Jaffas and a bag of Bath.   And she thanked their

Guardianesses for having come such a long way, and would they be offended if she paid the fare ? Only one was offended, but then her fare had cost only 3*d.*—2*d.* for herself, and 1*d.* (half price) for the little Peggoty Spalding she brought with her. And Miss Rawlings paid *her* sixpence.

She kept thirty little ten-year-olds altogether, and you never saw so many young fortunate smiling pigtailed creatures so much alike. And Miss Rawlings, having been so successful, withdrew her advertisements from the *Times* and the *Morning Post* and the *Daily Telegraph* and the *Spectator*, and she bought a most beautiful Tudor house called Trafford House, with one or two wings to it that had been added in the days of Good Queen Anne, and William and Mary, which stood in entirely its own grounds not ten miles from the Parish boundary. The forest trees in its park were so fine—cedars, sweet chestnuts, and ash and beech and oak—that you could only get a tiny glimpse of its chimneys from the entrance to the drive.

Things *are* often curious in this world, and coincidences are almost as common as centipedes. So Miss Rawlings was more happy than surprised when, on looking over this mansion, she counted—and to make sure counted again—exactly thirty little bedrooms, with some larger ones over for a matron, a nurse, some parlour-maids, some housemaids, some tweeny-maids, and a Boy to clean the button-boots and shoes. When her legal adviser explained to her that this establishment, what with the little chests-of-drawers, basins and ewers, brass candle-sticks, oval looking-glasses, dumpy beds, three-

legged stools, dimity curtains, woolly rugs, not to
speak of chiffoniers, whatnots, hot-water bottles,
soup ladles, and so on and so forth,—not to mention
a uniform with brass buttons for the man with
whiskers at the park gate,—would cost her at least
Six Thousand a year, that bee in Miss Rawlings's
bonnet buzzed as if indeed it *was* a whole hive gone
a-swarming.

' Well, now, my dear Mr. Wilkinson,' she said,
' I made a little estimate myself, being a *business*
woman, and it came to £6004 10s. od. How reason-
able ! I shall be at least four pounds-ten in
pocket.'

So in a few weeks everything was ready—new
paint, new gravel on the paths, geraniums in the
flower-beds, quilts as neat as daisies on a lawn on
the dumpy beds, and the thirty Barbara Allans
sitting fifteen a side at the immensely long oak table
(where once in Henry VIII.'s time monks had eaten
their fish on Fridays), the matron with the corkscrew
curls at the top and the chief nurse in her starched
cap at the bottom. And Miss Rawlings seated in
the South bow-window in an old oak chair, with her
ebony and ivory stick and her purple bonnet, smiling
at her Barbara Allans as if she had mistaken Trafford
House for the Garden of Eden.

And I must say every single pigtail of the complete
thirty bobbed as merrily as roses in June over that
first Grand Tea—blackberry jelly, strawberry jam,
home-made bread, plum cake, the best beef-dripping
for those who had not a sweet or a milk tooth, Sally
Lunns, heather honey, maids-of-honour, and an
enormous confection of marchpane, with cupids and

comfits and silver bells and thirty little candles
standing up in the midst of the table like St. Paul's
Cathedral on the top of Ludgate Hill in the great
city of London. It was a lucky thing for the
Thirty's insides that Grand Teas are not everyday
teas.

And so, when all the thirty Pigtails had sung a
Latin grace put out of English by Mr. Moffatt and
set to a tune composed by a beloved uncle of Miss
Rawlings's, who also was now no more, the Grand
Tea came to an end. Whereupon the Thirty—
looking themselves like yet another Crocodile with
very fat joints—came and said good-night to Miss
Rawlings, though some of them could scarcely speak.
And as Miss Rawlings knew that not *all* little girls
liked being kissed by comparative strangers, she just
shook hands with each, and smiled at them as if
her motherly heart would almost break. And Dr.
Sheppard was Medical Adviser to the thirty little
Pigtailers, and Mr. Moffatt came every other Sunday
to hear their catechisms.

Miss Rawlings had never been much attached to
rules and regulations for other people, though she
kept faithfully to a few for herself. She loved
everyone to be free and everything to be easy,
considering how hard most things are. And this
was the Order of the Day with the Pigtails in their
Home.

At half-past seven in Summer, and at nine in
Winter, the boy in buttons rang an immense bell,
its clapper tied round with a swab of cotton-wool to
prevent it from clanging too sonorously. This great
quiet bell was not only to waken from their last sweet

dreams the slumbering Pigtails in their little beds,
but to tell them they had yet another half-hour
between the blankets before they had to get up.
Then hairbrushes, toothbrushes, nailbrushes, as
usual. Then 'When morning gilds the sky,' and
breakfast in the wide white room with the primrose
curtains looking out into the garden. And if any
Pigtail happened to have been not quite so good as
usual on the previous day, she was allowed—if she
asked for it—to have a large plateful of porridge
with or without salt—for a punishment. No less than
ninety-nine such platefuls were served out in the
first year—the Pigtails were so high-spirited. Still,
it can be imagined what a thirtyfold sigh of relief
went up when breakfast on December 31st was over
and there hadn't been a hundredth.

From 9 a.m. to 12 p.m. the Pigtails were one and all
exceedingly busy. Having made their beds, they
ran out into the garden and woods—some to bathe
in the stream, some to listen to the birds, some to
talk, and some to sing ; some to paint, some to play,
and some to read, and some to dance ; some just
to sit ; and some high up in a beech tree to learn
poems, to make up poems, even to read each other's.
It all depended on the weather. The sun shone, the
rooks cawed, the green silken leaves whispered ;
and Miss Rawlings would stand looking up at them
in their verdurous perch as fondly as a cat at a
canary. There was not at last a flower or a tree or
an insect or a star in those parts, or a bird or a little
beast or a fish or a toadstool or a moss or a pebble,
that the little Pigtails did not know by heart. And
the more they knew them, closely the more they

looked at them, and the more closely they looked at them, the more they loved them and the more they knew them—round and round and round and round.

From twelve to one there were ' Lessons.' Then dinner, and tongues like jackdaws raiding a pantry for silver spoons. In the afternoon those who went for a walk toward the stranger parts went for a walk. Some stayed at home in a little parlour and sang in chorus together like a charm of wild birds. Some did their mending and darning, their hemming and featherstitching, and some did sums. Some played on the fiddle, and some looked after their bullfinches, and bunnies, and bees, and guinea pigs, and ducks. Then there were the hens and the doves and the calves and the pigs to feed, and the tiny motherless lambs, too (when lambs there were), with bottles of milk. And sometimes of an afternoon Miss Rawlings would come in and sit at a window just watching her Pigtails, or would read them a story. And Dr. Sheppard asseverated not once but three times over that if she went on bringing them sweetmeats and candies and lollipops and suckets to such an *extent*, not a single sound white ivory tooth of their nine hundred or so would be left in the Pigtails' heads. So Miss Rawlings kept to Sundays.

At five was tea-time : jam on Mondays, Wednesdays, and Fridays ; jelly on Tuesdays, Thursdays, and Saturdays ; and both on Sundays. From six to seven there were ' Lessons,' and when the little Pigtails were really tired, which was always before nine, they just skipped off to bed. Some of them had munched their supper biscuits and were snug in bed, indeed, even before the rest had sung the

evening hymn. And the evening hymn was always
' Eternal Father '—for being all of them so extremely
happy they could not but be ' in peril on the deep '
just as sailors are, for happiness may fly away like
birds in corn, or butterflies before rain. And on
Sundays they sang ' Lead, Kindly Light ' too,
because Miss Rawlings's mother had once been
blessed by the great and blessed Cardinal Newman.
And one Pigtail played the accompaniment on the
fiddle, and one on the sweet-tongued viola, and one
on the harpsichord ; for since Miss Rawlings had
read ' Barbara Allan ' she had given up pianofortes.
And then, sleepy and merry and chattering, they all
trooped up to bed.

So this was their Day. And all night, unseen, the
stars shone in their splendour above the roof of
Trafford House, or the white-faced moon looked
down upon the sleeping garden and the doves and
the pigs and the lambs and the flowers. And at
times there was a wind in the sky among the clouds,
and sometimes frost in the dark hours settled like
pollen wheresoever its cold brightness might find a
lodging. And when the little Pigtails awoke there
would be marvellous cold fronds and flowerets on
their windowpanes, and even sometimes a thin
crankling slat of ice in their water-jugs. On which
keen winter mornings you could hear their teeth
chattering like monkeys cracking nuts. And so
time went on.

On the very next June 1st, there was a prodigious
Garden Party at Trafford House, with punts on the
lake and refreshments and lemonade in a tent in
the park, and all the Guardianesses and Aunts and

Stepmothers and Matrons and Female Friends were invited to come and see Miss Rawlings's little Pig-tails. And some brought their sisters, and some their nieces and nephews. There were Merry-go-Rounds, Aunt Sallies, Frisk-and-Come-Easies, A Punch and Judy Show, a Fat Man, a fortune-teller, and three marvellous acrobats from Hongkong. And there were quantities of things to eat and lots to see, and Kiss-in-the-Ring, and all broke up after fireworks and ' God Save the Queen ' at half-past nine.

The house, as I keep on saying, was called Trafford House, but the *Home* was called ' The Home of All the Little Barbara Allans and Suchlike, with Brown Eyes, Narrow Cheek-bones, Beaver Hats, and Pigtails, Ltd.' And it was ' limited ' because there could be only thirty of them, and time is not Eternity.

And now there were only three things that pre-vented Miss Rawlings from being too intensely happy to go on being alive ; and these three were as follows : (*a*) She wanted to live always at the House : but how could the Parish get on without her ? (*b*) What was she going to do when the Pigtailers became twelve, thirteen, fourteen, fifteen, sixteen, seventeen, and so forth, and Grown-Up ? And (*c*) How could she ever possibly part with any of them or get any more ?

For, you see, Miss Rawlings's first-of-all Barbara Allan was aged ten, and had somehow managed to stay ten. But because, I suppose, things often go right in this world when we are not particularly noticing them, and don't know how, all these diffi-culties simply melted away like butter in the sun.

In the first place, Miss Rawlings did at last—in 1888, to be exact, one year after Queen Victoria's first Jubilee—did, I say, at last go to live at the Home of All the Little Barbara Allans and Suchlike, with Brown Eyes, Beaver Hats, and Pigtails, Ltd. She was called The Matron's Friend, so as not to undermine the discipline. When her Parish wanted her, which was pretty often, the Parish (Thirty or Forty strong) came to see her in her little parlour overlooking the pond with the punts and the water lilies.

Next—though how, who can say?—the little Pigtails somehow did not grow up, even though they must have grown older. Something queer happened to their Time. It cannot have been what just the clocks said. If there wasn't more of it, there was infinitely more *in* it. It was like air and dew and sunbeams and the South Wind to them all. You simply could not tell what next. And, apart from all that wonderful learning, apart even from the jam and jelly and the Roast Beef of Old England, they went on being just the right height and the right heart for ten. Their brown eyes never lost their light and sparkle. No wrinkles ever came in their three-cornered faces with the high cheek-bones, and not a single grey or silver hair into their neat little pigtails—that could at any rate be seen.

Next, therefore, Miss Rawlings never had to part with any of them or to look or advertise for any more.

Yet another peculiar thing was that Miss Rawlings grew more and more like a Pigtail herself. She grew younger. She laughed like a schoolgirl. Her face became a little narrower, even the cheek-bones seemed not to be so wide. As for her bonnets, as time ' went on ' they grew up instead of broadwise. And when she sat in Church with the Thirty, in the third pew down from Mrs. Tomlington's, you might almost have supposed she *was* a widish pigtail, just a little bit dressed up.

It is true that in the very secretest corner of her heart of hearts she was still looking for the one and only absolute little Barbara Allan of her lifelong daydream ; but that is how things go. And the thought of it brought only a scarcely perceptible grave glance of hope and inquiry into her round brown eyes. And underneath—oh, dear me, yes —she was almost too happy and ordinary and good-natured and homely to be telling this story about at all.

We all die at last—just journey on—and so did Miss Rawlings. And so did the whole of the Thirty, and the matron, and the chief nurse, and Mr. Moffatt, and Dr. Sheppard, and the Man with whiskers at the park gates, *and* the Boy who cleaned the button-boots ; parlour-maids, tweeny-maids, Mrs. Tomfoolington, and all. And if you would like to see the Old House and the little graves, you take the first turning on the right as you leave the Parish Church on your left, and walk on until you come to a gatepost beyond the milestone.

A path crossing the fields—sometimes of wheat, sometimes of turnips, sometimes of barley or clover or swedes—leads to a farm in the hollow with a duckpond, guinea fowl roosting in the pines at evening, and a lovely old thatched barn where the fantailed doves croon in the sunshine. You then

cross the yard and come to a lane beside a wood of
thorn and hazel. This bears a little East, and
presently, after ascending the hill beyond the hay-
stack, you will see—if it is still there—the Home of
All the Little Barbara Allans and Suchlike, with
Brown Eyes, Beaver Hats, and Pigtails, Ltd.

And not very far away is a little smooth-mown
patch of turf with a beautiful thatched wall around
it, which Mr. Moffat consecrated himself. And
there, side by side, sleep the Little Thirty, with their
pigtails beside their narrow bones. And there lie
the tweeny-maids, the parlour-maids, the Man with
whiskers at the park gate, and the Boy who cleaned
the button-boots. And there lies Miss Rawlings, too.
And when the last trump sounds, up they will get
as happy as wood larks, and as sweet and fresh
as morning mushrooms. But if you want to hear
any more about *that*, please turn to the Poems of
Mr. Wm. Blake.

THE DUTCH CHEESE

EVER so many years ago there
lived, with his sister Griselda,
in a cottage near the Great
Forest, a young farmer whose
name was John. Brother and
sister, they lived alone, except
for their sheep-dog, Sly, their
flock of sheep, the numberless
birds of the forest, and the
fairies. John loved his sister beyond telling; he loved
Sly; and he delighted to listen to the birds singing at
twilight round the darkening margin of the forest.
But he feared and hated the fairies. And, having
a very stubborn heart, the more he feared, the
more he hated them; and the more he hated them,
the more they pestered him.

Now these were a tribe of fairies, sly, small, gay-
hearted and mischievous, and not of the race of
fairies noble, silent, beautiful and remote from man.
They were a sort of gipsy fairies, very nimble and of
aery and prankish company, and partly for mischief and partly for love of her were always striving
to charm John's dear sister Griselda away, with
their music and fruits and dancing. He more than
half believed it was they who years ago had decoyed
into the forest his poor old father, who had gone out

c

faggot-cutting in his sheepskin hat with his ass ; and his mother too soon after who had gone out looking for him.

But fairies, even of this small tribe, hate no man. They mocked him and mischiefed him ; they spilt his milk, rode astraddle on his rams, garlanded his old ewes with sow-thistle and briony, sprinkled water on his kindling wood, loosed his bucket into the well, and hid his great leather shoes. But all this they did, not for hate—for they came and went like evening moths about Griselda—but because in his fear and fury he shut up his sister from them, and because he was sullen and stupid. Yet he did nothing but fret himself. He set traps for them, and caught starlings ; he fired his blunderbuss at them under the moon, and scared his sheep ; he set dishes of sour milk in their way, and sticky leaves and brambles where their rings were green in the meadows ; but all to no purpose. When at dusk, too, he heard their faint, far, elfin music, he would sit in the door blowing into his father's great bassoon till the black forest re-echoed with its sad, solemn, wooden voice. But that was of no avail either. At last he grew so sour that he made Griselda utterly miserable. Her cheeks lost their scarlet and her eyes their sparkling. Then the fairies began to plague John in earnest, lest their lovely, loved child of man, Griselda, should die.

Now one summer's evening—and most nights are cold in the Great Forest—John, having put away his mournful bassoon and bolted the door, was squatting, moody and gloomy, with Griselda on his hearth beside the fire. And he leaned back his great hairy head and stared straight up the chimney to where in the black sky the Seven Sisters sat aglitter. And suddenly, while he lolled there on his stool watching that tiny seven, there appeared against the dark sky a mischievous, elvish head secretly peeping down at him ; and busy hands sprinkling dew on his wide upturned face. He heard the laughter too of the fairies meeting and gambolling on his thatch, and in a rage he started up ; seized a great round cheese that lay on a platter, and with all his force threw it clean and straight up the sooty chimney at the faces of mockery clustered above. And after that, though Griselda sighed at her spinning wheel, he heard no more. Even the cricket that had been whistling all through the evening fell silent, and John supped on his black bread and onions alone.

Next day Griselda woke at dawn and put her head out of the little window beneath the thatch, and the day was white with mist.

' 'Twill be another hot day,' she said to herself, combing her beautiful hair.

But when John went down, so white and dense with mist were the fields, that even the green borders of the forest were invisible, and the whiteness went to the sky. Swathing and wreathing itself, opal and white as milk, all morning the mist grew thicker and thicker about the little house. When John went out about nine o'clock to peer about him, nothing was to be seen at all. He could hear his sheep bleating, the kettle singing, Griselda sweeping, but straight up above him hung only, like a small round fruit, a little cheese-red beamless sun ; straight up above him, though the hands of the clock were not yet got to ten. And he clenched his fists and stamped in his rage. But no one answered him, no voice mocked him but his own. For when these idle, mischievous fairies have played a trick on an enemy they soon weary of it.

All day long that little sullen lantern burned above the mist, sometimes red, so that the white mist was died to amber, and sometimes milky pale, the trees dropped water from every leaf. Every flower asleep in the garden was neckleted with beads ; and nothing but a drenched old forest crow visited the lonely cottage that afternoon to cry : ' Kah, Kah, Kah ! ' and fly away. But Griselda knew her brother's mood too well to speak of it, or to complain. And she sang on gaily in the house, though she was more sorrowful than ever.

The next day John went out to tend his flocks. And wherever he went the red sun seemed to follow. When at last he found his sheep they were drenched with the clinging mist and were huddled together in dismay. And when they saw him it seemed that they cried out with one unanimous bleating voice :

' O ma-a-a-ster ! '

And he stood counting them. And a little apart from the rest stood his old ram Soll, with a face as black as soot ; and there, perched on his back, impish and sharp and scarlet, rode and tossed and sang just such another fairy as had mocked John from the chimney-top. A fire seemed to break out in his body, and, picking up a handful of stones, he rushed at Soll through the flock. They scattered, bleating, out into the mist. And the fairy, all-acockahoop

on the old ram's back, took its small ears between
finger and thumb, and as fast as John ran, so fast
jogged Soll, till all the young farmer's stones were
thrown, and he found himself alone in a quagmire
so sticky and befogged that it took him till afternoon
to grope his way out. And only Griselda's singing
over her broth-pot guided him at last home.

Next day he sought his sheep far and wide, but
not one could he find. To and fro he wandered,
shouting and calling and whistling to Sly, till heart-
sick and thirsty, they were both wearied out. Yet
bleatings seemed to fill the air, and a faint, beautiful
bell tolled on out of the mist ; and John knew the
fairies had hidden his sheep, and he hated them
more than ever.

After that he went no more into the fields, brightly
green beneath the enchanted mist. He sat and
sulked, staring out of the door at the dim forests
far away, glimmering faintly red beneath the small
red sun. Griselda could not sing any more, she was
too tired and hungry. And just before twilight
she went out and gathered the last few pods of peas
from the garden for their supper.

And while she was shelling them John within doors
in the cottage heard again the tiny timbrels and the
distant horns, and the odd, clear, grasshopper voices
calling and calling her, and he knew in his heart that,
unless he relented and made friends with the fairies,
Griselda would surely one day run away to them
and leave him forlorn. He scratched his great head,
and gnawed his broad thumb. They had taken his
father, they had taken his mother, they might
take his sister—but he *wouldn't* give in.

So he shouted, and Griselda in fear and trembling came in out of the garden with her basket and basin and sat down in the gloaming to finish shelling her peas.

And as the shadows thickened and the stars began to shine, the malevolent singing came nearer, and presently there was a groping and stirring in the thatch, a tapping at the window, and John knew the fairies had come—not alone, not one or two or three, but in their company and bands—to plague him, and entice away Griselda. He shut his mouth and stopped up his ears with his fingers, but when, with great staring eyes, he saw them capering like bubbles in a glass, like flames along straw, on his very doorstep, he could contain himself no longer. He caught up Griselda's bowl and flung it—peas, water and all—full in the snickering faces of the Little Folk! There came a shrill, faint twitter of laughter, a scampering of feet, and then all was utterly still.

Griselda tried in vain to keep back her tears. She put her arms round John's neck and hid her face in his sleeve.

' Let me go ! ' she said, ' let me go, John, just a day and a night, and I'll come back to you. They are angry with us. But they love me ; and if I sit on the hillside under the boughs of the trees beside the pool and listen to their music just a little while, they will make the sun shine again and drive back the flocks, and we shall be happy as ever. Look at poor Sly, John dear, he is hungrier even that I am.' John heard only the mocking laughter and the tap-tapping and the rustling and crying of the fairies, and he wouldn't let his sister go.

And it began to be marvellously dark and still in the cottage. No stars moved across the casement, no waterdrops glittered in the candleshine. John could hear only one low, faint, unceasing stir and rustling all around him. So utterly dark and still it was that even Sly woke from his hungry dreams and gazed up into his mistress's face and whined.

They went to bed ; but still, all night long, while John lay tossing on his mattress, the rustling never ceased. The old kitchen clock ticked on and on, but there came no hint of dawn. All was pitch-black and now all was utterly silent. There wasn't a whisper, not a creak, not a sigh of air, not a footfall of mouse, not a flutter of moth, not a settling of dust to be heard at all. Only desolate silence. And John at last could endure his fears and suspicions no longer. He got out of bed and stared from his square casement. He could see nothing. He tried to thrust it open ; it would not move. He went downstairs and unbarred the door and looked out. He saw, as it were, a deep, clear, green shade, from behind which the songs of the birds rose faint as in a dream.

And then he sighed like a grampus and sat down, and knew that the fairies had beaten him. Like Jack's beanstalk, in one night had grown up a dense wall of peas. He pushed and pulled and hacked with his axe, and kicked with his shoes, and buffeted with his blunderbuss. But it was all in vain. He sat down once more in his chair beside the hearth and covered his face with his hands. And at last Griselda, too, awoke, and came down with her candle. And she comforted her brother, and told him if he would do what she bade she would soon make all right again. And he promised her.

So with a scarf she bound tight his hands behind him ; and with a rope she bound his feet together, so that he could neither run nor throw stones, peas or cheeses. She bound his eyes and ears and mouth with a napkin, so that he could neither see, hear, smell, nor cry out. And, that done, she pushed and pulled him like a great bundle, and at last rolled him out of sight into the chimney-corner against the wall. Then she took a small sharp pair of needlework scissors that her godmother had given her, and snipped and snipped, till at last there came a little hole in the thick green hedge of peas. And putting her mouth there she called softly through the little hole. And the fairies drew near the doorstep and nodded and nodded and listened.

And then and there Griselda made a bargain with them for the forgiveness of John—a lock of golden hair ; a dish of ewes' milk ; three and thirty bunches of currants, red, white and black ; a bag of thistle-down ; three handkerchiefs full of lambs' wool ; a jar of honey ; a peppercorn of spice ; and she to sit one full hour each evening of summer on the hillside in the shadow and still greenness that slope down from that great Forest towards the meadows, where the fairy mounds are, and their brindled cattle graze.

Her brother lay blind and deaf and dumb as a faggot. She promised all.

And then, instead of a rustling and a creeping, there came a rending and clattering and crashing. Instead of green shade, light of amber ; then white.

And as the thick hedge withered and shrank, and the merry and furious dancing sun scorched and scorched and scorched, there came, above the singing of the birds, the bleatings of sheep—and behold sooty Soll and hungry Sly met square upon the doorstep; and all John's sheep shone white as hoarfrost on his pastures; and every lamb was garlanded with pimpernel and eyebright; and the old fat ewes stood still, with saddles of moss; and their laughing riders sat and saw Griselda standing in the doorway in her bounteous yellow hair.

As for John, tied up like a sack in the chimney-corner, down came his cheese again crash upon his head, and, not being able to say anything, he said nothing.

MISS JEMIMA

T was a hot, still evening; the trees stood motionless; and not a bird was singing under the sky when a little old lady and a child appeared together over the crest of the hill. They paused side by side on the long, green, mounded ridge, behind which the sun was now descending. And spread out flat beneath them were the fields and farms and the wandering stream of the wide countryside. It was quite flat, and a faint thin mist was over it all, stretching out as if to the rim of the world. The stooping old lady and the child presently ventured a few further paces down the hillside, then again came to a standstill, and gazed once more, from under the umbrella that shaded them against the hot sun, on the scene spread out beneath them.

' Is *that* the house, Grannie,' said the child, ' that one near the meadow with the horses in it, and the trees ? And is that *queer* little grey building right in the middle of that green square field the church ? '

The old lady pressed her lips together, and continued to gaze through her thick glasses at the great solitary country scene. Then she drew her umbrella

45

down with a click, placed it on the turf beside her, and sat down on it.

' I don't suppose the grass *is* damp, my dear, after this long hot day ; but you never know,' she said.

' It's perfectly dry, Grannie dear, and *very* beautiful,' said the child, as if she could hardly spare the breath for the words. Then she too sat down. She had rather long fair hair, and a straight small nose under her round hat with its wreath of butter-cups. Her name was Susan.

' And *is* that the house, Grannie ? ' she whispered once more. ' And *is* that the church where you did really and truly see it ? '

The old lady never turned her eyes, but continued to overlook the scene as if she had not heard the small voice questioning ; as if she were alone with her thoughts. And at that moment, one after another, a troop of gentle-stepping, half-wild horses appeared on a path round the bluff of the hill. Shyly eyeing these two strange human figures in their haunts, one and another of them lifted a narrow lovely head to snort ; and a slim young bay, his mane like rough silk in the light, paused to whinny. Then one by one they trotted along the path, and presently were gone. Susan watched them out of sight, then sighed.

' This is a lovely place to be in, Grannie,' she said, and sighed again. ' I wish I had been here too when I was little. Please do tell me again about the— *you* know.'

Her voice trailed off faintly in the still golden air up there on the hill, as if she were now a little timid of repeating the question. She drew in closer beside her grannie, and pushing her small fingers between those of the bent-up, black-gloved hand in the old lady's lap, she stooped forward after yet another pause, looked up into the still grey face with its spectacles, and said very softly, ' *How* many years ago did you say ? '

There was a mild far-away expression in the slate-grey eyes into which Susan was looking, as if memory were retracing one by one the years that had gone. Never had Susan sat like this upon a green hill above so immense a world, or in so hushed an evening quiet. Her busy eyes turned once more to look first in the direction in which the trotting comely horses had vanished, then down again to the farmhouse with its barns and byres and orchard. They then rested once more on the grey stone church —which from this height looked almost as small as an old cottage—in the midst of its green field.

' *How* many years ago, Grannie ? ' repeated Susan.

' More than I scarcely dare think of,' said the old woman at last, gently pressing her fingers. ' Seventy-five, my dear.'

' Seventy-five ! ' breathed Susan. ' But that's not so very many, Grannie dear,' she added quickly, pushing her head against her grannie's black-caped shoulder. ' And now, before it is too late, please will you tell me the story. You see, Grannie, soon we shall have to be going back to the cab, or the man will suppose we are not coming back at all. *Please.*'

' But you know most of it already.'

' Only in pieces, Grannie ; and besides, to think that here we are—here, in the very place ! '

' Well,' began the old voice at last, ' I will tell it you all again, if you persist, my dear ; but it's a little *more* than seventy-five years ago, for—though you would not believe it of such an old person—I was born in May. My mother, your great-grandmother, was young then, and in very delicate health after my father's death. Her doctor had said she must go on a long sea voyage. And since she was not able to take me with her, I was sent to that little farm-house down there—Green's Farm, as it was called—to spend the months of her absence with my Uncle James and his housekeeper, who was called Miss Jemima.'

' Miss Jemima ! ' cried the little girl, stooping over suddenly with a burst of laughter. ' It *is* a queer name, you know, Grannie.'

' It is,' said the old lady. ' And it belonged to one to whom it was my duty to show affection, but who never much cared for the little girl she had in her charge. And when people don't care for you, it is sometimes a little difficult, Susan, to care for them. At least *I* found it so. I don't mean that Miss Jemima was unkind to me, only that when she was kind, she seemed to be kind on purpose. And when I had a slice of plum cake, her face always seemed to tell me it was *plum* cake, and that I deserved only plain. My Uncle James knew that his housekeeper did not think me a pleasant little girl. I was a shrimp in size, with straight black hair which she made me tie tightly back with a piece of velvet ribbon. I had small dark eyes and very skimpy legs. And though he himself was kind, and fond of me, he showed his affection only when we were

alone together, and not when she was present. He
was ill, too, then, though I did not know *how* ill.
And he lay all day in a long chair with a check rug
over his legs, and Miss Jemima had charge not only
of me, but of the farm.'

' *All* the milking, and the ploughing, and the
chickens, and the pigs, Grannie ' ? asked Susan.

The old lady shut her eyes an instant, pressed her
lips together and said, ' All.'

' The consequence was,' she went on, ' I was
rather a solitary child. Whenever I could, I used
to hide myself away in some corner of the house—
and a beautiful house it is. It's a pity, my dear, I
am so old and you so young and this hill so steep.
Otherwise we could go down and—well, never mind.
That row of small lattice windows which you can see
belong to a narrow corridor ; and the rooms out of
it, rambling one into the other, were walled in just
as the builders fancied, when they made the house
three hundred years or more ago. And that was in
the reign of Edward VI.'

' Like the Bluecoat boys,' said Susan, ' though I
can't say I like the yellow stockings, Grannie, not
that *mustard* yellow, you know.'

' Like the Bluecoat boys,' repeated her grandmother. ' Well, the house was simply a nest of
hiding-places ; and I was small—smaller even than
you. I would sit with my book ; or watch out of a
window, *lean* out too sometimes—as if to see my
mother in India. And whenever the weather was
fine, and sometimes when it was not, I would creep
out of the house and run away down that shaggy
lane to the little wood you see there. There is a

brook in it (though you can't see that) which brawls
continuously, all day long.   And sometimes I would
climb up this very hill.   And sometimes I would
creep across the field to that little church.

'It was there I most easily forgot myself and my
small scrapes and troubles—with the leaves and the
birds, and the blue sky and the clouds overhead, or
watching a snail, or picking kingcups and cowslips,
or staring into the stream at the fish.   You see I was
rather a doleful little creature :   first because I was
alone ;   next because my Uncle James was ill and
so could not be happy ;   and last because I was made
to feel more homesick than ever, by the cold glances
and cold tongue of Miss Jemima.'

'Miss Jemima !' echoed Susan, burying her face
in her amusement an instant in her hands.

'Miss Jemima,' repeated the old voice solemnly.
'But I was not only dismal and doleful.   Far worse :
I made little attempt to be anything else, and began
to be fretful too.   There was no company of my own
age, for, as you see, the village is a mile or two off—
over there where the sun is lighting the trees up.
And I was not allowed to play with the village
children.   The only company I had was a fat little
boy of two, belonging to one of the farm-hands.   And
he was so backward a baby, that even at that age
he could scarcely say as many words.'

'I began to talk at one,' said Susan.

'Yes, my dear,' said her grannie, 'and you are
likely, it seems, to go on talking the clock round.'

'Grannie, dear,' said Susan, 'I simply *love* this
story—until—*you* know.'

'Now of all the places where I was supposed not

to go to,' continued the old lady, ' that churchyard was the very one. My aunt, as I say, thought me a fantastic silly-notioned little girl, and she didn't approve of picking flowers that grow among tombstones. Indeed, I am not now quite sure myself if such flowers belong to the living at all. Still, once or twice in the summer the old sexton—Mr. Fletcher he was called, and a very grumpy old man he was— used to come with his scythe and mow the lush grasses down. And you could scarcely breathe for the sweet smell of them. It seemed a waste to see them lying in swaths, butterflies hovering above them, fading in the sun. There never were such buttercups and dandelion-clocks and meadow-sweet as grew beneath those old grey walls. I was happy there ; and coming and going, I would say a prayer for my mother. But you will please understand, Susan, that I was being disobedient ; that I had no business to be there at all—when I first came to know there was somebody else in the churchyard.'

' Ah ! somebody else,' sighed Susan, sitting straight up, her eyes far away.

' It was one evening, rather like this one, but with a mackerel sky. The day before I had been stood in the corner for wearing an orange ribbon in my hair ; and then sent to bed for talking to the grandfather's clock. I did it on purpose. And now —*this* evening, I was being scolded because I would not eat blackberry jam with my bread for tea. I was told it was because I had been spoilt, and was a little town child who did not know that God had made the wild fruits for human use, and who thought that the only things fit to eat grew in gardens.

' Really and truly I disliked the blackberry jam because of the pips, and I had a hollow tooth. But I told my aunt that my mother didn't like blackberry jam either, which made her still more angry.

' " Do you really think, James," she said to my uncle, " we should allow the child to grow up a dainty little minx like that ? Now, see here, Miss, you will just stay there until you have eaten up the whole of that slice on your plate."

' " Well, then, Miss Jemima," I said pertly, " I shall stay here till I am eighty."

' " Hold your tongue," she bawled at me, with eyes blazing.

' " I can't bear the horrid——" I began again, and at that she gave me such a slap on my cheek that I overbalanced, and fell out of my chair. She lifted me up from the floor with a shake, set me in my chair again, and pushed it against the table till the edge was cutting into my legs. "And now," she said, " sit there till you are eighty ! "

' A look I had never seen before came into my uncle's face ; his hands were trembling. Without another word to me, Miss Jemima helped him rise from his chair, and I was left alone.

' Never before had I been beaten like that. And I was almost as much frightened as I was hurt. I listened to the tall clock ticking, " Wick-ed child, stub-born child," and my tears splashed slowly down on the odious slice of bread-and-jam on my plate. Then all of a sudden I clenched and shook my ridiculous little fist at the door by which she had gone out, wriggled back my chair, jumped out of it, rushed out of the house, and never stopped to breathe or to look back, until I found myself sitting huddled up under the biggest tomb in the churchyard; crying there, if not my heart out, at least a good deal of my sour little temper.'

' Poor Grannie ! ' said Susan, squeezing her hand.

' There was not much " poor " about that,' was the reply. ' A pretty sight I must have looked, with my smeared face, green-stained frock and hair dangling. At last my silly sobbing ceased. The sky was flaming with the sunset. It was in June, and the air very mild and sweet. But instead of being penitent and realising what a bad and foolish child I was, I began to be coldly rebellious. I stared at the rosy clouds and vowed to myself I'd give Miss Jemima a fright. I'd rather die than go back to the house that night. And when the thought of my mother came into my mind, I shut it out, saying to myself that she could not have cared how much I loved her, to leave me like this. And yet only a fortnight before a long letter had come to me from India !

' Well, there I sat. A snail came out of his day's hiding-place ; moths began to appear ; the after-noon's butterflies had all gone to rest. Far away I heard a hooting—and then a step. Cautiously peering up above my tombstone, I saw Maggie, one of the girls that helped on the farm. Her face was burning hot, and she was staring about her round the corner of the little church tower with her saucer blue eyes. She called to me, and at that my mouth opened and I made a shrill yelping squeal. She screeched too ; her steel-tipped boot slipped on the flagstones ; in an instant she was gone. And once more I was alone.'

'Ah, but you weren't *really* alone, Grannie,' whispered Susan, 'were you?'

'That was just what I was going to tell you, my dear. Immediately in front of my face stood some tall dandelion stalks, with their beautiful clocks, grey in the late evening light. And there were a few other gently nodding flowers. As I stared across them, on the other side of the flat gravestone a face appeared. I mean it didn't rise up. It simply came into the air. A very small face, more oval than round, its gold-coloured hair over its wild greenish eyes falling on either side its head in a curious zigzag way—like this, I mean.' The old lady took the hem of her skirt, and three or four times folded it together, then loosened it out.

'You mean, Grannie, as if it had been pleated,' said Susan.

'Yes,' said her grannie. 'I noticed that most particularly. And very lovely it looked in the reddish light. The face was not smiling, and did not appear to see me sitting there, no more than a lion does when he looks out of his cage at the people gathered round to see him fed. And yet I knew *she* knew that I was there. And though I did not think she minded my being there, I felt more frightened than I had ever been in my life. My mouth opened; I was clutching tight the grass on either side. And I saw nothing else as I stared into that face.'

'That was the Fairy, Grannie,' said Susan, stooping forward again as if to make her words more impressive. The old lady glanced fixedly at the two blue eyes bent on her from under the brim of the round straw hat.

'At that moment, my dear, I did not know *what* it was. I was far too frightened to think. Time must have been passing, too, very quickly, for as I stared on, it was already beginning to be gloaming between us, and silent. Yes, much more silent even than this. Then, suddenly, behind me a low birdlike voice began to sing from out of the may-bushes, the notes falling like dewdrops in the air. I knew it was a nightingale. And at the very moment the thought came to me—That is a nightingale—the face on the other side of the rough grey stone vanished.

'For a few minutes I sat without moving—not daring to move. And then I ran, straight out of the churchyard by the way I had come, as fast as my legs could carry me. I hardly know what I thought, but as soon as I saw the lights in the upper windows of the farm, I ran even faster. Up under the ilexes, and round through the farmyard to the back door. It was unlatched. I slipped through, quiet as a mouse, into the kitchen, climbed into the chair, and at once devoured every scrap of that horrid bread-and-jam !

'And still, my dear, I don't believe I was really thinking, only dreadfully afraid, and yet with a kind of triumph in my heart that Miss Jemima should never know anything at all about the face in the churchyard. It was all but dark in the kitchen now, but I still sat on in my chair, even at last lifted the plate, and insolently licked up with my tongue every jammy crumb that was left.

'And then the door opened, and Miss Jemima stood there in the entry with a lighted brass candle-stick in her hand. She looked at me, and I at her.

" Ah, I see you have thought better of it," she said.
" And high time too.   You are to go straight to bed."

' If you can imagine, Susan, a cake made almost
entirely of plums, and every plum a black thought
of hatred, I was like that.   But I said never a word.
I got down from my chair, marched past her down
the flagstone passage, and she followed after.   When
I came to my uncle's door, I lifted my hand towards
the handle.   " Straight on, Miss," said the voice
behind me.   " You have made him too ill and too
unhappy to wish you good-night."   Straight on I
went, got into bed with all my clothes on, even my
dew-wet shoes, and stared at the ceiling till I fell
asleep.'

' You know, Grannie, said Susan, ' it was very
curious of you not even to undress at all.   Why do
you think you did that ? '

' My dear,' said her grannie, ' at that moment I
had such a hard, hot heart in me, that there was not
any room for a why.   But you see that little jutting
attic window above the trees—it was in the room
beyond that and on the other side of the house that
I lay.   And it's now seventy-five years ago.   It
may be there was even then a far-away notion in my
mind of getting up in the middle of the night and
running away.   But whether or not, I was awakened
by the sun streaming through my lattice window, for
my bedroom lay full in the light of the morning.

' I could think of but one thing—my disgrace of
the night before, and what I had seen in the churchyard.   It was a dream, I thought to myself, shutting
my eyes, yet knowing all the time that I did not
believe what I was saying.   Even when I was told

at breakfast that my uncle was no better, I thought
little of him, and gobbled down my porridge, with
the one wish to be out of the house before I could be
forbidden to go out. But the only sign of Miss
Jemima was my dirty jam-stained plate of the night
before, upon which she had put my hunch of breakfast bread. Yet although I was so anxious to get
out, for some reason I chose very carefully what I
should wear, and changed the piece of ribbon in my
hat from blue to green. A rare minx I was.'

'You were, Grannie,' said Susan, clasping her
knees. 'And then you went out to the churchyard
again?'

'Yes. But all seemed as usual there; except only
that a tiny bunch of coral-coloured berries lay on a
flat leaf, on the very tombstone where I had hid.
Now though I was a minx, my dear, I was also fairly
sharp for my age, and after the first gulp of surprise,
as I stood there among the nodding buttercups, the
sun already having stolen over the grey roof and
shining upon the hot tombstones, I noticed a beady
dewdrop resting on the leaf, and the leaf of as fresh
a green as lettuce in a salad. Looking at this
dewdrop I realised at once that the leaf could not
have been there very long. Indeed, in a few minutes
the sun had drunk up that one round drop of water,
for it was some little time before I ventured to touch
the berries.

'Then I knew in my heart I was not alone there,
and that the green dish had been put there on purpose, just before I had come. The berries were lovely
to look at, too; of a coral colour edging into rose.
And I don't think it was because I had long ago been

warned not to taste strange fruit, but because I was uneasy in conscience already, that I did not nibble one then and there.

' It was very quiet in that green place, and on and on I watched, as still as a cat over a mouse's hole, though I myself really and truly was the mouse. And then, all of a sudden, flinging back my green dangling hat-ribbon, I remember, over my shoulder, I said half aloud, in an affected little voice, ' Well, it's very kind of you, I am sure,' stretched my hand across, plucked one of the berries, and put it into my mouth.

' Hardly had its juice tartened my tongue when a strange thing happened. It was as if a grasshopper was actually sitting in my hair, the noise of that laughter was so close. Besides this, a kind of heat began to creep into my cheek, and it seemed all the colours around me grew so bright that they dazzled my eyes. I closed them. I must have sat there for a while quite unconscious of time, for when I opened them again, the shadow had gone perceptibly back from the stone, and it was getting towards the middle of the morning.

' But there was still that dazzle in my eyes, and everything I looked at—the flowers and the birds, even the moss and lichen on the old stones, seemed as if they were showing me secrets about themselves that I had not known before. It seemed that I could share the very being of the butterfly that was hovering near ; and could almost hear not only what the birds were singing, but what they were saying.'

' Just like the fairy-tales, Grannie.'

' Yes,' said the little old woman, ' but the difference is that I was not happy about it. The flush was still in my cheek, and I could hear my heart beating under my frock, and I was all of an excitement. But I knew in my inmost self that I ought not to feel like that at all ; that I had crept into danger through my wicked temper ; that these little unknown coral fruits on the tombstone had been put there for a trap. It was a bait, Susan ; and I was the silly fish.'

' O Grannie, a " silly fish " ! ' said Susan. ' I can see you *might* feel wicked,' she added, with a sage little nod, ' but I don't *exacaly* see why.'

' That is just when it's most dangerous, my child,' said her grandmother, sharply closing her mouth very much indeed like a fish. ' But I must get on with my story, or we shall never get home.

' I sat on, keeping my eyes as far as I could fixed on the invisible place in the air where I had seen the face appear, but nothing came, and gradually the scene lost its radiance, and the birds were chirping as usual again, and the buttercups were the same as ever. No, not the same as ever, because, although it was a burning, sunny day, it seemed now that everything was darker and gloomier than usual on so bright a morning, and I skulked away home, feeling not only a little cold, but dejected and ashamed.

' As I went in through the gate between those two stone pillars you can just see by the round green tree down there, I looked up at the windows. And a dreadful pang seized me to see that their curtains were all drawn over the glass. And though I didn't know then what that meant, I knew it meant something sorrowful and tragic. Besides, they seemed like shut eyes, refusing to look at me. And when I went in, Miss Jemima told me that my uncle was dead. She told me, too, that he had asked to see me an hour or two before he died. "He said, 'Where is my little Susan?'' And where you have been," added Miss Jemima, "is known only to your wicked wilful self." I stared at her, and seemed to shrink until she appeared to be twice as large as usual. I could not speak, because my tongue would not move. And then I rushed past her and up the stairs into a corner between two cupboards, where I used sometimes to hide, and I don't know what I did or thought there; I simply sat on and on, with my hands clenched in my lap, everything I looked at all blurred, and my lips trying to say a prayer that would not come.

'From that day on I became a more and more wretched and miserable little girl, and, as I think now, a wickeder one. It all came of three things. First, because I hated Miss Jemima, and that is just like leaving a steel knife in vinegar, it so frets and wastes the heart. Next, because of the thought of my poor uncle speaking of me so gently and kindly when he was at death's door; and my remorse that I could never now ask him to forgive me. And last, because I longed to see again that magical face in the churchyard, and yet knew that it was forbidden.'

'But, Grannie dear, you know,' said Susan, 'I never can see why you should have thought that then.'

'No,' replied the old lady. 'But the point was, you see, that I *did* think it, and I knew in my heart

that it would lead to no good. Miss Jemima made
me go next day into the room where my uncle lay
in his coffin. But try as she might to persuade
and compel me, she could not make me open my
eyes and look at him. For that disobedience she
sent me to my bedroom for the rest of the day.

'When all was still, I crept out across the corridor
into another room, and looked out over the trees
towards the little church. And I said to myself, as
if I were speaking to someone who would hear, ' I am
coming to you soon, and nobody, *nobody* here shall
ever see me again.'

'Think of it ; a little girl not yet nine, angry with
the whole world, and hardly giving a thought to the
mother who was longing to see her, and—though I
didn't know it then—was very soon to be in England
again.

'Well, then came the funeral. I was dressed—
I can see myself now, as I stood looking into the
looking-glass—in a black frock trimmed with crape,
with a tucker of white frilling round the neck, and
an edging of it at the sleeves ; my peaked white face
and coal-black eyes.

'It was, as you see, but a very little distance to
my poor uncle's last resting-place, and in those days
they used a long hand-cart on wheels, which the
men pushed in front of us, with its flowers. And
Miss Jemima and I followed after it across the field.
I listened to the prayers as closely as I could. But
at last my attention began to wander, and, kneeling
there beside Miss Jemima in the church, my hands
pressed close to my eyes, for an instant I glanced
out and up between my fingers.

' The great eastern window, though you cannot see it from here, is of centuries-old stained glass, crimson, blue, green.   But in one corner, just above the narrow ledge of masonry outside, it had been broken many, many years ago by the falling of a branch of a tree, and had been mended with clear *white* glass.   And there, looking steadily in and straight across and down at me, was the face and form of the being I had seen beside the tombstone.

' I cannot tell you, Susan, how beautiful that face looked then.   Those rich colours of the saints and martyrs surrounding that gold hair—living gold— and the face as pale and beautiful—far more beautiful than anything else I had ever seen in my life before. But even then I saw, too, that into the morning church a kind of shadowy darkness had come, and the stone faces on either side the window, with their set stare, looked actually to be alive.   I gazed between my fingers, hearing not a single word of what the old clergyman was saying, wondering when anyone else would see what I saw, and knowing that the smiling lips were breathing across at me, ' Come away, come away ! '

' My bones were all cramped, and at last I managed to twist my head a little and peep up at Miss Jemima. The broad face beneath her veil had its eyes shut, and the lips were muttering.   She had noticed nothing amiss.   And when I looked again, the face at the window had vanished.

' It was a burning hot day—so hot that the flowers beside the grave were already withering before Miss Jemima took me home.   We reached the stone porch together, and in its cold shadow she paused, staring down on me through her veil. " You will be staying on here for a while, because I don't know what else to do with you," she said to me. "But you will understand that this is my house now. I am telling your mother how bad a child you are making yourself, and perhaps she will ask me to send you away to a school where they will know how to deal with stubborn and ungrateful beings like yourself. But she will be sorry, I think, to hear that it was your wickedness that brought that poor kind body to its grave over there. And now, miss, as the best part of the day is over, you shall have your bread-and-butter and milk in your bedroom, and think over what I have said." '

' I think, Grannie,' cried Susan, bending herself nearly double, ' that that Miss Jemima was the most dreadful person I have ever heard of.'

' Well, my dear,' said her grandmother, ' I have lived a good many years, and believe it is wiser to try and explain to oneself people as well as things. Do you suppose she would have been as harsh to me if I hadn't hated her ? And now she lies there too, and I never had her forgiveness either.'

Susan turned her head away and looked out over the countryside to the north, to where the roving horses had vanished, and where evening was already beginning gradually to settle itself towards night.

' And *did* you think over what Miss Jemima had said, Grannie ? ' she asked in a low voice.

' The first thing I did was to throw the bread-and-butter out of the window, and while I watched the birds wrangling over it and gobbling it up, I thought of nothing at all. It was cooler in the shade on that

side of the house.   My head ached after the sorrowful
walk to the church and back.   I came away from
the window, took off my black frock, and sat there
on the edge of my bed, I remember, in my petticoat,
not knowing what to do next.   And then, Susan,
I made up my mind that I could not bear to be in
Miss Jemima's house for a day longer than I need.

' I was just clever enough to realise that if I wanted
to run away I must take care not to be brought back.
I grew hot all over at the thought of such a shame,
never thinking how weak and silly I was not to be
able to endure patiently what could only be a few
more days or weeks before another letter came from
my mother.   Then I tore a leaf from a book that
was in my room—a Prayer-Book—and scrawled a
few words to my mother, saying how miserable *and*
wicked I had been, and how I longed to see her again.
It's a curious thing, Susan, but I was pitying myself
while I wrote those words, and thinking how grieved
my mother would be when she read them, and how
well Miss Jemima would deserve whatever my
mother said to her.   But I didn't utter a word in
the letter about where I was going.'

' You didn't really *know* where you were going,
Grannie,' whispered Susan, edging a little nearer.
' Did you ?   Not *then*, I mean ? '

' No, but I had a faint notion whom I was going
to ; for somehow, from old fairy tales I had got to
believe that human children could be taken away to
quite a different world from this—a country of
enchantment.   And I remembered having read, too,
about two children that had come back from there,
and had forgotten their own English.'

' I know two poems about it,' said Susan. ' One about " True Thomas "—" Thomas the Rhymer," you know, Grannie, who stayed with the Queen of Elfland for seven whole years, and another about . . . I do wonder—— But please, *please*, go on.'

' Well, I hid my little letter in a cranny in the wainscot, after sewing a piece of cotton to it so that I might pull it out again when I wanted it. The next morning, I got up early, and slipping on my clothes, tiptoed out of the house before breakfast, and made my way to the church. I thought deceitfully that Miss Jemima would be sure to find out that I was gone, and that if for a morning or two she discovered me quietly sitting in the churchyard she would not suppose at another time, perhaps, that I was not safely there again. Plots, Susan, are tangled things, and are likely to tangle the maker of them too.

' The old man who took care of the church, Mr. Fletcher, to save himself the trouble of carrying the key of the door, used to hide it under a large stone beneath the belfry tower. I had watched him put it there. It was a fresh sparkling day, I remember, with one or two thin silver clouds high in the sky —angels, I used to call them—and I forgot for the moment in the brightness of it all my troubles, as I frisked along past the dewy hedges.

' My first thought was to make quite, quite sure about the strange being in the churchyard, my next to plan a way of escape. I gathered a bunch of daisies, and having come to the belfry door, I somehow managed to open it with the key which I fetched out from beneath its stone, and crept into the still,

E

empty coolness. I had come to the conclusion, too, Susan, young though I was, that if the elf or fairy or whatever she might be actually came into the church to me, it would be a proof there was no harm in her company, though I knew in my heart that I was in some mysterious danger.

' There are a few old oak pews in the little church, with heads carved upon them, and one or two have side seats that draw out from the wood into the aisle. On one of these I sat down, so that while I could be intent on my daisy-chain—just to show I had something to do there—I could see out of the corner of my eye the open door by which I had come in. And I hadn't very long to wait.

' In the midst of the faint singing of the wild birds, out of the light that lay beyond the stone church wall I spied her come stealing. My heart almost stopped beating, nor did I turn my head one inch, so that my eyes soon ached because they were almost asquint with watching. If you can imagine a figure—even now I cannot tell you how tall she was—that seems to be made of the light of rainbows, and yet with every feature in its flaxen-framed face as clearly marked as a cherub's cut in stone; and if you can imagine a voice coming to you, close into your ear, without your being able to say exactly where it is coming *from—that* was what I saw and heard beneath that grey roof down there on that distant morning, seventy-five years ago. The longer I watched her out of the corner of my eye, the more certain I became that she was using every device she knew to attract my attention, even that she was impatient at my stupidity, and yet that she could

not or that she dared not cross the threshold. And
so I sat and watched her, fumbling on the while with
my limpening daisy-stalks. Many strange minutes
must have passed like this.

' At last, however, having fancied I heard a footfall ; I was surprised out of myself, and suddenly
twisted my head. She too had heard, and was
standing stiller than a shadow on snow, gazing in
at me. I suppose thoughts reveal themselves in the
face more swiftly than one imagines. I was partly
afraid, partly longing to approach closer. I wished
her to realise that I longed for her company, but that
danger was near, for I was well aware whose step it
was I had heard. And, as I looked at her, there
came a sharpness into her face, a cold inhuman look
—not of fear, but almost of hatred—and she was
gone. More intent than ever, I stooped over my
daisies. And in the hush there was a faint sound as
of an intensely distant whistle.

' Then a shadow fell across the porch, and there
was Miss Jemima. It's a strange thing, Susan, but
Miss Jemima also did not enter the church. She
called to me from where she stood, in almost a
honeyed voice : " Breakfast is ready, Susan." '

' I can imagine *exacaly* how she said that, Grannie,'
said the little girl, ' because my name's Susan, too.'

' Yes, my dear,' said the old lady, squeezing her
hand. ' It was passed on to you from me by your
dear mother just because it was mine. And I hope
you will always be the Susan I have *now*.' ...From
near at hand upon the hill a skylark suddenly took
its flight into the evening blue. The old lady
listened a moment before going on with her story.

' Well,' she began again, ' I gathered up my apron and walked towards Miss Jemima down the aisle. Suddenly there came a slight rumbling noise, which I could not understand. Then instantly there followed a crash. And at Miss Jemima's very feet, in the sunlight, I saw lying a piece of stone about the size of a small plum pudding. Miss Jemima gave a faint scream. Her cheek, already pale, went white ; and she stared from me to the stone and back again, as I approached her.

' " You were talking in there—in God's church— to someone," she whispered harshly, stooping towards me. " To whom ? "

' I shook my head, and stood trembling and gazing at the stone.

' " Look into my face, you wicked child," she whispered. " Who were you talking to in there ? "

' I looked up at last. " It's empty," I said.

' " There's a lying look in your eyes ! " cried Miss Jemima. " And *you* are the child that goes into a sacred place to weave daisy-chains ! Turn your face away from me. Do you hear me, miss ? Miserable little *Sorceress* that you are ! "

' The word seemed to flame up in my mind as if it had been written in fire on smoke ; and still I stared at the stone. I felt but did not see Miss Jemima steadily turn her head and look around her.

' " A few inches," she added in a low voice, " and you would have killed me."

' " Me ! " I cried angrily. " What has it to do with *me*, Miss Jemima ? "

' " Ah ! " said she. ' We shall know a little more about that when you have told me what company

you find here where your poor uncle might hope to
be at rest."

' It's a dreadful thing to confess, Susan, but up to
that moment, though I had again and again cried
by myself at memory of him, though tears were
always in my heart for him, I hadn't thought of my
uncle that morning.

' " And perhaps," added Miss Jemima, " bread and
water and solitude for a day or two will help to
persuade your tongue."

' I followed her without another word across the
field, and in a few minutes was alone once more in
my bedroom with a stale crust and a glass of water
to keep me company.

' I should think if my angry tears had run into the
water that morning, they would have actually made
it taste salt. But I cried so that not even a mouse
could have heard me. Every other thought was
now out of my mind—for I dared not even talk
to myself about the stone—but that of getting away
from the house for ever. One thing I could not
forget, however, and that was the word " sorceress."
It terrified me far more than I can tell you. I knew
in my young mind that Miss Jemima was treating
me wickedly, however naughty I had been, and I knew
too, in fear and horror, that the stone might not
have fallen by accident. I had seen the look on the
Fairy's face and . . .' The old lady suddenly broke
off her story at this point, and looked about her in
alarm. ' My dear, we must go at once ; the dew is
beginning to fall, and the air is already colder.'

' Oh, Grannie,' said the child, ' how I wish we
might stay—a little, *little* longer ! '

' Well, my dear, so do I. For I am old, and I shall never see this place again. It brings many memories back. Who knows what might have happened if——'

' But, Grannie,' interrupted the child hastily, picking up the umbrella from the grass. ' Please tell me the rest of the story straight, straight, straight on as we go back.' It seemed to Susan, so rapt was her grandmother's face at that moment, and so absent her eyes—that she could not have heard her. The small aged eyes were once more looking carefully down on the scene below. For an instant they shut as if the old lady had thought so to remember it more completely. And then the two of them began slowly to climb the hill, and the story proceeded.

' No one disturbed me during that long morning,' continued the quiet voice, ' but in the afternoon the door was unlocked, and Miss Jemima opened it to show in a clergyman, Mr. Wilmot, who conducted the service in the church every other Sunday. I won't tell you all he said to me. He was a kind and gentle old man, but he didn't so much as think it possible there was any being or thing in the church-yard but its birds, its tombstones, and now and then a straying animal. He only smiled about all that, nor did he ask me Miss Jemima's question.

' He took my hand in his great bony one and begged me to be a good little girl. And I see his smiling face as he asked it. " Not only for your mother's sake," he said, " but *for goodness' sake*."

' " I am sure, my dear," he went on, " Miss Jemima *means* to be kind, and all *we* have to do is to mean to be good."

' I gulped down the lump in my throat, and said, " But don't you think *sorceress* is a very wicked word ? "

' He stood up, holding both my hands in his. "But my poor little lamb," he cried, " Miss Jemima is no more a sorceress than I am a Double Dutchman ! " And with that he stooped, kissed the top of my head, and went out of the room.

' In a minute or two his footsteps returned. He opened the door an inch and peeped in. " Why, we are better already ! " he smiled at me over his spectacles. Then he came in, carrying a plate with a slice of bread-and-jam upon it, and a mug of milk. " There," he said, " there's no sorcery in that, is there ? And now you will be an obedient and gentle child, and think how happy Mamma will be to see you ? " '

' I think,' said Susan stoutly, ' that that Mr. Wilmot is one of the kindest men I ever knew.'

Her grandmother looked down on her with a peculiar smile on her face. ' He was so kind, Susan, that I never mentioned to him that the blackberry-jam on the bread was not a great favourite of mine ! A moment after the sound of his footsteps had died away I heard the key once more in the lock. And what did I say to myself when he was gone ? I looked forlornly at the plate, then out of the window, and I believe, Susan, that I did what they sometimes describe in the story-books—I wrung my hands a little, repeating to myself, " *He doesn't understand. No ! He doesn't understand.*"

' In an hour or two, Miss Jemima herself opened the door and looked in. She surveyed me where I sat, and then her glance fell on the untouched slice of bread-and-jam.

' " Ah," said she, " a good man like Mr. Wilmot cannot realise the hardness of a stubborn heart. I don't want to be unkind to you, Susan, but I have a duty to perform to your mother and to your poor uncle. You shall not leave this room until you apologise to me for your insolence of this morning, and until you tell me whom you were speaking to in the church."

' The lie that came into my mind—" But I was not speaking to anyone, Miss Jemima "—faded away on my tongue. And I simply looked at her in silence.

' " You have a brazen face, Susan," said she, " and if you grow up as you are now, you will be a very wicked woman." '

' I think,' said Susan, ' that was a perfectly *dreadful* thing to say, Grannie.'

' Times change, my dear,' said the old lady. ' And now—well, it is fortunate there is very little more to tell. For this hill has taken nearly all the breath out of my body ! '

The two of them stood now on the crest of the hill. The light was beginning to die away in the sky, and the mists to grow milkier in the hollows of the flat country that lay around and beneath them. Far, far away, facing them across the wild, a reddish-coloured moon was rising. From far beneath them a dog barked—it might be from dead Miss Jemima's farmyard. The little church surrounded by its low wall seemed to have gathered in closer to its scattered stones.

' Yes, Grannie, dear ? ' breathed Susan, slipping
her hand into the cotton-gloved one that hung near.
' What then ? '

' Then,' replied her grandmother, ' the door was
locked again. Anger and hatred filled that silly
little body sitting in the bedroom, and towards
evening I fell asleep. And I must have dreamed a
terrifying dream, though when I awoke I could not
remember my dream—only its horror. I was
terrified at it in that solitude, and I knew by the
darkening at the window that it must be at least
nine or ten o'clock. Night was coming, then. I
could scarcely breathe at the thought. A second
mug of milk had been put beside the plate ; but
I could not even persuade myself to drink any of it.

' Then in a while I heard Miss Jemima's footsteps
pass my room. She made no pause there, and
presently after I knew that she had gone to bed,
having not even troubled to look in on her wretched
little prisoner. The hardness of that decided me.

' I tiptoed over to the door, and with both hands
softly twisted the handle. It was still locked. Then
I went to the window and discovered, as if the fairy
creature herself had magicked it there, that a large
hay-wain half full of hay, its shafts high in the air,
had been left drawn up within a few feet of my
window. It looked dangerous, but it was not
actually a very difficult jump even for a child of my
age ; and I think I would have attempted it even
if there had been no cart at all. My one thought was
to run away. *Any*where—so long as there was no
chance of Miss Jemima's finding me.

' But even in that excited foolish moment I had

sense enough left—before I jumped out of the window—to take a warm woollen jacket out of my chest-of-drawers, and to wrap my money-box up in a scarf so that it should not jangle too much. I pulled my letter up from its cranny in the wainscot by its thread, and put it on the pink dressing-table. And at that moment, in the half dark I saw my face in the looking-glass. I should hardly have recognised it. It looked nearly as old, Susan, as I do now.'

' Yes, dear Grannie,' said Susan.

' Then I jumped—without the slightest harm to myself. I scrambled down into the yard and, keeping close to the house, crept past the kennel, the old sheep-dog merely shaking her chain with her thumping tail a little as I passed. And then, as soon as I was beyond the tall gate-posts, I ran as fast as my legs would carry me.'

' But *not*,' cried Susan almost with a shout in the still air, ' *not* to the churchyard, Grannie. I think that was the most wonderful thing of all.'

' Not so very wonderful, my dear, if you remember that I was now intensely afraid of the fairy, after seeing that look of evil and hatred in her face when Miss Jemima was approaching the church. Something in me had all along, as you know, said, *Don't be deceived by her. She means you no good*. I cannot explain that ; but so it was. Yet all the time I had been longing to follow wherever she might lead. Why she should wish to carry off a human child I don't know, but that she really wanted me I soon discovered for certain.

' If you follow the tip of my umbrella, you will

just be able to see, Susan, a large meadow on the other side of the farm. But I don't think even your sharp eyes will detect the stones standing up in it. They are called the Dancers, and though I was dreadfully frightened of passing them in the darkness, this was the only way to take. Gradually I approached them, my heart beating beneath my ribs like a drum, until I had come near.

' And there, lovelier than ever, shining in that dark as if with a light of her own, and sitting beneath the largest of the Dancers directly in my path, was She. But this time I knew she was not alone. I cannot describe what passed in my heart I longed to go on, and yet was in anguish at the thought of it. I didn't dare to look at her, and all I could think to do was to pretend not to see anything. How I found the courage I cannot think. Perhaps it was the courage that comes when fear and terror are almost beyond bearing.

' I put my money box on to the grass ; the scarf was already wet with dew. Then, very slowly, I put my black jacket on and buttoned it up. And then, with my eyes turned away, I walked slowly on down the path, between the Dancers, towards the one that is called the Fiddler, in their midst. The night air here was cold and still. But as I approached the stone, it seemed as if it were full of voices and patterings and sounds of wings and instruments. It terrified and bewildered me ; I could think of nothing.

' I just kept saying, " Oh, please, God ; oh, please, God," and walked on. And when at last I came to the stone, the whole world suddenly seemed to turn

dark and cold and dead. Apart from the ancient
stone, leaning up out of the green turf as it had done
for centuries, there was not a sign or a symptom,
Susan, of anything or anybody there.'

' I think I can *just* see the stone, Grannie, but I
would not be there like that in the dark, not for
anything—anything in the world. . . . I expect
it was what you *said* made the Fairy go. And then,
Grannie ? '

' Then, Susan, my heart seemed to go out of me.
I ran on, stumbling blindly for a little way, then lost
my balance completely over a tussock of grass or a
mole-heap and fell flat on my face. Without any
words that I can remember, I lay praying in the
grass.

' But even that did not turn me back. I got up at
last and ran on more lightly, and without looking
behind me, across the field. Its gate leads into a
by-road. It was padlocked, and as I mounted to the
top my eyes could see just above a slight rise in the
ground, for the lane lies beneath a little hill there.

' And coming along the road towards me there
were shining the lamps of a carriage. I clambered
down and crouched in the hedge-side, and in a few
moments the lamps reappeared at the top of the
incline and the horse came plod-plodding along
down the hill. It was a wonderful summer night,
the sky all faint with stars. What would have
happened if it had been cold or pouring with rain I
cannot think. But because it was so warm, the air
almost like milk, the hood of the carriage was down.

' And as it came wheeling round by the hedge-side,
I saw in the filmy starlight who it was who was

sitting there. Neither horse nor coachman had seen me. I jumped to my feet and ran after the carriage as fast as my legs could carry me, screaming at the top of my voice, " Mother, Mother ! "

' Perhaps the grinding of the wheels in the flinty dust and the noise of the hoofs drowned my calling. But I still held tight to my money-box, and though it was muffled by the scarf in which it was wrapped, at each step it made a dull noise like a bird-scare, and this must at last have attracted my mother's attention. She turned her head, opened her mouth wide at sight of me—I see her now—then instantly jumped up and pulled the coachman's buttoned coat-tails. The carriage came to a standstill. . . .

' And that,' said the old lady, turning away her head for one last glance of the countryside around her, ' that is all, Susan.'

Susan gave a last great sigh. ' I can't think what you must have felt, Grannie,' she said, ' when you were safe in the carriage. And I can't——' But at this point she began to laugh very softly to herself, and suddenly stood still. ' And I can't think either,' she went on, ' what Miss Jemima must have thought when you and *Great*-Grannie knocked at the door. You did tell me once that she opened her bedroom window at the sound of the knocking, and looked out in her nightdress. I expect she was almost as frightened as you were amongst those Dancers.'

The two of them were now descending the hill on the side away from the farm and the church. And they could see not only their carriage standing beneath them, but the evening star had also come into

view.   There could not be a more peaceful scene—
the silver birches around them standing motionless
under the deep, pale sky, clothed with their little
leaves, and the rabbits at play among the gorse
and juniper.

'Bless me, Mum,' said the old cabman as he
opened the carriage door, 'I was just beginning to
think them fairises had runned away with you and
the young lady.'

Susan burst completely out laughing.   'Now don't
you think, Grannie,' she said, 'that is a very, very
curious quincidence ? '

THE THIEF

NCE upon a time there lived in a mansion in the Great City of London a Thief. There never was a thief of so much pomp and splendour. He had coaches and carriages — apple - green cardinal, scarlet, canary and maroon. He had stabling for forty horses—bay, cream, roan, and piebald. He had coachmen and footmen, link-boys, and outriders, white, yellow and black. Of servants to do his bidding there was a multitude. He never even attempted to remember their names. He clapped his hands, and they came; clapped his hands and they went.

His marbled rooms were crammed to their gilded ceilings with furniture of the utmost magnificence. Money was nought to him. Not only were his plates and dishes, jugs and basins of solid gold, but so were his chair-castors, locks, keys, and bell-pulls ; while his warming pans were of purest Thracian silver. There was Gobelin velvet on his floors ; there were tapestries of Arras and Bayeux on his walls with the date in each corner, 999. Silken mats from Persia and India, Bangkok and

Samarkand beflowered his marble and alabaster stair-cases.

As for his Pictures—he had a Siege of Athens fourteen yards by six even in his privy parlour, with frame to match. His cellars were full of wine, his attics—boards to rafters—with sacks of moidores, doubloons, diamonds, rubies, Orient pearls, and Pieces of Eight. There never was such a Thief since the world began, and he lived in his mansion all alone.

He had a fine constitution, too. He was a square heavy man with a large head and a slight squint in his little green eyes, and he dressed in a velvet doublet and rose-silk hose, like Henry VIII. And being now come to be about sixty years of age, and having stolen everything in the world he thought worth stealing, his one desire was to marry and settle down. He desired to be safe and comfortable and respectable and beloved. Better still, he longed beyond measure for a nursery of children ; he wanted to *share* his ill-gotten gains among them— ten at least : five strapping sons and five lovely flaxen daughters.

And then perhaps in full season, when he was ninety-nine or a hundred or so, he would die and be buried in an enormous tomb made of a hundred kinds of marble, inlaid with sardonyx, chrysopase and chalcedony. And he hoped by that time no one would have the faintest wish to remember where his wicked wealth had come from, he being by then so much beloved. On that day multitudes upon multitudes of mourners—men, women and children —in deepest black, with crape streamers and lilies in their hands, would attend him to his grave. And they would cut out upon his alabaster tomb in gold-filled lettering :

> Here lies at rest in our belief
> Of honourable men the Chief.
> He died respected of men all
> After a Splendid Funeral.

Just like Enoch Arden, who had never in his long solitary existence stolen a sixpence or even a yam !

But this of course was only a wicked hope and dream of folly in this Thief's head. He had many such dreams and he was still alive ; and one of them— much more enjoyable than tombstones and funerals — was how to be happy. But it was difficult for such a Thief as he even to be contented. It was difficult for such a Thief as he to be contented because it was impossible for such a Thief to be at ease. He hadn't a Friend to his name, and more enemies than he could count. He could not even stir out of his house except after dark, or in a thick fog, in case he should be recognised in the streets by someone whom he had robbed. He was therefore compelled to keep within doors all day. His only chance, that is, against being found out was always to stay in.

Even at night he would sit shivering in his coach on his way to a Ball or a Rout or a Banquet or a Levee or a Ceremony or a Function, with the gold-laced blinds tightly drawn, and his piebald horses heavily caparisoned in ear-nets and flowered velvet and silver tassels, so that nobody should notice their tell-tale spots. And as likely as not he put on a false beard and whiskers.

All this was second nature to him, but the one thing he could not understand—when lolling on some Persian divan he was safe at home sitting by himself and looking at the exquisite pictures in a beautiful book he had not yet learned to read, or playing over a tune with one finger on his American organ, or biting his nails and looking out of the window at the people walking in the streets, every one of whom was twenty-thousand times at least poorer than his chief footman—there was one thing he could not understand. Which was why he was not happy.

At first he supposed it was because he had not yet managed to marry a wife. But then for a Thief as rich as he only a very few wives could be fine enough. It must be a Great Lady. It must be a Lady of Wealth and of Title and of a Family as old as the Pyramids. He had asked all such of these as he could find or be told about, but not a single one would at last say, Yes.

First there was the Duchess of Anjou and Angelette. She was a duchess absolutely in her own right, with finer manners than a queen, and a nose so aristocratic that it rose up between her eyes like the Duke of Burgundy's, or like the wing of a seraph in full flight. The Thief sent her a most polite little note, copied out of a Guide to Letter Writing, and inscribed in the most beautiful Italian handwriting by his Writing-Master, Signor Babbinetti. At first the Duchess had said Yes—though not in such few words as that.

But when her High Chamberlain came to look over the Thief's mansion, and to count his sacks of diamonds and doubloons, and taste the wine in his cellar, he began to have suspicions. There was a coffer of ivory and ebony in one of the attics with mermaids in gold and silver at the four corners and dolphins with eyes of emerald all round that he *seemed* to remember to have seen in the Palace of the Emperor of Portugal. And there was a necklet of black duck's-egg pearls that he knew in his heart had once dangled round the neck of the fair Duchess of Anjou and Angelette herself. And as soon as he had returned home and had refreshed himself with a little sleep after his visit to the Thief's cellars, the Duchess addressed in the third person another little letter to the Thief, which said not Yes, but a most emphatic No.

So, too, with the Countess Couterau de Côtelette with the three golden plaits, one of whose ancestors had been King of Troy before Helen was born. *Her* first faint Yes was also followed by an emphatic No.

Indeed, the Thief grew more and more dejected and more and more anxious and miserable and angry. One after the other, these noble ladies : next a widowed Marchioness with a wig, and next a dowager Baroness without, and next the step-daughter of a Baronet, and next the aunt by marriage of a Knight, and so on and on and on—they one and all refused with disdain at last to accept his proffered hand. And it was by no means ever because he squinted or dressed like Henry VIII., but simply because he was no honest man but a Thief.

After a whole year's letter-writing the Thief was just as much a bachelor as ever and ten times more unhappy. Indeed news had long since gone abroad of his vain endeavours to find a bride. His neighbours were filled with suspicion; they looked askance at his chimneys; and one by one, leaving their houses vacant and staring, they removed far away out of his society. And ever more and more the vacancy grew about that infamous mansion until at length a newsboy crying the news sounded like the hollow booming of the bittern, and the streets were a desolation. And now, oftentimes, strangers from foreign parts, and peculiar-looking men like pirates and bandits might be seen standing and gazing up at his windows from the deserted pavements, only to turn away at last with a frown of contempt or a sudden grimace.

And the Thief peering down and out on them from behind his rich damask curtains, would tremble in his shoes, partly in rage and partly in fear. Yes, he began to be afraid of what might now befall him—what mishap. And he bought yet another twenty red Morocco leather buckets to be filled with water and hung in rows in his gilded marble vestibule in case an enemy should set his house on fire. Moreover, he had three heavy chains hung upon the door, and new locks fitted to all the windows. Why? To keep out Thieves!

Not only this, but his mind began to be gnawed by remorse. And now and then, especially at Christmastide and on St. Valentine's Day, a great empty van would draw up to the house and would carry away a sack or two of money, with cabinets, and carpets, and pictures and such like, for Christmas gifts and Valentines to people the Thief had never

seen. He would not even put his name and address
on the packages—but just 'X from X.' But at
last he wearied of copying out the names and
addresses of new strangers to send gifts to. And one
night a happy thought came to him. . With chisel,
hammer, and jemmy, he cut away the bars of some
of the lower windows and left them wide open to the
empty dark in the dead of night.

And one such dark night, as he sat listening,
muffled up in an Arabian shawl, three felons in
masks and felt slippers came creeping in through the
open windows and began to put treasures into their
sacks.

The Thief rubbed his hands together with a long
gentle sigh. ' Now at last,' he thought to himself, ' I
shall escape : I shall be free : I will begin again :
a new man : I shall be loved for my own sake only.'
And he shivered a little. But alas even as he
listened, he heard the first thief say to the second
thief, ' Silas, what have we here ? '

And the third thief said to the first thief, ' And
this, too ? Ay me ! Oh no ! Oh no ! '

And presently, leaving their bulging impious sacks
behind them, the three thieves crept out once more
through the open window and were swallowed up in
the darkness. And *the* Thief, with his little green
squinting eyes, muffled up in his Arabian shawl,
knew that these not wholly dishonest men had been
utterly ashamed even so much as to have coveted
such a bad man's goods. And for the first time in
his wicked life he blushed up to his eyes.

And so—and so—he grew more and more unhappy,
and more and more suspicious and sullen and sly and

stupid.   He never even dare stir out after dusk had fallen now, and his horses grew so fat over their mangers of wheat and oats and barley that they could scarcely stir in their stables.   And at last he sold them one and all—bay and cream, roan and piebald ; and he sold his coaches and carriages— apple-green, cardinal, scarlet, canary and maroon. And he dismissed his grooms and coachmen and outriders and linkboys, and his butler and cup-bearer, his three valets and all his servants.   And in a few days there was nobody left in that vast mansion but himself.   No-one at all.   He was alone.

But *still* he did not know where to turn or what to do to be at peace or in comfort ; while the streets and squares around him grew emptier and emptier, and there was scarcely a sound to be heard in his house but the interminable sawing of moths gnawing at his tapestries, mice at his cedar-wood, and rats at his butts.   His doublet hung looser and looser on his stooping shoulders, his rose-silk hose sagged in folds on his shanks.   He hiccoughed whenever he ate or drank.   He was a creature almost without hope.

And one late afternoon, as he sat on his striped marble staircase going down to the Hall, there came a tap.   *Tap, tap, tap.*   With his damascened silver-mounted blunderbuss in his left hand, the Thief opened the door on its chain and peered through the crevice.

' Who's there ? ' he said.

And a voice said, ' Pity the blind.'

'*I* didn't make your eyes,' muttered the Thief, peering through and clutching tighter his blunderbuss.

' Pity the blind,' repeated the voice. ' I starve.'

And there was a slip of moon standing over the house-tops by whose light the Thief could see the thin, white, trembling eyelids of the blind man and his fallen cheeks. He stared at him a while.

' Wait there,' he said.

So, ascending into his empty banqueting hall, he carried down from the table at which he had been sitting and looking at the pictures in the book of Jeremiah—he carried down to the blind man a manchet of white bread and a cup of water. And he thrust the manchet through the crevice of the door into the beggar's one hand ; and the cup of water into the other.

Whereupon, having drained the cup of water, the blind beggar, shaking there with palsy in the moonlight, inquired if there was anything he could do for the Thief in return for his charity. And the Thief shook a heavy head.

And the blind beggar, lifting his face in the moonlight, sniffed softly, and cried in a low, still voice, ' Ay, but I smell the Magic Egg.'

' What's that ? ' cried the Thief sharply.

' Hatched,' was the reply, ' it brings happiness ! ' And with that the blind beggar turned himself about, and clutching his loaf groped his way down from out of the Thief's marble porch.

From that day on, of course, the Thief's one thought, hope, desire and aim was to find the Magic Egg. From loft to cellar, from roof to drains, he searched his mansion through. There never was such a scene of riot and rummaging and disorder. The contents of a thousand drawers were strewn

upon the floor. His sacks of money and jewels
were slit from top to bottom and their contents
lay glittering and shimmering in heaps in the sunbeams that pierced through his upper windows.
He ripped up his ottomans, sawed through his
chair-legs, and disembowelled his divans.

And there was nobody to help, feed, encourage,
or watch over him but one puny scullery-maid with
eyes black as sloes and a shock of jet-black hair.
And why ?   Simply because she had refused to go.
Six times the Thief had barred her out at the area
steps, having given her, for fear of being talked
about, a fresh week's wages every time.   Yet still
for the seventh time, she had managed to creep
back again into the mansion, though by what
crevice or cranny her master never knew.

Being accustomed by this time to hearing only the
gnawing of the moths and the mice and the rats and
the hushing drift of dust in the vacant air, the Thief
could distinguish the least little trickle of sound in
his mansion at night.   So it was that for the seventh
time he had found himself creeping downstairs
with his candle, only to discover this stubborn
creature sitting on the scullery steps with the same
old band-box and broken umbrella as before.

' You ! you baggage !   Why do you keep coming
back, when I have told you to go ? ' he cried angrily
in the doorway.   ' *You* there !   do you hear me ?
It's against the law.   I shall send for the P—P—P—.'

But somehow or other the word stuck to the root
of his tongue.

Susan's black eyes, shining like pools of ink and
ebony beneath her mop of jet-black hair, looked up

at him from the scullery step. ' Oh, Master ! ' she
said. ' If I go, then you will starve to death, you
will. In all my life I never see anyone before so
drop away.'

And the Thief, shivering with cold as he stood in
the doorway, could feel at sound of these words
how loose his bones were in his body. ' What's
that to you ? ' he said. ' If I drop away, I drop
away. And why should you care ? '

' Oh, Master,' said she, ' You was less unkind to
me than to all the other servants put together, and
stay here I must and will, if only to see you comfortably into your coffin.'

' My coffin,' cried the Thief, staring at her out of
an empty face. ' My coffin ! '

' Oh, Master ! ' said she, ' they comes to all, they
do.'

And the Thief after mumbling and grumbling (for
he had never meant to be less unkind to anybody
than to everybody) simply because he was too weary
and unhappy and restless and befogged in his wits
to do anything else, let her stay on.

' Never let me set eyes on you ! ' says he ; ' nor
hear so much as a sneeze, nor sniff so much as a
candlewick. There's odds and ends in the larder, and
there's water in the cistern.' And once more he
returned to his search for the Magic Egg.

Now early one Spring morning, the Thief happened
to climb up on top of two gilt chairs in a forgotten
lumber room to look over the edge of an old oak
fifteenth-century Carnarvonshire wardrobe. It was
not an elegant or beautiful or valuable wardrobe, indeed it looked queer and ungainly and ugly standing

up there among all the other splendours which that
wicked Thief had acquired and discarded in his long
active life. But unlike the rest, it was an honest
wardrobe, for it had been left to him in her last
will and testament in his young and careless days by
a Welsh widow-woman. For one bright morning—
just such a morning as this—the Thief had been on
his way through East Honglingham to see a famous
Abbey in those parts in which in old days the Monks
had dined off silver dishes that had once belonged
to the Grand Kham of Tartary.

And as in the bright March weather he turned the
corner into the village street, he saw over an orchard
wall, hanging pegged upon a clothes-line, and spread
over the currant and gooseberry-bushes within, a
marvellous array of white laundered linen. The
sun flashed down on the cherry-trees and plums
in full blossom. But fairer, sweeter, whiter yet was
this array. Pausing—even on that rapid and
dangerous journey—to admire the scene, he had
with all his heart exclaimed out loud, ' My hat and
shoe-tags ! Now that's what I call WASHING.'

Now, by chance the widow-woman herself—her
sleeves tucked up to her elbow and a pink print cap
on her head—was standing at that moment on the
other side of the wall, and she heard these words.
She drank them in. And it kindled such burning
pleasure in her heart to hear her laundering thus
praised by a stranger, that she never forgot him.
And when she lay dying, she remembered him yet
again. Thus it was that the Thief had acquired
this ugly old fifteenth-century Carnarvonshire wardrobe.

All thought of the widow, however, had vanished completely out of his mind as he clambered heavily up on to the two chairs set one on top of the other that morning in the search that had now grown desperate for the Magic Egg. And as his squinting eyes came over the dog-tooth cornice, they fastened greedily upon a small square wooden box, its top at least an eighth of an inch thick with dust. For on the side of it they had detected in the dim light six scrawled letters : ' THE EGG.'

With a groan of joy he thrust out his hand, clutched the box, the upper chair slipped from under him ; and down he came toppling headlong, higgledy-piggledy, helter-skelter to the floor. He groaned and moaned and moaned and groaned. There was no doubt about it, his leg was broken in three places, and a rare trouble it was for Susan to get him into bed. But she bound the broken leg up at last with three old silk handkerchiefs and a broom-stick.

And after a while, with the wooden box under his pillow, the Thief fell asleep in his great four-post bed. For a full forty-eight hours—two whole days and two whole nights—he lay there fast asleep. At the first tick of the forty-ninth he woke up, and having lit his candle at the bed-side, he pushed his hand in under his pillow as he lay on his back and, with trembling fingers, drew out the box. And there within, sure enough, just twisted up in a twist of old newspaper and cotton-wool, was the Egg.

It was a small, usual-shaped egg and of the colour of a robin's. And as the broken-legged Thief held it between finger and thumb he heard a faint, faint,

faint tapping. *Tap, tap, tap!* And in another instant—hatched in slumber by the warmth of the Thief's swansdown pillow—the thin shell crumbled between his fingers and there flew out, full-fledged, a teeny, tiny, leetle Bird with feathers of gold and eyes like emeralds and claws like coral. And it perched on his bedrail; it tweeted a few frail notes sharper than a needle and tinier than a clover-seed; and it looked at the Thief.

At that moment there came the whisper of a whisper at the immense mahogany door. For the ninety-seventh time during that last forty-eight hours Susan was standing there in the doorway looking in on her master; but now her eyes under her black mop of hair were fixed on this Tiny One.

And she said ' O ! '

And it seemed to the Thief as he lay there shrunken to a shadow, and looking at Susan with her mouth open, that he had never seen a lovelier sight. And yet, nevertheless, the delight in her dark eyes, and on her smooth young sooty cheek as she smiled at the bird, was something no Thief—not even Ali Baba's brother himself—could *steal*. And his heart seemed to break into three times as many pieces as his leg, as he said, having forgotten how many times this question had been answered by the highborn with emphatic Noes, ' Susan, will you marry me ? '

And she said : ' Oh, Master ! It comes sudden. And I don't like anything in the house at all, at all, at all. I hates it. And particularly them bags of beads and brass upstairs in the attics. And all them rats a-capering on their hind-legs in the cellar. And

such a mort of carpets to sweep and marble to keep
clean and windows to keep curtained. But if you
truly love me, then I will marry you. And please
may I have the little bird on the bedrail for a
wedding-present.'

Now there was an old, old curate that lived in the
great Square nearby—the only human creature there,
because all that property was of no value now and
its rent a mere song. For what even comparatively
honest man ever wants to live next door to a Thief ?
But the curate had other views, and he had called
regularly at the Thief's mansion month after month
on their first Mondays for years and years, though in
Mr. Smoke's the butler's day he had never once been
let in. But Susan knew about him all right, oh yes ;
and he came round with his stole and his surplice
over his arm that May Day morning, and he married
them then and there.

And the Thief, having now given away everything
in his house, including the glass beads and the brass,
died presently after, of his broken leg. And though
he was not exactly happy or good—since no man can
be that for more than a moment or two together—
I must say that on the day of his death there was
much less of a squint than usual in his little green
eyes, and he looked far less like King Henry VIII.
(who could have married as many duchesses as he
pleased by cutting off their heads in turn) than he
had ever looked before. That may have been
because in his last moments there was a little gold
bird singing a song like a grasshopper on the towel
rail near the window to the left of his bed, while
on the right sat Susan, holding his crime-stained

hand and saying how sorry she was to bid him
good-bye.

And soon after the Thief had breathed his last, the
tiny inmate of the Magic Egg fluttered across the
bed and quite unbeknown to Susan, who had fallen
asleep with grief and fatigue, at once set to building
a little sort of a nest in her hair. But in spite of the
fact that she, being kind-hearted, was thus prevented
from combing out her hair *completely* every night
and morning, the kind curate managed to get her a
'place' with an elderly maiden lady living in a
charming villa near a village called Silleyton in
Suffolk. And this lady (seeing how good and happy
and willing a creature Susan was otherwise) did not
mind her maid looking like a Zulu with that extra-
ordinarily bunchy mop of hair. And when this old
lady died, having no nephews or nieces to whom to
leave her money, she left it all to Susan.

So Susan was a lady, too. And after residing
quietly in the villa for some little time, the High
Chamberlain of the Duchess of Anjou and Angelette,
who lived nearby, presented her with a gilt-edged
ticket admitting her every Tuesday, Thursday and
Saturday, to walk in the Great Park. And though
the children of the third under-gardener, when they
saw her in her neat black weeds, taking the air under
the pale-green beech-trees, would whisper audibly
to one another, ' Lawks, what a mop ! '—for some
reason Susan was as happy as a kingfisher.

And every foggy 5th of November she would take
a first-class ticket and be off by the Great Eastern
Railway, to a certain large cemetery near London,
and make her way to the south-east corner of it.

And there, under a weeping willow, stood a small rounded stone. Susan would lay her bunch of artificial forget-me-nots (the real not being yet abloom) beside the stone, and, with her black-edged handkerchief in her hand, she would once more, with tears in her eyes, spell out the epitaph on it :

'Here lies my poor deer husband. R.I.P.'

BROOMSTICKS

MISS CHAUNCEY'S cat, Sam, had been with her many years before she noticed anything unusual, anything *disturbing*, in his conduct. Like most cats who live under the same roof with but one or two humans, he had always been more sagacious than cats of a common household. He had learned Miss Chauncey's ways. He acted, that is, as nearly like a small mortal dressed up in a hairy coat as one could expect a cat to act. He was what is called an ' intelligent ' cat.

But though Sam had learned much from Miss Chauncey, I am bound to say that Miss Chauncey had learned very little from Sam. She was a kind, indulgent mistress ; she could sew, and cook, and crochet, and make a bed, and read and write and cipher a little. And when she was a girl she used to sing ' Kathleen Mavourneen ' to the piano. Sam, of course, could do nothing of this kind.

But then, Miss Chauncey could no more have caught and killed a mouse or a blackbird with her five naked fingers than she could have been Pope of Rome. Nor could she run up a six-foot brick wall,

or leap clean from the hearthmat in her parlour on
to the shelf of her chimney-piece without disturbing
a single ornament, or even tinkling one crystal-drop
against another.   Unlike Sam, too, she could not find
her way in the dark, or by her sense of smell ; or
keep in good health by merely nibbling grass in the
garden.   If, moreover, she had been carefully held
up by her feet and hands two or three feet above the
ground and then dropped, she would have at once
fallen plump on her back, whereas when Sam was
only three-months-old he could have managed to
twist clean about in the air in twelve inches and come
down on his four feet, as firm as a table.

While then Sam had learned a good deal from Miss
Chauncey, she had learned nothing from him.   And
even if she had been willing to be taught, it is
doubtful if she would ever have proved even a
promising pupil.   What is more, she knew much
less about Sam than he knew about his mistress—
until, at least, that afternoon when she was doing
her hair in the glass.   And then she could hardly
believe her own eyes.   It was a moment that
completely changed her views about Sam—and
nothing after that experience was ever quite the
same again.

Sam had always been a fine upstanding creature,
his fur jet-black and silky, his eyes a lambent green,
even in sunshine, and at night a-glow like green
topazes.   He was now full five years of age, and had
an unusually powerful miaou.   Living as he did quite
alone with Miss Chauncey at Post Houses, it was
natural that he should become her constant companion.   For Post Houses was a singularly solitary

house, standing almost in the middle of Haggurdsdon
Moor, just where two wandering byways cross each
other like the half-closed blades of a pair of shears
or scissors.

It was a mile and a half from its nearest neighbour,
Mr. Cullings, the carrier ; and yet another quarter of
a mile from the village of Haggurdsdon. Its roads
were extremely ancient. They had been sheep-tracks
long before the Romans came to England and had
cut *their* roads from shore to shore. But for many
years past few travellers or carts or even sheep with
their shepherd came Miss Chauncey's way. You
could have gazed from her windows for hours
together, even on a summer's day, without seeing so
much as a tinker's barrow or a gipsy's van.

Post Houses too was perhaps the ugliest house
there ever was. Its four corners stood straight up
on the moor like a house of nursery bricks. From
its flat roof on a clear day the eye could see for miles
and miles across the moor, Mr. Cullings's cottage being
out of sight in a shallow hollow. It had belonged
to Miss Chauncey's respectable ancestors for genera-
tions. Many people in Haggurdsdon indeed called
it Chauncey's. And though in a blustering wind it
was as full of noises as an organ, though it was a cold
barn in winter, and though another branch of the
family had as far back as the 'seventies gone to live
in the Isle of Wight, Miss Chauncey still remained
faithful to the old walls. In fact she loved the ugly
old place, for she had lived in it ever since she was a
little girl with knickerbockers showing under her
skirts and pale-blue ribbon shoulder knots.

This fact alone made Sam's conduct the more

reprehensible, for never cat had kinder mistress. Miss Chauncey herself was now about sixty years of age—fifty-five years older than Sam. She was five-foot ten-and-half-inches in height. On week-days she wore black alpaca, and on Sundays a watered silk. Her large round steel spectacles straddling across her high nose gave her a look of being keen as well as cold. But truly she was neither. For even so stupid a man as Mr. Cullings could take her in over the cartage charge of a parcel —just by looking tired or sighing as he glanced at his rough-haired, knock-kneed mare. And there was the warmest of hearts under her stiff bodice.

Post Houses being so far from the village, milk and cream were a little difficult. But Miss Chauncey could deny Sam nothing—in reason. She paid a whole sixpence a week to a little girl called Susan Ard, who brought these dainties from the nearest farm. They were dainties indeed, for though the grasses on Haggurdsdon Moor were of a dark sour green, the cows that grazed on it gave an uncommonly rich milk, and Sam flourished on it. Mr. Cullings called once a week on his round, and had a standing order to bring with him a few sprats or fresh herrings, or any toothsome fish that was in season. Miss Chauncey would not even withhold her purse from whitebait, if no other cheaper wholesome fish were procurable. And Mr. Cullings would eye Sam fawning about his cartwheel, or gloating up at his dish, and say, ' 'Ee be a queer animal, shure enough ; 'ee be a wunnerful queer animal, 'ee be.'

As for Miss Chauncey herself, she was a niggardly eater, though much attached to her tea. She made

her own bread and cookies. On Saturdays a
butcher-boy drove up in a striped apron with her
Sunday joint ; but she was no meat-lover. Her
cupboards were full of home-made jams and bottled
fruits and dried herbs—everything of that kind, for
Post Houses had a nice long strip of garden behind
it, surrounded by a high old yellow brick wall.

Quite early in life Sam, of course, had learned to
know his meal-times—though how he ' told ' them
was known only to himself, for he never appeared
even to glance at the face of the grandfather's clock
on the staircase. He was punctual, particular in
his toilet, and a prodigious sleeper. He had learned
to pull down the latch of the back door, if, in the
months when an open window was not to be found,
he wished to go out. Indeed at last he preferred
the latch. He never slept on Miss Chauncey's
patchwork quilt unless his own had been placed over
it. He was fastidious almost to a foppish degree in
his habits, and he was no thief. He had a mew on
one note to show when he wanted something to eat ;
a mew a semitone or two higher if he wanted drink
(that is, cold water, for which he had a great taste) ;
and yet another mew—gentle and sustained—when
he wished, so to speak, to converse with his mistress.

Not, of course, that the creature talked *English*,
but he liked to sit up on one chair by the fireside,
especially in the kitchen—for he was no born
parlour-cat—and to look up at the glinting glasses
of Miss Chauncey's spectacles, and then down awhile
at the fire-flames (drawing his claws in and out as
he did so, and purring the while), almost as if he
might be preaching a sermon, or reciting a poem.

But this was in the happy days when all seemed well. This was in the days when Miss Chauncey's mind was innocent of doubts and suspicions.

Like others of his kind, too, Sam delighted in youth to lie in the window and idly watch the birds in the apple-trees—tits and bullfinches and dunnocks—or to crouch over a mouse-hole for hours together. Such were his house amusements (he never ate his mice) while Miss Chauncey with cap and broom, duster and dishclout, went about her work. But he also had a way of examining things in which cats are not generally interested. He as good as told Miss Chauncey one afternoon that a hole was coming in her parlour carpet. For he walked to and fro and back and forth with his tail up, until she attended to him. And he certainly warned her, with a yelp like an Amazonian monkey, when a red-hot coal had set her kitchen mat on fire.

He would lie or sit with his whiskers to the North before noonday, and due South afterwards. In general his manners were perfection. But occasionally, when she called him, his face would appear to knot itself into a frown—at any rate to assume a low sullen look, as if he expostulated : ' Why must you be interrupting me, Madam, when I was attending to something else ? ' And now and then, Miss Chauncey fancied, he would deliberately secrete himself or steal out of (and into) Post Houses unbeknown.

Miss Chauncey too would sometimes find him trotting from room to room as if on a visit of inspection. On his second birthday he had brought an immense mouse and laid it beside the shiny toecap of her boot as she sat knitting by the fire. She smiled and nodded merrily at him, as usual, but on this occasion he looked at her intently, and then deliberately shook his head. After that he never paid the smallest attention to mouse or mouse-hole or mousery, and Miss Chauncey was obliged to purchase a cheese-bait trap, else she would have been overrun.

Almost any domestic cat may do things of this nature, and of course all this was solely on Sam's domestic side. For he shared house with Miss Chauncey and, like any two beings that live together, he was bound to keep up certain appearances. He met her half-way, as the saying goes. When, however, he was ' on his own,' he was no longer Miss Chauncey's Sam, he was no longer merely the cat at Post Houses, but just *himself*. He went back, that is, to his own free independent life ; to his own private habits.

Then the moor on which he roved was his own country, and the humans and their houses on it were no more to him in his wild privy existence than molehills or badgers' earths or rabbit warrens are to us. Of this side of his life his mistress knew practically nothing. She did not consider it. She supposed that Sam behaved like other cats, though it was evident that at times he went far abroad, for he now and again brought home a Cochin China chick, and the nearest Cochin China fowls were at the vicarage, a good four miles off. Sometimes of an evening, too, when Miss Chauncey was taking a little walk herself, she would see him—a swiftly-moving black speck—far along the road, hastening home. And there was more purpose expressed in his gait and appearance than ever Mr. Cullings or even the vicar showed !

It was pleasant to observe, too, when he came within miaouing distance how his manner changed. He turned at once from being a Cat into being a Domestic Cat. He was instantaneously no longer the Feline Adventurer, the Nocturnal Marauder and Haunter of Haggurdsdon Moor (though Miss Chauncey would not have so expressed it), but simply his mistress's spoiled pet, Sam. She loved him dearly. But as again with human beings who are accustomed to live together, she did not *think* very much about him. It could not but be a shock then that latish evening, when without the slightest warning Miss Chauncey discovered that Sam was deliberately deceiving her !

She was brushing her thin brown front hair before her looking-glass. At this moment it hung down over her face like a fine loose veil. And as she always mused of other things when she was brushing her hair, she was somewhat absent-minded the while. On raising her eyes from her reverie behind this mesh of hair, she perceived not only that Sam's reflection was in sight in the looking-glass, but that something a little mysterious was happening. Sam was sitting up as if to beg. There was nothing in that. It had been a customary feat of his since he was six months old. Still, for what might he be begging, no-one by ?

Now the window to the right of the chintz-valanced dressing-table was open at the top. Without, it was beginning to grow dark. All Haggurds-don Moor lay hushed and still in the evening's thick-

ening gloom. And apart from begging when there
was nothing to beg for, Sam seemed, so to speak, to
be gesticulating with his paws. He appeared, that
is, to be making signs, just as if there were someone
or something looking in at the window at him from
out of the air—which was quite impossible. And
there was a look upon his face that certainly Miss
Chauncey had never seen before.

She stayed a moment with hair-brush uplifted,
her long lean arm at an angle with her head. On
seeing this, Sam had instantly desisted from these
motions. He had dropped to his fours again, and
was now apparently composing himself for another
nap. No ; this too was a pretence ; for presently as
she watched, he turned restlessly about so that his
whiskers were once again due South. His backward
parts towards the window, he was now gazing
fixedly in front of him out of a far from friendly face.
Far indeed from friendly for a creature that has lived
with you ever since he opened the eyes of his first
kittenhood.

As if he had read her thoughts, Sam at that
moment lifted his head to look at his mistress ; she
withdrew her eyes to the glass only in the nick of
time, and when she turned from her toilet there sat
he—so serene in appearance, so puss-like, so ordinary
once more that Miss Chauncey could scarcely believe
anything whatever had been amiss. Had her eyes
deluded her—her glass ? Was that peculiar motion
of Sam's fore-paws (almost as if he were knitting),
was that wide excited stare due only to the fact
that he was catching what was, to her, an invisible fly ?

Miss Chauncey having now neatly arranged her
' window-curtains '—the sleek loops of hair she wore
on either side her high forehead—glanced yet again
at the window. Nothing there but the silence of
the Moor ; nothing there but the faint pricking of
a star as the evening darkened.

Sam's supper cream was waiting on the hearthrug
in the parlour as usual that evening. The lamp
was lit. The red blinds were drawn. The fire
crackled in the grate. There they sat, these two ;
the walls of the four-cornered house beside the
cross-roads rising up above them like a huge oblong
box under the immense starry sky that saucered in
the wide darkness of the Moor.

And while she sat so—with Sam there, seemingly
fast asleep—Miss Chauncey was thinking. What
had occurred in the bedroom that early evening had
reminded her of other odd little bygone happenings.
Trifles she had scarcely noticed, but which now
returned clearly to memory. How often in the
past, for example, Sam at this hour would be sitting
as if fast asleep (as now) his paws tucked neatly in,
looking much like a stout alderman after a high
dinner. And then suddenly, without warning, as if
a distant voice had called him, he would leap to his
feet and run straight out of the room. And somewhere in the house—door ajar or window agape, he
would find his egress and be up and away into the
night. This had been a common thing to happen.

Once, too, Miss Chauncey had found him squatting
on his hindquarters on the window-ledge of a little
room that had been entirely disused since, years ago,
Cousin Milly had stayed at Post Houses when Miss

Chauncey was a child of eight. She had cried out
at sight of him, ' You foolish Sam, you ; come in,
sir ! You will be tumbling out of the window next ! '
And she remembered as though it were yesterday
that though at this he had stepped gingerly in at once
from his dizzy perch, he had not looked at her. He
had passed her without a sign.

On moonlight evenings, too—why you could never
be sure where he was. You could never be sure
from what errand he had *returned*. Was she sure
indeed where he was on *any* night ? The longer
she reflected, the gloomier grew her doubts and
misgivings. This night, at any rate, Miss Chauncey
determined to keep watch. But she was not happy
in doing so. She hated all manner of spying. They
were old companions, Sam and she ; and she,
without him in bleak Post Houses, would be sadly
desolate. She loved Sam dearly. None the less
the sight of that afternoon haunted her, and it would
be wiser to know all that there was to be known,
even if for Sam's sake only.

Now Miss Chauncey always slept with her bedroom door ajar. She had slept so ever since her
nursery days. Being a rather timid little girl, she
liked in those far-away times to hear the grown-up
voices down stairs and the spoons and forks clinking.
As for Sam, he always slept in his basket beside her
fireplace. Every morning there he would be, though
on some mornings Miss Chauncey's eyes would open
gently to find herself gazing steadily into his pale-
green ones as he stood on his hind-paws, resting his
front ones on her bedside, and looking into her face.
' Time for breakfast, Sam ? ' his mistress would

murmur. And Sam would mew, as distantly almost as a seagull in the heights of the sky.

To-night, however, Miss Chauncey only pretended to be asleep. It was difficult, however, to keep wholly awake, and she was all but drowsing off when there came a faint squeak from the hinge of her door, and she realised that Sam was gone out. After waiting a moment or two, she struck a match. Yes, there was his empty basket in the dark silent room, and presently from far away—from the steeple at Haggurdsdon Village—came the knolling of the hour.

Miss Chauncey placed the dead end of the match in the saucer of her candlestick, and at that moment fancied she heard a faint *whssh* at her window, as of a sudden gust or scurry of wind, or the wings of a fast-flying bird—of a wild goose. It even reminded Miss Chauncey of half-forgotten Guy Fawkes days and of the sound the stick of a rocket makes as it slips down through the air—while its green and ruby lights die out in the immense heavens above. Miss Chauncey gathered up her long legs in the bed, drew on the flannel dressing-gown that always hung on her bedrail, and lifting back the blind an inch or two, looked out of the window.

It was a high starry night ; and a brightening in the sky above the roof seemed to betoken there must be a moon over the backward parts of the house. Even as she watched, a streak of pale silver descended swiftly out of the far spaces of the heavens, and fading into the darkness dwindled and vanished away. It was a meteorite ; and at that very instant Miss Chauncey fancied she heard again a faint remote dwindling *whssh* in the air. Was *that* the meteorite too? Could she have been deceived? Was she being deceived in everything? She drew back.

And then, as if in deliberate and defiant answer, out of the distance and from what appeared to be the extreme end of her long garden where grew a tangle of sloe bushes, there followed a prolonged and as if half-secret caterwaul: very low—contralto, one might say—*Meearou-rou-rou-rou-rou*!

Heaven forbid! Was *that* Sam's tongue? The caterwauling ceased. Yet still Miss Chauncey could not suppress a shudder. She knew Sam's voice of old. But surely not that! Surely not that!

Strange and immodest though it was to hear herself, too, in that solitary place calling out in the dead of night, she nevertheless at once opened the window and summoned Sam by name. There was no response. The trees and bushes of the garden stood motionless; their faint shadows on the ground revealing how small a moon was actually in the sky, and how low it hung towards its setting. The vague undulations of the Moor stretched into the distance. Not a light to be seen except those of the firmament. Again, and yet again, Miss Chauncey cried 'Sam, Sam! Come away in! Come away in, sir, you bad creature!' Not a sound. Not the least stir of leaf or blade of grass.

When, after so broken a night, Miss Chauncey awoke a little late the next morning, the first thing her eyes beheld when she sat up in bed was Sam—couched as usual in his basket. It was a mystery, and an uneasy one. After supping up his morning bowl, he slept steadily on until noonday. This

happened to be the day of the week when Miss
Chauncey made bread. On and on she steadily
kneaded the dough with her knuckled hands, glancing ever and again towards the motionless creature.
With fingers clotted from the great earthenware
bowl, she stood over him at last for a few moments,
and eyed him closely.

He was lying curled round with his whiskered
face to one side towards the fire. And it seemed to
Miss Chauncey that she had never noticed before
that faint peculiar grin on his face. 'Sam!' she
cried sharply. An eye instantly opened, fiercely
green as if a mouse had squeaked. He stared at
her for an instant; then the lid narrowed. The
gaze slunk away a little, but Sam began to purr.

The truth of it is, all this was making Miss
Chauncey exceedingly unhappy. Mr. Cullings called
that afternoon, with a basket of some fresh comely
young sprats. 'Them'll wake his Royal Highness
up,' he said. 'They'm fresh as daisies. Lor, m'm,
what a Nero that beast be!'

'Cats *are* strange creatures, Mr. Cullings,' replie
Miss Chauncey reflectively; complacently supposing
that Mr. Cullings had misplaced an *h* and had meant
to say, *an hero.* And Sam himself, with uplifted tail,
and as if of the same opinion, was rubbing his head
gently against her boot.

Mr. Cullings eyed her closely. 'Why, yes, they
be,' he said. 'What I says is is that as soon as
they're out of your sight, you are out of their mind.
There's no more gratitood nor affection in a cat than
in a pump. Though so far as the pump is concerned,
the gratitood should be on our side. I knew a

family of cats once what fairly druv their mistress
out of house and home.'

'But you wouldn't have a cat *only* a pet?' said
Miss Chauncey faintly; afraid to ask for further
particulars of this peculiar occurrence.

'Why no, m'm,' said the carrier. 'As the Lord
made 'em, so they be. But I'll be bound they could
tell some knotty stories if they had a human tongue
to their heads!'

Sam had ceased caressing his mistress's foot, and
was looking steadily at Mr. Cullings, his hair roughed
a little about the neck and shoulders. And the
carrier looked back.

'No, m'm. We wouldn't keep 'em,' he said at
last, 'if they was *four* times that size. Or, not for
long!'

Having watched Mr. Culling's little cart bowl away
into the distance, Miss Chauncey returned into the
house, more disturbed than ever. Nor did her
uneasiness abate when Sam refused even to sniff at
his sprats. Instead, he crawled in under a low table
in the kitchen, behind the old seaman's chest in
which Miss Chauncey kept her kindling-wood. She
fancied she heard his claws working in the wood now
and again, and once he seemed to be expressing his
natural feelings in what vulgar people with little
sympathy for animals describe as 'swearing.'

Her caressing 'Sams,' at any rate, were all in vain.
His only reply was a kind of sneeze which uncom-
fortably resembled 'spitting.' Miss Chauncey's feelings had already been hurt. It was now her mind
that suffered. Something the carrier had said, or
the way he had said it, or the peculiar look she had

noticed on his face when he was returning Sam's stare in the porch, haunted her thoughts. She was no longer young, was she becoming fanciful? Or must she indeed conclude that for weeks past Sam had been steadily circumventing her, or at any rate concealing his wanderings and his interests? What nonsense. Worse still. was she now so credulous as to believe that Sam had in actual fact been making signals—and secretly, behind her back—to some confederate that must either have been up in the sky, or in the moon!

Whether or not, Miss Chauncey determined to keep a sharper eye on him. Their future was at stake. She would at least make sure that he did not leave the house that night. But then: Why not? she asked herself. Why shouldn't the creature choose his own hour and season? Cats, like owls, *see* best in the dark. They go best a-mousing in the dark, and may prefer the dark for their private, social, and even public affairs. Post Houses, after all, was only rather more than two miles from Haggurdsdon Village, and there were cats there in plenty. Poor fellow, her own dumb human company must sometimes be dull enough!

Such were Miss Chauncey's reflections; and as if to reassure her, Sam himself at that moment serenely entered the room and leapt up on to the empty chair beside her tea-table. As if, too, to prove that he had thought better of his evil temper, or to insinuate that there had been nothing amiss between himself and Mr. Cullings, he was licking his chops, and there was no mistaking the odour of fish which he brought in with him from his saucer.

' So you have thought better of it, my boy ? '
thought Miss Chauncey, though she did not utter the
words aloud. And yet as she returned his steady
feline gaze, she realised how difficult it was to read
the intelligence behind those eyes. You might say
that Sam, being only a cat, there was no meaning
in them at all. But Miss Chauncey knew better.
There would be meaning enough if such eyes had
looked out of a *human* shape at her !

Unfortunately, and almost as if Sam had overheard
his mistress's speculations regarding possible cat
friends in the Village, there came at that moment a
faint wambling mew beneath the open window. In
a flash Sam was out of his chair and over the window
ledge, and Miss Chauncey rose only just in time to
see him in infuriated pursuit of a slim sleek tortoiseshell creature that had evidently come to Post
Houses in hope of a friendlier reception, and was now
fleeing in positive fear of its life.

Sam returned from his chase as fresh as paint, and
Miss Chauncey was horrified to detect—caught up
between the claws of his right forefoot—a tuft or
two of tortoiseshell fur, which, having composed
himself by the fire, he promptly removed by licking.

Still pondering on these disquieting events, Miss
Chauncey took her usual evening walk in the garden.
Candytuft and virginia stock were seeding along
the shell-lined path, and late roses were already
beginning to blow on the high brick wall which shut
off her narrow strip of land from the vast lap of the
Moor. Having come to the end of the path, Miss
Chauncey pushed on a little further than usual, to
where the grasses grew more rampant, and where

wild headlong weeds raised their heads beneath her
few lichenous apple trees.   Still further down, for
hers was a long, though narrow, garden—there grew
straggling bushes of sloe, spiny whitethorn.   These
had blossomed there indeed in the moor's bleak
springs long before Post Houses had raised its
chimney pots into the sky.   Here, too, flourished a
dense drift of nettles—their sour odour haunting
the air.

And it was in this forlorn spot that—like Robinson
Crusoe, before her—Miss Chauncey was suddenly
brought to a standstill by the sight of what appeared
to be nothing else than a strange footprint in the
mould.   Nearby the footprint, moreover, showed
what might be the impression of a walking-cane or
possibly of something stouter and heavier—a crutch.
Could she again be deceived ?   The footprint, it was
true, was unlike most human footprints, the heel
sunk low, the toe square.   Might it be accidental ?
Was it a footprint ?

Miss Chauncey glanced furtively across the bushes
towards the house.   It loomed gaunt and forbidding
in the moorland dusk.   And she fancied she could
see, though the evening light might be deceiving her,
the cowering shape of Sam looking out at her from
the kitchen-window.   To be watched !   To be herself spied upon—and watched !

But then, of course, Sam was always watching
her.   What oddity was there in that ?   Where else
would his sprats come from, his cream, his saucer
of milk, his bowl of fresh well-water ?   Nevertheless,
Miss Chauncey returned to her parlour gravely
discomposed.

It was an uncommonly still evening, and as she went from room to room locking the windows, she noticed there was already a moon in the sky. She eyed it with misgiving. And at last bedtime came ; and when Sam, as usual, after a lick or two, had composed himself in his basket, Miss Chauncey, holding the key almost challengingly within view, deliberately locked her bedroom door.

When she awoke next morning Sam was asleep in his basket as usual, and during the day-time he kept pretty closely to the house. So, too, on the Wednesday and the Thursday. It was not until the following Friday that having occasion to go into an upper bedroom that had no fireplace, and being followed as usual by Sam, Miss Chauncey detected the faint rank smell of soot in the room. No chimney, and a smell of soot ! She turned rapidly on her companion : he had already left the room.

And when that afternoon she discovered a black sooty smear upon her own patchwork quilt, she realised not only that her suspicions had been justified, but that for the first time in his life Sam had deliberately laid himself down there in her absence. At this act of sheer defiance she was no longer so much hurt as exceedingly angry. There was no doubt now. Sam was deliberately defying her. No two companions could share a house on such terms as these. He must be taught a lesson.

That evening, in full sight of the creature, having locked her bedroom door, she stuffed a large piece of mattress ticking into the mouth of her chimney and pulled down the register. Having watched these proceedings, Sam rose from his basket, and with an easy spring, leapt up on to the dressing-table. Beyond the window, the Moor lay almost as bright as day. Ignoring Miss Chauncey, the creature squatted there steadily and openly staring into the empty skies, for a whole stretch of them was visible from where he sat.

Miss Chauncey proceeded to make her toilet for the night, trying in vain to pretend that she was entirely uninterested in what the animal was at. A faint sound—not exactly mewings or growlings—but a kind of low inward caterwauling, hardly audible, was proceeding from his throat. But whatever these sounds might mean, Sam himself can have been the only listener. There was not a sign of movement at the window or in the world without. And then Miss Chauncey promptly drew down the blind. At this Sam at once raised his paw for all the world as if he were about to protest, and then, apparently thinking better of it, he pretended instead that the action had been only for the purpose of commencing his nightly wash.

Long after her candle had been extinguished, Miss Chauncey lay listening. Every stir and movement in the quiet darkness could be clearly followed. First there came a furtive footing and tapping at the register of the fireplace, so closely showing what was happening that Miss Chauncey could positively see in her imagination Sam on the hearth-stone, erecting himself there upon his hindlegs, vainly attempting to push the obstacle back.

This being in vain, he appeared to have dropped back on to his fours. Then came a pause. Had he given up his intention? No: now he was at the door, pawing, gently scratching. Then a leap, even, towards the handle : but one only—the door was locked. Retiring from the door, he now sprang lightly again on to the dressing-table. What now was he at ? By covertly raising her head a little from her pillow, Miss Chauncey could see him with paw thrust out, gently drawing back the blind from the moon-flooded window-pane. And even while she listened and watched, she heard yet again—and yet again—the faint *whssh* as of a wild swan cleaving the air ; and then what might have been the cry of a bird, but which to Miss Chauncey's ears resembled a thin shrill pealing cackle of laughter. At this Sam hastily turned from the window, and without the least attempt at concealment pounced clean from the dressing-table on to the lower rail of her bed.

This unmannerly conduct could be ignored no longer. Poor Miss Chauncey raised herself in her sheets, pulled her night-cap a little closer down over her ears, and thrusting out her hand towards the chair beside the bed, struck a match and relit her candle. It was with a real effort that she then slowly turned her head and faced her night-companion. His hair was bristling about his body as if he had had an electric shock. His whiskers stood out at stiff angles with his jaws. He looked at least twice his usual size, and his eyes blazed in his head, as averting his face from her regard he gave vent to a low sustained *Miariou-rou-rou* !

' I say you shall *not*,' cried Miss Chauncey at the creature. At the sound of her words, he turned slowly and confronted her. And it seemed that until that moment Miss Chauncey had never actually seen Sam's countenance as in actual fact it really was. It was not so much the grinning tigerish look it wore, but the sullen assurance upon it of what he wanted and that he meant to get it.

All thought of sleep was now out of the question. Miss Chauncey could be obstinate too. The creature seemed to shed an influence on the very air which she could hardly resist. She rose from her bed and thrusting on her slippers made her way to the window. Once more a peculiar inward cry broke out from the bed-rail. She raised the blind and the light of the moon from over the moor swept in upon her little apartment. And when she turned to remonstrate with her pet at his ingratitude, and at all this unseemliness and the deceit of his ways, there was something so menacing and pitiless in his aspect that Miss Chauncey hesitated no more.

' Well, mark me ! ' she cried in a trembling voice, ' go out of the *door* you shan't. But if you enjoy soot, soot it shall be.'

With that she thrust back the register with the poker, and drew down the bundle of ticking with the tongs. And before the fit of coughing caused by the smotheration that followed had ceased, the lithe black shape had sprung from the bedrail, and with a scramble was into the hearth, over the fire-bars, up the chimney, and away.

Trembling from head to foot, Miss Chauncey sat down on a cane rocking-chair that stood nearby to reflect what next she must be doing. *Wh-ssh !* *Wh-ssh !* Again at the window came that mysterious rushing sound, but now the flurrying murmur as of a rocket shooting up with its fiery train of sparks

thinning into space, rather than the sound of its
descending stick. And then in the hush that followed, there sounded yet again like a summons from
the foot of the garden—a caterwauling piercing and
sonorous enough to arouse the sleeping cocks in the
Haggurdsdon hen-roosts and for miles around. Out
of the distance their chanticleering broke shrill on
the night air ; to be followed a moment afterwards
by the tardy clang of midnight from the Church
steeple. Then once more, silence ; utter quiet.
Miss Chauncey returned to bed, but that night she
slept no more.

Her mind overflowed with unhappy thoughts.
Her faith in Sam was gone. Far worse, she had lost
faith even in her affection for him. To have wasted
that !—all the sprats, all the whitebait in the wide,
wide seas were as nothing by comparison. That
Sam had wearied of her company was at last beyond
question. It shamed her to think how much this
meant to her—a mere animal ! But she knew what
was gone ; knew how dull and spiritless the day's
round would seem—the rising, the housework, the
meals, a clean linen collar in the afternoon, her
evening slippers, a dish of tea, her candle, prayers,
bed. On and on. In what wild company was her
cat, Sam, now ? At her own refusal to answer this
horrid question, it was as if she had heard the hollow
clanging slam of an immense iron door.

Next morning—still ruminating on these strange
events, grieved to the heart at this dreadful rift
between herself and one who had been her honest
companion for so many years : ashamed too that
Sam should have had his way with her when she had

determined not to allow him to go out during the night—next morning Miss Chauncey, as if merely to take a little exercise, once again ventured down to the foot of her garden. A faint, blurred mark (such as she had seen on the previous evening) in the black mould of what *might* be a foot-print is nothing very much.

But now—in the neglected patch beyond the bushes of white-thorn and bramble—there was no doubt in the world—appeared the marks of many. And surely no cats' paw-prints these ! Of what use, too, to a cat could a crutch or a staff be ? A staff or a crutch which—to judge from the impression it had left in the mould—must have been at least as thick as a broomstick.

More disquieted and alarmed than ever over this fresh mystery, Miss Chauncey glanced up and back towards the chimney-pots of the house clearly and sharply fretted against the morning light of the eastern skies. And she realised what perils even so sure-footed a creature as Sam had faced when he skirred up out of the chimney in his wild effort to emerge into the night. Having thus astonishingly reached the rim of the chimney-pot—the burning stars above and the wilderness of the moor spread out far beneath and around him—he must have leaped from the top of the pot to a narrow brick ledge not three inches wide. Thence on to the peak of the roof and thence down a steep, slippery slope of slates to a leaden gutter.

And how then ? The thick tod of ivy, matting the walls of the house, reached hardly more than half-way up. Could Sam actually have plunged from gutter to tod ? The very thought of such a peril drew Miss Chauncey's steps towards the house again, in the sharpest anxiety to assure herself that he was still in the land of the living.

And lo and behold, when she was but half-way on her journey, she heard a succession of frenzied cries and catcalls in the air from over the Moor. Hastily placing a flower-pot by the wall, she stood on tiptoe and peered over. And even now, at this very moment, in full flight across the nearer slope of the Moor she descried her Sam, not now in chase of a foolishly trustful visitor, but hotly pursued by what appeared to be the complete rabblement of Haggurds-don's cats. Sore spent though he showed himself to be, Sam was keeping his distance. Only a few lank tabby cats, and what appeared to be a grey-ginger Manx (unless he was an ordinary cat with his tail chopped off) were close behind.

'Sam ! Sam !' Miss Chauncey cried, and yet again, 'Sam !' but in her excitement and anxiety her foot slipped on the flower-pot and in an instant the feline chase had fallen out of sight. Gathering herself together again, she clutched a long besom or garden broom that was leaning against the wall, and rushed down to the point at which she judged Sam would make his entrance into the garden. She was not mistaken, nor an instant too soon. With a bound he was up and over, and in three seconds the rabble had followed, in vehement pursuit.

What came after Miss Chauncey could never very clearly recall. She could but remember plying her besom with might and main amid this rabble and mellay of animals, while Sam, no longer a fugitive,

turned on his enemies and fought them man to man.
None the less, it was by no means an easy victory.
And had not the over-fatted cur from the butcher's
in Haggurdsdon—which had long since started in
pursuit of this congregation of his enemies—had
he not at last managed to overtake them, the
contest might very well have had a tragic ending.
But at sound of his baying, and at sight of the cur's
teeth snapping at them as he vainly attempted to
surmount the wall, Sam's enemies turned and fled
in all directions.   And faint and panting, Miss
Chauncey was able to fling down her besom and
to lean for a brief respite against the trunk of
a tree.

At last she opened her eyes again.   ' Well, Sam,'
she managed to mutter at last, ' we got the best of
them, then ? '

But to her amazement she found herself uttering
these friendly words into a complete vacancy.   The
creature was nowhere to be seen.   His cream
disappeared during the day, however, and by an
occasional rasping sound Miss Chauncey knew that
he once more lay hidden in his dingy resort behind
the kindling-wood box.   And there she did not
disturb him.

Not until tea-time of the following day did Sam
reappear.   And then—after attending to his hurts—
it was merely to sit with face towards the fire,
sluggish and sullen and dumb as a dog.   It was not
Miss Chauncey's ' place ' to make advances, she
thought.   She took no notice of the beast except to
rub in a little hog's-fat on the raw places of his
wounds.   She was rejoiced to find, however, that

he kept steadily to Post Houses for the next few days, though her dismay was re-awakened at hearing on the third night a more dismal wailing and wauling than ever from the sloe-bushes, even while Sam himself sat motionless beside the fire. His ears twitched ; his fur bristled ; he sneezed or spat, but remained otherwise motionless.

When Mr. Cullings called again, Sam at once hid himself in the coal-cellar, but gradually his manners towards Miss Chauncey began to recover their usual suavity. And within a fortnight after the full-moon, the two of them had almost returned to their old friendly companionship. He was healed, sleek, confident and punctual. No intruder of his species had appeared from Haggurdsdon. The night noises had ceased. Post Houses to all appearance—apart from its strange ugliness—was as peaceful and calm as any other solitary domicile in the United Kingdom.

But alas and alas. With the very first peeping of the crescent moon, Sam's mood and habits began to change again. He mouched about with a sly and furtive eye. And when he fawned on his mistress, purring and clawing, the whole look of him was a picture of deceit. If Miss Chauncey chanced to enter the room wherein he sat, he would at once leap down from the window at which he had been perched as if in the attempt to prove that he had *not* been looking out of it. And once, towards evening, though she was no spy, she could not but pause at the parlour door. She had peeped through its crack as it stood ajar. And there on the hard sharp back of an old prie-Dieu chair that had belonged to her

I

pious great-aunt Miranda, sat Sam on his hind quarters. And without the least doubt in the world he was vigorously signalling to some observer outside with his forepaws. Miss Chauncey turned away sick at heart.

From that hour on Sam more and more steadily ignored and flouted his mistress, was openly insolent, shockingly audacious. Mr. Cullings gave her small help indeed. ' If I had a cat, m'm, what had manners like that, after all your kindness, fresh fish and all every week, and cream, as I understand, not skim, I'd—I'd give him away.'

' To whom ? ' said Miss Chauncey shortly.

' Well,' said the carrier, ' I don't know as how I'd much mind to who. Just a home, m'm.'

' He seems to have no friends in the village,' said Miss Chauncey, in as light a tone as she could manage.

' When they're as black as that, with them saucer eyes, you can never tell,' said Mr. Cullings. ' There's that old trollimog what lives in Hogges Bottom. She's got a cat that might be your Sam's twin.'

' Indeed no, he has the mange,' said Miss Chauncey, loyal to the end. The carrier shrugged his shoulders, climbed into his cart, and bowled away off over the Moor. And Miss Chauncey returning to the house, laid the platter of silvery sprats on the table, sat down and burst into tears.

It was, then, in most ways a fortunate thing that the very next morning—five complete days, that is, before the next full-moon-tide—she received a letter from her sister-in-law in Shanklin, in the Isle of Wight, entreating her to pay them a long visit.

'My dear Emma, you must sometimes be feeling very lonely [it ran] shut up in that great house so far from any neighbours. We often think of you, and particularly these last few days. It's very nice to have that Sam of yours for company, but after all, as George says, a pet's only a pet. And we do all think its high time you took a little holliday with us. I am looking out of my window at this very moment. The sea is as calm as a mill-pond, a sollemn beautiful blue. The fishing boats are coming in with their brown sails. This is the best time of the year with us, because the *tripper* season is drawing to a close and there are fewer of those horrid visitors to be seen, and no crowds. George says you *must* come. He joins with me in his love as would Maria if she weren't out shoping, and will meet you at the station in the trap. And we shall all be looking forward to seeing you in a few days. Emmie is now free of her cough—only whooping when the memory takes her, and never sick. . . .'

At this kindness, and with all her anxieties, Miss Chauncey all but broke down. When the butcher drove up in his cart an hour or two afterwards, he took a telegram for her back to the Village, and on the Monday her box was packed, and all that remained was to put Sam in his basket in preparation for the journey. But I am bound to say it took more than the persuasions of his old protectress to accomplish this. Indeed Mr. Cullings had actually to hold the creature with his gloved hands and none too gently, while Miss Chauncey pressed down the lid and pushed the skewer in to hold it close. 'What's done's durned done,' said the carrier, as he rubbed a pinch of earth into his scratches. 'But what *I* says is, better done for ever. Mark my words, m'm!'

Miss Chauncey took a shilling out of her large leather purse; but made no reply.

Indeed, all this trouble proved at last in vain. Thirty miles distant from Haggurdsdon, at Blackmoor Junction, Miss Chauncey had to change trains. Her box and Sam's basket were placed together on the station platform beside half-a-dozen empty milk-cans and some fowls in a crate, and Miss Chauncey went to make enquiries of the station-master in order to make sure of her platform.

It was the furious panic-stricken cackling of these fowls that brought her hastily back to her belongings, only to find that by hook or by crook Sam had managed to push the skewer of the basket out of its cane loops. The wicker lid gaped open—the basket was empty. Indeed one poor gasping hen, its life fluttering away from its helpless body, was proof enough not only of Sam's prowess but of his cowardly ferocity.

A few days afterwards, as Miss Chauncey sat in the very room to which her sister-in-law had referred in her invitation, looking over the placid surface of the English Channel, the sun gently shining in the sky, there came a letter from Mr. Cullings. It was in pencil and written upon the back of a baker's bag.

'Dear madam, i take the libberty of riteing you in reference to the Animall as how i helped put in is bawskit which has cum back returned empty agenn by rail me having okashun to cart sum hop powles from Haggurdsden late at nite ov Sunday. I seez him squattin at the parlour windy grimasin out at me fit to curdle your blood in your vanes and lights at the upper windies and a yowling and screetching as i never hopes to hear agen in a Christian lokalety. And that ole wumman from Hogges Botom sitting in the porch mi own vew being that there is no good in the place and the Animall be bewhitched. Mister flint the boutcher agrees with me as how now only last mesures is of any use and as i have said afore i am willing to take over the house the rent if so be being low and moddrit considering of the bad name it as in these parts around haggurdsden. I remain dear madam waitin your orders and oblige yours truely William Cullings.'

To look at Miss Chauncey you might have supposed she was a strong-minded woman. You might have supposed that this uncivil reference to the bad name her family house had won for itself would have mortified her beyond words. Whether or not, she neither showed this letter to her sister-in-law nor for many days together did she attempt to answer it. Sitting on the esplanade, and looking out to sea, she brooded on and on in the warm, salt, yet balmy air. It was a distressing problem. But ' No, he must go his own way,' she sighed to herself at last ; ' I have done my best for him.'

What is more, Miss Chauncey never returned to Post Houses. She sold it at last, house and garden and for a pitiful sum, to the carrier, Mr. Cullings. By that time Sam had vanished, had been never seen again. He had gone his way.

Not that Miss Chauncey was faithless of memory. Whenever the faint swish of a sea-gull's wing

sounded in the air above her head ; or the crackling
of an ascending rocket for the amusement of visitors
broke the silence of the nearer heavens over the sea ;
whenever even she became conscious of the rustling
frou-frou of her Sunday watered silk gown as she
sallied out to Church from the neat little villa she
now rented on the Shanklin Esplanade—she never
noticed such things without being instantly trans-
ported back in imagination to her bedroom at Post
Houses, and seeing again that strange deluded
animal, once her Sam, squatting there on her bed,
and as it were knitting with his fore-paws the while
he stood erect upon his hind.

LUCY

ONCE upon a time there were three sisters, the Misses Mac-Knackery—or, better still, the Miss MacKnackeries. They lived in a large, white, square house called Stoneyhouse; and their names were Euphemia, Tabitha, and Jean Elspeth. They were known over Scotland for miles and miles, from the Tay to the Grampians—from the Tay to the Grumpy Ones, as a cousin who did not like Euphemia and Tabitha used to say.

Stoneyhouse had been built by the Miss Mac-Knackeries's grandfather, Mr. Angus MacKnackery, who, from being a poor boy with scarcely a bawbee in his breeches pocket, had risen up to be a wealthy manufacturer of the best Scotch burlap, which is a kind of sacking. He made twine, too, for tying up parcels. He would have made almost anything to make money. But at last, when he was sixty-six, he felt he would like to be a gentleman living in the country with a large garden to walk about in, flowers in beds, cucumbers in frames, pigs in sties, and one or two cows for milk, cream, and butter.

So he sold his huge, smoky works and warehouse,

and all the twine and burlap, hemp, jute, and whale-bone still in it, for £80,000. With this £80,000 he built Stoneyhouse, purchased some fine furniture and some carriages and horses, and invested what was over.

Jean Elspeth, when she was learning sums, and when she had come to Interest—having sometimes heard her father and mother speak of her grandfather and of his fortune, and how he had invested it—just to please her governess, Miss Gimp, thought she would make a sum of it. So she wrote down in her rather straggly figures in an exercise book :

£80,000 @ £4 per centum per annum
=£80,000 × 4 ÷ 100 =£52,000.

It was the first really enjoyable sum she had ever done. And yet Miss Gimp was a little put about when Jean Elspeth showed it to her father. Still, Mr. MacKnackery, senior, had been a really rich man, and regretted that the gentleman who bought his factory could never afterwards make such fine burlap as himself, nor even such admirable twine.

He lived to be eighty, and then he died, leaving his money to his son, Robert Duncan Donald David, Jean Elspeth's father. And when *he* died, his dear wife Euphemia Tabitha being dead too, he left all that was over of the £80,000 (for, alas and alas ! he had lost a good part of it) to his three daughters : Euphemia, Tabitha, and Jean Elspeth.

When Jean Elspeth was old enough to breakfast with the family in the big dining-room with the four immense windows, she used to sit opposite the portraits of her grandfather, her father, and her mother. They hung in heavy handsome gilt frames on the wall opposite the windows. And while in her high chair she gobbled up her porridge—and gobbled it up quickly, not so much because she liked it as because she hated being put in the corner for not eating it—she would sit and look at them.

Her grandfather's was by far the largest of the three portraits, and it hung in the very middle of the lofty wall, under the moulded ceiling. He was a stout and imposing man, with bushy whiskers and cold bright blue eyes. The thumb and first finger of his right hand held a fine thick Albert watch-chain, which the painter had painted so skilfully that you could see it was eighteen-carat gold at a single glance. So he hung, for ever boldly gazing.

What was more, her grandfather always looked exactly as if he was on the point of taking out his watch to see the time ; and Jean Elspeth had the odd notion that, if he ever did succeed in so doing, its hands would undoubtedly point to a quarter to twelve. But she could no more have told you why, than she could tell you why she used to count each spoonful of her porridge, or why she felt happier when the last spoonful was an odd number.

The portrait of her father was that of a man much less stout and imposing than her grandfather. He was dark, and smiling, and he had no whiskers. But Jean Elspeth had loved him dearly, and each morning when she had finished her breakfast (and if nobody was looking) she would give a tiny little secret wave of the spoon towards him, as if he might be pleased at seeing her empty plate.

On the other side of her grandfather's portrait hung a picture of her mother. And the odd thing about this picture was that, if you looked long enough, you could not help seeing—as if it were almost the ghost of Jean Elspeth—her very own small face, peeping out of the paint at you, just like a tiny little green marmoset out of a cage all to itself in the Zoo. Jean Elspeth had discovered this when she was only seven; but Euphemia and Tabitha had never noticed it at all.

They knew they were far less like their mother (who had been a Miss Reeks MacGillicuddy of Kelso) than their grandfather, and they were exceedingly proud of *that*. As for Jean Elspeth, they didn't think she was like any of the family at all. Indeed, Euphemia had more than once remarked that Jean Elspeth had ' nae deegnity,' and Tabitha that ' she micht jist as weel ha' been a changeling.' Even now, when they were elderly ladies, they always treated her as if she were still not very far from being a child, though, after all, Jean Elspeth was only five years younger than Tabitha.

But then, how different she was in looks! For while Tabitha had a long pale face a little like a unicorn, with mouse-coloured hair and green-grey eyes, Jean Elspeth was dark and small, with red in her cheek and a tip to her nose. And while Tabitha's face changed very little, Jean Elspeth's was like a dark little glancing pool on an April morning. Sometimes it looked almost centuries older than either of her sisters', and then, again, sometimes it looked simply no age at all.

It depended on what she was doing—whether she

was sitting at seven o'clock dinner on Great Occasions, when the Bults, and the McGaskins, and Dr. Menzies were guests, or merely basking idly in the sunshine at her bedroom window. Jean Elspeth would sometimes, too, go wandering off by herself over the hills a mile or two away from the house. And *then* she looked not a minute older than looks a harebell, or a whinchat, perched with his white eyebrow on a fuzz-bush near a lichenous half-hidden rock among the heather.

However sad, too, she looked, she never looked grim. And even though (at dinner parties) she parted her hair straight down the middle, and smoothed the sides over as sleek as satin, she simply could not look what is called ' superior.' Besides, she had lips that were the colour of cherries, and curious quick hands that she was sometimes compelled to clasp together lest they should talk even more rapidly than her tongue.

Now in Stoneyhouse nobody—except perhaps the tweeny-maid and the scullery-maid, Sally and Nancy McGullie, who were cousins—ever talked *much*. It was difficult even to tell exactly how wise and sagacious and full of useful knowledge Euphemia and Tabitha were, simply because they so seldom opened their mouths, except at meals. And never to sing.

This, maybe, was because it is impossible to keep order if everybody's tongue keeps wagging. It wastes time, too, for only very few people can work hard and talk hard both at the same moment. And in Stoneyhouse everything was in apple-pie order (except the beds), and nobody ever wasted any time.

And yet, although time was never wasted, nobody seemed to be very much the better off for any that was actually 'saved.' Nobody had ever managed to pack some of it up in neat brown-paper parcels, or to put it in a bank as Mr. MacKnackery, senior, had put his money, or to pour it into jars like home-made jam. It just went. And in Stoneyhouse (until, at least, Euphemia one morning received a certain letter) it went very very slowly. The big hands of its clocks seemed to be envious of the little ones. They crept like shadows. And between their 'tick' and their 'tock' at times yawned a huge hole, as dark as a cellar. So, at least, Jean Elspeth fancied.

One glance at Stoneyhouse, even from the outside, would tell you how orderly it was. The four high white walls, with their large square slate roof fixed firmly on top of them, stood stiff as bombardiers on extremely solid foundations, and they on even solider rock. No tree dared cast a shadow upon them, no creeper crept. The glossy windows, with their straight lines of curtains behind them, just stared down on you as if they said, ' Find the faintest speck or smear or flaw in us if you can ! ' And you hadn't the courage even to try.

It was just so inside. Everything was in its place. Not only the great solid pieces of substantial furniture which Mr. MacKnackery had purchased with his burlap money—wardrobes, coffers, presses, four-posters, chests-of-drawers, sideboards, tables, sofas, chairs—but even all the little things, bead-mats, footstools, candle-snuffers, boot-trees, ornaments, knick-knacks, Euphemia's silks and Tabitha's water-colours. There was a place for everything, and everything was in its place. Yes, and kept there.

Except in Jean Elspeth's room. She could never learn to be tidy, not even in her sums. She was constantly taking things out, and either forgetting to put them away again, or putting them away again in their wrong places. And do you suppose she blamed herself for this? Not at all. When she lost anything and had been looking for it for hours and hours—a book, or a brooch, or a ribbon, or a shoe—she would say to herself, laughing all over, 'Well now, there! That *Lucy* must have hidden it!' And presently *there* it would be, right in the middle of her dressing-table or under a chair, as if it had been put back there just for fun.

And who was this '*Lucy*'? There couldn't be a more difficult question ; and Jean Elspeth had never attempted to answer it. It was one of those questions she never even asked herself, at least, not out loud. This, perhaps, was because she hated the thought of hurting anybody's feelings. As if Lucy —but, never mind!

It was Lucy, at any rate, who so unfortunately came into that dreadful talk over the porridge on the morning when the fatal letter came to Euphemia. It arrived just like any other letter. The butler, with his mouth as closely shut as usual, laid it beside Euphemia's plate. Judging from its large white envelope, nobody could possibly have thought it was as deadly as a poison and sharper than a serpent's tooth. Euphemia opened it, too, just as usual— with her long, lean forefinger,and her eyebrows lifted a little under her grey front of hair. And then she read it, and turned to ice.

It was from her lawyer, or rather from her Four Lawyers, for they all shared the same office, and at the foot of the letter one of them had signed all their four names. It was a pitch-black letter—a thunderbolt. It said at the beginning that the Miss MacKnackeries must expect in future to be a little less well off than they had been in the past, and it said at the end that they were ruined.

You see, Euphemia's grandfather had lent what remained of his £80,000 (after building Stoneyhouse and buying furniture, cucumber-seed, horses, cows, and so on) to the British Government, for the use of the British nation. The British Government of that day put the money into what were called the Consolidated Funds. And to show how much obliged they were to Mr. MacKnackery for the loan of it, they used every year to pay him interest on it —so many shillings for every hundred pounds. Not so much as £4 per annum, as Jean Elspeth had put down in her sum, but as much as they could afford —and that was at least 1,000,000 bawbees. There couldn't have been a safer money-box ; nor could Mr. MacKnackery's income have ' come in ' more regularly if it had come in by clockwork. So far the British Government resembled Stoneyhouse itself.

But the Miss MacKnackeries's father was not only a less imposing man than their grandfather, he had been much less careful of his money. He delighted in *buying* things and giving presents, and the more he spent the more he wanted to spend. So he had gradually asked for his money back from the British Government, using some of it and lending the rest to persons making railways and gasworks in foreign parts, and digging up gold and diamonds, and making scent out of tar, and paint which they said would never wear off or change colour, and everything like that.

These persons paid him for helping them like this a good deal more than the Consolidated Funds could pay him. But then gasworks are not always so *safe* as the British nation. It is what is called a speculation to lend gentlemen money to help them to dig up diamonds or to make waterworks in Armenia, which means that you cannot be perfectly sure of getting it back again. Often and often, indeed, the Miss MacKnackeries's father had not got *his* money back.

And now—these long years after his death—the worst had befallen. The Four Lawyers had been suddenly compelled to tell the Miss MacKnackeries that nearly every bit left of their grandfather's savings was gone ; that their bright gold had vanished like the glinting mists of a June morning. They had for some time been accustomed to growing less and less rich ; but that's a very different thing from becoming desperately poor. It is the difference between a mouse with a fat slice of cheese and a mouse without a bread-crumb.

Euphemia, before opening the letter, had put on her pince-nez. As she read, the very life seemed to ebb out of her countenance, leaving it cold and grey. She finished it to the last word, then with a trembling hand took the glasses off her nose and passed the letter to Tabitha. Tabitha could still read without

spectacles. Her light eyes passed rapidly to and
fro across the letter, then she, too, put it down, her
face not pale, but red and a little swollen. ' It is
the end, Euphemia,' she said.

Jean Elspeth was sitting that morning with her
back to the portraits, and at the moment was gently
munching a slice of dry toast and Scotch marmalade
(made by the Miss MacKnackerle's's cook, Mrs.
O'Phrump). She had been watching a pied wagtail
flitting after flies across the smooth shorn lawn on
the white stone terrace. Then her gaze had wandered off to the blue outline of the lovely distant
hills, the Grumpy Ones, and her mind had slid into
a kind of day-dream.

Into the very middle of this day-dream had broken
the sound of Tabitha's words, ' It is the end, Euphemia ' ; and it was as if a trumpet had uttered them.

She looked round in dismay, and saw her sisters,
Euphemia and Tabitha, sitting there in their chairs
at the table, as stiff and cold as statues of stone.
Not only this, which was not so very unusual, but
they both of them looked extremely unwell. *Then*
she noticed the letter. And she knew at once that
this must be the serpent that had suddenly bitten
her sisters' minds. The blood rushed up into her
cheeks, and she said—feeling more intensely sorry
for them both than she could possibly express—' Is
there anything wrong, Euphemia ? '

And Euphemia, in a voice Jean Elspeth would
certainly not have recognised if she had heard it
from outside the door, replied, ' You may well ask
it.' And then in a rush Jean Elspeth remembered
her strange dream of the night before, and at once

went blundering on : ' Well, you know, Euphemia,
I had a dream last night, all dark and awful, and, in
it, *there* was *Lucy* looking out of a crooked stone
window over some water. And she said to me——'

But Tabitha interrupted her : ' I think, Elspeth,
neither myself nor Euphemia at this moment wish
to hear what Lucy, as you call her, said in your
dream. We have received exceedingly bad news
this morning, that intimately concerns not only
Tabitha and me, but even yourself also. And this
is no time for frivolity.' And it sounded even more
tragic in her Scots tongue.

Jean Elspeth had not meant to be frivolous. She
had hoped merely, and if but for a moment, to turn
her sisters' minds away from this dreadful news that
had come with the postman, and to explain what
her dream had seemed to promise. But no. It was
just her way. Whenever she said anything to her
sisters, anything that came from the very bottom
of her heart, she always made a muddle of it. It
sounded as small and meaningless as the echo of
a sparrow's cheeping against a bare stone wall.
They would look at her out of their green-grey eyes,
down their long pale noses, with an expression either
grim or superior, or both. Of course, too, at such a
moment, any mention of Lucy was a dreadfully silly
mistake. Even at the best of times they despised
Jean Elspeth for such ' childishness,' and now it must
seem like a hideous joke.

For there never was and there never could be any
real Lucy. It was only a name. And yet Jean
Elspeth still longed to find any word of hope or
comfort that would bring back a little colour into

poor Euphemia's cheeks, and make her look a little less like an image in marble. But no word came. She had even failed to hear what her sisters were saying. At last she could bear herself no longer.

'I am sure, Euphemia, that you would like to talk the letter over with Tabitha in quiet, and that you will tell me if I can be of any help. I think I will go out into the garden.'

Euphemia bowed her head. And though, by trying to move with as little noise as possible, Jean Elspeth made her heavy chair give a loud screech on the polished floor, she managed to escape at last.

It was a cold, clear spring morning, and the trees in the distance were just tipped with their new green buds. The gardeners were already mapping out their rows of plants in the herbaceous borders, in preparation for the summer. There never was a garden ' kept ' so well. The angles of the flower-beds on the lawn—diamonds and lozenges, octagons, squares, and oblongs—were as sharp as if they had been cut out of cardboard with a pair of scissors. Not a blade of grass was out of place.

If even one little round pebble pushed up a shoulder in the gravel path, up came an immense heavy roller and ground him back into his place. As for a weed, let but one poke her blunt green nose above the black mould, she would soon see what happened.

The bright light from the sky streamed down upon the house, and every single window in the high white wall of it seemed to be scornfully watching Jean Elspeth as she made her way down to a little straight green seat under the terrace. Here, at least, she was out of view.

She sat down, folded her hands in her lap, and looked straight in front of her. She always so sat when she was in trouble. In vain she tried to compose and fix her mind and to *think*. It was impossible. For she had not been there more than a moment or two before she knew that Lucy was haunting somewhere close beside her. So close and so much on purpose, it seemed that it was almost as if she wanted to whisper something in her ear.

Now it has been said that Lucy was only a name. Yet, after all, she was a little more than that. Years and years ago, when Jean Elspeth was only seven, she ' sort of ' made Lucy up. It was simply because there was no one else to play with, for Tabitha was five years older, and at least fifty-five times more sensible and intelligent and grown-up. So Jean Elspeth had just pretended.

In those days she would sometimes sit on one flower-pot on the long hot or windy terrace, and she would put another flower-pot for Lucy. And they would talk, or rather she would talk, and Lucy would look. Or sometimes they sat together in a corner of the great bare nursery. And sometimes Jean Elspeth would pretend she was holding Lucy's hand when she fell asleep.

And the really odd thing was that the less in those days she tried to ' pretend,' the more Lucy came. And though Jean Elspeth had never seen her with what is called her naked eye, she must have seen her with some other kind of eye, for she knew that her hair and skin were fairer than the fairest of flax, and that she was dressed in very light and queer fashioned clothes, though she could not say *how* queer.

Another queer thing was that Lucy always seemed to come and appear entirely out of nothing, and entirely of herself, when anything very odd or unexpected or sad or very beautiful happened, and sometimes just before it happened. That had been why she told Euphemia her dream of the night before. For though everything else in the dream had been dark and dismal, and the water had roared furiously over its rocks, breaking into foam like snow, and Jean Elspeth had been shaken with terror, Lucy herself appearing at the window had been more beautiful than moonlight and comforting as a star.

It was a pity, of course, that Jean Elspeth had ever so much as mentioned Lucy at all. But that had been years and years ago, and then she could not really help doing so. For Tabitha had crept up behind her one morning—it was on her eighth birthday—while she was sitting in a corner by the large cupboard, with her back to the nursery door, and had overheard her talking to someone.

' Aha ! little Miss Toad-in-the-hole ; and who are *you* talking to ? ' Tabitha had asked.

Jean Elspeth had turned cold all over. ' Nobody,' she said.

' Oh, Nobody, is it ? Then you just tell me Nobody's name,' said Tabitha.

And Jean Elspeth had refused. Unfortunately, she had been wearing that morning a high-waisted frock, with sleeves that came down only to the

elbow, and though Tabitha, with nips and pinches
of her bare skinny arm, could not make Jean Elspeth
cry, she had at least made her tell.

'Oh, so its name's Lucy, is it?' said Tabitha.
'You horrid little frump. Then you tell her from
me that if *I* catch her anywhere about, I'll scratch
her eyes out.'

After another pinch or two, and a good 'ring-of-
the-bells' at Jean Elspeth's plait, Tabitha had gone
downstairs to her father.

'Papa,' she said, 'I am sorry to interrupt you,
but I think poor Elspeth must be ill or in a fever.
She is "rambling." Had we better give her some
Gregory's powder, or some castor-oil, do you think?'

Mr. MacKnackery had been worried that morning
by a letter about a Gold Mine, something like that
which poor Euphemia so many years afterwards
was to receive from the Four Lawyers. But when
he was worried he at once tried to forget his worry.
Indeed, even at sight of what looked like an ugly
letter, he would begin softly whistling and smiling.
So it was almost with a sigh of relief that he pushed
the uncomfortable letter into a drawer and climbed
the stairs to the nursery.

And when Jean Elspeth, after crying a little as
she sat on his knee, had told him about Lucy, he
merely smiled out of his dark eyes, and, poking his
finger and thumb into a waistcoat pocket, had
pulled out, just as if it had been waiting there
especially for this occasion, a tiny little gold locket
with a picture of a moss-rose inside, which he asked
Jean Elspeth to give to Lucy the very next time she
came again. 'My dear,' he had said, 'I have my

Lucy, too, though I never, never talk about her. I keep her " for best." '

As for Tabitha, he thanked her most gratefully that morning at luncheon for having been so thoughtful about her sister. ' But I fear, my child,' he said, ' you must be fretting yourself without need. And for fretting there is nothing so good as Gregory's powder. So I have asked Alison to mix a good dose for you at bedtime, and if you are very generous, perhaps Jenny would like to lick the spoon.'

The very moment he turned his face away, with as dreadful a grimace as she could manage Tabitha had put out her long pale tongue at Jean Elspeth —which was about as much use as it would have been to put out her tongue for their old doctor— Dr. Menzies—after he had gone out of the room.

Whenever Jean Elspeth thought of those far-away years she always began to day-dream. And whenever she began to day-dream Lucy was sure to seem more real to her than at any other time. The gravel path, the green lawn, the distant hills vanished away before her eyes. She was lost as if in a region of light and happiness. There she was happy awhile. But cold spattering raindrops on her cheeks soon called her back to herself. A dark cloud had come over the world, and for the first time a dark dread came into her mind of what Euphemia's letter might mean.

She turned sharply on the little green seat almost as if she had been caught trespassing. And at that instant she could have vowed that she actually saw —this time with her real naked eye—a child standing and looking at her a few paces beyond. It was mere

make-believe, of course ; but what most surprised
Jean Elspeth was that there should be such a peculiar
smile on the child's face—as if she were saying :
' Never mind, my dear ; whatever happens, whatever
they say, I am going to be with you more than *ever*
before. You just see ! '

And then, not for the first time in her life, Jean
Elspeth felt almost ashamed of having a phantom
friend. When they were all in such trouble, was it
quite fair to Euphemia and Tabitha ? Was it even
quite right ? She actually went so far as to turn
away in the opposite direction, and would have
hastened straight back to the house if, at that
moment, she had not heard a small, curious fluttering
behind her. She turned her head on her shoulder,
but it was to find only that a robin had stolen in on
her to share her company, and was now eyeing her
with his bead-black eye from his perch on the green
seat which she had but just vacated.

For lunch that day the butler brought in a small
soup-tureen of porridge. When he had attended to
each of the ladies, and had withdrawn, Euphemia
explained to Jean Elspeth precisely what the lawyer's
letter meant. It was a long letter, not only about
the gentlemen who had failed to find water enough
for their waterworks in Armenia, but also about
some other gentlemen in Madagascar whose crops
of manioc and caoutchouc had been seized with chor-
blight. Jean Elspeth did not quite grasp the details ;
she did not quite understand why the lawyers had
ever taken such a fancy to caoutchouc ; but she
did perfectly understand Euphemia's last sentence :
' So you see, Elspeth, we are ruined ! '

And would you believe it? Once more Jean Elspeth said the wrong thing. Or rather it was her voice that was wrong. Far away in it was the sound as of a bugle bugling at break of day. 'And does that mean, Euphemia, that we shall have to *leave* Stoneyhouse?'

'It means,' said Tabitha tartly, 'that Stoneyhouse may have to leave *us*.'

'In either case we are powerless,' added Euphemia. And the tone in which Euphemia uttered these words—sitting there straight and erect, with her long white face, in her sleek grey silk morning gown with its pattern of tiny mauve flowers—brought tears, not to Jean Elspeth's eyes, but to somewhere deep down inside her. It was as if somebody was drawing water out of the very well of her heart.

'It is the disgrace,' said Tabitha. 'To have to turn our backs, to run away. We shall be the talk, the laughing-stock of the county.'

'Laugh at us because we are ruined!' cried Jean Elspeth.

But this time Tabitha ignored her. 'This is the house,' she said, 'our noble grandfather built for us. And here I will die, unless I am positively driven out of it by these systematic blood-suckers.'

'Tabitha!' pleaded Euphemia. 'Surely we should not demean ourselves so far as even to call them by their right name.'

'Systematic blood-suckers,' cried Tabitha fiercely. 'I will sell the very rings off my finger rather than be an exile from the house where I was born. And *he*—*he* at least shall never witness the ruin into which our father's folly has betrayed us.'

She rose from her seat, and mounting on one of
the maroon damask chairs that, unless guests were
present, were accustomed to stand in a demure row
along the wall, she succeeded, after one or two vain
attempts, in turning the immense gilt portrait of
her grandfather with its face to the wall.

Then tears really came into Jean Elspeth's eyes.
But they were tears of anger rather than of pity.
' I think,' she said, ' that is being intensely unkind
to father.'

' By this time,' said Tabitha sternly, ' I should
have supposed that you would have given up the
notion that you are capable of thinking. What right
have you to defend your father, pray, simply
because you take after him ? '

Jean Elspeth made no answer. Her father at any
rate continued to smile at her from his nail—though
it was not a very good portrait, because the painter
had been unable to get the hair and the waistcoat
quite right. And if—even at this unhappy moment
—Jean Elspeth had had her porridge spoon in her
hand, she would certainly have given it a little secret
wave in his direction.

But he was not to smile down for very long. The
Miss MacKnackeries's grandfather continued to hang
with his face to the wall. But the two other portraits, together with the wardrobes, coffers, presses,
sideboards, bead-mats, bureaus, and even the Indian
workboxes, were all taken off in a few weeks, to be
sold for what they would fetch. And Euphemia
now, instead of five, wore but one ring, and that of
turquoises.

In a month all the servants, from the butler to

Sally McGullie, and all the gardeners were gone.
Mrs. O'Phrump alone remained—first because she
was too stout to be likely to be comfortable in any
new place, and next, because she wasn't greedy about
wages. That was all. Just Mrs. O'Phrump and
the gardener's boy, Tom Piper, whose mother lived
in the village, and who slept at home. But he was
a lazy boy, was Tom Piper, and when he was not
fast asleep in the tool-shed, he was snoring in the
deserted orchard.

It was extraordinary to be alive and to be living
in so empty a house. The echoes! Why, if you
but walked alone along a corridor, you heard your
own footsteps pit-a-patt-a after you all the way
down. If by yourself, in ' your ain, ain companie,'
you but laughed out in a room, it was like being
the muffled clapper of a huge hollow bell. All
Stoneyhouse seemed empty now ; and yet perhaps
the emptiest place of all was the coach-house.

And then the stables. It was simply astonishing
how quickly stray oats, that had fallen by chance
into the crannies, sprang up green among the cobble-
stones in front of their walls. And if for a little
while you actually stood in the stables beside one
of the empty mangers, the note of a bird was like
the sound of a hundred. And you could almost see
ghostly horses with their dark eyes looking round at
you out of their long narrow heads, as if to say : ' So
this is what you have done with us ! '

Not that Jean Elspeth had very much time to
linger over such experiences. Somehow, she seemed
to have grown even smaller in the empty house.
But she was ten times more active. And, though

she tried not to be selfish by showing it, she was more than ten times happier. Between Jean Elspeth herself and the eagle-surmounted gateposts, indeed, she now secretly confessed that she had always hated Stoneyhouse. How very odd, then, that the moment it ceased to be a place in which any fine personage would care to stay a moment, she began to be friends with it. She began to pity it.

No doubt Tabitha was right. Their grandfather would assuredly have ' turned in his grave,' poor creature, at the sound of those enormous vans, those hideous pantechnicons, as their wheels ground down the gravel in the lingering twilight evenings. And yet, after all, that grandfather had been born— a fact that very much shocked Tabitha, whenever her father had smilingly related it—their grandfather had been born in a two-roomed cottage so minute that, if only you could have got it through the windows, it would have fitted quite comfortably into the great dining-room at Stoneyhouse.

There was not a single bawbee then in his breeches pocket, and having been such a good man, as both Euphemia and Tabitha agreed, he did not need a bawbee now. *Would* he then—once the pantechnicons were out of the way—would he, thought Jean Elspeth, have been so very miserable to see all this light in the house and to hear all these charming echoes ?

There were other advantages, too. It was easy to sweep the dining-room now ; and much easier to dust it. There was peace in its vacancy, and it was not stagnant. And one day, more out of kindness than curiosity, after busily whisking over its gilt

frame with her feather cornice-broom, Jean Elspeth
climbed on to a chair, and, tilting it, looked in at the
portrait.   A spider had spun its web in one corner,
but otherwise (it was almost disappointing) the
picture was unchanged.   Nor had Mr. MacKnackery
yet taken his watch out of his pocket, even though
(for his three granddaughters at any rate) the time
was now long—long past twelve.

Jean Elspeth had had ridiculous thoughts like
these as long as she could remember.   But now they
came swarming into her mind like midsummer bees
into a hive.   Try as she might, she could not keep
them all to herself, and though on this account alone
Tabitha seemed to dislike her more than ever,
Euphemia seemed sometimes to wish for her company.   But then, Euphemia was by no means well.
She had begun to stoop a little, and sometimes did
not hear what was said to her.   To watch her
visibly grow older like this gave Jean Elspeth dreadful anxiety.   Still, in most things she confessed to
herself almost every dawn, looking down from her
upper window, she was far far happier than when
Stoneyhouse stood in all its glory.

Indeed, there was no time to be anything else ;
and even if there had been a complete cupboard *full*
of neat packages of time *saved*, she would have used
them all up in a week.   Euphemia, being so poorly,
did very little.   She helped to make the beds and
to do the mending.   Only the mending, for, fortunately, the making of any new clothes would be
unnecessary for years and years to come ; they had
so many old ones.   Tabitha did what she could
manage of the lighter work, but although she had a

quick tongue, she had slow, clumsy hands. And it
is quite certain, though nobody, of course, would
have been so unkind as to say so, that she would
never have got even as low wages as Sally McGullie,
if she had been in need of a place.

Mrs. O'Phrump did the cooking ; but sat on one
chair in the kitchen for so many hours together that
she became almost like a piece of furniture—the
heaviest piece in the house. For the cooking of
water-porridge and potatoes does not require very
much time, and that was pretty much all that the
Miss MacKnackeries had to eat, except for the eggs
from Jean Elspeth's three Cochin-Chinas. And
Mrs. O'Phrump needed most of these, as there was so
much of her to sustain. As for the apples and pears
in the orchard, since Mrs. O'Phrump was too stout
to stoop to make dumplings, Jean Elspeth, having
two wonderful rows of small sharp teeth, shared
these raw with Tom Piper—though *he* had all the
stomachaches.

All the rest of the work fell to Jean Elspeth. She
slaved from morning till night. And to slave the
more merrily, she had taught herself to whistle. She
never asked herself why she was so happy. And
no doubt it was chiefly by contrast of having been so
cramped-in, and kept-under, and miserable in days
gone by.

Still, certain things did now happen in Stoneyhouse
that had not happened before, and some of these
may have helped. For one thing, Jean Elspeth had
always dreaded ' company.' Dressing-up made her
feel awkward. The simplest stranger made her shy.
She would have much preferred to say Boh to a

goose. None came now, except Dr. Menzies, who of his kindness sometimes called to feel Euphemia's pulse and look at her tongue.

Jean Elspeth, too, had never liked servants, not because they were servants, but because Euphemia and Tabitha seemed to think they oughtn't to be talked to much. Just given their orders. Now Jean Elspeth could easily have given everything else in the world : but not orders. And if there ever *had* been an interesting creature in Stoneyhouse, even though she was so stupid in some things, it was Sally McGullie.

Then, again, Jean Elspeth, being by nature desperately untidy, never showed it now. For it's all but impossible to be untidy in a room that contains only a table and three chairs !

Then, yet again, Jean Elspeth, before the gentlemen in Armenia and Madagascar had been disappointed in their waterworks and caoutchouc, had had very little to do. She was scarcely even allowed to read. For Tabitha was convinced that most reading was a waste of time, and trash at that ; while improving books had never the least bit improved Jean Elspeth. But now she had so many things to do that it was a perfect joy to fit them all in (like the pieces of a puzzle). And the perfectest joy of all was to scramble into her truckle bed, which had formerly been Sally McGullie's bed, and, with a tallow candle stuck by its own grease to the left-hand knob, to read and read and read.

The hours she spent like this, with no living company but mice and moths and bats and scritch-owls ! When her upper parts in the winter were cold, she put her skirt over the quilt. One thin blanket, indeed, is not much comfort on cold nights when one is lying up North there, almost in positive view of the Grumpy Ones. As for her feet, she used to boil some water in a kettle and fill a wine-bottle.

This, of course, broke a good many bottles ; and it was an odd thing that until there was only one left, Tabitha (whose feet were like slabs of ice) refused to think of such a vulgarity. And *then* she changed her mind. And medicine-bottles are too small.

Apart from all this, queer things now happened in Stoneyhouse. Little things, but entrancing. The pantechnicon men, for example, had broken a window on a lower staircase as they were heaving down old Mr. MacKnackery's best wardrobe. A pair of robins in the springtime noticed this hole, and decided to build their nest in a nook of the cornice. Jean Elspeth (with her tiny whistling) was accepted as the bosom friend of the whole family.

There was, too, a boot cupboard, one too far from the kitchen for Mrs. O'Phrump to use. Its window had been left open. And when, by chance, Jean Elspeth looked in one sunny afternoon, there hung within it a marvellous bush of Traveller's Joy, rather pale in leaf, but actually flowering there ; and even a butterfly sipping of its nectar. After that, not a day passed now but she would peep in at this delicate green visitor, and kiss her hand. It was, too, an immense relief to Jean Elspeth to have said good-bye for ever to lots of things in the house that seemed to her to have been her enemies ever since she was a child.

L

She wandered up into rooms she had never seen before, and looked out of windows whose views had never before lain under her eyes. Nor did she cease to day-dream, but indulged in just tiny ones, that may come and go, like swifts, between two ticks of a clock. And although, of course, Tabitha strongly disapproved of much that delighted Jean Elspeth now, there was not nearly so much time in which to tell her so.

Besides, Jean Elspeth was more useful in that great barracks of a place than ten superior parlour-maids would have been. She was much more like a steam-engine than a maiden lady. And, like a steam-engine, she refused to be angry; she refused to sulk; and she usually refused to answer back. But when nowadays she *did* answer back, her tongue had a sting to it at least as sharp (though never so venomous) as that of the busy bee.

And last, but not least, there was the *outside* of the house. As soon as ever Mr. McPhizz and his under-gardeners had departed with their shears and knives and edging-irons and mowing-machines, wildness had begun to creep into the garden. Wind and bird carried in seeds from the wilderness, and after but two summers, the trim barbered lawns sprang up into a marvellous meadow of daisies and butter-cups, dandelions, meadowsweet and fools' parsley, and then dock, thistle, groundsel and feathery grasses. Ivy, hop, briony, convolvulus crept across the terrace; Hosts of the Tiny blossomed between the stones. Moss, too, in mats and cushions of a green livelier than the emerald, or even than a one-night-old beech-leaf. Rain stains now softly coloured the white walls, as if a stranger had come in the night and begun to paint pictures there. And the roses, in their now hidden beds, rushed back as fast as ever they could to bloom like their wild-briar sisters again.

And not only green things growing. Jean Elspeth would tiptoe out to see complete little immense families of rabbits nibbling their breakfast or supper of dandelion leaves on the very flagstones under the windows. Squirrels nutted ; moles burrowed ; hedgehogs came beetle-hunting ; mice of every tiny size scampered and twinkled and danced and made merry.

As for the birds—birds numberless ! And of so many kinds and colours and notes that she had to sit up half the night looking out their names in the huge bird-book her father had given her on her eleventh Christmas. This was the one treasure she had saved from the pantechnicon men. She had wrapped it up in two copies of *The Scotsman*, and hidden it in the chimney. She felt a little guilty over it at times, but none the less determined that the Four Lawyers should never hear of *that*.

It was strange, exceedingly strange, to be so happy ; and Jean Elspeth sometimes could hardly contain herself, she was so much ashamed of it in the presence of her sisters. Still, she drew the line, as they say, at Lucy.

And that was the strangest and oddest thing of all. After the dreadful shock of the Four Lawyers' letter, after the torment and anxiety and horror, the pantechnicons and the tradespeople, poor Tabitha and Euphemia—however brave their faces and stiff their backs—had drooped within like flowers in autumn nipped by frost. In their pride, too, they had renounced even the friends who would have been faithful to them in their trouble.

They shut themselves up in themselves more than ever, like birds in cages. They scarcely ever even looked from the windows. It was only on Sundays they went out of doors. Euphemia, too, had sometimes to keep to her bed. And Jean Elspeth would cry to herself, ' Oh, my dear ! oh, my dear ! ' at the sight of Tabitha trailing about the house with a large duster and so little to dust. To see her sipping at her water-porridge as if she were not in the least hungry, as if it was the daintiest dish in Christendom, was like having a knife stuck in one's very breast.

Yet, such was Tabitha's ' strength of mind ' and hardihood, Jean Elspeth never dared to comfort her, to cheer her up, to wave her spoon by so much as a quarter of an inch in *her* direction.

In these circumstances it had seemed to Jean Elspeth it would be utterly unfair to share Lucy's company, even in her hidden mind. It would be like stealing a march, as they say. It would be cheating. At any rate, it might hurt their feelings. They would see, more stark than ever before, how desolate they were. They would look up and realise by the very light in her eyes that her old playmate had not deserted her. No. She could wait. There was plenty of time. She would keep her wishes down. And the little secret door of her mind should be left, not, as it once was, wide open, but just ajar.

How, she could not exactly say. And yet, in spite

of all this, Lucy herself, just as if she were a real
live ghost, seemed to be everywhere. If in her
scrubbing Jean Elspeth happened to glance up out
of the window, as like as not that fair gentle face
would be stealthily smiling in. If some moonlight
night she leaned for a few precious sweet cold
moments over her bedroom sill, as like as not that
pale phantom would be seen wandering, shadowless,
amid the tall whispering weeds and grasses of the
lawn.

Spectres and ghosts, of course, may be the most
forbidding company. But Lucy was nothing but
gaiety and grace. The least little glimpse of her
was like hearing a wild bird singing—even the
Southern nightingale, though without those long,
bubbling, grievous notes that seem to darken the
darkness. Having this ghost, then, for company,
however much she tried not to heed it, all that Jean
Elspeth *had* to do in order just to play fair—and she
did it with all her might—was not to *look* for Lucy,
and not to *show* that she saw her, when there she was,
plain to be seen, before her very eyes. And when
at last she realised her plot was succeeding, that
Lucy was gone from her, her very heart seemed to
come into her mouth.

And so the years went by. And the sisters became
older and older, and Stoneyhouse older and older
too. Walls, fences, stables, coach-house, hen-house,
and the square lodge crept on steadily to rack and
ruin. Tabitha kept more and more to herself, and
the sisters scarcely spoke at meal-times.

Then at last Euphemia fell really ill; and everything else for a while went completely out of Jean

Elspeth's life and remembrance. She hadn't a moment even to lean from her window or to read in her bed. It was unfortunate, of course, that Euphemia's bedroom was three stair-flights up. Jean Elspeth's legs grew very tired of climbing those long ladders, and Tabitha could do little else than sit at the window and knit knit the wool of worn-out shawls and stockings into new ones. So she would stay for hours together, never raising her eyes to glance over the pair of horn-rimmed spectacles that had belonged to her grandfather, and now straddled her own lean nose. Dr. Menzies, too, was an old man now, and could visit them but seldom.

Jean Elspeth seldom even went to bed. She sat on a chair in Euphemia's room and snatched morsels of sleep, as a hungry dog snatches at bits of meat on a butcher's tray. It was on such a night as this, nodding there in her chair, that, after having seemed to fall into a long narrow nightmare hole of utter cold and darkness, and to have stayed there for centuries without light or sound, she was suddenly roused by Euphemia's voice.

It was not Euphemia's usual voice, and the words were following one another much more rapidly than usual, like sheep and lambs running through a gate. Daybreak was at the window. And in this first chill eastern light Euphemia was sitting up in bed— a thing she had been unable to do for weeks. And she was asking Jean Elspeth to tell her who the child was that was now standing at the end of her bed.

Euphemia described her, too—' A fair child with straight hair. And she is carrying a bundle of gorse, with its prickles and flowers wide open. I can smell the almond smell. And she keeps on looking and smiling first at me, and then at you. Don't you *see*, Elspeth ? Tell her, please, to go away. Tell her I don't want to be happy like that. She is making me afraid. Tell her to go away at once, please.'

Jean Elspeth sat there shivering, like a snail in its shell. The awful thing was to know this visitor must be Lucy, and yet not to be able to see her— not a vestige, nothing but the iron bed and the bed-post, and Euphemia sitting there, gazing. How, then, could she tell Lucy to go away ?

She hastened across the room, and took Euphemia's cold hands in hers. ' You are dreaming, Euphemia. *I* see nothing. And if it is a pleasant dream, why drive it away ? '

' No,' said Euphemia, in the same strange, low, clear voice. ' It is not a dream. You are deceiving me, Elspeth. She has come only to mock at me. Send her away ! '

And Jean Elspeth, gazing into her sister's wide light eyes, that now seemed deeper than the deepest well that ever was on earth, was compelled to answer her.

' Please, please, Euphemia, do not think of it any more. There is nothing to fear—nothing at all. Why, it sounds like Lucy—that old silly story ; do you remember ? But I have not seen her myself for ever so long. I couldn't while you were ill.'

The lids closed gently down over the wide eyes, but Euphemia still held tight to Jean Elspeth's work-roughened hand. ' Never mind, then,' she

whispered, ' if that is all.   I had no wish to take her
away from you, Elspeth.   Keep close to me.   One
thing, we are happier now, you and I.'

' Oh, Euphemia, do you mean that ? ' said Jean
Elspeth, peering closer.

' Well,' Euphemia replied ; and it was as if there
were now two voices speaking : the old Euphemia's
and this low, even, dreamlike voice.   ' I mean it.
There is plenty of air now—a different place.   And
I hope your friend will come as often as she pleases.
There's room for us all.'

And with that word ' room,' and the grim smile
that accompanied it, all the old Euphemia seemed to
have come back again, though a moment after she
had dropped back upon her pillow and appeared to
be asleep.

Seeing her thus still once more, Jean Elspeth very,
very cautiously turned her head.   The first rays of
the sun were on the window.   Not the faintest scent
of almond was borne to her nostrils on the air.
There was no sign at all of any company.   A crooked
frown had settled on her forehead.   She was cold
through and through, and her body ached, but she
tried to smile, and almost imperceptibly lifted a
finger just as if it held a teaspoon, and she was
waving it in her own old secret childish way to her
father's portrait on the wall.

Now and again after that Jean Elspeth watched
the same absent far-away look steal over Euphemia's
face, and the same smile, dour and grim, and yet
happy—like still deep water under waves.   It was
almost as if Euphemia were amused at having stolen
Lucy away.

'You see, my dear,' she said suddenly to Jean Elspeth one morning, as if after a long talk, 'it only proves that we all go the same way home.'

'Euphemia, please don't say that,' whispered Jean Elspeth.

'But why not?' said Euphemia. 'So it is. And *she* almost laughing out loud at me. The hussy!'...

None of their old friends knew when Euphemia died, so it was only Dr. Menzies and his sister who came to Stoneyhouse for the funeral. And though Jean Elspeth would now have been contented to do *all* the work in the house and to take care of Tabitha and her knitting into the bargain, they persuaded her at last that this would be impossible. And so, one blazing hot morning, having given a little parting gift to Tom Piper and wept a moment or two on Mrs. O'Phrump's ample shoulder, Jean Elspeth climbed with Tabitha into a cab, and that evening found herself hundreds of miles away from Stoneyhouse, in the two upper rooms set apart for the two ladies by Sally McGullie, who had married a fisherman and was now Mrs. John Jones.

Jean Elspeth could not have imagined a life so different. It was as if she had simply been pulled up by the roots. Whenever Tabitha could spare her—and that was seldom now—she would sit at her window looking on the square stone harbour and the sea, or in a glass shelter on its narrow front. But now that time stretched vacantly before her, and she was at liberty if she pleased to 'pretend' whenever she wished, and to fall into day-dreams one after another, just as they might happen to come, it was just life's queer way that she could scarcely picture Lucy now, even with her inward eye, and never with her naked one.

It was, too, just the way of this odd world that she should pine and long for Stoneyhouse beyond words to tell. She felt sometimes she must die— suffocate—of homesickness, and would frown at the grey moving sea, as if that alone were the enemy who was keeping her away from it. Not only this, but she saved up in a tin money-box every bawbee which she could spare of the little money the Four Lawyers had managed to save from the caoutchouc. And all for one distant purpose.

And at length, years and years afterwards, she told Mrs. Jones that she could bear herself no longer, that—like the cat in the fairy-tale—she must pay a visit, and must go alone. . . .

It was on an autumn afternoon, about five o'clock, and long shadows were creeping across the grasses of the forsaken garden when Jean Elspeth came into sight again of Stoneyhouse, and found herself standing some little distance from the gaunt familiar walls by a dank pond that had formed itself in a hollow of the garden. Her father had delighted in water, and, making use of a tiny stream that coursed near by, had made a jetting fountain and a fishpond. The fountain having long ceased to flow and the pond having become choked with water-weeds, the stream had pushed its way out across the hollows, and had made itself this last dark resting-place. You might almost have thought it was trying to copy Jean Elspeth's life in Sally Jones's seaside cottage. On the other hand, the windows of the great house did not stare so fiercely now ; they were blurred and empty, like the eyes of a man walking in his sleep. One of the chimney-stacks had toppled down, and creepers had rambled all over the wide expanse of the walls.

Jean Elspeth, little old woman that she now was, in her dingy black bonnet and a beaded mantle that had belonged to Euphemia, stood there drinking the great still scene in, as a dry sponge drinks in salt water.

And after hesitating for some little time, she decided to venture nearer. She pushed her way through the matted wilderness of the garden, crossed the terrace, and presently peered in through one of the dingy dining-room windows. Half a shutter had by chance been left unclosed. When her eyes were grown accustomed to the gloom within, she discovered that the opposite wall was now quite empty. The portrait of her grandfather must have slowly ravelled through its cord. It had fallen face upwards on to the boards beneath.

It saddened her to see this. She had left the picture hanging there simply because she felt sure that Euphemia would so have wished it to hang. But though she wearied herself out seeking to find entry into the house, in order, at least, to lean her grandfather up again against the wall, it was in vain. The doors were rustily bolted; the lower windows tight shut. And it was beginning to be twilight when she found herself once more beside the cold stagnant pool.

All this while she had been utterly alone. It had been a dreadful and sorrowful sight to see the great house thus decaying, and all this neglect. Yet she was not unhappy, for it seemed with its trees and greenery in this solitude to be uncomplaining and at peace. And so, too, was she. It was as if her whole life had just vanished and flitted away like a dream, leaving merely her body standing there in the evening light under the boughs of the heavy chestnut-tree overhead.

And then by chance, in that deep hush, her eyes wandered to the surface of the water at her feet, and there fixed themselves, her whole mind in a sudden confusion. For by some strange freak of the cheating dusk, she saw gazing back at her from under a squat old crape bonnet, with Euphemia's cast-off beaded mantle on the shoulders beneath it, a face not in the least like that of the little old woman inside them, but a face, fair and smiling, as of one eternally young and happy and blessed—Lucy's. She gazed and gazed, in the darkening evening. A peace beyond understanding comforted her spirit. It was by far the oddest thing that had ever happened to Jean Elspeth in all the eighty years of her odd long life on earth.

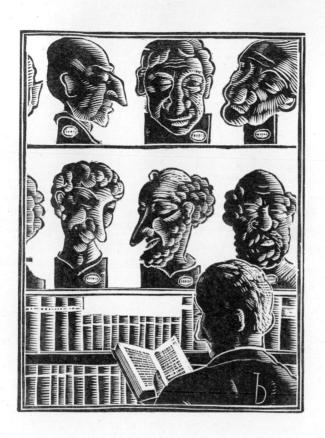

A NOSE

WHEN little Sam Such was christened, a host of aunts, uncles, cousins, second - cousins, and cousins once, twice and many times removed, came to the christening feast. There was hot veal-and-ham pie and cold roast leg-of-pork; there was lobster, cherry-tart, trifle, custard, and Devonshire cream, with bottled ale for the gentlemen to drink and lemonade for the ladies. And when the company had at last finished eating and drinking, little Sam in his long clothes, with the wrinkles on his forehead, the silky down on the back of his head, his tiny ears and his pouting mouth, was brought in by an exceedingly large nurse; and everyone present stood up, clinked glasses, and drank his health.

Sam's father was a prosperous clothier and haberdasher. He was Such & Such: it was written up over his fine shop in the best gilt lettering. He had two assistants, Mr. Hopper and George, who at the christening feast each took it in turn to mind the shop while the other looked in on the company. There were two wide plate-glass windows to the shop front in the High Street—one for the dummies in suits, boys and gents., and one for shirts, gloves, hose, ties, and chest-protectors. There, too, hung an elegantly gilded square of cardboard close against the glass with the invitation : ' Why go to So and So's when you can get ALL you will ever want from Such & Such ! '

Sam's mother was a shy little woman with a small face and large brown eyes. She was so shy that she had never even had the courage to serve in the shop and say ' A nice bright morning, sir,' or ' That will be 2s. 11¾d., madam.' Once even rather than serve a gentleman who wanted a blue poplin tie with white spots, she had hidden under the counter. She had four sisters, however, who were entirely different from herself in looks, figure, voices, nerves, and everything else. They were tall and thin and high-spirited, with large features and drooping chins, and whatever dresses they wore they always resembled flags flying in the wind. They were like war-horses, and laughed Ha Ha.

They brought little Sam, their first and only nephew, the handsomest of christening gifts—a pink coral comforter with silver bells ; a silver knife and fork in a maroon leather case ; a whistle also of hall-marked silver, and an embossed silver mug, with a beautiful inscription exquisitely engraved with all the proper flourishes on the bottom of it :

> Welcome Sam, to earth you came,
> Ring Heaven's bell, we wish you well.
> Many years and long to thrive
> May Providence to Samuel give.   Aunt Sarah.

For Aunt Sarah was one of the modestest of poets and had refused, though the silversmith suggested

it, to have her poem engraved round the mug's
margin.

Apart from all this—for Mr. Such had no Infants'
Department—his sisters-in-law bestowed on their
minute nephew a triple-complete outfit of woollen
mits, woollen boots, woollen over-breeches, bibs,
caps, veils and shawls. If Sam had been a prince his
christening gifts might have been more expensive,
but they could not have been of purer wool.

Sam's Aunt Lollie on his father's side, brought
him *her* little present too—a long large German
meerschaum pipe beautifully painted with woodland
scenes and peasants dancing. It was a peculiar
gift for one so young and tender, but, then, Aunt
Lollie was a little peculiar herself, and stood up
drinking Sam's health a long time after the others
had all sat down, even though she had only been
given lemonade in her glass.

With so many aunts to consider, the question of
who should be godmother had been a difficult one
for Sam's father and mother. To prevent the
faintest tinge of jealousy they had at last chosen a
Miss Catten, who wore the most charming little
gold belfries in her ears for earrings. She was not
so much as even a relative of the family's by marriage,
only a very old friend. Sam's godfathers were
easier (for he had no uncles). One was Mr. Hobble,
Mr. Such's partner in the haberdashery business,
the other Mr. Slant, a neighbour in the wine trade.
And Mr. Slant's christening present had been rather
to the company in general than to little Sam in
particular. It was six old cobwebby bottles of a
rich crusted port. None the less, and very much to

the amusement of the company, Sam's nurse insisted on just dipping her littlest finger into her glass and moistening Sam's underlip with the wine. He lapped it up like a blind kitten over its first taste of cream ; and yet—strangely enough—he became in after life a strict teetotaller.

Silver linings, alas, are apt to be at the edge of the darkest of clouds. And the cloud at Sam's christening was his great-aunt Keren-happuch (so called because her father's name had been Job). How Sam's great-aunt Keren-Happuch came to hear of his christening or even of his coming into the world at all, is a mystery. She lived in a crooked old country cottage miles away from Mr. Such's shop and even well outside the town. She was lame and walked with two sticks. She hated the streets ; she hated the people in them ; she hated everything and everybody ; and she had long since quarrelled with every relative she had.

But just like the wicked fairy godmother in the old stories, she came stumping into the house long after the ceremony was over, and in such a rage and fury she did not so much as say thank-you to Mr. Hopper, who having spied her from the shop-window ran out (with George) to help her in at the door. And she sat in a corner of the parlour glowering out of her horn spectacles at the merry party, and eyeing little Sam in his nurse's arms as if he were some horrid little wild animal.

She refused cold pork, she refused veal pie, and she scowled at the lobster. She told poor Aunt Lollie to mind her own business, laughed like a hyaena at Mr. Hobble's christening speech, and then

—at last—on leaving the house, turned back an
instant on her two sticks in the porch and muttered
a few words into Sam's mother's ear.

There couldn't have been more than half a dozen
of them altogether ; and yet on hearing them poor
little Mrs. Such turned a ghastly greenish white.
' Oh no, oh no,' she cried ; sat down on a hard
mahogany chair in the hall, and burst into tears.

Fortunately by this time only a few of the guests
invited to the christening were still in the house.
These gathered round her, some with smelling-salts,
some with cold water and some with feathers, all of
them fearing that she was just about to faint. But
try as she might, she couldn't. Her heart ceased to
palpitate at last, and a little pink crept back into her
cheek. But though she was still shaken and horrified,
nothing would induce her to breathe even a whisper
of what the cantankerous old woman had said.
Not until she was alone with her husband did she
manage to share her dreadful news with another
human soul. ' Oh, Samuel, Samuel,' she cried, ' how
can I bear it ? What will you say ? How can I
bear it ? That wicked old woman says that our poor
little Sam's nose is made of wax.'

' Of wax ! ' cried her husband, ' of wax ! ' his face
turning a deep mulberry red instead of ashen white.
' The old collop, the old ragbag ! For goodness'
sake, Matilda, pull yourself together. Don't carry
on like this ! You are spoiling the whole day for me.
Wax indeed ! Why—why your own sister Sarah's
very last words to me were that the child has *all*
the family features. You must be dreaming Matilda
—or the—the—what did you say she actually said ? '

'She said,' replied Mrs. Such, ' " I've looked and I've seen ; I've been where I've been ; though it grows where it grows—the brat *has a wax nose*." Oh, Samuel, I feel I shall never recover from it.'

The curious thing was that Mr. Such had never up to that moment really examined his infant son's nose. He had taken only a bird's-eye view of its tiny face. Nor was he an expert in noses. He blew his own like a trumpet and had admired Matilda's when she was a girl. But he was no nose *knower*, and when he stooped over his cradle and gazed down at Sam's, he discovered first, that it was exceedingly minute ; next, that it had no bridge to speak of ; and last, that it was not a deep cherry-pink, as he had supposed it would be, but as colourless as a candle. Indeed, the tip of it that stuck up out of Sam's face was scarcely larger than the seed of a bean.

When, then, Sam's mother turned her imploring round brown eyes on him and besought him, ' Oh, Samuel, what do you *think* ? ' Mr. Such had turned as white as Sam's own small sheets. He could only look away. He groaned inside him. ' Think, Matilda,' he blurted at last, ' think !—I think it's all stuff and nonsense ! all *bosh*, Matilda. The old harridan ! The collop ! The trollop ! The witch ! '

At this poor Mrs. Such burst out crying. The more names Mr. Such called her great-aunt Keren-Happuch, the more firmly she believed that what she had said was true. It *looked* true. Indeed, as if poor little Sam, seeing his father's rage and his mother's tears, had realised what was amiss, he began twisting and contorting his features as though he were

trying to explore his own face. But his nose
remained central and immovable. There was no
doubting it, Mrs. Such moaned to herself, it *was*
wax. It *was* wax. With tears streaming down her
face, she there and then made Mr. Such swear and
vow for ever and ever that he would never never
mention this dreadful secret even to the doctor,
even to the nurse—not to a living soul in the whole
wide world. And he—poor Mr. Such—to save her
feelings, took out his large handkerchief, dried
her eyes, and vowed his vow. It was a dreadful
moment, but he did his best.

This did not, however, prevent him at the first
opportunity from asking the nurse one or two
innocent round-about questions. ' For his age, now,
Nurse, he has remarkably blue eyes, Nurse, don't
you think ?—*blue* blue, I mean,' he said to her that
evening after Sam's bath.

' Blue, sir ! I never before see in a hinfant's face
what I should call such *hazure* eyes, sir—they remind me of Mr. Gladstone's, sir, if his portricks are
anything to go by.'

Mr. Such recalled Mr. Gladstone's face with ease,
for in politics he was an ardent Tory, and his next
remark was in even fainter tones. ' Ay, and he
looks *healthy*, don't he, Matilda ? '

Sam's mother hid her face in her handkerchief ;
but the nurse replied with alacrity : ' Healthy, sir,
why bless his 'eart, the very bloom of it's all hover
of 'im.'

' I have heard say,' said Mr. Such, thrusting his
thumbs into the openings of his waistcoat, ' that
what you may call *character* in the human face

comes foremost out in the nose—I've heard *say*,
I mean.'

' Oh, Samuel,' moaned poor Matilda, ' it's just like
asking for the Evil Eye.'

' Why no, mum,' said the nurse, ' asking your
pardon, mum. Truth's truth, mum, all the world
over. I've proved it on the face. And what I
should say, sir, is that that there nose there is what
you might call the finishing feature of the hangel's
'ole face. Bless his heart! *there's* character, if you
like. My first 'usband had a nose the very twin
of it, though he never lived, poor man, to make it
good. That nose might have been carved out of a
piece of hallyblaster, it might, sir, it's so, as you
might say, conspictious.'

It seemed to Mr. Such as if at this the very floor
of his inside had fallen in. The rich colour on his
round face faded to a dim purple as he led Matilda,
lost to all knowledge of the world, in a tempest of
sobs from the room.

Now if only Sam's mother had had a tinge more
courage ; if only Sam's father had not been so easily
led by his own far from wax-like nose, they might
have been wiser parents ; they might have treated
Sam's trouble with a little more simple common-
sense.

But no. Poor little Sam, from his very earliest
days, grew up in the belief that there was something
amiss with him ; that he had been somehow set
apart by ill-fortune from all other small creatures
of his age. Far beyond the time during which most
babies survey the world in perfect freedom, he wore
a thick fleecy veil over his young face. Visitors were

never allowed to look close at him and never even to see him in full daylight. Not even his aunts who of their generous natures continued to shower presents upon him at every opportunity—on his birthday, at Christmas and Michaelmas, on St. Valentine's, St. Swithin's, St. George's, St. Patrick's and Oak Apple days, and on any other day in between for which they could find the least excuse.

By hook or by crook it was always towards evening when he was brought down to be inspected even by the doctor. And when the doctor asked for lamp or gaslight there were no matches to be found. Nor could his mother resist from just *seeing* if her great-aunt Keren-Happuch's miserable visit had been anything more than a dream. Hardly an hour went by but betwixt finger and thumb she very very gently and cautiously stroked, pressed and pinched the tiny nose just in the hope of discovering for good and all whether it was not as other noses are. And on every occasion she became more and more convinced that there was no hope at all, that it was the same in substance and consistency as it had been the day before and the day before that and the day before that ; that, in fact, it was of wax.

The consequence was that even at the age of six this particular feature in Sam's rather long and sallow face was the very first object you noticed when you glanced at him. And why not ?—a stranger might enquire. The Duke of Marlborough had a famous nose ; so had most of the Roman Emperors ; so had Queen Elizabeth ; so had Cyrano de Bergerac ; so had Mr. Gladstone (between his blue eyes) ; so had poor Long-Nose in the fairy-tale. But then all these noses were real, all were human ; all were their owner's own. . . . Poor little Sam !

Not that Sam's actually resembled Master Long-Nose's. It was in no sense a funny nose, a laughable nose. It stood out bravely from his face like the bows of a brig. It was not excessively long, or unpleasingly wide or broad, nor had it a bump in the middle, or a hump at the tip. It did not turn up, or down, or sideways, or wag at all. Even though it was a trifle over-prominent, it was a *fine* nose, for his mother had caressed it every day with the gentlest of maternal fingers. Such a nose indeed might have been the pride of any human being, boy or man. Whatsoever it was made of, it might in Sam's later years have become the world's admiration, if only his parents had let well alone.

But, alackaday, when Sam was seven, they came to the decision that the dreadful news could be kept from him no longer. They let his actual birthday go happily by. ' It's the last he will have, Samuel, with a nose that seems his own,' Mrs. Such had pleaded. And then, one September evening—the leaves of the tree outside Mr. Such's shop were beginning to fall, and the lamp of the lamp-post had been lit—after Sam's prayers had been said, and Sam was in his flannel nightshirt, the secret was disclosed. He was told that though his heart was of gold, and all the rest of him of the blessedest description, that though mamma and papa loved him twice as dearly for it—his poor nose was of *wax*. He mustn't grieve. He mustn't brood over his nose. He must try and forget he even had one ; and yet must take every possible care of it and of his miserable secret, and keep both closely and continually guarded from the thousand and one risks that might await them in the cold careless world of men.

Little Sam cried himself to sleep that night, not so much because he fully realised what this news meant as because his tender heart was torn by seeing his mother so much grieved about him. He hid his nose in his wet pillow, and dreamed he was a fish. He woke, cried himself to sleep again, and dreamed he was a pelican. The very next morning, as soon as he came downstairs, he changed his place at the breakfast-table to a chair behind the aspidistra so as to be even further than usual from the heat of the fire, and he waited not only until his bread and milk had a skin on it but was cold. And the moment the meal was over he begged from the maid-servant a stub of candle—having first of all asked her if there was anything in the house made of wax—and this being a very warm and sunny day for the time of year, he was able to experiment with it at once, and all by himself.

Having fixed the stub to the prongs of a toasting-fork, he held it for some minutes an inch or two from the hot window glass, and was horrified to discover how rapidly it responded to the beams of the autumnal sun—even in England. In a minute or two, indeed, it was as plastic as a piece of putty. With ashen cheek averted he at once climbed up on to a stool, pulled the blind of his nursery window two-thirds of the way down, and retired, poor lamb, in this gloaming, into its remotest corner to read his book. From that day on he wore, autumn and winter and till June was out, two layers of underclothes, for nothing would persuade him even to look at a fire ; and on highly sunny days he lived behind his mother's drawn red damask window-curtains, and on Dog Days read his book in the cellar.

Now, if, perhaps, his father had been less occupied in his trade and could have had entirely his own way with his small son, Sam would have led a less solitary life. But being an only child his mother treasured him beyond words. And above all things she was anxious, of course, that not only his nose but also his feelings should be protected from all possible hurt. She would have burned at the stake rather than reveal this minute portion of a family skeleton-in-the-cupboard to a living soul. Sam was therefore kept as close at home as a bullfinch in its cage.

Again and again his anxious aunts—with housed-in little Sam pulling at their heart-strings—came all four of them to afternoon tea and did their utmost to persuade Mrs. Such to let little Sam be and do as do and are other small boys of his age. They reasoned and argued with her, they said this and they said that until Dorinda, the youngest, almost lost her temper. And Mrs. Such, poor soul, had no more words in her mouth than a fish.

' He's so timid,' said one. ' He's in the cellar now,' said another. ' He daren't even follow his own nose,' said a third. And as for devil-may-care Dorinda, she broke out in grim earnest. ' He's so pale and quiet, Matilda, the darling mite, he might as well be a wax dummy in Samuel's shop,' she said. ' You don't seem to see that he is growing *up*,' she said. ' And like a potato in a cellar ! ' she said. ' I see little boys wherever I go, sailing their painted boats, playing at bat-and-ball, leap-frogging, tip-in-the-ringing, hop-scotching. They go out with *their* aunts and have a " tuck-in " and a " blow-out " in a pastry-cook's—ices and jam-puffs and cream-tarts and bull's-eyes. They eat green apples and stickjaw. They bowl their hoops. They "swap," what they call, the dears, their alley-tors and their conkers. They scuffle and quarrel over their whip-tops and knuckle bones. What does a black eye matter now and then, or—or a patch on their breeches ? Surely, Matilda, you cannot want our poor little Sam to become like a bearded hermit in his cavern, or a rabbit in its hutch. He will ! mark my words, he will ! Give us only one rational *reason* why you coop him up like this, never even allowing that poor wan face to look out of the window and wave its hand to us as he used to do when we came out of the door—only one, and we shall be satisfied.'

' Only one ! ' cried her three sisters as if at a signal. ' Only one ! ' they cried, sitting there like eager lions waiting to be fed.

And Mrs. Such, driving back the tears that were pricking her eyelids, not only made the most absurd replies to all such arguments, but could not bring herself to confess in the smallest degree what was amiss with her Sam. ' Sammie is naturally a quiet boy,' she would say. ' He was not made for horrid rough games. He would hate to bite and scuffle and go patched. He loves his books. Why, you know perfectly well, Dorinda, he learnt to read in half the time you took to learn your alphabet. Please leave me alone to bring up my own son in my own way. You'll drive me clean distracted, you will.'

At this, Dorinda's heart would instantly melt in her kind angular body. She would toss her head— and, with *her* fine nose, she was remarkably like a pale brown horse—and take Matilda to her bosom while the others gathered round their small married sister and dabbed at her eyes with their pocket-handkerchiefs, and brought out their lavender water and vinaigrettes.

When indeed, if only in gratitude for all his aunts' generosity and kindness, Sam's mother gave way so far as to send him at the age of eight to a Dame School, it was with the saddest possible results. In a neat pepper-and-salt suit, a black-speckled straw-hat on his head, button-boots on his feet, a green satchel strapped tight to his back, he set out hand in hand with his mother.

He arrived at the school at half-past eight. By a quarter-to-nine half the pupils had pulled his hair, and by 8.55 the whole school was dancing around him like a tribe of Chocktaws or Cherokees to the tune of ' Nosey Such.' All the way home that morning he was followed by horrid little urchins— many of them not even his own schoolfellows— chanting in catlike chorus :

> Peacock, peacock, there he goes !
> Mammie's Sam from So-and-Soes ;
> Nosey, Nosey, Nosey, Nose !

He stumbled across the threshold, trembling and shaking, scuttled in through the shop instead of knocking at the private door, and scurried up to his old nursery at the very top of the house. There his mother found him, sitting in a chair before the empty grate, his chin on his hands and his eyes tight shut.

' Why, Sam! Sam, dear, Sam darling, mother's own own! ' she cried, ' what is the matter? Why are you shutting your eyes, Sammie? '

' Oh mother, if only I could never never see myself again! ' he replied, one solitary tear coursing down his face in the shadow of the very organ that had caused him such heartbreak.

Mrs. Such, with bursting heart, at once hurried downstairs and sent off there and then, a letter to Sam's school-mistress, mentioning by name all the little boys who had treated her son so ill.

Mow Miss Moss had only with the utmost reluctance agreed to accept Sam as a pupil at all. For Mrs. Such, almost at her wits' end to preserve her secret and Sam's nose, had made such absurd conditions. He was never to attend school on days when the sun was shining. He was to be kept at home during the months of May, June, July, August and September. In Winter he was never to sit within six paces of the fire. And whenever the temperature of the schoolroom rose above 62° he was to sit in the passage. All this was so fussy that even before his mother's letter came, Miss Moss was doubtful if Sam was worth his fees. The letter decided the matter.

' Dear Mrs. Such,' was her reply, ' I regret to hear of the behaviour of one or two of my pupils this morning. There runs an old *proverb*, however: " There is no smoke without a *fire*." There are, too, black sheep in *every* school, *however* well conducted it may be, as there are also in *some* families. I gather—though no doubt your son never *intended* it—that Samuel *himself* was not without blame in the matter. *Every* new pupil has to endure a little teasing ; every *popular* pupil soon wins an endearing nickname. Little Hubert Macnaughten, for example, the son of our late *Mayor*, is called " Carrots." Harold Simpkins, whose uncle is a *lawyer*, is known as " Simmy," and little Solomon Abrams, whose father, I believe, is a neighbour of your *own*, has for patronymic the peculiar name of " Rags and Bones." Why, then, little Samuel should have attempted to kick and scratch and even to bite some of his class-mates simply because they asked him questions about his *nose* (a feature for which *he* at least is in no way responsible), I fail to understand.

' He is excessively *backward*, though not, I think, a hopelessly stupid boy, and he is handicapped by having been kept so much at home. He has the pallid *waxen* appearance of a child who hasn't enough fresh air, and I am a great believer in *air*. Samuel *cannot* be well to be such a weeper. It is the *air*less boy who is the tell-tale-tit.

' I feel in the circumstances that a boarding-school would be a more fitting outlet for his temperament, and as he has spent only a single morning with us I am charging only one half-term's fees.

' Believe me, Yours faithfully,

' HANNAH MOSS.'

Mr. Such—his face a vivid purple—answered this letter himself. He stayed up till long after midnight doing so. But Miss Moss was experienced in the ways of parents, cashed Mr. Such's cheque, and took no further notice.

Sam's three brief hours at school, then, served only to make his existence more secluded than ever. Nevertheless he gained in some respects what the other pupils of Miss Moss's day-school may have missed. Every evening, as soon as the heats of the day were over, he would accompany his mother, arm in arm, on a long gentle walk, during which they talked happily together about everything under the sun—the sun of which our Sam was to see so little in this world. But there never were two more loving companions—walking together there. They might have been sweethearts.

As for reading, the profits of Mr. Such's haber-dashery business could hardly keep pace with Sam's hunger for books. Before he was eleven he had read and all but digested the whole of the works of Thomas Babington Macaulay, Sir Walter Scott, Dr. Johnson, Joseph Addison, William Paley, and most of William Shakespeare. He had long known *Little by Little* and *Brewer's Guide to Knowledge* almost by heart. He considered what he had seen of such writers as Ainsworth and Henty and Kingston and Ballantyne and Cooper hardly worth serious notice. By thirteen he had taught him-self enough Latin to read *Caesar* in the original and had mastered a few words of Hebrew, and he was so clever at sums that he helped his mother with her accounts, and his father with his ledgers, and could tell how many yards of calico at 4¾d. you could get for £1 16s. 9d., while most of his customers were getting out a pencil and a piece of paper.

In reading too the plays of William Shakespeare
he had discovered all by himself that the words
sound very much better if they are said aloud. And,
better still, if one has an audience. For this reason
he delighted in creeping down to the shop after
closing hours. With the immense blue calico blinds
drawn down over the sheeted glass, he would un-
fasten the little door by which Mr. Hopper sidled in
when he dressed the windows, and standing with
his back to the street outside, would march up and
down as far as the space permitted, taking the parts
now of Hamlet, now of Othello and now even of
Sir John Falstaff or King Lear, while the staring wax
dummies in their doeskin, broadcloth, serge and
cashmere gazed unmovedly on.

Their smirking glossy faces, it is true, were at
best not very expressive, and at worst were as
vacant as a mangel-wurzel or a pumpkin. Nor had
they any hands, poor things, with which to applaud.
But what mattered such trifles to Sam ? If his
nose was of wax, he could at least to that extent
share his sympathy with creatures made wholly of
that substance. And never having tasted the
flatteries of the public, he never so much as noticed
the profound hush that greeted even his wildest
sallies.

What cared Sam indeed ? ' My kingdom for a
horse ! ' he would cry at the top of his voice, lifting
his long-nosed face into the dusky air, and stalking
up and down with humped-up shoulders and a scowl
far more cruelly ferocious than could ever have
distorted the royal countenance of Richard Crook-
back. He was at least as happy with his father's

secret dim-lit shop-front for stage and his dummies
for audience as ever Edmund Kean or David
Garrick had been on theirs, with all the world of
rank and fashion in the stalls and boxes.

And his father and mother, having crept on tiptoe
into the inner recesses of the shop, or stooping behind
the counter, would, all unbeknown to himself, listen
enthralled to the marvellous speeches flowing from
his lips, and watch every strutting pace and animated
gesture ; convinced that their son was a genius of
the first water.

Not that Mr. and Mrs. Such, even if he had tried
to persuade them, would ever have consented to
Sam's becoming an actor. Even if they had
approved of miming and mummery, there was the
heated air, the paint, the footlights to consider.
One single torrid midnight hour of such an existence
might wreck all the loving care they had lavished
on him since his infancy.

Sam indeed never did become an actor. When
the saddest days of his life overtook him ; when,
having lost his dear father and mother he became an
orphan, he was thirty-five, and though his rather
lank hair was still as black as a raven's wing against
the intense pallor of his face, he looked to be a good
deal older.

He was tall but very narrow at the shoulders.
Like his father, he usually attired himself in a long
black frock-coat and (unlike his father) in quiet-
patterned trousers. With one sweeping lock of
ink-black hair descending on each side of his high
rounded forehead, he might have been taken for
a musician or a poet or a statesman or a barber.

Indeed in looks and deportment he in many respects resembled Mr. Cinquevalli, the juggler, and that famous fiddler, Signor Niccolo Paganini.

In figure he was singularly elegant and gentlemanly and, being accustomed to dark rooms (and he could read even moderate-sized print by starlight) his eyes had an unusual brilliance. His piercing glance darted to and fro when he talked even to himself, and his nose, now come to its fullest maturity, was a feature which (if any chance had been given of observing it) not even the most careless passer-by could fail to mark or to respect. It would at any rate have passed even in the most genteel *conversazione* or *soirée* without suspicion.

If only his Aunt Dorinda could have seen him now ! Not for a moment would she have regretted that her nephew had not been brought up in full daylight or in the common sheepish fashion. He seldom suffered from any ailment except a slight nervous cough, due to breathing through his mouth, and an occasional twinge of neuralgia between his eyes. He had the most modest of appetites, and perhaps for this reason consisted (though maybe with one trifling exception) of skin and bone. But these were skin and bone of the finest quality.

His father had all his life been a prudent and sagacious haberdasher, and so had saved a comfortable little competence from the profits of his business. Sam inherited every penny of it. He sold the shop, he sold the business. He allowed Mr. Hopper's widow two guineas a week, and paid her pigtailed daughter's fees for lessons on the pianoforte at the Royal Academy of Music. He bestowed on George

a round £100 down—and then made it guineas.
He retired to a small villa on the outskirts of the
town, furnished it by night, and settled down as a
private—a very private—citizen.

Books were still his hobby.   In a snug little attic
at the top of his villa he put up a quantity of shelves
(apart from more substantial book-cases), and on
these he displayed his library.   There were con-
siderably more than seven hundred books in the
neat catalogue he compiled, the authors in red ink,
the titles in black.   Most of his treasures were in the
brightest of cloth bindings, some were in calf, mottled
or plain, and a few even in vellum and morocco.
Books, indeed, were all but his only company, for
he had very few acquaintances and not one intimate
friend.

He was less sensitive now about his little secret.
But never having enjoyed any society but that of
his father and mother, their old servant, the two
shop-assistants, and his four aunts, he was unlikely
to miss it now.   He realised that his nose had cut
him off from many of the interests and pleasures
which other haberdashers' sons enjoy.   Unlike his
father, for example, he would never have a little
Sammie Wax-Nose of his own.   On the other hand,
this unfortunate organ had brought him delights
which many people miss altogether—solitude and
his own company (of which he never wearied), his
play-acting and his books.   He taught himself other
little amusements—to saw out a pretty air or two on
the fiddle, and to jig for indoor exercise to his own
whistling.   He kept a cat of the name of Tom, and
he delighted in modelling little pots and dishes and

even faces in clay which he dug up from a foot or two below the surface of his small back-yard.

One other hobby was Sam's. Above his chimney-piece was displayed a collection of casts and models of all the world's most famous noses. If the price was within his means he could not resist buying any head or bust or torso, whether in stone or wood or bronze or earthenware, the midmost feature of which was of an unusual size, shape or appearance. So, too, with engravings, etchings, mezzotints; for oil he could not afford. The dealers in such things sent him their catalogues. They knew his fancy, and kept him well supplied. And since, as is well known, the majority of the great men in history have been finished off with unusual noses, this end-side of his attic-library was a perfect hornet's-nest of these organs.

By far the larger number of them were high-arched, or long, or massive, or aquiline, or hooked, or noble, or haughty, or formidable, or indomitable noses. There were a few others—delicate, fastidious, feminine, witty, neat, eloquent, or jimp. Noses of ladies Sam had no interest in. Besides the rest, he possessed a plaster-cast or two—that of Mr. Sayers, the prize-fighter, for example, that of Socrates, the philosopher, and that of Mr. Thackeray, the author—whose noses had by some mischance been irreparably broken at some crisis in their careers. He prized these specimens by no means the least, realising what a tragedy such an event must have meant to their owners and their friends—a tragedy such as he himself had escaped solely by keeping well out of the Summer sun and at a stoical distance from the Winter fire.

Strangely enough, Sam had been unable to procure
a single specimen of a nose which, like his own, as
he supposed, consisted solely of some foreign
material—some material, that is, other than skin,
gristle and bone—such as wood or marble or cork
or china, or—above all—*wax*. Not that Sam now
suffered much from his own drawback, or even
thought about it. He would stalk up and down his
small library, reciting to a far more intelligent-
looking audience than in his young days his father's
shop-window had been able to display, his favourite
passages from Shakespeare, from the poets, even
from Seneca, even from Molière, whom, by reason
of some little freak of mind, it was his custom to
think of only by his actual name—Jean Baptiste
Poquelin.

Sam seldom now indulged in any fire at all, even
in the coldest weather, except in the kitchen. There
he cooked his frugal but tasty meals in a mask he
had made out of layers of paper, by steeping them
in water and moulding them with his fingers over
his face. He was as neat as an old maid. He could
have shaved in his frying-pan ; and his brass candle-
sticks were so brightly burnished he hardly needed
a candle. These candlesticks, indeed, were the
unfailing admiration of his friend, Mr. John Jones,
the Sweep—for Sam was no respecter of persons.

Mr. Jones was a man of the world. He went
about in the early hours in houses great and small—
boudoir and banqueting chamber, attic and pantry,
and maybe because of his black face was less noticeable than most men. Even if he had been by nature
as silent and taciturn as he was hoarse by trade ;

even if he had had no tales to tell about the rich and the gentry, and of the strange things he had found hidden away in his chimneys—mummies and bags of money and wigs and birds' bones and magpies' hoards, Sam would have delighted in his company. For Sam had an inexhaustible horror of fire. He would wake yelling Fire! He would dream he was a tallow candle—and alight; that he was *all* of wax—and shut in an oven!

Nothing pleased him better than to hear Mr. Jones's broom rattling its way up his empty chimney, and to hear its faint *plff* as it issued into the sky. Mr. Jones, that is, meant safety to Sam and to Sam's nose. He came often; did little; stayed long; and though Sam made a point of concealing his cooking-mask from observation, he would talk with Mr. Jones —if not exactly *nez-á-nez*—at least face to face, while he drank his glass of ale and duskily recounted what the World was now at. Mr. Jones never had the smallest suspicion or mistrust of Sam's nose. He thought him a quiet, liberal gentleman, and would have cleaned his chimneys three times a day if Sam's anxieties against fire had carried him to lengths so extreme.

Sam, indeed, was the gayest and cheerfullest of beings when safe within his own walls; sprightly and nimble, in spite of his long black coat and rather melancholy visage; and especially when with his cat, Tom, for company, he would sit for a full hour or more over his supper talking now to this un-answering yet not irresponsive animal, now to himself.

No less contented was he when, of mornings, out

of sight of prying eyes, his rooms swept, his bed made, his books and noses dusted, he could dream at ease over his Keats or Shelley, his Smiles or his Felicia Hemans; sit scraping at his fiddle; or— attired in a handsome Paisley-patterned dressing-gown presented to him on his twenty-first birthday by his wine-merchant godfather, Mr. Tobias Slant —once more forget himself and his queer fate by feigning in fancy to be the sorrowful Lear, the doubtful Hamlet, dreadful Prospero in his enchanted island, or young Orlando under the green beeches in the forest of Arden.

When the heat and curiosity of the daytime kept him indoors, he would stand for an hour at a time, stock still, his face edged forward—peering out between the curtains from so far within the room that not a bee at the window could have seen him. Thence he would stare into the street. And though he knew so few human creatures to talk to, a wonderful affection grew up in Sam for all kinds of people, young, old, prosperous, poor, odd, ugly, lovely and sad, who had never so much as dreamed of his existence; though he himself had watched their comings and goings, and their to's and fro's, with the closest heed and with unwearying interest again and again. He had discovered, too, a little flaw in one of the panes of his window which magnified all that he saw through it. And he dearly liked to kneel down when a stranger was passing so that he could thus see that stranger's nose—immensely elongated or broadened out. It amused and comforted him.

There wasn't a four-footed beast either, frequenting his parts of the town that Sam in this

window-gazing had not come to know by sight, if
not by name.   Indeed, he gave them names of his
own—' Ah, here comes Rover ! ' or ' Softly now,
Slyboots ! ' or ' Now's your chance, Scuttletail ! '—
and would smile and even laugh out at their ways
and customs and antics.   He would dearly like to
have kept a cockatoo or even a canary : but then,
there was Tom to consider ; and besides, he *might*
in his affection one day approach his face too close
to the bars, and beaks peck !   When the shades of
dusk were fallen, unless the night were dangerously
sultry and torrid, Sam would venture out on his
daily walk, muffled up to the eyes in Winter in a
sombre comforter, and in late Spring and Autumn
in one that had belonged to his grandmother Such,
made of Spitalfields silk.   With hands thrust deep
into the pockets of his skimpy overcoat, in his patent-
leather shoes, he would stalk in rapture through the
lamplit streets, drinking in the romance of night,
muttering over long fragments of the books he
loved best, pausing to hearken after squawking owl
or squeaking bat, at ease with himself, his retiring and
unknown neighbours, the world, and the universe.

What mattered it to Sam no human ear could
share these transports ?   He had for company the
peering moon, the midnight stars, the wandering
planets ; and now and then for music the flutes and
fiddles of a distant festivity, or maybe a May-time
nightingale or a churring nightjar.   But however
late the hour his last duty was never scamped.
With a partridge feather broom he carefully dusted
every bust and nose that was his before retiring in
peace and blessing to his truckle bed.

How strange, Sam would think to himself at such moments, are the caprices of fortune! Even in the history of our own small island there are heroes and poets by the score and statesmen by the hundred. And yet how few of their famous or notorious noses are to be seen in our picture-shops. Where is King Alfred's? Where the Lion-hearted's? Where valiant Drake's, unhappy Chatterton's, wild Turpin's? Where else but in our *Wax*-works! It was a jest after Sam's heart. He roared with laughter whenever it recurred to him.

As for the Noses of the Illustrious still living— Sam tried to be generous in his reflections on them, but often failed to be quite fair. Great noses, he found, were rarer even than great men. It may be argued that Nature has now no need to grow noses so noble as were those of old. Sam could hardly believe it.

He had once in his young days visited with his father the Monkey-House in the Zoological Gardens in Regent's Park. But one glance at its inmates had convinced him how far superior in shape and appearance is the human nose by comparison with that even of the larger apes—whom certain credulous persons suppose to have been our own ancestors. Even in those young days Sam had smiled at such a suggestion.

'I'm glad, Dad,' he had whispered, squeezing his father's hand, 'I'm glad, Dad, I haven't a tail. Not all by myself, I mean.' And Mr. Such, noticing the sadness behind his smile, had at once taken him off to the Buns and the Bears.

Monkey or no monkey, ape or no ape, the street

noses of his own times, Sam thought, as seen at any rate from his window, were nothing very much to talk about, though many of them were uncommonly likeable. And to judge merely from their features, he could hardly suppose that *all* the famous living men whose photographs he saw in the newspapers were quite as remarkable as their admirers seemed to think. Try as he might to increase his store, Sam in fact had very few noses on his chimney-piece which had come into the world after Mr. Gladstone's had left it. But then, Sam was fastidious.

Sam seldom ventured into the country on his nocturnal excursions : ' By came a blackbird and snipped off her nose ' had been one of the favourite dandling rhymes of an early nurse of his. And though—fortunately for Sam—this bird is seldom abroad after nightfall, it was wiser not to stray into the wild. On the other hand, he knew every by-way, every green court and garden wall of his native town by heart. In one direction, however, he never strayed. There was a street named Lovers' Walk which he avoided as he would have avoided a glass-blower's furnace. For *there* lived his great-aunt Keren-Happuch.

Not that he much thought of the cantankerous old woman now, or nursed any bitter grudge against her. After all, she had merely told his mother a secret which it might have hurt her a great deal more to discover for herself—or, worse still, to have had from the lips of a stranger. Still, the memory of that evening in his seventh year when with tears running down her cheeks his mother had broken the dreadful News, had never quite lost its sting.

Nor could he recall without a pang that next unhappy morning when, after having experimented in the hot sunlight with Susan's stub of tallow-candle, he had once and for all drawn down his nursery blinds and retired into his corner, with only his poor nose for company. No, it would be merely rubbing salt into an old wound to venture anywhere in the neighbourhood of his great-aunt Keren-Happuch.

Thus Sam's quiet uneventful life slipped away; so it might have continued to the end but for an unforeseen mischance. One Thursday evening—a 20th of October— he found himself treading a by-street into which he seldom turned, simply because it contained not a single bust-and-picture shop or bookseller's. St. Luke's brief summer was over; the wind blew bleak over the cobbles, and the muffler under his old tall silk hat had pushed itself somewhat higher than usual over the bridge of Sam's nose. He had paused a moment before the dingy window-panes of a marine store to gaze in upon a chipped cheap china bust of the poet Dante, and had smiled to himself in his pleasant fashion at sight of it. ' Ah, Master,' he whispered, ' the little less and how much away,' for the chip was where the face could least afford it—at the extreme tip of that astonishing nose.

A sigh followed close after the smile, such a sigh as Jaques sighed in pity of the wounded stag by the wooded brook. Sam turned abruptly away from the fusty window, and then caught a glimpse over his muffler of a slim taut figure hastening along in the gloaming on the other side of the street—a figure birdlike, erect, with a patch over its left

eye and the sleeve of the right arm pinned to its
breast.

Now there is a nose in history which no English-
man will ever forget : that of the Admiral of
Trafalgar. A flame seemed to leap up in Sam's
bosom. Was this figure real or a ghost ? Were his
eyes deceiving him ? Or was there indeed now
stalking the streets of his native town in front of
him one to whom his country could surely resort
if ever danger once more threatened her shores ?
Sam burned with curiosity. There could be no
hesitation : he must follow this stranger and make
sure.

Had the evening been warmer and his muffler in
its usual position, he might have heard or seen his
danger. But alas, heedless of all else, Sam at once
stepped off the pavement into the street and started
off in pursuit. At this precise moment an empty
carrier's van came careering at a foot-gallop out of
the neighbouring alley—its horses elated by the
lightness of their load and the prospect of their
stables. There was a shout, a shuddering crash, a
shower of dizzying sparks in Sam's eyes, and he
knew no more. . . .

When he came to, he found himself stretched out
upon his mother's horsehair sofa in his own neat
sitting-room. He was muffled, chin to toes, in
blankets and walled in with hot-water bottles ;
while his clammy countenance lay not more than two
paces distant from an immense blazing fire ! Sam
had not been at close quarters with such a fire since
his very earliest infancy. The sheer splendour of it
fairly took his breath away. He lay transfixed,

gazing into its flaming terraces and caves and
grottoes in the wildest astonishment and horror.

' Oh me ! oh me ! ' a voice sounded within him, as
his dazzled eyeballs rolled up and away from this
ill-boding sight and at once found themselves fixed on
the face of a complete stranger. It was a face with
an abrupt nose, a short brown beard, and quiet
blue eyes which were gazing into his own with
intense attention. ' Oh me ! oh me ! A doctor ! '
groaned Sam to himself. And Sam was right. He
shut his eyes.

' And how are we feeling now ? ' enquired a quiet
gruff voice.

A pain racked Sam's leg. His head was throbbing.
But he gave little thought to either. His one
concern was with the fire and with the middle of
his own face. What was happening—what *had*
happened—there ? These were the two dreadful
questions in his mind. What but one particular
calamity could have fixed this stranger's eyes in
so engrossed a stare ?

' Am I ill ? Am I dying ? ' he muttered in a
voice he scarcely recognised.

' Nothing as serious as that, my dear sir,' replied
the doctor. ' We just picked you up from under
the van, and, finding your address on Messrs.
Bumpus's envelope in one pocket and a latchkey
in the other, we brought you home.'

' Oh, doctor ! my N—, my N—, my N— ! Spare
my N— ! ' was Sam's unintelligible reply.

' Compose yourself, *please*,' replied the doctor,
for Sam seemed to be rambling. ' There is nothing
gravely wrong ; nothing—I assure you. Merely

a twisted ankle and slight concussion. Presently you may be sick. But at least you are no longer stone-cold.'

With this he gently pushed up the sleeve of Sam's black doeskin coat and took out his gold watch. Sam stared up into the eyes which no longer met his own. What had they seen? What was the mind behind them thinking about, apart from the feeble *tick-tock, tick-a-tock* which his shocked heart was beating out beneath his ribs?

Stone-cold indeed! Sam's body seemed to be on fire. Even if the grate had been empty, surely this internal heat alone must long since have converted that lofty peak in the middle of his face into a flat plateau. He was incapable of stirring, hand or foot. He lay mute and gasping, at the mercy of any tidings this stranger had to give.

' Hm ! ' the doctor snapped-to the lid of his watch, pushed down the sleeve of Sam's coat and smiled. ' It's pumping along a little faster, now. That's all to the good. What we need at present is complete rest and quiet. Just lie here, and enjoy the fire. Don't worry ; don't even think. Presently your thoughts will begin to wander off of themselves, then just follow your nose and you'll soon be safe in dreamland ! Meanwhile, *there* is the basin ; and not far off our excellent Mrs. Hobbs is busy in the kitchen. She will come at once if you call loud enough even to scare a mouse. I will look in again in the morning.'

He cast one more steady look round Sam's spotlessly neat parlour and yet another at the patient's remarkable countenance.

' I must apologise for having no ardent spirits in
the house, Doctor,' whispered Sam. ' But won't
you please refresh yourself with a cup of Epps's
cocoa ? The tin is on the dresser-shelf. It was, you
know, only my N—, N—, my . . . " but *still* the
fateful word refused to pass Sam's lips.

A far-away smile was in the doctor's glance. He
gently pressed his patient's hand, nodded Good-
night, and left the room. For five minutes—for
three hundred enormous seconds—Sam lay on the
sofa as inert as if he were an inanimate staring model
in the basement of Madame Tussaud's—as if he
were wax all over, *cap-à-pie*. He then slipped
into a profound childlike slumber.

It was full daylight when he opened his eyes
again. A stout homely body in a stiff print dress
was bustling about the room. The fire burned as
merrily as ever. And as if sleep had filled him with
some secret elixir, Sam called out instantly in a loud
bold voice : ' Good morning, ma'am. Would you,
please, kindly fetch me the hand-glass you will find
on the dressing-table in the room above this.'

' Of all the Peacocks !' thought Mrs. Hobbs to
herself, but she at once hastened away to do his
bidding.

Sam lay transfixed, listening first to her ascending,
and then to her descending, footsteps. His mind
was made up. He had as a child faced one supreme
disaster in his life ; he would now at least as manfully
face another. With trembling fingers he raised the
hand-glass to his face, prepared for any shock.

For any shock, that is, except that of finding his
familiar feature absolutely unchanged. But so it

was. The fire overnight had been fierce enough to roast an ox. His poor defenceless nose had lain there on the sofa in a direct line with its most furious glances maybe for an hour together. A slight flush on the bridge and tip suggested that it had been ever so slightly scorched. But otherwise it rose up in his face as lofty, as bony, as delicately arched, as formidable as ever. Wax indeed! hardly granite itself could have borne such an ordeal more triumphantly. Falsest of noses it had proved in sober truth—for it was real!

Sam—though a timid—was at heart a brave man; but good news may be as hard to bear as bad, and he had suffered a severe shaking. He covered his brow with his hands and tried in vain to think calmly. What wonder? He had at that moment survived the second severest shock of his whole life. It was as if the gates of his prison house had been flung wide open and he had walked out into Freedom.

Nosed like any other human being, he could now do *all* that can become a man. No more peeping from behind thick curtains, no more masked cooking, no more nocturnal skulking, no more overcoated shiverings on mornings of hard frost, no more fears, humiliations, precautions. All careers were now at his feet—ocean stoker, cannon-moulder, bell-founder, tea-planter, or even that of an equatorial buccaneer. Now, if he so wished—like Speke and Livingstone, Bates and Sven Hedin before him—he could explore the burning tropics; and summer in the wildest heats of the Sahara. He was free.

In a day or two Sam was on his feet again, and seemingly not one whit the worse for his accident.

What is more curious, he was at first conscious of little change in his mind or in himself. His relief, his gratitude had been inexpressible. And then, as time went on, and the novelty of having a nose which he might really call his own began to wane, his spirits flagged. At times he even pined for the ' good old days.' He no longer seemed to fit his customary solitude. His old hobbies, even his books, even his Shakespeare, were no longer quite the same as of old. With the knowledge that he possessed a merely natural nose, it seemed that the noisy interfering world outside had drawn a good deal nearer.

Talks with the doctor, a gossip now and then with homely Mrs. Hobbs, earnest and husky confabulations with Mr. Jones, had disturbed him far more than would have been possible if he had remained the old Sam of these long years past, or if even he had stayed the same old Sam but with his secret for ever obliterated and no nose at all to call his own. Even John Jones observed the change. ' That Mr. Such,' he told his wife, ' seems to have lost his interest even in sutt. He ain't the man he were.'

Sam indeed had begun to realise in what a backwater he had spent his days. How narrow were his pursuits ; how peculiar his habits. He became depressed in mind. He lost his appetite. He was less and less inclined to chatter to himself, and to indulge in a fandango across the floor of his library. Not even the brave spouting of ' To be or not to be,' or ' The quality of mercy is not strained,' not even ' A horse, a horse, my kingdom for a horse ! ' could now rouse him to his former gaiety and ardour.

o

For whatever his feelings towards his nose had been, it was as a nose of *wax* that he had all these years regarded it. As such he owed it his happy solitude, his hobbies, the serene tenour of his life— out of the glare and dust and heat of the bustling, giddy, world. Without his being aware of it, then, a deep affection had at last grown up in Sam for the very nose that might have been his ruin. He had been, indeed, his nose's only friend. He had forgiven it everything. There was an understanding between them. They had been through storm and stress together, and in the last few years had found a calm, if outlandish, haven. Poor Sam, for days together he desisted even from shaving. How face a nose that told him only of wasted grief and shame, of lost opportunities.

From his earliest days, too, Sam had believed that his nose was the only sham—the only piece of make-believe—in a world where everything else was real. Two homesick horses and a van had at a blow cruelly robbed him of this belief. And now, his trust and confidence in the one thing false having gone, doubts were beginning to arise in his mind regarding everything real.

For some little time after his accident he simply could not get this absurd notion out of his mind. Though still by choice a nightbird, he now occasionally ventured on his walks abroad in the daylight, or rather in the latish afternoon. At such times he frequently found his eyes dwelling rather fixedly on other men's faces. His own unassailable nasal organ rising like Ararat between his piercing eyes, he would discover himself in an omnibus or a

railway carriage, his gaze rudely set—all but gloating
on—some fellow-passenger's nose.   It was astonishing to find how seldom any such nose was *unquestion-
able*.   Surely *that* old gentleman's over there in the
corner *must* be fictitious ! Could Nature *really*
have been responsible for *this* unshapely lump and
that mere snub, and *that* and *that* ! !

Now Sam in his private life had never been
accustomed to be rude and ill-mannered.   When he
talked to himself he talked as gentleman with
gentleman.   To realise then that he could be guilty
of such conduct filled him with shame.   And when
detected in it, he would rapidly fix his eyes on some
other object near by, or thrust his hand into the
pocket of his frock coat as if his stare had been
absent-minded and he had suddenly discovered that
his pocket-book had been stolen.   Or he would cast
upon his fellow-traveller the most ample and amiable
of smiles and remark upon the weather.   In spite
of these precautions he more than once narrowly
escaped a lasting injury to his own nose simply
because of his intense interest in the noses of others.

All this had two unhappy results.   First, Sam
began to look with suspicion on every nose he saw ;
and then on their owners.   Even the pleasing noses
of the most charming of young ladies—when he
found courage to glance at them—caused him the
gravest misgivings.   Why, he wondered, should so
many of them attempt to conceal by means of a
powder-puff a *real* nose, however minute, however
pink, however glossy ? The bloom, thought Sam,
upon a nectarine, a cherry or a plum is proof
positive in a fruiterer's shop that his fruit is fresh

and genuine. But powder? Sam wondered. But as time went on, these misgivings, these doubts vanished in their turn. Sam began to pity the noses to which he had been unkind. He began to learn that a good seaworthy honest ship, so to speak, has not necessarily been given an elegant figure-head. He grew sorry for folk with noses not a patch on his own in shape or seemliness, and realised that to be really real in the world may be not only the hardest thing a man can attempt, but also the least flattering.

By this time he had begun to acquire the reputation of being a little peculiar in his head, simply because of this habit of staring at noses, and then of looking aside with an almost audible click of his eyelids! Now that there was in sober fact nothing really odd about him at all, the whole of him had begun to appear a little fantastic.

In part, too, from what was now a natural pride, in part because of his great muffler, Sam had a little way of dipping his own nose up and down while he walked—like a hen in the act of drinking. Or he would stand, like little Johnny-head-in-air, lost maybe in reflections on the works of Shakespeare, when he should have been leaving the pavement free for other pedestrians. One may do such things at dead of night and pass unobserved; but in broad day! Small boys in particular are sharp observers; and (however absurd their own half-shaped features may be) they make no allowances for the grown-up. So it came about that small boys were at last responsible for yet another crisis in Sam's life.

He had ventured out a good deal earlier than usual one cold sunny afternoon in December—two months

after that momentous 20th of October. For, though
direct daylight still tried his eyes, he felt it would
hardly be fair to his nose nowadays not to accustom
it to sunshine. For the same reason he now cooked
not over a gas-stove but over a kitchener, and had
laid in for roaring winter fires no less than three tons
of best screened domestic coal from Cannock Chase,
and a solid yard of ships' logs.

As, this particular morning, he made his way
towards an outlying bookshop, a large wicker cage
at an upper window took his eye. Squatting upon
a perch in it, and surveying the street below, was a
jackdaw—a bird as black and sleek of plumage as
he was himself in garb. Sam had never before
seen a bird with such a bill. He came to a standstill
on the kerbstone, his eyes fastened on this interesting
spectacle, and remained for so long in this oddish
attitude for a gentleman in the street, that he
attracted the attention of a fishmonger's errand-boy.

This lad in turn attracted the attention of a friend
in the butchering line, and after a moment or two
—gently at first under their breaths, but presently
ever more and more openly they began to chaunt
together :

> Here and there and everywhere,
> Nosey, Nosey, stand and stare !
> Somewhere, nowhere, everywhere,
> Nosey, Nosey, stand and stare !
> Night and morning, foul or fair,
> Tail in the dust, and head in the air,
> Stare ! Stare ! Stare ! Stare !

In a flash Sam had become eight again. In a
flash he was back once more in the pepper-and-salts,

the speckled straw hat and buttoned kid boots of his early childhood. For a while he was too much confused and overcome to move. Then he abruptly turned on his tormentors. When the Great Duke was out of favour with the fickle mob, they smashed his windows. When they repented and yelled with rapture to see him come riding home, he mutely shook his whip at the mended panes and rode on.

Sam had as fine a profile as the great Duke, but was less of a philosopher. After all, the very nose which was the object of this ridicule was also a sign of a spirited nature. Brandishing his malacca cane in the air he gave a whoop and at once started in pursuit. The urchins fled—and fled in a direction in which Sam himself had never before ventured. In half-an-hour or so he found himself at length at his last puff—his quarry out of sight—on the very outskirts of the street in which lived who but his old enemy, his great-aunt Keren-Happuch !

Sam was now a little beyond the town. It was quiet and green here, and, though the trees were leafless and the dahlias and Michaelmas daisies were long since over, a touch of frost in the air gave a lively sparkle to the cottage gardens, and the sun shone out like a red lantern in the rose of the west. If the errand-boys had at this moment reappeared they would have had even better cause than before to mock at their victim. For full five minutes at least Sam gazed up at the two simple words which had been painted on a board nailed to the nearest wall—*Lovers' Walk*.

A handsome prickly holly-tree grew at the street corner—crammed with berries. A robin, as if in imitation of a Christmas card, was whistling from its uppermost spray, and a hundred thoughts had meanwhile flitted through Sam's odd mind. But though many of them were wistful, and tinged with regret, none was vindictive. For somehow his long years of seclusion, far from souring his nature, had left his inward temper queer but sweet.

He thought again of his spinster Aunt Dorinda ; of her sisters, Sarah, Dora and Isabella ; of his father in his black coat and well-filled waistcoat, with that one long last lock of hair sleeked out over the bald expanse of his head. He thought of George and his chilblains, of cold-nosed Mr. Hopper at the shirt-counter, and of Mr. Hopper's widow in her frilling and her weeds. And last he thought of his mother.

Once, long ago, he had vowed he would revenge himself on the old woman who had so grieved that gentlest and most harmless of souls and led his own life so far astray. Just that one malignant couplet muttered into his mother's ear—' Though it grows where it grows, The brat *has a wax nose* ' had certainly been the cause of extreme unhappiness. It had cost her son endless shame and vexation.

And yet—well, time at last heals every wound which is not kept open by attention or hatred. And supposing—Sam thought—supposing if by accident he had never discovered the truth—what then ?

Most of all his other relatives were gone—Isabella had married a saddler and was now in New Zealand with a family of five little New Zealanders. Sarah had become a bonnet-maker in Birmingham. Dora was companion to the relict of a wealthy bead-manufacturer, and gay, high-spirited, sharp-tongued Dorinda was dead. How dismal a thing it would be if his great-aunt Keren-Happuch should die too, still believing that her lie had never been found out; still believing that she was responsible for her nephew's long retirement from the world, his shyness, his seclusion, his solitude!

Sam's slow, deep-cut, peculiar smile stole once more over his features. He might, if he wished, look in and give the malignant old woman a piece of his mind. He might call a policeman and confront her with the Law! But, bless me, he could do better than that. And he knew *how*.

With a hasty tap on the top of his silk-hat and a whisk of his cane, he at once turned homewards. If indeed he had at that moment met the fishmonger's boy there is no doubt he would have given him—not a hiding, but—a shilling. For the one thing in his strange noddle just now was to do anybody, everybody, a good turn, even including his wicked old aunt.

Now for some time past Sam had realised that his collection of famous nose-casts had somehow lost its old savour. Those old gentle reveries—feather-broom in hand—over the kindnesses which Providence had shown to other men's physiognomies but had withheld from his own had for Sam lost their impulse. He hadn't added a single new specimen—wood, brass, marble or alabaster—to his shelves since the 14th of October. His treasures had ceased to charm him. But they must now be worth a handsome sum.

This sum proved to be not quite so handsome as
Sam surmised. Still, when he had called in the
Dealer in Antiques from whom he had purchased
his finest examples of noble noses, and though he
learned from him that nasal appendages of every
kind, and even his own, were now out of fashion, the
cheque the dealer gave in exchange for what he
selected was at least a third as much as Sam had
expended on them. 'Why, sir,' the hook-beaked
creature lisped as he stuffed them into the old
Gladstone bag he had brought with him, ' fashion
or no fashion, a nose is still a nose ; and yet by any
other name, as the poet says, 'twould smell as sweet.'

Early the very next morning Sam visited his
bank and converted the dealer's cheque into gold.
Two large canvas bags were barely capacious enough
to contain it, and when Sam lifted them down from
the zinc counter they were almost as much as he
could carry.

When, then, that same afternoon he turned once
more towards *Lovers' Walk*, bound for his great-
aunt's cottage, he had been compelled to leave his
malacca cane behind. This deed of mercy was one
that needed both hands. Fortunately, it was a
Saturday, a day when errand-boys have little leisure
for mocking at gentlemen with peculiar habits.
Sam hastened along, stooping every now and then
to rest his bags on the pavement awhile, while he
sat and recovered his breath on any garden railing
that afforded him a seat. The perspiration even on
this frosty afternoon soon came trickling from
under the brim of his high hat, and coursed its way
down the deep furrows beneath his eyes. But an

errand such as Sam's is somehow pleasant going, even though one has blisters on one's heels or a hair-shirt on one's back. Besides, he intended to heap coals of fire on his old relative's head—and they would be far hotter than any winter sun.

About a quarter-to-four Sam arrived within twenty paces or so of his aunt's cottage. Once more he took a ' breather,' and looked about him. At first sight the cottage had a neglected look. The garden was a forest of frozen weeds ; a twisted old grey-barked apple-tree whose mossy branches showed above the palings was bushed with mistletoe. Only the thinnest plume of smoke was ascending from one of the broken chimney-pots. So much the better, thought Sam ; he would be the more welcome. Once more he heaved up his money-bags, and as he neared the rustic gate cast a glance at the upper windows. A shiver ran down his spine. He went cold all over. Every single blind in the house was down !

It is yet another proof of Sam's habitual absent-mindedness that never for a moment had he antici-pated his great-aunt Keren-Happuch might be no longer in this world. The marvel was indeed—had he only known it—that she had just managed only the very week before to attain her ninety-ninth birthday. Her hundredth was not for here.

Sam, as he searched the blank and blinded case-ments, groaned aloud ; both in sorrow at the doleful tidings they conveyed to him, and in sheer fatigue and disappointment. It is indeed the worst of luck to be cheated of doing any human creature a good turn. Besides, the bags were incredibly heavy by now. Sam was not a camel. He had come along rejoicing in his burden, but the thought of the long journey home was well-nigh insupportable. He would at least knock and enquire. He would venture a word or two with his aunt's successor. He would ask for a glass of water.

Pushing open the rickety gate he rapped softly on the door of the cottage. A little woman with an exceedingly small head and skimpy bare arms opened to him. She appeared to have been weeping. Indeed at the very mention of Sam's aunt's name she instantly flung her apron over her head and burst into tears. Sam was consumed with self-reproach.

'Hush, hush! my poor poor, good good woman,' he exclaimed, hastily seizing his money-bags and pushing his way into the dingy little sitting-room that lay beyond. 'You must not grieve for my dear aunt like this. She has gone to a better world. Pray dry your eyes. I am her nephew, you must understand, and I came but to wish her " Many happy returns of the day "—though I see I am a little late.'

Sam hoped to comfort the poor creature with these words ; they merely made her tears course down anew. But at last her fit of weeping began to subside, and with Sam seated before her on a horse-hair chair, the little woman sobbingly explained to him precisely what the position was. It was not exactly grief, he learned, that was the cause of her lamentations. It was not grief, but bitter disappointment.

She had been in his aunt's service, she told him, since she was a mere child of twelve, and during the thirty-two years that had since elapsed she had been paid in wages exactly £2 8s. 4¼d. in all. For this simple creature of so tender an age had scarcely set foot in the house when her crafty mistress had begun to persuade her that a fat bird in the bush is worth a complete flock in the hand. 'Wait, Sallie, till I die,' she would say; 'and that won't be long. Then you shall see what you *shall* see. What's wages, you silly chit—what's wages, compared with a snug little cottage like this, a garden full of gooseberry bushes, and a nest-egg in the Bank ? '

Bolt upright on his chair, his eyes fixed on either side his high-arched nose, Sam listened to this doleful story. Doleful indeed, for not only had his aunt gone to her last resting-place the day before, but her last Will and Testament had been read, and she had left her faithful servant not even a halfpenny. ' Not so much as an ole scrubbin'-brush or a snub of soap,' the poor creature exclaimed with a sob from the very depths of her being. ' Lor, sir, I ain't even had the strenth to hoise up the blinds ! '

Sam listened and listened and thought and thought. He then placed the tips of his long fingers together and stooping his sallow lean face over them he began to tell the one and only lie he had ever told in his life. But—as if to make up for it—it was a pretty long lie.

' Ah, but my dear madam,' he began, ' we must not always judge by *appearances*. I grant you, things in this world often *seem* to be what in truth they are not. I am not blaming you, heaven forbid ! You naturally thought that my poor dear deceased relative was nothing but a skinflint, if not

a miser and a cheat. Nothing of the sort. Nothing
of the sort. She was the gentlest, kindest, fairest,
justest, generousest, magnanimousest great-aunt
man ever had! She was a blessing—a *thousand*
blessings—in disguise.

'What's more, I have known of your patience and
industry and self-sacrifice ever since I was a little
lad but so high : but scarce in breeches. "When
and that I was but a little tiny boy," you know, and
so on. And you must understand that my poor
dear aunt—little though my looks may suggest such
a thing—believed me to be a *business*-man, and
prudent. Every Lady Day, Midsummer Day,
Michaelmas Day, Christmas Day for the last thirty-
two years—punctual as the rent collector himself—
she has made over to me no less a sum than £3
sterling, and on Boxing Day she habitually added
what she called a little *makeweight* as well. "Keep
it safe for me, my dear Samuel," she would entreat
me, " keep it as safe as you would the apple of your
eye. It is intended at last for the most amiable
creature in the world. Her name is Sallie—Sarah,
you know. She has been with me since she was a
pretty blushing slip of twelve. Not if I were the
old lady of Threadneedle Street herself could I ever
hope to leave behind me anything resembling a true
token of my livelong affection and gratitude. Still,
when I am myself no more, she will know I have
never forgotten her." These, I assure you, were
my aunt's very words. Only last week, my dear
madam (and pray continue to dry your eyes)—only
last Thursday she sent me a postcard bidding me
visit the Bank and bring these trifles along. Death,

Sallie, is no respecter of times or persons. It grieves me to the heart that my aunt herself was unable to present you with this small tribute of her thanks. Still, I am her only nephew and here it is.'

With that he stooped low, hoisted his two bulging bags from the floor and placed them on the table.

' Oh sir, oh *sir*,' Sallie cried at sight of them. ' And them all for the likes of me ! ' and could say no more.

Extreme happiness is almost as difficult a thing to face as the bitterest of disappointments. Sam rose to his feet and hastily withdrew. A mist blurred his eyes ; he could but follow his nose.

The darkness of a December evening was now down upon the streets. The lamplighter had long since gone his way. Even the robin had hopped into cover for the night. Sam felt a little faint after so many revulsions of feeling. That long ' story '— so blameless in intention that it hardly deserved to be called even a *white* lie, had tired him out. The consequence was that five minutes after leaving behind him *Lovers' Walk*—a sight of wonder with its hoarfrost in the starshine—Sam ventured to make yet another precedent in his strange see-saw life, for he sidled into ' The Three Jolly Wagoners '— a cosy little ale-house that stood on the outskirts of the town, and called for a stone bottle of ginger-beer.

And as he sipped it, ruminating on his afternoon's work, his eye chanced to wander to the mirror that backed the row of gaudy holly-decked bottles behind the bar ; and there he saw a human being in a high hat, with two wisps of silvering black hair descending on either side his cheeks, a full black cravat, two piercing black eyes, and a nose of a shape and magnitude that might have been the pride and glory of Charlemagne himself.

It was a figure you might first have mistaken for the great Cinquevalli and next for Nicolo Paganini. In fact, he saw our Sam. And yet once more he smiled—a long, genial, indefatigable smile—and lifting his frothing glass to his lips he solemnly and silently drank both Noses' health.

THE THREE SLEEPING BOYS OF WARWICKSHIRE

 IN a low-ceiled white-washed room on the uppermost floor of a red brick building in Pleasant Street, Cheriton, standing there in their glazed cases, is a collection of shells, conchs, seaweeds, dried salty sea-flowers, fossils, staring birds, goggling fish with glass eyes, dried mermaids, coffers, too, and anchors, and old guns, and lumps of amber and coral and quartz. And there for years and years— the narrow windows with their carved brick fruits and flowers and old leaden gutters, showering the day's light upon their still retreat—there for years and years slumbered on in their glass case the Three Sleeping Boys of Warwickshire. The tale of them goes a long way back. But so, too, do all tales, sad or merry, if you follow them up.

About the year 1600, when Queen Elizabeth was sixty-seven, and William Shakespeare was writing his play called ' Julius Caesar,' there died, twenty-four miles from Stratford-on-Avon, a rich miller— John James Nollykins by name. His was the handsomest mill in Warwickshire. But none of his neighbours—or none at least of his poorer neigh-hours—could abide the sight of him. He was a morose, close-fisted, merciless man. He cheated his customers and was pitiless to those whom he got in his clutches.

As he grew older he had grown ever more mean and churlish until at last he had even begun to starve his own horses. Though he died rich, then, few of his neighbours mourned him much. And as soon as he was gone his money began to go too. For his three sons gobbled up what he left behind him like jackals a lion's supper bones. It slipped through their fingers like water through a sieve. They coursed, they diced, they gambled high and low. They danced, and capered and feasted in their finery, but they hardly knew offal from grain. Pretty soon they began to lose not only their father's trade but also all his savings. Their customers said that there was not only dust but stones in the flour; and tares too. It was fusty; it smelt mousey. What cared they? They took their dogs rat-hunting, but that was for the sake of the sport and not of the flour. Everything about the Mill got shabbier and shabbier —went to rack and ruin. The sails were patched. They clacked in the wind. The rain drove in. There were water-weeds in the mill stream where should have been nothing but a crystal looking-glass; and when the farmers and peasants complained they were greeted with drunken jeers and mockery.

And at length, three years after the death of the miller's last poor half-starved mare, his sons were ruined. They would have been ruined just the same if as one foul windy night they sat drinking and singing in the Mill-house the youngest of them had not knocked over the lamp on the table, and so burned the Mill to the ground.

The eldest—with what he could pick up—went off to Sea, and to foreign parts, and died of yellow fever in Tobago. The second son was taken in by an uncle who was a goldsmith in London. But he was so stupid and indolent that he frequently put the wrong works in the right watch, or *vice versa*, and at last, by swallowing an exquisitely carved cherry-stone from China, which had actually been brought back to Europe by Marco Polo, so enraged his master that he turned him off then and there. He went East and became a fishmonger in Ratcliff Highway, with a shop like a booth, and a long board in front of it. But he neglected his fish too, and at last became a man-of-all-work (or of none) at the old Globe Theatre in Southwark, where he saw Shakespeare dressed up as the ghost in ' Hamlet ' and was half killed as if by accident while taking the part of the Second Murderer in ' Macbeth.'

The youngest son, named Jeremy, married the rich widow of a saddler. She was the owner of a fine gabled house in the High Street of the flourishing town of Cheriton—some eight miles from Bishops Hitchingworth. He had all the few good looks of the family, but he was sly and crafty and hard. The first thing he did after he came home from his honeymoon was to paint a long red nose to the portrait of the saddler. The next thing he did was to drown his wife's cat in the water-butt, because he said the varmint had stolen the cheese. The third thing he did was to burn her best Sunday bonnet, then her wig—to keep it company. How she could bear to go on living with him is a mystery. Nevertheless she did.

This Jeremy had three sons : Job, John and (another) Jeremy. But he did not flourish. Far from it. The family went ' down the ladder,' rung by rung, until at long last it reached the bottom. Then it began to climb up again. But Jeremy's children did best. His youngest daughter married a well-to-do knacker, and *their* only son (yet another Jeremy), though he ran away from home because he hated water-gruel and suet pudding, went into business as assistant to the chief sweep in Cheriton ; and at last, having by his craft and cunning and early rising and hard-working inherited his master's business, he bought his great uncle's fine gabled house, and himself became a Master Sweep and ' Sweep by Appointment,' to the Mayor and Corporation and the Lords of three neighbouring Manors. And *he* never married at all. In spite of his hard childhood, in spite of the kindness shown him by his master, in spite of his good fortune with the three Lords of the Manors, he was a skinflint and a pick-halfpenny. He had an enormous brush over his door, a fine brass knocker, and—though considering all things, he had mighty few friends, he was the best, as well as the richest master-sweep in those parts.

But a good deal of his money and in later years most of his praise was due to his three small 'prentices—Tom, Dick and Harry. In those days, hearths and fireplaces were as large as little rooms or chambers, or at any rate, as large as large cupboards or closets. They had great warm com-

fortable ingle-nooks, and the chimney was like a deep
well running up to the roof, getting narrower and
narrower towards the top.   And the chimneys were
swept by hand.

These 'prentices then (like Tom in *The Water
Babies*) had to climb from brick to brick with a
brush, and sweep till they were as black as blackest
blackamoors inside and out.   Soot, soot, soot !
Eyes, mouth, ears and nose.   And sometimes the
bricks were scorching hot, and their hands got blistered.   And sometimes they were all but suffocated
in the narrow parts, and sometimes they were nearly
wedged there, to dry like mummies in the dark.
And sometimes in the midst of the smother a leg
would slip, and down they would come tumbling
like apples out of a tree or hailstones out of a
cloud.

And Jeremy Nollykins, after tying up all the
money they brought him in in fat canvas and leather
bags, served them out water-gruel for supper, and
water-gruel for breakfast.   For dinner on Tuesdays
and Thursdays he gave them slabs of suet-pudding
with lumps of suet in it like pale amber beads ; what
he called soup on Mondays and Wednesdays and
Fridays ; and a bit of catsmeat (bought cheap from
his second cousin) on Sundays.   But then you can't
climb chimneys on *no* meat.   On Saturdays they
had cold pease-pudding and potage : because on
Saturdays the Mayor's man might look in.   You
would hardly believe it : but in spite of such poor
mean living, in spite of their burns and their bruises,
and the soot in their eyes and lungs and in their
close lint-coloured hair, these three small boys, Tom,

Dick and Harry, managed to keep their spirits up. They even rubbed their cheeks rosy when the week's soot was washed off under the pump on a Saturday night.

They were like Tom Dacre in the poem:

There's little Tom Dacre, who cried when his head
That curled like a lamb's back was shav'd: so I said
'Hush, Tom! never mind it, for when your head's bare
You know that the soot cannot spoil your white hair.'

And so he was quiet, and that very night
As Tom was a-sleeping, he had such a sight!
That thousands of sleepers, Dick, Joe, Ned, and Jack
Were all of them lock'd up in coffins of black. . . .

Still, they always said 'Mum' to the great ladies. and 'Miss' to the maids, and they kept their manners even when some crabbed old woman said they were owdacious, or imperent, or mischeevious. And sometimes a goodwife would give them a slice of bread pudding, or a mug of milk, or a baked potato, or perhaps a pocket-full of cookies or a slice of white bread (which did not remain white very long). And now and then, even a sip of elderberry wine. After all, even half-starved sparrows sometimes find tit-bits, and it's not the hungry who want the richest sauce!

When they *could* scuttle away too they would bolt off between their jobs to go paddling in the river, or bird-nesting in the woods, or climbing in an old stone quarry not very far from the town. It is lovely country thereabouts—near ancient Cheriton.

Whether they played truant or not, Jeremy Nolly-

kins the Fourth—Old Noll, as his neighbours called
him—used to beat them morning, noon and night.
He believed in the rod. He said it was a fine sauce
for the saucy. Tom, Dick and Harry simply hated
their master : and that's a bad thing enough.
But, on the other hand, they were far too much
alive and hearty and happy when they were not
being beaten, and they were much too hungry even
over their water-gruel to *think* or to brood over how
they hated him ; which would have been a very
much worse.

In sober fact—with their bright glittering eyes and
round cheeks and sharp white teeth, and in spite
of their skinny ribs and blistered hands, they were
a merry trio. As soon as ever their teeth stopped
chattering with the cold ; and their bodies stopped
smarting from Old Noll's sauce, and their eyes from
the soot ; they were laughing and talking and
whistling and champing like grasshoppers in June
or starlings in September. And though they sometimes quarrelled and fought together, bit and
scratched too, never having been taught to fight
fair, they were very good friends. Now and again
too they shinned up a farmer's fruit-trees to have a
taste of his green apples. Now and again they played
tricks on old women. But what little chimney-
sweeps wouldn't ?

They were just young ragamuffins, as wild as colts,
as nimble as kids, though a good deal blacker. And,
however hard he tried, Old Noll never managed to
break them in. Never. And at night they slept as
calm and deep as cradled babies—all three of them
laid in a row up in an attic under the roof on an

immense wide palliass or mattress of straw, with a straw bolster and a couple of pieces of old sacking for blankets each.

Now Old Noll, simply perhaps because he was— both by nature as well as by long practice—a mean old curmudgeonly miser, hated to see anybody merry, or happy, or fat. There were moments when he would have liked to skin his three 'prentices alive. But then he wanted to get out of them all the work he could. So he was compelled to give them *that* much to eat. He had to keep them alive—or the Mayor's man would ask Why. Still, it enraged him that he could not keep their natural spirits down ; that however much he beat them they " came up smiling." It enraged him to know in his heart (or whatever took its place) that though (when they had nothing better to do, or were smarting from his rod and pickle) they hated him, they yet had never done him an ill-turn.

Every day he would gloat on them as they came clattering down to their water-gruel just as Giant Despair looked at Faithful and Christian in the dungeon. And sometimes at night he would creep up to their bed chamber, and the stars would show him the three of them lying there fast asleep on their straw mattress, the sacking kicked off, and on their faces a faint far-away smile as if their dreams were as happy as swans in the Hesperides. It enraged him beyond measure. What could the little urchins be dreaming about ? What made the little blacka- moors grin in sleep ? You can thwack a wake boy, but you can't thwack a dreamer ; not at least while he is positively dreaming. So Old Noll was helpless. He could only grind his teeth at the sight of them. Poor Old Noll.

He ground his teeth more than ever when he first heard the music in the night. And he might never have heard it at all if hunger hadn't made him a mighty bad sleeper himself. Two or three hours was the most he got, even in winter. And if Tom, Dick and Harry had ever peeped in on *him* as he lay in his four-post bed, they would have seen no smile on his old sunken face with its long nose and long chin and straggling hair—but only a sort of horrifying darkness. They might even have pitied him, lying there with nightmare twisting and darkening his features, and his bony fingers twitching.

Because, then, old Noll could not sleep of nights, he would sometimes let himself out of his silent house to walk in the streets. And while so walking, he would look up at his neighbours' windows, all dark beneath the night-sky, and he would curse them for being more comfortable than he. It was as if instead of marrow he had malice in his bones, and there is no fattening on that.

Now one night, for the first time in his life, except when he broke his leg at eighteen, Old Noll had been unable to sleep at all. It was a clear mild night with no wind, and a fine sharp fragment of a moon was up aloft, and the stars shone bright. There was a sweet balmy air in Cheriton, borne in from the meadows that then stretched in within a mile of the town, and so silent was the hour you could almost hear the rippling of the river among its osiers that far away.

And as Old Nollykins was sitting like a gaunt

shadow all by himself on the first milestone that comes into the town—and he was too niggardly even to smoke a pipe of tobacco—a faint thin wind came drifting along the street. And then on the wind a fainter music—a music which at first hardly seemed to be a music at all. None the less it continued on, and at last so filled and trembled in the air that even Old Nollykins, who was now pretty hard of hearing, caught the strains and recognised the melody. It came on, that music—a twangling as of harps or citherns, and a breathing as of shawms and horns waxing merrier and merrier in the quick mild night October air :—

> Girls and boys come out to play,
> The moon doth shine as bright as day ;
> Leave your supper, and leave your sleep,
> And come with your playfellows into the street. . .

Girls and boys come out to play : on and on and on, now faint now shrill, now in a sudden rallying burst of music as if it came from out of the skies. Not that the moon just then was shining as bright as day. It was but barely in its first quarter. It resembled a bent bit of intensely shining copper down low among the stars ; or a gold basin, of which little more than the edge showed, resting atilt. But full moon or no, the shapes that were now hastening along the street, running and hopping and skipping and skirring and dancing, had heard the summons, had obeyed the call ! From by-lane and alley, court, porch and house-door the children of Cheriton had come pouring out like water-streams in April. Running, skipping, hopping, dancing, they kept time

to the tune.   Old Noll fairly gasped with astonishment as he watched them.   What a tale to tell—and
all the comfortable and respectable folks of Cheriton
fast asleep in their beds.   To think such innocents
could be such arch deceivers.   To think that
gluttonous and grubby errand and shop and boot-
and-shoe and pot boys could look so clean and nimble
and happy and free.   He shivered ; part with the
night air and part with rage.

But real enough though these young skip-by-nights
appeared to be, there were three queer things about
them.   First there was not the faintest sound of
doors opening or shutting, or casement windows
being thrust open with a squeal of the iron rod.   Next,
there was not the faintest rumour of footsteps even,
though at least half the children of Cheriton were
now bounding along the street, like leaves borne on
a great wind, and all with their faces towards the
East and the water-meadows.   And last, though Noll
could see the very eyes in their faces in the faint
luminousness of starshine and little moon, not a
single one of that mad young company turned head
to look at him, or seemed in the least particular to
be aware that he was there.   Clockwork images of
wood or wax could not have ignored him more
completely.

Old Noll, after feeling at first startled, flabber-
gasted, a little frightened even, was now in a fury.
His few old teeth began to grind together as lustly
as had the milestones of Jeremy the First when he
was rich and prosperous.   Nor was his rage
diminished when, lo and behold, even as he turned
his head, out of his own narrow porch with its three

rounded steps and fluted shell of wood above it, came leaping along who but his own three half-starved 'prentices, Tom, Dick and Harry—now seemingly nine-year-olds as plump and comely to see as if they had been fed on the fat of the land, as if they had never never in the whole of their lives so much as tasted rod-sauce. Their mouths were opening and shutting, too, as if they were whooping calls one to the other and to their other street-mates, though no sound came from them. They flung their fingers in the air. They came cavotting and skirling along in their naked feet to the strains of the music as if scotched shins and cramped muscles and iron-bound clogs had never once pestered their young souls. Yet not a sound, not a whisper, not a footfall could the deaf old man hear—nought but that sweet shrill terrifying infuriating music.

In a few minutes the streets were empty, a thin fleece of cloud had drawn across the moon and only one small straggler was still in sight, the small son of the Mayor. He was last merely because he was least, and had no young sister to take care of him. And Old Noll, having watched this last night-truant out of sight, staring at him with eyes like saucers beneath his bony brows, hobbled back across the street to his own house, and after pausing awhile at the nearest post to gnaw his beard and think what next was to be done, climbed his three flights of shallow oak stairs until he came to the uppermost landing under the roof. There at last with infinite caution he lifted the pin of the door of the attic and looked in on what he supposed would be an empty bed. Empty! It was far from being that. For lying there, in the dim starlight of the dusty dormer window, he could see as plain as can be the motionless shapes of his three 'prentices, breathing on so calmly in midnight's deepmost sleep that he even ventured to fetch in a tallow candle in a pewter stick in order that he might examine them more closely.

With its smoky beams to aid him he searched the three young faces utterly unconscious that the old skinflint was stooping as close over them as a bird-snarer over his note. There were traces of soot on their chubby cheeks, but though every few weeks their heads were regularly shaved by the barber, the hair still continued to grow on them in tight short ringlets like lamb's wool. And all three were smiling away, gently and distantly as if they were sitting in their dreams in some wondrous orchard supping up strawberries and cream, as though the spirits within them were untellably happy though the bodies of them were as fast asleep as peg-tops or pigs in a July sun. Moreover, their expressions showed no change at all. Like this had these faces been left a few moments ago ; and like this they would remain until the midnight tryst was over.

Stair by stair Old Nollykins crept down again, blew out his candle, and sat on his great bed to think. He was a cunning old miser, which is as far away from being generous and wise as moonlight is from a dip. His fingers had itched to wake his three sleeping chimney-boys with a smart taste of his rod, just to ' learn them a lesson.' He hated to think of that quiet happy smile resting upon their faces while the shadow-shapes or ghosts of them were out and

away, pranking and gallivanting in the green water-
meadows beyond the town. How was he to know
that his dimming eyes had not deluded him. Supposing he went off to the Mayor himself in the morning
and told his midnight tale, who would believe it ?
High and low, everybody hated him, and as like as
not they would shut him up in the town dungeon for a
madman or burn his house about his ears supposing
him to be a wizard. ' No, no, no ! ' he muttered
to himself, ' We must watch and wait, friend
Jeremy, and see what we shall see.'

Next morning his three 'prentices, Tom, Dick
and Harry, were up and about as sprightly as grasshoppers, a full hour before daybreak. You might
have supposed from their shining eyes and apple
cheeks that they had just come back from a long
holiday in the Islands of the Blest. Away they
tumbled—as merry as frogs—to their work, with their
brushes and bags, still munching away at their
gritty oatcakes—three parts bran to one of meal.

So intent had Old Noll been on watching from
his chimney-corner what he could see in their faces
at breakfast, and on trying to overhear what they
were whispering to each other, that he forgot to
give them their usual morning dose of stick. But
not a word had been uttered about the music or the
dancing or the company at the water-meadows.
They just talked their usual scatter-brained gibberish
to one another—except when they saw that the old
creature was watching them ; and he was speedily
convinced that whatever adventures their dream-
shapes may have had in the night-hours, they had
left no impression on their waking minds.

Poor Old Noll. An echo of that music and the sight he had seen kept him awake for many a night after, and his body was already shrunken up by age and his miserly habits to nothing much more substantial than a bag of animated bones. And yet all his watching was in vain. So weary and hungry for sleep did he become, that when at last the hunter's moon shone at its brightest and roundest over the roofs of Cheriton, he nodded off in his chair. He was roused a few hours afterwards by a faint glow in his room that was certainly not moonlight, for it came from out of the black dingy staircase passage. Instantly he was wide awake—but too late. For, even as he peeped through the door-crack, there flitted past his three small 'prentices—just the ghosts or the spirits or the dream-shapes of them— faring merrily home. They passed him softer than a breeze through a willow tree and were out of sight up the staircase before he could stir.

The morning after the morning after that, when Tom, Dick and Harry woke up at dawn on their mattress, there was a wonderful rare smell in the air. They sniffed it greedily as they looked at one another in the creeping light of daybreak. And sure enough, as soon as they were in their ragged jackets and had got down to their breakfast, the old woman who came to the house every morning to do an hour or two's charing for Old Nollykins came waddling in out of the kitchen with a frying-pan of bacon frizzling in its fat.

' There, me boys,' said Old Noll, rubbing his hands together with a cringing smile, ' there's a bit of bacon for ye all, and sop in the pan to keep the cold out, after that long night run in the moonlight.'

Q

He creaked up his eyes at them, finger on nose ; but all three of them, perched up there on their wooden stools the other side of the table, only paused an instant in the first polishing up of their plates with a crust of bread to stare at him with such an innocent astonishment on their young faces that he was perfectly sure they had no notion of what he meant.

' Aha,' says he, ' do ye never dream, me boys, tucked up snug under the roof in that comfortable bed of yours ? D'ye never dream ?—never hear a bit of a tune calling, or maybe see what's called a nightmare ? Lordee, when I was young there never went a night but had summat of a dream to it.'

' Dream ! ' said they, and looked at one another with their mouths half open. ' Why, if you ax me, Master,' says Tom, ' I dreamed last night it was all bright moonshine, and me sitting at supper with the gentry.'

' And I,' says Dick, ' I dreamed I was dancing under trees and bushes all covered over with flowers. And I could hear 'em playing on harps and whistles.'

' And me,' says Harry, ' I dreamed I was by a river, and a leddy came out by a green place near the water and took hold of my hand. I suppose, Master, it must have been my mammie, though I never seed her as I knows on.'

At all this the cringing smile on Old Nollykins' face set like grease in a dish, because of the rage in his mind underneath. And he leaped up from where he sat beside the skinny little fire in the immense kitchen hearth. ' " Gentry " ! " Harps " ! " Mammie " ! ' he shouted, ' ye brazen, ungrateful, greedy little deevils. Be off with ye, or ye shall have such a taste of the stick as will put ye to sleep for good and all.'

And almost before they had time to snatch up their bags and their besoms, he had chased them out of the house. So there in the little alley beside the house, sheltering as close to its wall as they could from the cold rain that was falling, they must needs stand chattering together like drenched starlings, waiting for the angry old man to come out and to send them about the business of the day.

But Old Nollykins' dish of bacon fat had not been altogether wasted. He knew now that the young rapscallions only dreamed their nocturnal adventures, and were not in the least aware that they themselves in actual shadow shape went off by night to the trysting-place of all Cheriton's children to dance and feast and find delight. But he continued to keep watch, and would again and again peer in at his three 'prentices laid together asleep on their mattress on the attic floor, in the hope of catching them in the act of stealing out. But though at times he discerned that same quiet smile upon their faces, shining none the less serenely for the white gutter-marks of tears on their sooty cheeks, for weeks together he failed to catch any repetition of the strains of that strange music or the faintest whisper of their dream-shapes coming and going on the wooden stairs.

Nevertheless, the more he brooded on what he had seen, the more he hated the three urchins, and the more bitterly he resented their merry ways. The one thing he could not decide in his mind was whether when next, if ever, he caught them at their midnight tricks, he should at once set about their slumbering bodies with his stick or should wait until their dream-wraiths were safely away and so try to prevent them from coming back. Then indeed they would be at his mercy.

Now there was an old crone in Cheriton who was reputed to be a witch. She lived in a stone hovel at the far end of a crooked alley that ran beside the very walls of Old Nollykins' fine gabled house. And Old Nollykins, almost worn to a shadow himself by his gnawing thoughts and night watching, determined to ask her counsel. She was no dainty to look at. Her nose and chin nearly met over her toothless gums. She might have been the old man's grandmother as she sat there, hunched up in her corner like a bundle of rags, listening to his questions and leering at Old Nollykins over an iron pot smoking on the fire. And the old miser haggled with her over his purse, thinking he could cheat her. But she watched him close ; mumbling. Waken a sleeper, she told him, before his dream-shape can get back into his mortal frame, it's as like as not to be sudden death. But if you just keep the dream-shape out *without* rousing his sleeping body, then he will for ever more be your slave, and will never grow any older. And what keeps a human's dream-shape out—or animal's either for that matter—she said, is a love-knot twist of steel or a horseshoe upside down, or a twisted wreath of elder and ash fastened up with an iron nail over the keyhole—and every window shut. Brick walls and stone and wood are nothing to such wanderers. But they can't abide iron. And what she said was partly true and partly false ; and it was

in part false because the foolish old man had refused
to pay the crone her price.

Now Old Nollykins knew well that there was only
a wooden latch to his door, because he had been too
much of a skinflint to pay for one of the new iron
locks to be fixed on. He had no fear of thieves,
because he had so hidden his money that no thief
on earth would be able to find it, not if he searched
for a week. So he asked the old woman again, to
make assurance doubly sure, how long a man would
live and work if his dream-shape never got back.
' Why, that,' she mumbled, leering at him out of her
wizened up old face, ' that depends how young they
be ; what's the blood, and what's the heart. Take
'em in their first bloom,' she said, ' and so they
keeps ' ; for she had long since seen what the old
man was after, and had no more love for him than
for his three noisy whooping chimney-sweeps.

So Old Nollykins very unwillingly put his bits of
money into her skinny palm and went back to his
house, not knowing that the old woman, to avenge
herself on his skinflint ways, had told him only half
the story. That evening the three 'prentices had a
rare game of hide-and-seek together in the many-
roomed old rat-holed house ; for their master had
gone out. The moment they heard his shuffling
footsteps on the porch steps they scampered off to
bed, and were to all appearance fast asleep before
he could look in on them.

And Old Nollykins had brought back with him
some switches of elder and ash, a tenpenny nail and
an old key, and a cracked horseshoe. And, strange
to say, the iron key which he had bought from a

dealer in broken metal had once been the key of the Mill of rich old Jeremy the First at Stratford-on-Avon. He had pondered all day on what the old woman had said, and 'surely,' said he to himself, 'their blood's fresh enough, my old stick keeps them out of mischief, and what is better for a green young body than a long day's work and not too much to eat, and an airy lodging for the night?' The cunning old creature supposed indeed, that if only by this sorcery and hugger-mugger he could keep their wandering dream-shapes from their bodies for good and all, his three young 'prentices would never age, never weary, but stay lusty and nimble perhaps for a century. Ay, he would use them as long as he wanted them, and sell them before he died. *He'd* teach them to play truant at night, when honest folk were snoring in their beds. For the first time for weeks his mangy supper off a crust and a hambone and a mug of water tasted like manna come down from heaven.

The very next day chanced to be St. Nicholas's Day. And those were the times of old English winters. Already a fine pattering of snow was on the ground, like minute white lumps of sago, and the rivers and ponds were frozen hard as iron. Moreover, there was three parts of a fine moon that night, and the puddles in Cheriton High Street shone like Chinese crystal in the beams slanting down on them from between the eaves of the houses.

For five long hours of dark, after his seven o'clock supper, Old Nollykins managed to keep himself awake. Then, a little before midnight, having assured himself that his three 'prentices were sound

aslcep in their bed, he groped downstairs again,
gently lifted the latch and looked out. There never
was such a shining scene before. The snow on the
roofs and gables and carved stone-work of the houses
gleamed white and smooth as the finest millers' meal.
There was not a soul, not even a cat, to be seen in
the long stretch of the lampless street. And the
stars in the grey-blue sky gleamed like dewdrops on
a thorn.

Sure enough, as soon as ever the last stroke of
midnight had sounded out from St. Andrew's tower,
there came faintly wreathing its way out of the
distance the same shrill penetrating strains of the
ancient tune. Lord bless me, if Old Nollykins had
had but one sole drop of the blood of his own youth
left in his veins he could not have resisted dancing
his old bones out of his body down his steps and into
the crudded High Street at the sound of it :

> Girls and boys come out to play,
> The moon doth shine as bright as Day ;
> Leave your supper, and leave your sleep,
> And come with your Playfellows into the street.

But, instead, he shuffled like a rat hastily back into
the house again ; pushed himself in close under the
staircase ; and waited, leaving the door ajar.

Ho, ho, what's that ? Faint flitting lights were
now showing in the street, and a sound as of little
un-human cries, and in a minute or two the music
loudened so that an old glass case on a table nearby
containing the model of a brig which had belonged
to Old Nollykins's wicked grandfather who had died
in Tobago, fairly rang to the marvellous stirrings

on the air. And down helter-skelter from their bed, just as they had slipped in under its sacking—in their breeches and rags of day-shirts, barefoot, came whiffling from stair to stair the ghosts of his three small 'prentices. Old Nollykins hardly had time enough to see the wonderful smile on them, to catch the gleam of the grinning white teeth shining beneath their parted lips, before they were out and away.

Shivering all over, as if with a palsy, the old man hastened up the staircase, and in a minute or two the vacant house resounded with the strokes of his hammer as he drove in the tenpenny nail into the keyhole above the attic door, and hung up key and horseshoe by their strings. This done, he lowered his hammer and listened. Not the faintest whisper, sigh or squeak came from within. But in dread of what he might see he dared not open the door.

Instead, curiosity overcame him. Wrapping a cloak round his skinny shoulders he hurried out into the street. Sure enough, here, there, everywhere in the fine snow were traces of footprints—traces distinct enough for his envious eyes though hardly more than those of the skirring of a hungry bird's wing on the surface of the snow. And fondly supposing in his simplicity that he had now safely cheated his 'prentices, that for ever more their poor young empty bodies would be at his beck and call, Old Noll determined to follow up out of the town and into the water-meadows the dream-shapes of the children now all of them out of sight. On and on he went till his breath was whistling in his throat and he could scarcely drag one foot after another.

And he came at last to where, in a loop of the Itchin, its waters shining like glass in the moon, there was a circle of pollard and stunted willows.   And there, in the lush and frosty grasses was a wonderful company assembled, and unearthly music ascending, it seemed, from out of the bowels of a mound nearby, called Caesar's Camp.   And he heard a multitude of voices and singing from within.   And all about the meadow wandered in joy the sleep-shapes not only of the children from Cheriton, but from the farms and cottages and gipsy camps for miles around.   Sheep were there too, their yellow eyes gleaming in the moon as he trod past them.   But none paid any heed to the children or to the strangers who had called them out of their dreams.

Strange indeed were these strangers : of middle height, with garments like a spider-web, their straight hair of the colour of straw falling gently on either side their narrow cheeks, so that it looked at first glimpse as if they were grey-beards.   And as they trod on their narrow feet, the frozen grasses scarcely stirring beneath them, they turned their faces from side to side, looking at the children.   And then a fairness that knows no change showed in their features, and their eyes were of a faint flame like that of sea-water on nights of thunder when the tide gently lays its incoming wavelets on the wide flat sandy strand.

And at sight of them Old Nollykins began to be mortally afraid.   Not a sign was there of Tom, Dick or Harry.   They must have gone into the sonorous mound—maybe were feasting there—if dream-shapes feast.   The twangling and trumpeting and incessant music made his head spin round. He peered about for a hiding-place, and at length made his way to one of the old gnarled willows beside the icy stream. There he might have remained safe and sound till morning, if the frost, as he dragged himself up a little way into the lower branches of the tree, had not risen into his nostrils and made him sneeze. There indeed he might have remained safe and sound if he had *merely* sneezed, for man's sneeze is not so very much unlike a sheep's wheezy winter cough. But such was the poor old man's alarm and terror at the company he had stumbled into that he cried ' God bless us ! ' after his sneeze—just as his mother had taught him to do.

That was the end of wicked old Nollykins ; that was his first step on the long road of repentance. For the next thing he remembered was opening his eyes in the first glimpse of stealing dawn and finding himself perched up in the boughs of a leafless willow-tree, a thin mist swathing the low-lying water-meadows, the sheep gently browsing in the grasses, leaving green marks in the frosty grass as they munched onwards. And such an ache and ague was in Old Noll's bones as he had never since he was swaddled felt before. It was as if every frosty switch of every un-polled willow in that gaunt fairy circle by the Itchin had been belabouring him of its own free will the whole night long. His heart and courage were gone. Sighing and groaning, he lowered himself into the meadow, and by the help of a fallen branch for staff made his way at last back into the town.

It was early yet even for the milkman, though

cocks were crowing from their frosty perches, and
the red of the coming sun inflamed the eastern skies.
He groped into his house and shut the door.   With
many rests on the way from stair to stair he hoisted
himself up, though every movement seemed to
wrench him joint from joint, until at last he reached
the attic door.   He pressed his long ear against the
panel and listened a moment.   Not a sound.   Then
stealthily pushing it open inch by inch, he thrust
forward his shuddering head and looked in.

The ruddy light in the East was steadily increasing,
and had even pierced through the grimy panes of the
casement window as though to light up the faces of
his small chimney sweeps.   It was a Sunday morning,
and the three faces and lamb's-wool heads showed
no sign of the week's soot.   But while at other times
on spying in at them it looked to Old Nollykins as
if their smiling faces were made of wax, now they
might be of marble.   For each one of the three—
Tom, Dick and Harry—was lying on his back, their
chapped, soot-roughened hands with the torn and
broken nails resting on either side their bodies.   No
smile now touched their features, but only a solemn
quietude as of images eternally at rest.   And such
was the aspect of the three children that even Old
Nollykins dared not attempt to waken them because
he knew in his heart that no earthly rod would ever
now bestir them out of this sound slumber.   Not at
least until their spirits had won home again.   And
the soured old crone was not likely to aid him in
that.

He cursed the old woman, battering on her crazy
door, but she paid him no heed.   And at last, when

the Cheriton Church bells began ringing the people
to morning service, there was nothing for it, if there
was any hope of saving his neck, but to go off to the
Mayor's man, dragging himself along the street on
a couple of sticks, to tell him that his 'prentices
were dead.

Dead they were not, however. The Mayor's
man fetched a doctor, and the doctor, after putting a
sort of wooden trumpet to their chests asseverated
that there was a stirring under the cage of their ribs.
They were fallen into a trance, he said. What is
called a catalepsy. And though the old midwife the
doctor called in heated up salt, for salt-bags, and
hour by hour put a hot brick fresh from the fire to
each 'prentice's stone-cold feet, by not a flutter of
an eyelid nor the faintest of sighs did any one of
the three prove that he was alive or could heed.

There they lay, on their straw mattress, quiet as
mummies, unchanging, lovely as any mother might
wish, with their solemn Sunday-morning soap-
polished cheeks and noses and foreheads and chins,
and as motionless as statues in stone.

And the Mayor of the Town, after listening to all
Old Nollykins could say, fined him Five Bags of
Guineas for allowing his three 'prentices to fall into
a catalepsy for want of decent food and nourishment. And what with the pain of his joints and the
anguish of having strangers tramping all over his
house, and of pleading with the Mayor, and of seeing
his money fetched out from its hiding-places and
counted out on the table, the miserable old man was
so much dazed and confused that he never thought
to take down the wreath of ash and elder and the

horseshoe and the key. That is why, when a week
or two had gone by and no sign had shown how
long this trance would continue, the Mayor and
Councillors decided that as Tom, Dick and Harry
could be of no further use to the town as chimney-
sweeps, they might perhaps earn an honest penny
for it as the Marvels of the Age.

So the Mayor's man with a flowing white muslin
band round his black hat, and his two mutes—carrying bouquets of lilies in their hands—came with his
hand-cart and fetched the three bodies away. A
roomy glass case had been made for them of solid
Warwickshire oak, with a fine lock and key. And by
the time that the Waits had begun to sing their carols
in the snow, the three children had been installed in
their glass case on the upper floor of the Cheriton
Museum and lay slumbering on and on, quiet as
Snowwhite in the dwarfs' coffin, the gentle daylight
falling fairly on their quiet faces—though during the
long summer days a dark blind was customarily
drawn over the glass whenever the sun shone too
fiercely at the window.

News of this wonder spread fast, and by the
following Spring visitors from all over the world
—even from cities as remote as Guanojuato and
Seringapatam—came flocking into Warwickshire
merely to gaze awhile at the sleeping Chimney-
Sweeps, at 6d. a time. After which a fair proportion
of them went on to Stratford to view the church
where lie William Shakespeare's honoured bones.
Indeed Mrs. Giles, the old woman who set up an
apple and ginger-bread stall beside the Museum, in
a few years made so much money out of her wares

that she was able to bring up her nine orphaned grand-children in comfort, and to retire at last at the age of sixty to a four-roomed cottage not a hundred yards from that of Anne Hathaway's herself.

In course of time the Lord-Lieutenant and the Sheriffs and the Justices of the Peace and the Bishop and the mayors of the neighbouring towns, jealous no doubt of this fame and miracle in their midst, did their utmost to persuade and compel the Mayor and Corporation of Cheriton to remove the Boys to the county-town—the Earl himself promising to house them in an old Inn not a stone's-throw distant from the lovely shrine of his ancestors, Beauchamp Chapel. But all in vain. The people of Cheriton held tight to their rights : and the Lord Chief Justice after soberly hearing both sides at full length wagged his wigged head in their favour.

For fifty-three years the Sleeping Boys slept on. During this period the Town Council had received One Hundred and Twenty-Three Thousand, Five Hundred and Fifty-Five sixpences in fees alone (*i.e.* £3088 17s. 6d.), and nearly every penny of this vast sum was almost clear profit. They spent it wisely too—planted lime-trees in the High Street and ash and willow beside the river, built a fountain and a large stone dove-cot, and opened a small shady Zoo with every comfort wild creatures can hope to have bestowed on them by their taskmaster, Man.

Then, one fine day, the curator—the caretaker—of the Museum, who for forty years had never once missed dusting the 'prentices glass case first thing in the morning, fell ill and had to take to his bed. And his niece, a fair young thing with straight yellow hair, came as his deputy for a while, looked after the Museum, sold the tickets, and kept an eye on the visitors in his stead. She was but twenty-three, and was the first person who had ever been heard to sing in the Museum—though of course it was only singing with her lips all but closed, and never during show-hours.

And it was Summer-time, or rather the very first of May. And as each morning she opened the great door of the Museum and ascended the wide curved staircase and drew up the blinds of the tall windows on the upper floor, and then turned—as she always turned—to gaze at the Three Sleepers (and not even a brass farthing to pay), she would utter a deep sigh as if out of the midst of a happy dream.

' You lovely things ! ' she would whisper to herself. ' You lovely, lovely things ! ' for she had a motherly heart ; and the fair wisps of her hair were as transparent as the E-string of a fiddle in the morning light. And the glance of her blue eyes rested on the glass case with such compassion and tenderness that if mere looking could have awakened the children they would have been dancing an Irish jig with her every blessed morning.

Being young, too, she was inclined to be careless, and had even at times broken off a tiny horn of coral, or a half-hidden scale from the mermaid's tail for a souvenir of Cheriton to any young stranger that particularly took her fancy. Moreover, she had never been told anything about the magicry of keys or horseshoes or iron or ash or elder, having been brought up at a School where wizardry and witchcraft were never so much as mentioned during school hours. How could she realise then that the little key of the glass case and the great key of the Museum door could keep anybody or anything out, or in, even when the doors were wide open?

And one morning there was such a pomp of sunshine in the sky, and the thrushes were singing so shrilly in the new-leafed lime trees as she came along to her work, that she could resist her pity and yearning no longer. Having drawn up the blinds on the upper floor, in all that silence she took out the little key from its secure repository, turned it softly in the lock, and *opened* the case. And one by one —after first listening at their lips as stealthily as if in hope of hearing what their small talk or song might be in dream, she kissed the slumbering creatures on their stone-cold mouths. And as she kissed Harry she thought she heard a step on the stair.

In her haste and apprehension she dropped the key of the case—the great iron key of the Museum door itself being already in the pocket of her alpaca apron. And she ran out to see who was there. No-one. Then, as she stood on the wide staircase listening, her fair face tilted and intent, on a sudden there came a waft up as of spiced breezes from the open spaces of the street. Not a sound but just a breath, faint and yet almost unendurably sweet of Spring—straight across from the bird-haunted, sheep-grazed meadows skirting the winding river— the perfume of a whisper. It was as if a distant memory had taken presence and swept in delight across her eyes. Then stillness again, broken by the sounding as of a voice smaller than the horn of a gnat. And then a terrible sharp crash of glass. And out pell-mell came rushing our three young friends, the chimney-sweeps, their dream-shapes home at last.

Now Old Nollykins by this time had long been laid in his grave. So even if he had been able to catch them, Tom, Dick and Harry would have swept no more chimneys for him. Nor could even the new Mayor manage to catch them ; nor even the complete Town Council, nor the Town Crier, though he cried twice a day to the end of the year : ' O-yèss ! O-yèss ! ! O-yèss ! ! ! Lost, stolen, or strayed. The Three All-Famous and Notororious Sleeping Boys of Warwickshire.' Nor even the Lord-Lieutenant, nor the mighty Earl.

As for the mound by the pollard willows—well, what bright Wide-awake was to know about that ?

R

THE LOVELY MYFANWY

In an old castle under the forested mountains of the Welsh Marches there lived long ago Owen ap Gwythock, Lord of Eggleyseg. He was a short, burly, stooping man with thick black hair on head and face and small restless eyes. And he lived in his great castle alone, but for one only daughter, the lovely Myfanwy.

Lovely indeed was she. Her hair red as red gold hung in plaits to her knees. When she laughed it was like bells in a far-away steeple. When she sang, Echo forgot to reply. And her spirit would sit gently looking out of her blue eyes like cushats out of their nest in an ivy bush.

Myfanwy was happy, too, in most things. All that her father could give her for her ease and pleasure was hers—everything indeed but her freedom. She might sing, dance, think and say, eat, drink and delight in whatsoever she wished or willed. Indeed her father loved her so dearly that he would sit for hours together merely watching her—as you may watch wind over wheat, sea-birds in the air, or clouds in the heavens. So long as she was safely and solely his all was well.

But ever since Myfanwy had been a child a miserable foreboding had haunted his mind. Supposing she should some day leave him ? Supposing she were lost or decoyed away ? Supposing she fell ill and died ? What then ? The dread of this haunted his mind day and night. His dark brows loured at the very thought of it. It made him morose and sullen ; it tied up the tongue in his head.

For this sole reason he had expressly forbidden Myfanwy even to stray but a few paces beyond the precincts of his castle with its battlemented towers, its galleries and corridors and multitudinous apart ments, its high garden and courtyard, its alleys, fountains, fish-pools and orchards. He could trust nobody. He couldn't bear her out of his sight. He spied, he watched, he walked in his sleep, he listened and peeped ; and all for fear of losing Myfanwy.

So it was she might have for company the doves and swans and peacocks, the bees and butterflies, the swallows and swifts and jackdaws and a multitude of birds of every song and flight and feather that haunted the castle ; but of humans, except her father, none. The birds and butterflies could hie away at will wherever their wings could carry them. Even the fishes in the fish-pools and in the fountains had their narrow alleys of marble and alabaster through which on nimble fin they could win back to the great river at last. But not so Myfanwy.

She was her father's unransomable prisoner ; she was a bird in a cage. She might feast her longing eyes on the distant horizon beyond whose forests lay the sea, but knew she could not journey thither. While as for the neighbouring township, with its busy streets and marketplace—not more than seven country miles away—she had only dreamed of its marvels and dreamed in vain. A curious darkness at such times came into her eyes, and her spirit would look out of them not like a dove but as might a dumb nightingale out of its nest—a nightingale that has had its tongue cut out for a delicacy to feed some greedy prince.

How crisscross a thing is the heart of man. Solely because this lord loved his daughter so dearly, if ever she so much as sighed for change or adventure, like some plodding beast of burden he would set his feet together and refuse to budge an inch. Beneath his louring brows he would gaze at the brightness of her unringleted hair as if mere looking could keep that gold secure ; as if earth were innocent of moth and rust and change and chance, and had never so much as hearkened after the restless footfall of Time.

All he could think of, then, to keep her his own was hers without the asking : delicate raiment and meats and strange fruits and far-fetched toys and devices and pastimes, and as many books as would serve a happy scholar a long life through. He would sit alone too in a corner of the great banqueting hall and play on his harp while she listened—play every wistful and ancient strain of music that came into his head, striving only to express with the plucking of the strings how much he loved and treasured her. But there is a hunger of the heart and of the spirit no *thing* in the world can ever surely ease or satisfy. And Myfanwy listened, and sighed.

Besides which, Myfanwy grew up and grew older as a green-tressed willow grows from a sapling ; and now that she was come to her eighteenth spring she was lovelier than words could tell. But seeing his daughter thus come into her utmost fairness only added yet another and sharper dread and foreboding to her father's mind. It sat like a skeleton at his table whenever he broke bread or sipped wine. Even the twittering of a happy swallow from distant Africa reminded him of it like a knell. It was this : that some day a lover, a suitor, would come and carry her off.

Why, merely to *see* her, even with her back turned —to catch but a glimpse of her slim shoulders, of her head stooping over a rosebush would be enough. Let her but laugh—two notes—and be a listener ! Nobody—prince nor peasant, knight nor squire— brave, foolish, young or weary, would be able to resist her. Owen ap Gwythock knew it in his bones. But one look, and instantly the looker's heart would be stolen out of his body. He would fall in love with her—fall as deep and irrevocably as the dark spark- ling foaming water crashing over into the gorge of Modwr-Eggleyseg, scarcely an arrow's flight beyond his walls.

And supposing any such suitor should *tell* Myfanwy that he loved her, might she not—forgetting all his own care and loving-kindness—be persuaded to flee away and leave him to his solitude ? Solitude—now that old age was close upon him ! For thought of it, for fear of it, he would sigh and groan within : and he would bid the locksmiths double their locks and bolts and bars, and would sit for hours watching the highroad that swept up past his walls, scowling at sight of every stranger that passed his way.

He even at last forbade Myfanwy to walk in the garden except with an immense round mushroom hat on her head, a hat of so wide a brim that it concealed from any trespasser who might be spying over the wall even the glinting of her hair—everything of her indeed except her two velvet shoes beneath the hem of her dress as they stepped in turn—and softly as moles—one after the other from blossoming alley to alley and from lawn to lawn.

And because Myfanwy loved her father almost as dearly as he loved her, she tried her utmost to be gay and happy and not to fret or complain or grow pale and thin and pine. But as a caged bird with a kind mistress may hop and sing and flutter behind its bars as if it were felicity itself, and yet be sickening at heart for the wild wood and its green haunts, so it was with Myfanwy.

If only she might but just once venture into the town, she would think to herself ; but just to see the maids in the streets, and the pedlars in the market-place, and the cakes and sweetmeats and honey-jars in the shops, and strangers passing to and fro, and the sunshine in the high gables, and the talking and the singing and the bargaining and the dancing—the horses, the travellers, the bells, the starshine.

Above all, it made her heart ache to think her father should have so little faith in her duty and love for him that he would not consent to let her wander a snail's journey out of his sight. When, supper over, she leaned over his great chair as he sat there in his crimson—his black hair dangling on his shoulders, his beard hunched up on his breast—to kiss him Good-night, this thought would be in her eyes even if not on the tip of her tongue. And at such times he himself—as if he knew in his heart what he would never dare to confess—invariably shut down his eyelids or looked the other way.

Now servants sometimes have long tongues, and gossip flits from place to place like seeds of thistle-down. Simply because Myfanwy was never seen abroad, the fame of her beauty had long since spread through all the countryside. Minstrels sang of it, and had even carried their ballads to countries and kingdoms and principalities far beyond all Wales.

Indeed, however secret and silent men may be concerning rare beauty and goodness, somehow news of it sows itself over the wide world. A saint may sit in his cave or his cell, scarcely ever seen by mortal eye, quiet as sunshine in a dingle of the woods or seabirds in the hollows of the Atlantic, doing his deeds of pity and loving-kindness, and praying his silent prayers. And he may live to be a withered-up, hollow-cheeked old man with a long white beard, and die, and his body be shut up in a tomb. But nevertheless, little by little, the fame of his charity, and of the miracles of his compassion will spread abroad, and at last you may even chance on his image in a shrine thousands of leagues distant from the hermitage where he lived and died, and centuries after he has gone on his way.

So it was with the loveliness and gentleness of Myfanwy. That is why, when the Lord of Eggleyseg himself rode through the streets of the neighbouring town, he perceived out of the corner of his eye strangers in outlandish disguise whom he suspected at once must be princes and noblemen from foreign climes come thither even if merely to set eyes on his daughter. That is why the streets were so full of music and singing that of a summer evening you could scarcely hear the roar of its cataracts. That is why its townsfolk were entertained with tumblers and acrobats and fortune-tellers and soothsayers and tale-tellers the whole day long. Ever and again, indeed, grandees visited it *without* disguise. They lived for weeks there with their retinues of servants, their hawks and hounds and tasselled horses in some one of its high ancient houses. And their one sole hope and desire was to catch but a glimpse of the far-famed Myfanwy.

But as they came, so they went away. However they might plot and scheme to gain a footing in the castle—it was in vain. The portcullis was always down; there were watchmen perpetually on the look-out in its turrets; and the gates of the garden were festooned with heavy chains. There was not in its frowning ancient walls a single window less than twenty feet above the ground that was not thickly, rustily, and securely barred.

None the less, Myfanwy occasionally found herself in the garden alone. Occasionally she stole out if but for one breath of freedom, sweeter by far to those who pine for it than that of pink, or mint, or jasmine, or honeysuckle. And one such early evening in May, when her father—having nodded off to sleep in an arbour from sheer exhaustion of watching and listening and prying and peering—was snoring in an arbour or summer-house, she came to its western

gates, and having for a moment lifted the brim of
her immense hat to look at the sunset, she gazed
wistfully awhile through its bars out into the green
woods beyond.

The leafy boughs in the rosy light hung still as
pictures in a deep water. The skies resembled a
tent of silk blue as the sea. Deer were browsing
over the dark turf; and a wonderful charm and
carolling of birds was rising out of the dingles and
coverts.

But what Myfanwy had now fixed her dark eyes
on was none of these, but the figure of a young man
leaning there, erect but fast asleep, against the bole
of a gigantic beech-tree, not twenty paces distant
from the gate at which she stood. He must, she
judged, have been slumbering so for some little time.
His eyelids were dark with watching; his face pale.
Slim and gentle does were treading close beside him;
the birds had clean forgotten his presence; and a
squirrel was cracking the nut it held between its
clawed forepaws not a yard above his head.

Myfanwy had never before set eyes on human
stranger in this chace beyond the gates. Her father's
serving-men were ancients who had been in his
service in the castle years before she was born. This
young man looked, she imagined, like a woodman, or
a forester, or a swine-herd. She had read of them
in a handwritten book of fantastic tales which she
chanced on among her mother's belongings.

And as Myfanwy, finger on brim of her hat, stood
intently gazing, a voice in her heart told her that
whoever and whatever this stranger might be, he
was someone she had been waiting for, and even

dreaming about, ever since she was a child. All else
vanished out of her mind and her memory. It
was as if her eyes were intent on some such old story
itself, and one well-known to her. This unconscious
stranger was that story. Yet he himself—stiff as a
baulk of wood against the beech-trunk, as if indeed
he had been nailed to its bark—slumbered on.

So he might have continued to rest his weary
watchworn senses until she had vanished as she had
come. But at that moment the squirrel squatting
there on its haunches immediately above his head,
having suddenly espied Myfanwy beyond the bars
of the gate, in sheer astonishment let fall his nut,
and the young man—as if at a tiny knock on the
door of his mind—opened his eyes.

For Myfanwy it was like the opening of a door into
a house, strange and marvellous, or into Ali Baba's
cavern of precious stones. Her heart all but ceased
to beat. She went cold to her fingertips. And the
stranger too continued to gaze at Myfanwy—as if
out of an incredible dream.

And if could be expressed in words *all* that that
one quiet exchanged look told Myfanwy of things
strange that yet seemed more familiar to her than
the pebbles on the path and the thorns on the rose-
bushes and the notes of the birds in the air and the
first few drops of dew that were falling from the
heavens, then it would take a book ten times as long
as this in which to print it.

But even as she gazed Myfanwy suddenly remembered her father. She sighed ; her fingers let fall
the wide brim of her hat ; she turned away. And
oddly enough, by reason of this immense ridiculous

hat, her father who but a few moments before had awakened in his arbour and was now hastening along the path of the rosery in pursuit of her, caught not a single glimpse of the stranger under the beech-tree. Indeed, before the squirrel could scamper off into hiding, the young man had himself whisped round the trunk of the tree out of sight like a serpent into the grass.

In nothing except in this, however, did he resemble a serpent. For that very evening at supper her father told Myfanwy that yet another letter had been delivered at the castle, from some accursed Nick Nobody, asking permission to lay before him his suit for her hand. His rage was beyond words. He spilt his wine and crumbled his bread—his face a storm of darkness ; his eyes like smouldering coals.

Myfanwy sat pale and trembling. Hitherto, such epistles, though even from Princes of renowned estate and of realms even of the Orient, had carried less meaning to her heart than the cuckooing of a cuckoo, or the whispering of the wind in a tree. Indeed, the cuckoo of those Welsh mountains and the wind from over their seas were voices of a language which, though secret, was yet not wholly incommunicable. Not so these pompous declarations. Myfanwy would laugh at them—as though at the clumsy gambollings of a bear. She would touch her father's hand, and smile into his face, to assure him they had no meaning, that she was safe as safe can be.

But this letter—not for a single moment had the face of the young stranger been out of her mind. Her one sole longing and despair was the wonder whether she would ever in this world look upon him again.   She sat like stone.

' Ay, ay, my dear,' said her father at last, laying his thick, square hand on hers as she sat beside him in her high-backed velvet chair—' Ay, ay, my gentle one.   It shows us yet again how full the world is of insolence and adventurers.   This is a *cave*, a warning, an *alarum*, my dear—maledictions on his bones! We must be ten times more cautious ; we must be wary ; we must be lynx and fox and Argus—all eyes!   And remember, my all, my precious one, remember this, that while I your father live, no harm, no ill can approach or touch you.   Believe only in my love, beloved, and all is well with us.'

Her cold lips refused to speak.   Myfanwy could find no words with which to answer him.   With face averted she sat in a woeful day-dream, clutching her father's thumb, and only vaguely listening to his transports of fury and affection, revenge and adoration.   For her mind and heart now welled over with such a medley of thoughts and hopes and fears and sorrows that she could find no other way but this dumb clutch of expressing that she loved her father too.

At length, his rage not one whit abated, he rose from his chair, and having torn the insolent letter into thirty-two tiny pieces he flung them into the huge log fire burning in the stone chimney.   ' Let me but lay a finger on the shameless popinjay,' he muttered to himself ; ' I'll—I'll cut his tongue out ! '

Now the first thing Myfanwy did when chance offered was to hasten off towards the Western Gate if only to warn the stranger of her father's rage and menaces, and bid him go hide himself away and never never come back.

But when once more she approached its bars the deer were still grazing in the forest, the squirrel was nibbling another nut, the beech had unfolded yet a few more of its needle-pointed leaves into the calm evening light ; but of the stranger, not a sign. Where he had stood was now only the assurance that he was indeed gone for ever. And Myfanwy turned from the quiet scene of the forest, its sunlight faded, all its beauty made forlorn. Try as she might in the days that followed to keep her mind and her thoughts fixed on her needle and her silks, her lute and her psalter, she could see nothing else but that long look of his.

And now indeed she began to pine and languish in body a little, haunted by the fear that maybe the stranger had met with disaster. And simply because her father loved her so jealously, he knew at once what worm was in her mind, and he never ceased to watch and spy upon her, and to follow her every movement.

Now Myfanwy's bed-chamber was in the Southern tower of this lord's castle, beneath which a road from the town to the Eastward wound round towards the forests and distant mountains. And it being set so high above the ground beneath there was no need of bars to its windows. While then from these window slits Myfanwy could see little more than the tops of the wayfarers' heads on the turf below, they were wide and lofty enough to let the setting sun in its due hour pour in its beams upon her walls and pictures and coloured Arabian bed. But the stone walls being so thick, in order to see out of her chamber at all, she must needs lie along a little on the cold inward sill, and peer out over the wide verdant countryside as if through the port-hole of a ship.

And one evening, as Myfanwy sat sewing a seam— and singing the while a soft tune to herself, if only to keep her thoughts from pining—she heard the murmur of many voices. And, though at first she knew not why, her heart for an instant or two stopped beating. Laying her slip of linen down, she rose, stole over the mats on the flagstones, and gently pushing her narrow shoulders onwards, peeped out and down at last through the window to look at the world below. And this was what she saw. In an old velvet cloak, his black hair dangling low upon his shoulders, she saw in the evening light beneath her window a juggler standing, and in a circle round and about him was gathered a throng of gaping country-folk and idlers and children, some of whom must even have followed him out of the town. And they were lost one and all in wonder at his tricks.

Myfanwy herself indeed could not have imagined such skill could be, and so engrossed did she become in watching him that she did not catch the whisper of a long-drawn secret sigh at her key-hole; nor did she hear her father as he turned away on tip-toe to descend the staircase again into the room below.

Indeed one swift glance from Myfanwy's no longer sorrowful eyes had pierced the disguise—wig, cloak, hat, and hose—of the juggler. And as she watched him she all but laughed aloud. Who would have imagined that the young stranger, whom she had

seen for the first time leaning dumb, blind, and fast
asleep against the trunk of a beech-tree could be
possessed of such courage and craft and cunning
as this !

His head was at the moment surrounded by a
halo of glittering steel—so fast the daggers with
which he was juggling whisked on from hand to hand.
And suddenly the throng around him broke into a
roar, for in glancing up and aside he had missed a
dagger. It was falling—falling : but no, in a flash
he had twisted back the sole of his shoe, and the
point had stuck quivering into his heel while he
continued to whirl its companions into the golden
air.

In that instant, however, his upward glance had
detected the one thing in the world he had come
out in hope to see—Myfanwy. He flung his daggers
aside and fetched out of his travelling box a net-ful
of coloured balls. Holloing out a few strange
foreign words to the people he straightway began
to juggle with these. Higher and higher the seven
of them soared into the mellow air, but one of the
colour of gold soared on ever higher and higher than
any. So high, indeed, that at last the people could
watch it no longer because of the dazzle of the
setting sun in their eyes. Presently, indeed, it
swooped so loftily into the air that Myfanwy need
but thrust out her hand to catch it as it paused for
a breath of an instant before falling, and hung within
reach of her lichenous stone window-sill.

And even as she watched, enthralled, a whispering
voice within her cried ' Take it ! ' She breathed a
deep breath, shut her eyes, paused, and the next

instant she had stretched out her hand into the air.
The ball was hers.

Once more she peeped down and over, and once
more the juggler was at his tricks. This time with
what appeared to be a medley of all kinds and
varieties of fruits : pomegranates, quinces, citrons,
lemons, and others as outlandish, and soaring high
above them, what looked to be an English apple.
Once again the whisperer in Myfanwy's mind cried
'Take it!' And she put out her hand and took
the apple too.

Yet again she peeped and peered over, and this
time it appeared that the juggler was flinging
serpents into the air, for they writhed and looped
and coiled around him as they whirled whiffling
on from hand to hand. There was a hissing, too,
and the people drew back a little, and a few of the
timider children ran off to the other side of the highroad. And now, yet again, one of the serpents was
soaring higher and higher above the rest. And
Myfanwy could see from her coign of vantage that
it was no live serpent but a strand of silken rope.
And yet again and for the third time the whisperer
whispered, 'Take it!' And Myfanwy put out her
hand and took it.

And it happening that a little cloud was straying
across the sun at that moment, the throng below
had actually seen the highestmost of the serpents
thus mysteriously vanish and they cried out as if
with one voice, 'Gone!' 'Vanished!' 'Vanished!'
'Gone!' 'Magician, magician!' And the coins
that came dancing into the juggler's tambourine
in the minute that followed were enough to make

him for that one minute the richest man in the
world.

And now the juggler was solemnly doffing his hat
to the people. He gathered his cloak around him
more closely, put away his daggers, his balls, his
fruits, his serpents, and all that was his, into a long
green narrow box. Then he hoisted its strap over his
shoulder, and doffing his cap once more, he clasped
his tambourine under his elbow and seizing his staff,
turned straight from the castle tower towards the
hazy sun-bathed mountains. And, it beginning to
be towards nightfall, the throng of people soon dis-
persed and melted away ; the maids and scullions,
wooed out by this spectacle from the castle, returned
to their work ; and the children ran off home to tell
their mothers of these marvels and to mimic the
juggler's tricks as they gobbled up their supper-
crusts and were packed off to bed.

In the stillness that followed after the juggler's
departure, Myfanwy found herself kneeling in her
chamber amid the still golden twilight beside a
wooden chair, her hands folded in her lap and her
dark eyes fixed in wonderment and anxiety on the
ball, and the apple and the rope ; while in another
such narrow stone chamber only ten or more stone
steps beneath, her father was crouching at his window
gnawing his beard, and seeing in his imagination
these strange gifts from the air almost as clearly as
Myfanwy could see them with her naked eye.

For though the sun had been as much a dazzle
to himself as to the common people in the highway,
he had kept them fastened on the juggler's trickeries
none the less, and had counted every coloured ball

and every fruit and every serpent as they rose and
fell in their rhythmical maze-like network of circlings
in the air. And when each marvellous piece of
juggling in turn was over, he knew that in the first
place a golden ball was missing, and that in the
second place a fruit like an English apple was missing,
and that in the third place a silken cord with a
buckle-hook to it like the head of a serpent had
been flung into the air but had never come down to
earth again. And at the cries and the laughter and
the applause of the roaring common people and
children beneath his walls, tears of rage and despair
had burst from his eyes. Myfanwy was deceiving
him. His dreaded hour was come.

But there again he was wrong. The truth is, his
eyes were so green with jealousy and his heart so
black with rage that his wits had become almost
useless. Not only his wits either, but his courtesy
and his spirit ; for the next moment he was actually
creeping up again like a thief from stair to stair, and
presently had fallen once more on to his knees outside
his beloved Myfanwy's chamber door and had fixed
on her one of those green dark eyes of his through
its immense gaping pin-hole. And there he saw a
strange sight indeed.

The evening being now well advanced, and the
light of the afterglow too feeble to make more than
a glimmer through her narrow stone window-slits,
Myfanwy had lit with her tinder box (for of all
things she loved light), no less than seven wax
candles on a seven-branched candlestick. This
she had stood on a table beside a high narrow mirror.
And at the moment when the Baron fixed his eye

to the pin-hole, she was standing, a little astoop, the apple in her hand, looking first at it, and then into the glass at the bright-lit reflected picture of herself holding the apple in her hand.

So now there were two Myfanwy's to be seen— herself and her image in the glass. And which was the lovelier not even the juggler could have told. And the cold miserable lord at the door-crack could all but hear the words she was silently repeating to herself as she gazed at the reflected apple : ' Shall I, shan't I ?   Shall I, shan't I ? '   And then suddenly —and he dared not stir or cry out—she had raised the fruit to her lips and had nibled its rind.

What happened then he could not tell, for the *sovran* part of what happened was deep in Myfanwy herself.   The sharp juice of the fruit seemed to dart about in her veins like flashing fishes in her father's crystal fountains and water-conduits.   It was as if happiness had begun gently to fall out of the skies around her like dazzling flakes of snow.   They rested on her hair, on her shoulders, on her hands, all over her.   And yet not snow, for there was no coldness, but a scent as it were of shadowed woods at noonday, or of a garden when a shower has fallen.   Even her bright eyes grew brighter ; a radiance lit her cheek ; her lips parted in a smile.

And it is quite certain if Myfanwy had been the Princess of Anywhere-in-the-World-at-All, she would then and there—like Narcissus stooping over his lilied water-pool—have fallen head over ears in love with herself !   ' Wonder of wonders ! ' cried she in the quiet ; ' but if this is what a mere nibble of my brave juggler's apple can do, then it were wiser indeed to nibble no more.' So she laid the apple down.

The Baron gloated on through the pin-hole—watching her as she stood transfixed like some lovely flower growing in the inmost silent solitude of a forest and blossoming before his very eyes.

And then, as if at a sudden thought, Myfanwy turned and took up the golden ball, which—as she had suspected and now discovered—was no ball, but a small orb-shaped box of rare inlaid woods, covered with golden thread. At touch of the tiny spring that showed itself in the midst, its lid at once sprang open, and Myfanwy put in finger and thumb and drew out into the crystal light a silken veil—but of a gossamer silk so finely spun that when its exquisite meshes had wreathed themselves downward to the floor the veil in appearance was nought but a silvery grey mist in the candle-light.

It filmed down from her fingers to the flagstones beneath, well nigh as light as the air in which it floated. Marvellous that what would easily cover her head to heel could have been packed into so close a room as that two-inch ball. She gazed in admiration of this exquisite fingerwork. Then, with a flick of her thumb, she had cast its cloudlike folds over her shoulders.

And lo!—as the jealous lord gloated on—of a sudden there was nothing to be seen where Myfanwy had stood but seven candles burning in their stick, and seven more in the mirror. She had vanished.

She was not gone very far, however. For presently he heard—as if out of nowhere—a low chuckling childlike peal of laughter which willy-nilly had

broken from her lips at seeing that this Veil of
Invisibility had blanked her very looking-glass.
She gazed on into the empty glass, lost in wonder.
Nothing at all of her whatsoever was now reflected
there !—not the tip of her nose, not a thumb, not
so much as a button or a silver tag. Myfanwy had
vanished ; and yet, as she well knew, here she truly
was in her body and no other though tented in
beneath the folds of the veil, as happy as flocks on
April hills, or mermaids in the deep blue sea.   It was
a magic thing indeed, to be there and yet not there ;
to be herself and yet transparent as water.

Moreover, besides all this, her thoughts were at
the same time flitting about like quick and nimble
birds in her mind.   This veil, too, was the gift of
the juggler ; her young sleeping stranger of the
beech-tree in a strange disguise.   And she could
guess in her heart what use he intended her to make
of it, even though at thought of it that heart
misgave her.   A moment after, and as swiftly as she
had gone, she had come back again—the veil in her
fingers. Laughing softly to herself she folded and
refolded it and replaced it in its narrow box.   Then
turning, she took up from the chair the silken cord,
and as if in idle fancy twined it twice about her
slender neck.   And it seemed the cord took life into
itself, for lo, showing there in the mirror, calm now
as a statue of coloured ivory, stood Myfanwy ; and
couched over her left temple the swaying head of the
Serpent of Wisdom, whispering in her ear.

Owen ap Gwythock could watch no more.   Groping his way with trembling fingers through the thick
gloom of the staircase he crept down to the Banquet-

ing Hall where already his Chief Steward awaited
his coming to announce that supper was prepared.

To think that his Lovely One, his pearl of price,
his gentle innocent, his Myfanwy—the one thing on
earth he treasured most, and renowned for her
gentleness and beauty in all countries of the world,
had even for an instant forgotten their loves, forgotten her service and duty, was in danger of leaving
and forsaking him for ever !   In his rage and despair
tears rolled down his dark cheeks as he ground his
teeth together, thinking of the crafty enemy that
was decoying her away.

Worse still ; he knew in his mind's mind that in
certain things in this world even the most powerful
are powerless.   He knew that against true love all
resistance, all craft, all cunning at last prove of no
avail.   But in this grief and despair the bitterest
of all the thoughts that were now gnawing in his
brain was the thought that Myfanwy should be
cheating and deceiving him, wantonly beguiling him ;
keeping things secret that should at once be told !

A black and dismal mind was his indeed.   To
distrust one so lovely !—*that* might be forgiven
him.   But to creep about in pursuit of her like a
weasel ; to spy on her like a spy ; to believe her
guilty before she could prove her innocence !   Could
that be forgiven ?   And even at this very moment
the avenger was at his heels.

For here was Myfanwy herself. Lovely as a
convolvulus wreathing a withered stake, she was
looking in at him from the doorpost, searching his
face.   For an instant she shut her eyes as if to breathe
a prayer, then she advanced into the room, and,

with her own hand, lay before him on the oak table
beside his silver platter, first the nibbled apple, next
the golden ball, and last the silken cord. And
looking at him with all her usual love in her eyes and
in her voice, she told him how these things had
chanced into her hands, and whence they had come.

Her father listened ; but durst not raise his eyes
from his plate. The scowl on his low forehead grew
blacker and blacker ; even his beard seemed to
bristle. But he heard her in silence to the end.

' So you see, dear father,' she was saying, ' how
can I but be grateful and with all my heart to one
who takes so much thought for me ? And if you
had seen the kindness and courtesy of his looks, even
you yourself could not be angry. There never was,
as you well know, anybody else in the whole wide
world whom I wished to speak to but to you. And
now there is none other than you except this stranger.
I know nothing but that. Can you suppose indeed
he meant these marvellous gifts for me ? And why
for me and no other, father dear ? And what would
you counsel me to do with them ? '

Owen ap Gwythock stooped his head lower. Even
the sight of his eyes had dimmed. The torches
faintly crackled in their sconces, the candles on the
table burned unfalteringly on.

He turned his cheek aside at last like a snarling
dog, ' My dear,' he said, ' I have lived long enough
in this world to know the perils that beset the young
and fair. I grant you that this low mountebank
must be a creature of infinite cunning. I grant
you that his tricks, if harmless, would be worth a
charitable groat. If, that is, he were only what he

seems to be. But that is not so. For this most
deadly stranger is a Deceiver and a Cheat. His lair,
as I guess well, is in the cruel and mysterious East,
and his one desire and stratagem is to snare you into
his company. Once within reach of his claws, his
infamous slaves will seize on you and bear you away
to some evil felucca moored in the river. It seems,
beloved, that your gentle charms are being whispered
of in this wicked world. Even the beauty of the
gentlest of flowers may be sullied by idle tongues.
But once securely in the hands of this nefarious
mountebank, he will put off to Barbary, perchance, or
to the horrid regions of the Turk, perchance, there
to set you up in the scorching market-place and to
sell you for a slave. My child, the danger, the peril
is gross and imminent. Dismiss at once this evil
wretch from your mind and let his vile and dangerous
devices be flung into the fire. The apple is pure
delusion ; the veil which you describe is a mere toy ;
and the cord is a device of the devil.'

Myfanwy looked at her father stooping there with
sorrow in her eyes, in spite of the gladness sparkling
and dancing in her heart of hearts. Why, if all that
he was saying he deemed true—why could he not
lift his eyes and meet her face to face ?

' Well then, that being so, dear father,' she said
softly at last, ' and you knowing ten thousand times
more of God's world than I have ever had opportunity of knowing, whatever my desire, I must ask
you but this one small thing. Will you promise me
not to have these pretty baubles destroyed at once,
before, I mean, you have thought once more of *me* ?
If I had deceived you, then indeed I should be

grieved beyond endurance. But try as I may to darken my thoughts of him, the light slips in, and I see in my very heart that this stranger cannot by any possibility of nature or heaven be all that you tell me of him. I have a voice at times that whispers me yes or no : and I obey. And of him it has said only yes. But I am young, and the walls of this great house are narrow, and you, dear father, as you have told me always, are wise. Do but then invite this young man into your presence ! Question him, test him, gaze on him, hearken to him. And that being done, you will believe in him as I do. As I know I am happy I know he is honest. It would afflict me beyond all telling to swerve by a hair's-breadth from my dear obedience to you. But, alas, if I never see him again, I shall wither up and die. And that—would it not——' she added smilingly—' that would be a worse disobedience yet ? If you love me, then, as from my first hour in the world I *know* you have loved me, and I have loved you, I pray you think of me with grace and kindness —and in compassion too.'

And with that, not attempting to brush away the tears that had sprung into her eyes, and leaving the juggler's three gifts amid the flowers and fruit of the long table before him, Myfanwy hastened out of the room and returned to her chamber, leaving her father alone.

For a while her words lay like a cold refreshing dew on the dark weeds in his mind. For a while he pondered them, even ; while his own gross fables appeared in all their ugly falseness.

But alas for himself and his pride and stubbornness, these gentler ruminations soon passed away. At thought once more of the juggler—of whom his spies had long since brought him far other tidings than he had expressed—rage, hatred and envy again boiled up in him, and drowned everything else. He forgot his courtesy, his love for Myfawny, his desire even to keep her love for him. Instead, on and on he sipped and sipped and sate fuming and plotting and scheming with but one notion in his head—by hook or by crook to defeat this juggler and so murder the love of his innocent Myfanwy.

' Lo, now,' whispered at last a small shrill voice within him, ' Lo, now, if thou taste of the magic apple, may it not be that it will give thee courage and skill to contend against him, and so bring all his hopes to ruin ? Remember what a marvel but one merest nibble of the outer rind of it wrought in thy Myfanwy ! '

And the foolish creature listened heedfully to this serpent voice, not realising that the sole virtue of the apple was that of making any human who tasted it more like himself than ever. He sat there—his fist over his mouth—staring intently at the harmless-looking fruit. Then he tiptoed like a humpback across the room and listened at the entry. Then having poured out, and drained at a draught, yet another cup of wine, he cautiously picked up the apple by its stalk between finger and ringed thumb and once more squinted close and steadily at its red and green, and at the very spot where Myfanwy's small teeth had rasped away the skin.

It is in a *moment* that cities fall in earthquake, stars collide in the wastes of space, and men choose between good and evil. For suddenly—his mind made up, his face all turned a reddish purple—this foolish lord lifted the apple to his mouth and, stalk to dried blossom, bit it clean in half. And he munched and he munched and he munched.

He had chawed for but a few moments, however, when a dreadful and continuous change and transformation began to appear upon him. It seemed to him that his whole body and frame was being kneaded and twisted and wrung in much the same fashion as dough being made into bread, or clay in a modeller's fingers. Not knowing what these aches and stabbings and wrenchings meant, he had dropped as if by instinct upon his hands and knees, and thus stood munching, while gazing blankly and blindly, lost in some inward horror, into the great fire on the hearth.

And meanwhile, though he knew it not in full, there had been sprouting upon him grey coarse hairs—a full thick coat and hide of them—in abundance. There had come a tail to him with a tassel that hung down; long hairy ears had jutted out upon his temples; the purple face turned grey, lengthening as it did so until it was at least full eighteen inches long, with a great jaw-full of large teeth. Hoofs for his hands, hoofs where his feet used to be, and behold!— standing there in his own banqueting hall—this poor deluded Owen ap Gwythock, Lord of Eggleyseg, transformed into an Ass!

For minutes together the dazed creature stood in utter dismay—the self within unable to realise the change that had come over its outer shape. But, happening to stretch his shaggy and unfamiliar neck

a little outward, he perceived his own image in a
scoured and polished suit of armour that stood on
one side of the great chimney. He shook his head,
the ass's head replied. He shook himself, the long
ears flapped together like a wood pigeon's wings.
He lifted his hand—a hoof clawed at nowhere !

At this the poor creature's very flesh seemed to
creep upon his bones as he turned in horror and
dismay in search of an escape from the fate that had
overtaken him. That Ass *he* ? he *himself* ? His
poor wits in vain endeavoured to remain calm and
cool. A panic of fear all but swept him away. And
at this moment his full, lustrous, long-lashed,
asinine eye fell by chance upon the golden ball
lying ajar on the table beside his wine-cup—the
Veil of Invisibility glinting like money-spider's web
from within.

Now no Ass is quite such a donkey as he looks.
And this Owen ap Gwythock, though now completely shut up in this uncouth hairy body was in his
mind no more (though as much) of a donkey than
he had ever been. His one thought, then, was to
conceal his dreadful condition from any servant
that might at any moment come that way, while he
himself could seek out a quiet secluded corner in the
dark wherein to consider how to rid himself of his
ass's frame and to regain his own usual shape. And
there lay the Veil ! What thing sweeter could there
be than to defeat the juggler with his own devices.

Seizing the veil with his huge front teeth, he jerked
it out of the ball and flung it as best he could over
his shaggy shoulders. But alas, his donkey's muzzle
was far from being as deft as Myfanwy's delicate

fingers. The veil but half concealed him. Head, neck, and forelimbs were now vanished from view; but his hinder parts remained wholly unhidden; and a strange spectacle he now appeared. In vain he tugged; in vain he wriggled and wrenched; his hard hoofs thumping on the hollow flagstones beneath. Half of him stubbornly remained in this world and the other half out of sight.

At last, breathless and wearied out with these exertions, trembling and shuddering, and with not a vestige of sense left in his poor donkey's noddle, he wheeled himself about once more and caught up with his teeth from beneath the veil the silken cord. It was his last hope. But this having been woven of wisdom—it being indeed itself the Serpent of Wisdom in disguise—at touch of his teeth at once, converted itself into a strong hempen halter, and, before he could so much as rear out of the way to escape its noose or even bray for help, it had tethered him to a large steel hook in his own chimney-piece.

Bray he did, none the less: ' Hee-haw! Hee-haw!! Hee-ee-ee-ee Haw-aw-aw!!!' His prolonged, sea-saw, dismal lamentations shattered the silence. So harsh and hoarsely that the sound rose up through the echoing stone walls and even pierced into Myfanwy's own bedchamber, where she sat in the darkness at her window, looking out half in sorrow, half in unspeakable happiness, at the shining stars.

Filled with alarm at this dreadful summons, in an instant or two she had descended the winding stone steps and a strange scene met her eyes.

There, before her, in the full red light of the flaming brands in the hearth and the torches on the walls, stood the fore-legs, the neck, head, and ears of a fine, full-grown Ass, and a yard or so behind him his back-legs and dangling tail. And only vacancy in between! Poor Myfanwy—she could but wring her fair hands in grief and astonishment; for there could be no doubt in her mind of who it was in truth now stood before her—her own dear father. And on his face such a look of despair, entreaty, shame and stupefaction as never man has seen on ass's countenance before. At sight of her the creature tugged even more furiously at his halter, and shook his shaggy shoulders; but still in vain. His mouth opened and a voice beyond words to describe, brayed out upon the silence, these words: ' Oh Myfanwy, see into what a pass your sorceries and deceits have reduced me.'

' Oh, my dear father,' she cried in horror, ' speak no more, I beseech you—not one syllable—or we shall be discovered. Or if you utter a sound, let it be but in a whisper.'

She was at the creature's side in an instant, had flung her arms about his neck, and was whispering into his long hairy ear all the comfort and endearments and assurances that loving and tender heart could say. ' Listen, listen, dear father,' she was entreating him, ' I see indeed that you have been meddling with the apple, and the ball, and the cord. And I do assure you, with all my heart and soul, that I am thinking of nothing else but how to help you in this calamity that has overtaken us. Have patience. Struggle no more. All will be well. But

T

oh, beloved, was it quite just to me to speak of my
deceits ? '

Her bright eyes melted with compassion as she
looked upon one whom she had loved ever since she
could remember (though he had not always been of
an unfaltering kindness), so dismally transmogrified.

' How can you hesitate, ungrateful creature ? ' the
see-saw voice once more broke out. ' Relieve me
of this awful shape, or I shall be strangled on my own
hearthstone in this pestilent halter.'

But now, alas, footsteps were sounding outside
the door. Without an instant's hesitation Myfanwy
drew the delicate veil completely over the trembling
creature's head and hinder-quarters and thus
altogether concealed him from view. So—though
it was not an instant too soon—when the Lord of
Eggleyseg's Chief Steward appeared in the doorway
nothing whatever was changed within, except that
his master no longer sat in his customary chair,
Myfanwy stood solitary at the table, and a mysterious
cord was stretched out between her hand and the
hook in the chimney-piece.

' My father,' said Myfanwy, ' has withdrawn for
a while. He is indisposed, and bids me tell you that
not even a whisper must disturb his rest. Have a
hot posset prepared at once, and see that the room
beneath is left vacant.'

The moment the Steward had gone to do her
bidding Myfanwy turned at once to her father, and
lifting the veil, whispered into the long hairy ear
again that he must be of good cheer. ' For you see,
dear father, the only thing now to be done is that
we set out together at once in search of the juggler

who, meaning no unkindness, presented me with these strange gifts. He alone can and will, I am assured, restore you to your own dear natural shape. So I pray you to be utterly silent—not a word, not a murmur—while I lead you gently forth into the forest. Once there I have no doubt I shall be able to find our way to where he is. Indeed he may be already expectant of my coming.'

Stubborn and foolish though the Baron might be, he realised, even in his present shape, that this was his only wisdom. Whereupon, withdrawing the end of the bridle from the hook to which it was tethered, Myfanwy softly led the now invisible creature to the door, and so, gently onward down the winding stone staircase, on the stones of which his shambling hoofs sounded like the hollow beating of a drum.

The vast room beneath was already deserted by its usual occupants, and without more ado the two of them, father and daughter, were soon abroad in the faint moonlight that now by good fortune bathed the narrow bridle-path that led into the forest.

Never before in all her years on earth had Myfanwy strayed beyond the Castle walls ; never before had she stood lost in wonder beneath the dark emptiness of the starry skies. She breathed in the sweet fresh night air, her heart blossoming within her like an evening primrose, refusing to be afraid. For she knew well that the safety of them both—this poor quaking animal's and her own—depended now solely on her own courage and resource, and that to be afraid would almost certainly lead them only from one disaster into another.

Simply, however, because a mere ownerless Ass

wandering by itself in the moonlit gloom of the forest would be a sight less strange than that of a solitary damsel like herself, she once more drew down her father's ear to her lips and whispered into it, explaining to him that she herself must now be veiled and that if he would forgive her such boldness —for after all, he had frequently carried her in his arms when she was a child—she would mount upon his back and in this way they would together make better progress on their journey.

Her father dared not take offence at her words, whatever his secret feelings might be. ' So long as you hasten, my child,' he gruffed out in the hush, striving in vain to keep his tones no louder than a human whisper, ' I will forgive you all.' In a moment then there might be seen jogging along the bridle-path, now in moonlight, now in shadow, a sleek and handsome Ass, a halter over its nose, making no stay to browse the dewy grass at the wayside, but apparently obeying its own whim as it wandered steadily onward.

Now it chanced that night there was a wild band of mountain robbers encamped within the forest. And when of a sudden this strange and pompous animal unwittingly turned out of a thicket into the light of their camp fire, and raised its eyes like glowing balls of emerald to gaze in horror at its flames, they lifted their voices together in an uproarious peal of laughter. And one of them at once started up from where he lay in the bracken, to seize the creature's halter and so make it his prize.

Their merriment, however, was quickly changed into dismay when the robbers saw the strange creature being guided, as was evident, by an invisible and mysterious hand. He turned this way, he turned that, with an intelligence that was clearly not his own and not natural to his kind, and so eluded every effort made by his enemy to get a hold on his halter, his teeth and eyeballs gleaming in the flame.

At this awe and astonishment fell upon these outlaws. Assuredly sorcery alone could account for such ungainly and unasslike antics and manœuvres. Assuredly some divine will must have the beast in keeping, and to meddle with it further might only prove their own undoing.

Fortunate indeed was it that Myfanwy's right foot, which by a mischance remained uncovered by the veil, chanced to be on the side of the animal away from the beams of the camp fire. For certainly had these malefactors seen the precious stones blazing in its buckle their superstitions would have melted away like morning mist, their fears have given place to cupidity, and they would speedily have made the Ass their own and held its rider to an incalculable ransom.

Before, however, the moon had glided more than a soundless pace or two on her night journey, Myfanwy and her incomparable Ass were safely out of sight : and the robbers had returned to their carousals. What impulse bade her turn first this way, then that, in the wandering and labyrinthine glades and spaces of the forest, she could not tell. But even though her father—not daring to raise his voice in the deep silence—ever and again stubbornly tugged upon his halter in the belief that the travellers

had taken a wrong turning and were irrevocably
lost, Myfanwy kept steadily on her way.

With a touch of her heel or a gentle persuasive pat
of her hand on his hairy neck she did her best to
reassure and to soothe him. ' Only trust in me, dear
father : I vow all will be well.'

Yet she was haunted with misgivings. So that
when at last a twinkling light, sprinkling its beams
between the boughs, showed in the forest, it refreshed
her heart beyond words to tell. She was reaching
her journey's end. It was as if a voice in the secrecy
of her heart had murmured, ' Hst ! He draws
near ! '

There and then she dismounted from off her
father's hairy back and once more communed with
him through that long twitching ear. ' Remain here
in patience awhile, dear father,' she besought him,
' without straying by a hair's-breadth from where
you are ; for everything tells me our Stranger is not
far distant now, and no human being on earth, no
living creature, even, must see you in this sad and
unseemly disguise. I will hasten on to assure myself
that the light which I perceive beaming through the
thicket yonder is his, and no other's. Meanwhile—
and this veil shall go with me in case of misadventure
—meanwhile do you remain quietly beneath this
spreading beech-tree, nor even stir unless you are
over-wearied after our long night journey and you
should feel inclined to rest awhile on the softer turf
in the shadow there under that bush of fragrant
roses, or to refresh yourself at the brook whose
brawling I hear welling up from that dingle in the
hollow. In that case, return here, I pray you ;

contain yourself in patience, and be your tongue as
dumb as a stone. For though you may *design* to
speak softly, dearest father, that long sleek throat
and those great handsome teeth will not admit
of it.'

And her father, as if not even the thick hairy hide
he wore could endure his troubles longer, opened his
mouth as if to groan aloud. But restraining himself,
he but sighed, while an owl out of the quiet breathed
its soft call as though in mocking response. For
having passed the last hour in a profound and
afflicted reverie, this poor Ass had now regained in
part his natural human sense and sagacity. But
pitiful was the eye, however asinine the grin, which
he now bestowed as if in promise on Myfanwy who,
with veil held delicately in her fingers stood there,
lovely as snow, beside him in the moonlight.

And whether it was because of her grief for his
own condition or because of the expectancy in her
face at the thought of her meeting with the Stranger,
or because maybe the Ass feared in his despair and
dejection that he might never see her again, he could
not tell ; but true it was that she had never appeared
in a guise so brave and gay and passionate and
tender. It might indeed be a youthful divinity gently
treading the green sward beside this uncouth beast
in the chequered light and shadow of that unearthly
moonshine.

Having thus assured herself that all would be well
until her return, Myfanwy kissed her father on his
flat hairy brow, and veil in hand withdrew softly
in the direction of the twinkling light.

Alas, though the Baron thirsted indeed for the chill

dark waters whose song rose in the air from the
hollow beneath, he could not contain himself in her
absence, but unmindful of his mute promise followed
after his daughter at a distance as she made her
way to the light, his hoofs scarce sounding in the
turf. Having come near, by peering through the
dense bushes that encircled the juggler's nocturnal
retreat in the forest, he could see and hear all that
passed.

As soon as Myfanwy had made sure that this
stranger sitting by his glowing watch-fire was indeed
the juggler and no man else—and one strange leap
of her heart assured her of this even before her eyes
could carry their message—she veiled herself once
more, and so, all her loveliness made thus invisible, she drew stealthily near and a little behind
him, as he crouched over the embers. Then pausing, she called gently and in a still low voice, ' I
beseech you, stranger, to take pity on one in great
distress.'

The juggler lifted his dreaming face, all ruddied
with the light of his fire, and peered cautiously but
in happy astonishment all around him.

' I beseech you, stranger,' cried again the voice
from the unseen, ' to take pity on one in great
distress.'

And at this it seemed to the juggler that now ice
was running through his veins and now fire. For he
knew well that this was the voice of one compared
with whom all else in the world to him was nought.
He knew also that she must be standing near,
though made utterly invisible to him by the veil of
his own enchantments.

'Draw near, traveller. Have no fear,' he cried
out softly into the darkness. 'All will be well. Tell
me only how I may help you.'

But Myfanwy drew not a hair's-breadth nearer.
Far from it. Instead, she flitted a little across the
air of the glade, and now her voice came to him from
up the wind towards the South, and fainter in the
distance.

'There is one with me,' she replied, 'who by an
evil stratagem has been transformed into the shape
of a beast, and that beast a poor patient ass. Tell
me this, sorcerer—how I may restore him to his
natural shape, and mine shall be an everlasting
gratitude. For it is my own father of whom I
speak.'

Her gentle voice faltered on the word as she longed
almost beyond bearing to reveal herself to this unknown one, trusting without doubt or misgiving
indeed that he would serve her faithfully in all she
asked of him.

'But *that*, gentle lady,' sang out the juggler, 'is
not within my power, unless he of whom you speak
draws near to show himself. Nor—though the voice
with which you speak to me is sweeter than the
strings of a harp twangling on the night air—nor
is it within my power to make promises to but a
bodiless sound only. For how am I to be assured
that the shape who utters the words I hear is not
some dangerous demon of the darkness who is bent
on mocking and deluding me, and who will bring
sorcery on myself?'

There was silence for a while in the glade, and then
'Nay, nay!' cried the juggler. 'Loveliest and

bravest of all that is, I need not see thy shape to know thee. Thou art that fair one, the lovely Myfanwy, and all that I am and have has ever been and ever shall be in thy service. Tell me, then, where is this poor Ass that was once thy noble father ? '

And at this, and at one and the same moment, Myfanwy, withdrawing the veil from her head and shoulders, disclosed her fair colt standing there in the faint rosy glow of the slumbering fire, and there broke also from the neighbouring thicket so dreadful and hideous a noise of rage and anguish—through the hoarse and unpractised throat of the eavesdropper nearby—that it might be supposed the clamour was not of one but of a chorus of demons—though it was merely our poor Ass complaining of his fate.

' Oh, sir,' sighed Myfanwy, ' my poor father, I fear, in his grief and anxiety has been listening to what has passed between us. See, here he comes.'

Galloping hoofs were indeed now audible as the Lord of Eggleyseg in ass's skin and shape drew near to wreak his vengeance on the young magician. But being at this moment in his stubborn rage and folly more ass than human, the glaring of the watch-fire dismayed his heavy wits, and he could do no else than paw with his fore-hoof, lifting his smooth nose with its gleaming teeth into the night air, snuffing his rage and defiance some twenty paces distant from the watch-fire.

The young magician, being of nature as courteous as he was bold, did not so much as turn his head to scan the angry shivering creature, but once more addressed Myfanwy. She stood bowed down a little, tears in her eyes in part for grief at her father's broken promise and the humiliation he had brought upon himself, in part for joy that their troubles would soon be over and that she was now in the very company of the stranger who unwittingly had been the cause of them all.

' Have no fear,' he said, ' the magic that changed the noble Baron your father into a creature more blest in its docility, patience, and humbleness than any other in the wide world, can as swiftly restore him to his natural shape.'

' Ah then, sir,' replied the maid, ' it is very certain that my father will wish to bear witness to your kindness with any small gift that is in our power. For, as he well knows, it was not by any design but his own that he ate of the little green apple of enchantment. I pray you, sir, moreover, to forgive me for first stealing that apple, and also the marvellous golden ball and also the silken cord from out of the air.'

The juggler turned and gazed strangely at Myfanwy. ' There is but one gift I desire in all this starry universe,' he answered. ' But I ask it not of *him*—for it is not of his giving. It is for your own forgiveness, lady, that I pine.'

' *I* forgive you ! ' she cried. ' Alas, my poor father ? '

But even as she spoke a faint smile was on her face, and her eyes wandered to the Ass standing a few paces beyond the margin of the glow cast by the watch-fire, snuffing the night air the while and shaking dismally the coarse grey mane behind his ears. For now that her father was so near his deliverance her young heart grew entirely happy again, and the future seemed as sweet with promise as a garden of roses in May.

Without further word the juggler drew from out of his pouch, as if he always carried about with him a little privy store of vegetables, a fine, tapering, ripe, red carrot.

' This, lady,' said he, ' is my only wizardry. I make no bargain. My love for you will never languish, even if I never yet again refresh my sleepless eyes with the vision of your loveliness in this solitary glade. Let your noble father the Lord of Eggleyseg draw near without distrust. There is but little difference, it might be imagined, between a wild apple and a carrot. But then, when all is said, there is little difference in the long sum between any living thing and another in this strange world. There are creatures in the world whose destiny it is in spite of their gentleness and humility and lowly duty and obedience to go upon four legs and to be in service of masters who deserve far less than they deserve, while there are men in high places of whom the reverse might truly be said. It is a mystery beyond my unravelling. But now all I ask is that you bid the ass whom you tell me is hearkening at the moment to all that passes between us to nibble of this humble but useful and wholesome root. It will instantly restore him to his proper shape. Meanwhile, if you bid, I will myself be gone.'

Without further speech between them, Myfanwy accepted the proffered carrot, and returned once more to the Ass.

' Dear father,' she cried softly, ' here is a root, raw and vulgar—a carrot ; yet nibble of it and you will

be at once restored, and will forget you were ever an
—as you are. For many days to come, I fear, you
will not wish to look upon the daughter that has been
the unfortunate cause of this night's woeful experience. There lives, as you are aware, in a little green
arbour of the forest yonder, a hermit. This young
magician has promised to place me in his care awhile
until all griefs are forgotten between us. You will
consent to this, dear father, will you not ? ' she
pleaded, guilefully keeping the while the tasteful
carrot well out of his outstretched nose's reach.

A prolonged prodigious bray resounded dreadfully
in the hollows of the far-spread forest's dells and
thickets. The Lord of Eggleyseg had spoken.

' Indeed, father,' smiled Myfanwy, ' I have never
before heard you say " Yes " so heartily. What
further speech is needed ? '

Whereupon the Ass, with more dispatch than
gratitude, munched up the carrot, and in a few
hours Owen ap Gwythock, once more restored to his
former, though hardly his more appropriate, shape,
returned in safety to his Castle. There for many
months he mourned his woeful solitude, but learned,
too, not only how true and faithful a daughter he
had used so ill, but the folly of a love that is fenced
about with mistrust and suspicion and is poisoned
with jealousy.

And when May was come again, a Prince, no longer
in the disguise of a wandering juggler, drew near
with his beloved Princess to the Lord of Eggleyseg's
ancient castle. And Owen ap Gwythock, a little
older but a far far wiser man, greeted them with such
rejoicings and entertainment, with such feastings

and dancing and minstrelsy and jubilations as are squandered only on beloved and dutiful sons-in-law and no less beloved and devoted daughters. In sober truth he would have been donkey unadulterated if he had done else.

ALICE'S GODMOTHER

THOUGH Alice sat steadily looking out of the small square pane of glass in the railway carriage, she was not really seeing the green undulating country through which the train was clattering on its way. While everything near—quickening hedges, grazing cattle, galloping calves, wood, farm and stony foaming brook—swept past far too swiftly for more than a darting glance; everything in the distance—hill, tree and spire—seemed to be stealthily wheeling forward as if to waylay the puffing engine and prevent it from reaching her journey's end.

' If only it would ! ' sighed Alice to herself, ' How much—much happier I should be ! ' Her blue eyes widened at the fancy. Then once more a frown of anxiety drew her fair eyebrows together ; but she said nothing. She sat on in her corner gently clasping her mother's hand and pondering in dismay on what might happen to her in the next few hours.

Alice and her mother prided themselves on being just ' two quiet people,' happy in each other's company, and very seldom going out or paying calls and visits. This particular visit that Alice was about to make when they reached the little country station

of Freshing, she was to make alone. It was this
that alarmed her. The invitation in that queer
scrabbling handwriting had been to herself only.
So though her mother was with her now, soon they
would be parting. And every now and again Alice
would give the hand she held in hers a gentle squeeze
of self-reassurance. It was the Good-bye—though
it would be only for a few hours—that she dreaded.

And yet their plans had all been talked over and
settled again and again. Alice must, of course, take
a fly from the station—whatever the expense. After
telling the cabman when she would need him again,
she would get into it and her mother would wait for
her in a room at the village Inn until she herself
returned in the early evening from her visit. Then
everything would be safely over. And to imagine the
joy of seeing all these fields and woods come racing
back the other way round almost made Alice ill.

It was absurd to be so nervous. Alice had told
herself that a hundred times. But it was no use.
The very thought of her great-great-great-great-
great-great-great-great-grandmother filled her mind
with a dreadful foreboding. If only she were a
little stronger-minded ; if only the old lady, who
was also her godmother too, had asked her mother
to come with her ; if only her heart would stop
beating so fast ; if only a wheel would come off the
engine !

But then, after all, Alice had never before so much
as seen this old old lady. Even now she could not
be quite certain she had the number of ' greats ' to
the ' grandmother ' quite right. Not even strong-
minded people, she supposed, are often suddenly

invited to tea with relatives aged three-hundred-and-forty-nine. And not only that either ; for this day—this very Saturday, was her godmother's birthday—her three-hundred-and-fiftieth !

Whenever Alice remembered this, a faint smile came into her face. At seventeen a birthday is a real ' event.' Life is galloping on. You are sprouting up like a beanstalk. Your hair is ' put up ' (or at least it was when Alice was a girl), your skirts ' come down,' and you're soon to ' come out.' In other words you are beginning to be really and truly grown-up. But three-hundred-and-fifty ! Surely by that time. . . . It must even be difficult to be certain you have the total right. Surely there can't be *any* kind of a change then. Surely not !

Still, Alice thought, it is perhaps the *name* of the number that counts. She herself had known what an odd shock it had been to slip into her teens, and could guess what the shivers would be like of the plunge into her twenties. Yet even if it were only the name of the number—why, at the end of three centuries you must begin to be getting accustomed to birthdays.

It was odd too that her godmother had never asked to see her before. Years ago she had sent her a squat parcel-gilt mug—a mug that her godmother herself used to drink her beer out of when she was a child of ten in Queen Elizabeth's reign. A little sheepskin, illuminated Prayer Book, too, that had once been given to her godmother by Charles the First, and a few delicious little old trinkets had come too. But receiving presents is not the same thing as actually meeting and talking with the mysterious giver of them. It is one thing to imagine the unknown ; another thing altogether to meet it face to face. What would her godmother look like ? What *could* she look like ? Alice hadn't the faintest notion. Old ladies of eighty and upwards are one thing ; but you can't just multiply 80 by 4 as if growing older were merely a sum in arithmetic.

Perhaps when you are very old indeed, Alice supposed, you have no wish left to sit for a portrait or to be photographed. It is a petrifying experience even when you are young. When you are as old as all that you may prefer to—well, to keep yourself *to* yourself. *She* would.

'Mamma dear,' she suddenly twisted round on her hard seat, her straight straw-coloured hair slipping over in one smooth ripple on her shoulder as she did so. 'Mamma dear, I can't think even now what I ought to do when I go into the room. Will there be anybody there, do you think ? Do I shake hands ? I suppose she won't kiss me ? I simply can't think what I ought to do. I shall just hate leaving you— being left, I mean.'

She stroked hard with her fingers the hand that was in her own, and as she gazed at her mother's face in this dreadful anxiety, she knew that the smile on it was just like a pretty blind over a window, and that her mother's self within was almost as much perturbed over this visit as she was herself.

'It's getting nearer, darling, at any rate, isn't it ? ' her mother whispered. And the fat old farmer in the opposite corner of the carriage emitted yet another grunt, for he was fast asleep. 'I think, you know,' her mother continued softly, 'I should first

enquire of the maid if she is quite well—your godmother, I mean, my dear. Say, " Do you think
Miss Cheyney is well enough to see me ? " She will
know what you ought to do. I am not even certain
whether the poor old lady can speak ; though her
handwriting is simply marvellous.'

' But Mummie darling, how are we to know that
there *will* be a maid ? Didn't they, in godmother's
time, always have "retainers"? Supposing there are
rows of them in the hall ! And when ought I to get
up to say Good-bye ? If she is deaf and blind *and*
dumb I really don't know what I *shall* do ! '

A dozen questions at least like this had been asked
and answered during the last few days, and though
Alice's skin, with that light hair, was naturally very
pale, her mother watched it grow paler yet as the
hard-seated old-fashioned railway-carriage they sat
in jogged steadily on its way.

' Whenever I am in any difficulty, sweetheart,' she
whispered close up to her daughter's ear, ' I always
say a little prayer.'

' Yes, yes, dear dearest,' said Alice, gazing at the
fat old farmer, fast asleep. ' But if only I weren't
going quite alone. I don't think, you know, she can
be a very good godmother : she never said a word
in her letter about my Confirmation. She's at least
old enough to know better.' Once more the ghost
of a smile flickered over her face. But she clasped
her mother's fingers yet a little tighter, and the
hedges and meadows continued to sidle by.

They said Good-bye to one another actually inside
the cab, so as to be out of sight of the Inn and the
cabman.

' I expect, my sweet,' breathed Alice's mother, in
the midst of this long embrace, ' we shall both soon
be smiling away like two turtledoves at the thought
of all our worry. We can't tell what kind things
she may not be thinking of, can we ? And don't
forget, I shall be waiting for you in the " Red Lion "
—there's the sign, my dear, as you see. And if
there is time, perhaps we will have a little supper
there all to ourselves—a little soup, if they have it ;
or at any rate, an egg. I don't suppose you will have
a very *substantial* tea. Not in the circumstances.
But still, your godmother wouldn't have asked you
to visit her if she had not really wanted to see
you. We mustn't forget that, darling.'

Alice craned her head out of the window till her
mother was out of sight behind the hedge. And the
fly rolled gently on and on and on along the dusty
lanes in the direction of the Grange. On and on
and on. Surely, thought Alice at last, we must
have gone miles and miles. At this she sprang up
and thrust her head out of the window, and called
up to the cabman, ' the Grange, you know, please.'

' That's it, Miss, the Grange,' he shouted back,
with a flourish of his whip. ' Not as how I can take
you in to the Park, Miss. It ain't allowed.'

' Mercy me,' sighed Alice as she sank back on the
fusty blue cushions. ' Supposing there are miles of
avenue, and the front door's at the back ! '

It was a pleasant sunny afternoon. The trim
hedgerows were all in their earliest green ; and
young spring flowers—primroses, violets, jack-in-
the-hedge, stitchwort—in palest blossom starred the
banks. It was only half-past three by Alice's little

silver watch.   She would be in good time then.   In
a few minutes, indeed, the fly drew up beside an
immense rusty wrought-iron gate on the four posts
of which stood heavy birds in stone, with lowered
heads, brooding with outstretched wings.

' And you will be sure to come back for me at six,'
Alice implored the cabman, though she tried to keep
her voice natural and formal.   ' Not a minute later
than six, please.   And then wait here until I come.'

The cabman ducked his head and touched his
hat ; drew his old horse round in the shafts, and off
he went.   Alice was alone.

With one last longing look at the strange though
friendly country lane—and there was not a house in
sight—Alice pushed open the little gate at the side
of the two large ones.   It emitted a faint, mocking
squeal as it turned slowly upon its hinges.   Beyond
it rose a hedge of yew at least twenty feet high, and in
a nook there stood a small square lodge, its windows
shuttered, a scurry of dead leaves in its ancient
porch.   Alice came to a standstill.   This was a
difficulty neither she nor her mother had foreseen.
Ought she to knock or to go straight on ?   The
house looked as blind as a bat.   She stepped back,
and glanced up at the chimneys.   Not the faintest
plume of smoke was visible against the dark foliage
of the ilex behind the house.   Some bird flew into
the shadows with a jangling cry of alarm.

Surely the lodge was empty.   None the less it
might be good manners to make sure, so she stepped
into the porch and knocked—but knocked in vain.
After pausing a minute or two, and scanning once
more the lifeless windows, in a silence broken only

by the distant laughing of a woodpecker, Alice determined to go on.

So thick now grew the tufted moss in the gravel of the narrow avenue that her footsteps made no sound. So deep was the shade afforded by the immense trees that grew on either side she could have fancied evening was already come, though it was yet early afternoon. Mammoth oaks lifted their vast boughs into the air; the dark hollows in their ancient boles capacious enough for the dwelling house of a complete family of humans. In the distance Alice could see between their branches gigantic cedars, and others still further, beneath which grazed what she supposed was a herd of deer, though it was impossible to be quite certain from so far.

The few wild creatures which she interrupted in these haunts were uncommonly tame. They did not so much as trouble to run away; just turned aside and watched her as she passed, the birds hopping a little further out of her reach while yet continuing on their errands. In sheer curiosity indeed Alice made an attempt to get as near as she possibly could to a large buck rabbit that sat nibbling under the broken rail of the fence. With such success that he actually allowed her to scratch his furry head and stroke his long lopping ears.

'Well,' thought she with a sigh as she straightened herself, 'there can't be very much to be afraid of in great-great-great-great-great-great-great-great-grandmother's house if the rabbits are as tame as all that. Au revoir, Mr. Bunny,' she whispered to the creature; 'I hope to see you again very very soon.' And on she went.

Now and then a hunchbacked thorn-tree came into view, and now and then a holly. Alice had heard long ago that hollies are wise enough not to grow prickles where no animal can damage their leaves by browsing on them. These hollies seemed to have no prickles at all, and the hawthorns, in spite of their bright green coats, speckled with tight buds, were almost as twisted out of shape as if mischievous little boys had tied knots in them when they were saplings. But how sweet was the tranquil air. So much indeed this quiet avenue with its towering branches and the child-like blue of the skies overhead pacified her mind, that she had almost forgotten her godmother when, suddenly, at a break in the avenue there came into view a coach.

Not exactly a coach, perhaps, but a large painted carriage of a faded vermilion and yellow, drawn by two cream-coloured horses—a coachman on the box in a mulberry livery and a footman beside him. What was really strange, this conveyance was being steadily driven round a circular track so overgrown with moss and weeds that it was hardly discernible against the green of the grass. Alice could not but watch it come nearer and nearer—as she stood drawn up close to the furrowed bark of an oak that towered overhead. This must be her godmother's carriage. She must be taking her daily drive in concealment from the wide wide world. But no : it had drawn near ; with a glimpse of the faded red morocco within, it had passed ; it was empty. Only the backs of coachman and footman now showed above its sun-bleached panels—their powdered hair, their cockaded hats.

All Alice's misgivings winged back into her mind at sight of this curious spectacle. She tiptoed out of her hiding-place, and hastened on. Her one wish now was to reach her journey's end. Presently after, indeed, the House itself appeared in sight. The shorn flowerless turf gently sloped towards its dark low walls and grey chimneys. To the right of it lay a pool as flat as a huge looking-glass in the frame of its trees. Behind it rose a smooth green hill.

Alice paused again behind yet another of the huge grey boles to scan it more closely before she herself could be spied out from any of the many windows. It looked as if it had stood there for ever. It looked as if its massive stones had of their own weight sunken a few feet into the ground. Not a blossoming shrub, not a flower nearby—except only a powder of daisies and a few yellow dandelions.

Only green turf and trees, and the ancient avenue on which she stood, sweeping gently towards its low-porched entrance. ' Well,' she sighed to herself, ' I'm thankful I don't live *there*, that's all—not even if I were a thousand-and-one ! ' She drew herself up, glanced at her shoes, gave a little push to her ribboned straw hat, and, with as much dignity as she could manage, proceeded straight onwards.

A hoarse bell responded, after a whole second's pause, to the gentle tug she had given the iron pull that hung in the porch. It cried ' Ay, ay ! ' and fell silent. And Alice continued to look at the immense iron knocker which she hadn't the courage to use.

Without a sound the door opened at last, and there,

as she had feared, stood, not a friendly parlour-maid
with a neat laundered cap, but an old man in a
black tail-coat who looked at her out of his pale grey
eyes as if she were a stuffed bird in a glass case.
Either he had been shrinking for some little time, or
he must surely have put on somebody else's clothes,
they hung so loosely on his shoulders.

'I am Miss Alice Cheyney—Miss Alice Cheyney,'
she said. 'I think my great-great . . . Miss Cheyney
is expecting me—that is, of course, if she is quite
well.' These few words had used up the whole of
one breath, and her godmother's old butler continued
to gaze at her, while they sank into his mind.

'Will you please to walk in,' he said at last.
'Miss Cheyney bade me express the wish that you
will make yourself at home. She hopes to be with
you immediately.' Whereupon he led the way,
and Alice followed him—across a wide hall, lit
with low, greenish, stone-mullioned windows. On
either side stood suits of burnished armour, with lifted
visors. But where the glittering eyes of their long-
gone owners once had gleamed, nothing now showed
but a little narrow darkness. After a hasty glance
or two on either side, Alice kept her eyes fixed on
the humped back of the little old butler. Up three
polished stairs, under a hanging tapestry, he led
her on, and at length, at the end of a long gallery,
ushered her into what she supposed was her godmother's sitting-room. There, with a bow, he left
her. Alice breathed one long deep sigh, and then,
having unbuttoned and buttoned up again one of
her grey silk gloves, she sat down on the edge of a
chair near the door.

It was a long, low-pitched, but not very wide room, with a moulded ceiling and panelled walls, and never before had Alice seen such furniture. In spite of the dreadful shyness that seemed to fill her to the very brim, at thought of her mother's little pink-and-muslin drawing-room compared with this, she almost burst out laughing.

'Make herself at home!' Why, any one of those coffers would hide her away for ever, like the hapless young bride in the 'Mistletoe Bough.' As for the hanging portraits in their great faded frames, though she guessed at once they must be by 'old masters,' and therefore eyed them as solemnly as she could, she had never supposed human beings could look so odd and so unfriendly. It was not so much their clothes : their stomachers, their slashed doublets and wide velvet caps, but their faces. Ladies with high bald foreheads and tapering fingers and thumb-rings, and men sour and dour and glowering.

'Oho! Miss Nobody!' they seemed to be saying, 'And pray, what are *you* doing here?'

The one single exception was the drawing of a girl of about her own age. A dainty cap with flaps all but concealed the yellow hair ; a necklet dangled at her breast ; the primrose-coloured bodice sloped sharply to the waist. So delicate were the lines of this drawing and so faint the tinted chalk, they hardly stained the paper. Yet the eyes that gazed out across the low room at Alice seemed to be alight with life. A smile half-mocking, half-solemn, lingered in their depths. See, I am lovely, it seemed to be hinting, and yet how soon to be gone! And even though Alice had never before seen a face so lovely, she could not but confess it bore a remote resemblance to herself. Why this should have a little restored her confidence she could not tell. None the less, she deliberately smiled back at the drawing as if to say, ' Well, my dear, I shall have *you* on my side, whatever happens.'

The lagging minutes ticked solemnly by. Not a sound to be heard in the great house ; not a footfall. But at last a door at the further end of the room softly opened, and in the greenish light of the deep mullioned window appeared what Alice knew was She. She was leaning on the arm of the butler who had admitted Alice to the house. Quiet as shadows they entered the room ; then paused for a moment, while yet another man-servant arranged a chair for his mistress. Meanwhile the old lady was peering steadily in search of her visitor. She must once have been as tall as Alice herself, but now time had shrunken her up into the stature of a child, and though the small head was set firmly on the narrow shoulders, these stooped like the wings of the stone birds upon her gates.

' Ah, is that you, my dear ? ' cried a voice ; but so minute was the sound of these words that Alice went suddenly hot all over lest she had merely imagined them.

' I say, is that you, my dear ? ' repeated the voice. There was no mistaking now. Alice ventured a pace forward into the light, her knees shaking beneath her, and the old lady thrust out a hand—its shrunken fingers closed in one upon the other like the cold claws of a bird.

For an instant Alice hesitated. The dreadful moment was come. Then she advanced, made the old lady a curtesy, and lifted the icy fingers to her lips.

' All I can say *is*,' she confided to her mother when they met again, ' all I can say *is*, Mamma, if it had been the Pope, I suppose I should have kissed his toe. And really, I would have much rather.'

None the less, Alice's great-great-great-great-great-great-great-great-grandmother had evidently taken no offence at this gesture. Indeed what Alice thought might be a smile crinkled, as it were, across the exquisite web of wrinkles on her face. On her acorn-shaped head rose a high lace and silver cap resembling the gown she wore ; and silk mittens concealed her wrists. She was so small that Alice had to bend almost double over her fingers. And when she was seated in her chair it was as if a large doll sat there—but a marvellous doll that had voice, thought, senses and motion beyond any human artificer's wildest fancy. The eyes in this dry wizened-up countenance—of a much fainter blue than the palest forget-me-not—steadily continued to look at Alice, the while the butler and footman with head inclined stood surveying their mistress. Then, as if at a secret signal, they both bowed and retired.

' Be seated, my dear,' the tinkling voice began when they had withdrawn. And there fell a horrifying pause. Alice gazed at the old lady, and like half-transparent glass the aged eyes continued to survey herself, the bird-like hands crossed daintily over the square lace handkerchief held in the narrow lap.

Alice grew hotter and hotter. ' What a very beautiful old house this is, great-grandmama,' she suddenly blurted out. ' And those wonderful trees ! '

No flicker of expression showed that Miss Cheyney had heard what she had said. And yet Alice could not help thinking that she *had* heard, and that for some reason she had disapproved of her remark.

' Now come,' she cried sharply, ' now come ; tell me what you have been doing this long time. And how is your Mother ? I think I faintly remember seeing her, my dear, soon after she married your father, Mr. James Beaton.'

' Mr. Beaton, I *think*, was my great-grandfather, great-grandmama,' Alice breathed softly. ' My father's name, you know was John—John Cheyney.'

' Ah well, your great *grand*father, to be sure,' said the old lady. ' I never pay much attention to dates. And has anything been happening lately ? '

' Happening, great-grandmama ? ' echoed Alice.

' Beyond ? ' said the old lady, ' in the world ? '

Poor Alice ; she knew well the experience of nibbling a pen over impossible questions in history examinations, but this was far worse than any she had ever encountered.

' There, you see ! ' continued the piping voice, ' I hear of the wonderful things they are doing, and yet when I ask a simple question like that no one has anything to say. Have you travelled on one of these steam railway trains yet ? Locomotives ? '

' I came that way this afternoon, great-grandmama.'

' Ah, I thought you looked a little flushed. The smoke must be most disagreeable.'

x

Alice smiled. ' No, thank you,' she said kindly.

' And how is Queen Victoria ? ' said the old lady.
' She is still alive ? '

' Oh yes, great-grandmama. And that is just,
of course, what *has* been happening. It's her
Diamond Jubilee this year — sixty years — you
know.'

' H'm,' said the old lady. ' Sixty. George III.
reigned sixty-three. But they all go in time. I
remember my dear father coming up to my nursery
after the funeral of poor young Edward VI. He was
one of the Court pages, you know—that is, when
Henry VIII. was King. Such a handsome lad—
there is his portrait . . . somewhere.'

For a moment Alice's mind was a whirlpool of
vague memories—memories of what she had read
in her history-books.

But Miss Cheyney's bead-like voice had hardly
paused. ' You must understand that I have not
asked you to come this long way by one of those
horrid new-fangled steam-engines just to gossip
about my childhood. Kings and Queens come and
go like the rest of things. And though I have seen
many changes, it seems to me the world is pretty
much the same as ever. Nor can I believe that the
newspaper is a beneficial novelty. When I was a
girl we managed well enough without, and even in
Mr. Addison's day one small sheet twice a week was
enough. But there, complaint is useless. And you
cannot exactly be held responsible for all that.
There were changes in my girlhood—great changes.'
Her eyes wandered, to rest a moment on the portrait
of the young woman in the primrose gown. ' The

truth is, my dear,' she continued, ' I have to tell
you something, and I wish you to listen.'

Once more she remained silent a moment, clutching
the handkerchief she held between her fingers.
' What I desire you to tell me,' she said at last,
leaning stealthily forward in her great chair, ' what I
am anxious that you should tell me is, How long
do you wish to live ? '

For a few moments Alice sat cold and motionless.
It was as if an icy breath straight from the North Pole
had swept across the room, congealing with its horror
the very air. Her eyes wandered vacantly from
picture to picture, from ancient object to ancient
object—aged, mute and lifeless—to rest at last on a
flowering weed that reared its head beyond one of
the diamond-shaped panes of glass in the window.

' I have never thought of that, great-grandmama,'
her dry lips whispered. ' I don't think I know.'

' Well, I am not expecting an old head on young
shoulders,' retorted the old lady. ' Perhaps if
King Charles had realised that—so learned, so
generous, so faithful a monarch—I doubt if that
vulgar creature Oliver Cromwell would ever have
succeeded in having his off.'

The acorn head drew down into its laces like a
snail into its shell. Until this moment Alice might
have been conversing with an exquisite image, or
an automaton—the glittering eyes, the bird-claw
hands, the voice from afar. But now it seemed life
itself was stirring in it. The tiny yet piercing tones
sank almost to a whisper, the head stirred stealthily
from side to side as if to be sure no eavesdropper
were within earshot.

' Now listen close to me, my child : I have a secret.
A secret which I wish to share only with you. You
would suppose, wouldn't you, that this being the
three-hundred-and-fiftieth anniversary of my natal
day '—and at this the dreadful realisation suddenly
swept over Alice that she had quite forgotten to wish
her godmother ' Many happy returns '— ' you might
suppose that you are about to meet a gay and
numerous company here—young and happy creatures
like yourself. But no ; not so. Even your dear
mother is, of course, only my great-great-great-great-
great-great-great-granddaughter-*in-law*. She was a
Miss Wilmot, I believe.'

' Woodcot, great-grandmama,' smiled Alice.

' Well, Woodcot,' said the old lady ; ' it is no
matter. You yourself, however, are my chosen
female great-great-great-great-great-great-great-great-
grandchild, to be precise. In mere men I take no
interest. Not only that, but you must now be of
the age I was when the portrait you see on yonder
wall was painted. It is the work of a pupil of Hans
Holbein's. Hans Holbein himself, I believe, was
dead at the time. Dear me, child, I remember
sitting for that portrait in this very room—as if it
were yesterday. It was much admired by Sir
Walter Raleigh, who, you may remember, came to
so unhappy an end. That was, I recollect, in my
early seventies. My father and his father were boys
together in Devonshire.'

Alice blinked a little—she could not take her eyes
off the old lady—that mammet-like face, those
minute motionless hands.

' Now glance at that picture, please ! ' the old lady

bade her, pointing a tiny crooked-up forefinger towards the further wall. ' Do you see any re-semblance ? '

Alice looked long and steadily at the portrait. But she had neither the courage nor vanity to deny that the fair smiling features were at least a *little* like her own. ' To whom, great-grandmama ? ' Alice whispered.

' Well, well, well ! ' cried the old lady, the words sounding like the chiming of a distant silver bell. ' I see it. I see it. . . . But never mind that now. Did you perhaps look at this *house* as you made your way up the avenue ? '

' Oh yes, great-grandmama—though I couldn't, of course, look close, you know,' Alice managed to reply.

' Did you *enjoy* its appearance ? '

' I don't think I thought of that,' said Alice. ' The trees and park were very lovely. I have never seen such—*mature* trees, great-grandmama. And yet all their leaves were budding and some were fully out. Isn't it wonderful for trees so —so long in the world to—why to come out at all ? '

' I was referring to the house,' said the old lady. ' *Springs* nowadays are not what they used to be. They have vanished from the England I once knew. I remember once an April when angels were seen on the hilltops above London. But that is no matter for us now : not now. The house ? '

Once again Alice's gaze wandered—to rest on the green nodding weed at the window.

' It is a very very quiet house,' she said.

The child-like tones died between the thick stone walls ; and a profound silence followed them, like

that of water in an unfathomable well. Meanwhile,
as Alice fully realised, her great-great-great-great-
great-great-great-great-grandmother had been fixedly
searching her face with her needle eyes.

'Now please listen to me very carefully,' she
continued at last. 'Such a countenance as yours—
one bearing the least resemblance to that portrait
over there, must be the possessor of a fair share of
wits. I am old enough, my child, not to be accused,
I hope of the folly of vanity. In my girlhood I
enjoyed a due share of admiration. And I have a
proposal to make to you which will need all the
sagacity you are capable of. Don't be alarmed.
I have every faith in you. But first I want you
to go into the next room, where you will find a meal
prepared. Young people nowadays, I hear, need
continuous nourishment. What wonder ! since they
have forgotten all the manners of a lady as *I* know
them and are never still for a moment together.
What wonder ! with all those dreadful machines I
hear of, the discontent, the irreligion, all these years
of unrest and confusion. In my young days the
poor were the poor and the humble the humble, my
child ; and knew their place. In my young days
I would sit contented for hours at a time over a
simple piece of embroidery. And if I needed it,
my mother never thought to spare the rod. But
there, I didn't invite you to visit an old woman
merely to preach you a sermon. When you have
refreshed yourself you are to take a little walk
through the house. Go wherever you please ; look
well about you ; no one will disturb you. And in
an hour's time come back to me here again. Now-

adays I take a little sleep in the afternoon. I shall
be ready for you then.'

Alice, with a relief beyond words, rose from her
chair. She curtseyed again towards the small,
motionless figure in the distance, and retired
through the dark oak door.

The room in which she at once found herself was
small, hexagonal, and panelled with the blackest of
old oak. A copper candelabrum hung from the
moulded ceiling, and out of the leaded panes she
could see the gigantic trees in the park. To her
dismay the footman who had accompanied the
butler into the room when her great-great-great-
great-great-great-great-great-grandmother had first
made her appearance, was stationed behind the
chair at the table. Never had Alice supposed that
it was proper for men-servants, except perhaps
gardeners, to wear long grey beards. But there he
was, with his dim sidling eyes. And she must needs
turn her back on him to seat herself at the table.
She nibbled the fruit and bread which he presented
in the heavy silver dishes, and she sipped her sweet
drink. But it was a hasty and nervous meal, and
she tasted nothing of what she had eaten.

As soon as it was over the servant opened the
door for her, and she began her voyage of discovery
through the great, deserted house. It was as if her
very ghost had come with her. Never had solitude
so oppressed her, never had she been so acutely
conscious of being in her own small company. The
long corridors, the low and crooked lintelled doors,
the dark uneven floors, their Persian mats, their
tapestries and hangings only the lovelier in that their

colours had been dimmed by so many suns, the
angled flights of stairs, the solemn air that brooded
between the walls, the multitude of pictures, the
huge beds, the endless succession of superannuated
coffers, daybeds, cabinets—all this in but a few
minutes had tired and fatigued Alice far more even
than the long journey from the home of her childhood that morning. Upstairs and downstairs on
she wandered, for all the world like the goosey goosey
gander of the old nursery rhyme.

And when at last with a sigh she glanced at the
bright little silver watch which had been her mother's
birthday gift, its slender hands told her that she
had still a full quarter-of-an-hour before she need
return to her great-great-great-great-great-great-
great-great-grandmother.

The room in which she now found herself seemed
to be a small library. Its walls were ranged from
ceiling to floor with old leather and lambskin
folios and quartos and squat duodecimos, while
between them hung portraits and the loveliest
miniatures and medallions of scores upon scores of
persons whom she guessed must be her ancestors
of goodness knows how many Henries ago.

One or two of them indeed, as the crabbed inscrip-
tions showed, had been gifts to the family from
those Henries themselves. In their various cos-
tumes, wigs, turbans and furbelows they looked as
if they must have been the guests at an immense
fancy-dress ball.

In this room a low recess filled the shallow bow
window and on this lay a strip of tapestry. The
leaded pane of the window was open. The sun was

already westering, its light slanting in on the gilt
and ebony and ivory of the frames suspended from
their nails. Alice knelt down at the window ; and
her mind slipped into a day-dream, and her gaze
wandered far away over the golden budding tops
of the enormous oaks, the flat dark palms of cedars
—descendants, no doubt, of those which Sir Philip
Sidney had brought home to his beloved England
from the East.

The thoughts that had all day been skittering in
her mind like midges over a pool, gradually fell
still, and she sank deeper and deeper into the hush
that lay over the ancient house. It was as if its
walls were those of an enormous diving-bell sunken
beyond measure in the unfathomable ocean of
Time. So still was the sweet April air beyond the
window that she could actually detect the sound of
the browsing of the herd of fallow deer that had now
closely approached the dark green lawns of the
house itself.

And as, lost in this reverie she sat entranced, she
became conscious that a small living animal—the
like of which she had never seen before—had crept
up within a pace or two of her on the window-sill,
and was now steadily regarding her with its clear
bead-brown eyes. In size it was rather larger than
a mole, its dark thick fur was soft as a beaver's,
and it had a short, furry, and tufted tail. Its ears
were cocked on its head, its silvery whiskers turned
downwards above its jaws, and Alice could see
its tiny ivory claws as it sat there erect on its
haunches like a tame cat or a dog begging for
a tidbit of meat. Alice, alas, had nothing to

offer her visitor, not even a cherry-stone, not even a crumb.

'Well, you pretty thing,' she whispered, 'what is it?'

The creature's whiskers moved ever so slightly, its eyes fixed more intently than ever on the face of this strange visitor. Very very delicately Alice thrust out her finger, and to her astonishment found herself gently caressing the furry nose. 'It was as if I was in Wonderland, myself, she explained long afterwards to her mother. Perfectly mute and still, the owner of it seemed to enjoy this little courtesy. And when she had withdrawn her finger, it looked at her more closely and searchingly than ever, as if bidding her take heed. It then tapped repeatedly with its ivory-clawed paw on the oak casement, glanced searchingly at her yet again, then shook its furry head vehemently three times, paused, turned swiftly about and pattered away into hiding behind a huge carved Moorish cabinet before Alice could so much as bid it adieu.

Quiet little events in this life, even though we cannot understand what exactly they mean, are apt to *seem* to mean a great deal. So with this small animal and Alice. It was as if—though she was not aware of it—she had been brooding over a problem in Algebra or a proposition in Euclid, and it had ventured out of its living-place to tell her the answer. How fantastic a notion!—when Alice knew neither the problem nor what its solution was.

She glanced at her watch once more; her fair cheeks pinking all over at realising that she was now ten minutes late for her assignation with her

great-great-great-great-great-great-great-great-grandmother. She must be gone. None the less, she had
time to wave her hand at the huge dreaming park
before she set out on her return journey.

Before at last finding her way, however, she
irretrievably lost it. For the house was a perfect
maze of deceiving passages and corridors. Every
fresh attempt only increased her confusion, and then
suddenly she found herself looking into a room
utterly different from any she had yet seen. Its
low walls were of stone, its dusty windows shuttered ;
it contained nothing but a chair. And in that chair
sat what appeared to be the life-size image of the
smiling lovely creature she had seen in the portrait—
eyes shut, cheeks a faint rose, hair still shimmering
with gold, its hands laid idly in the lap, the fingers
of one of them clutching what seemed to be the
dried-up fragments of a bunch of flowers. What
there was to alarm her in this harmless image she
could not tell ; but she gazed awhile at it in horror,
closed-to the door and ran off as if pursued by
a nightmare, down one corridor and up another,
to find herself at last by good fortune once more in
the room where she had had her meal. It seemed,
as she stood there, her hand upon her breast, as if
she would never again recover her breath ! She was
no longer nervous, no longer merely timid : she was
afraid. ' If only, if only I had never come to this
house ! ' was her one terrified thought.

She discovered with relief on re-entering Miss
Cheyney's presence that her godmother was still
asleep. Alice could see awhile without being seen.

Now one of her mother's brothers—one of Alice's

uncles, that is—was an old bachelor who delighted in birthday gifts. Alice had therefore been richer in dolls than most children : wooden, wax, china, Dutch, French, Russian, and even one from the Andaman Islands. But no single one of them had shown a face so utterly still and placid as that now leaning gently aside in its lace and silver cap and mantle. There was no expression whatever on its features. No faintest smile ; no shadow of a frown. And yet, the tiny wrinkles all over it, crooking down even from the brows over the eyelids, gave it the appearance of an exquisitely figured map.

And Alice was still surveying it as closely as some old treasure-hunter might the chart of his secret island, when the minute eyes reopened and her great-great-great-great-great-great-great-great-grand-mother was instantly wide awake.

' Ah,' whispered the old lady, ' I have been on a long journey, but I heard you calling. What happens, I wonder,' and the tones sank lower, ' what happens when one has ventured on too far to hear any such rumours. Answer me that, eh ? But no matter. There is a more important question first. Tell me, if you please, what you think of my house.'

Alice moistened her lips. ' That, great-grand-mama,' she managed to reply at last, ' that would take *ages*. It is marvellous : but oh, so very still.'

' What should there be to disturb it ? ' asked the old lady.

Alice shook her head.

' Tell me,' and the voice tinkled across the air

with a peculiar little tang, ' would you like it for your own ? '

' This House—for my own ? ' breathed the young girl.

' Ay, for your own, and for always—humanly speaking.'

' I don't quite understand,' said Alice.

The little head leaned sidelong like a bird's.

' Naturally, my child. You *cannot* until I have gone a little further. The gift I am now offering you is one that few human beings in this world conceive to be possible. It is not merely this house, my child, with all that it contains—much as that may be. It is life. My father, you must understand, was a traveller, and in days when danger was a man's constant companion. In this very room on his return from a many years' journey, he told me as a girl of a dismal mountainous region of snow and ice and precipices that lies there—West of China, I believe. It was from thence that he brought back his secret. You will realise there may come a day when the wish to live on may have somewhat dimmed in my mind. I confess to feeling a little weariness at times. But before I go, it is my privilege—my obligation—to confer the secret on another. Look at me : ' the voice rose a little ; it was as though a wren had uttered its shrill song in the low resounding room, ' I am offering this inestimable benefit to *you*.'

Alice sat straight as a dart in her chair, not venturing to turn her eyes aside even for a moment

' A secret, great-grandmama ? '

' Ay,' continued the old woman, closing her eyes, ' you heard me aright. A secret. I will whisper it into your ear. Imagine, my child, the wonder of infinite time ! Imagine a life in such surroundings as these, far from all the follies and vexations of the world—and one fear—the most terrible of all fears —gone, or at any rate so remote as to be of no consequence. Imagine that, I say.'

For an instant Alice's gaze wavered. Her eyes glanced swiftly towards the window where shone the swiftly changing colours of the sunset ; where sang the wild birds, and Spring was flooting on her way.

' Take your own time : and do not be afraid of me. I shall make few conditions. Only that you must vow silence, to breathe not one syllable of what I shall tell you—not even to your own mother. All else will be easy—comparatively easy. All else. You will come here and live with me. Rooms are prepared for you—books, music, horses to ride, servants to wait on you, all that you need. And in due season this house, this accumulation of things precious and old and beautiful, this wide park stretching for many more miles than you can see from my topmost windows, will be yours alone. You may pine awhile for old friends. It is an unhappy thing to say goodbye, as I have heard. But all fades, all goes. And in time you will not wish for company. Servants as aged as mine are not difficult to find ; they are discreet, and have need to remain faithful. We shall have many a quiet talk together. I have much to tell you. I long, my dear child, to share memories with you that I have never breathed to a living soul. There are wings to this house into which you cannot have penetrated, simply because they are shut off by bolts

and bars. They contain much to see : much to
linger over ; much to wonder at. Tell me now,
what do you think of my proposal ? And remember
this :—Not even Solomon in all his glory could have
conferred on you what I now offer.'

The aged head was nodding—as if in fatigue. The
cramped fingers fumbled aimlessly with the lace
handkerchief, and Alice's poor wits were once more
in a desperate confusion. The room swam dizzily
before her eyes. She shut them a moment ; en-
deavouring in vain to consider calmly what that
remote unhuman voice had been saying to her.
She might as well have struggled in sleep to shake
off the veils and nets of a dream, the snares of a
nightmare. One thing only was audible to her
now, the sound of her shoe tapping on the floor.
She came to with a jerk.

' You mean,' she whispered, ' on and on and on—
like you, great-grandmama ? '

The old lady made no reply.

' May I, do you think, then, if you would be so kind,
may I have time to think it over ? '

' Think what over ? ' said the old lady. ' Are
you supposing a child of your age can think over
three complete centuries before a single moment of
them has come into view ? '

' No,' said Alice, her courage returning a little,
' I meant think over what you have said. It is
so very difficult to realise what it means.'

' It means,' said the old lady, ' an immeasurable
sea, an infinite garden, an endless vista—of time. It
means freedom from the cares and anxieties and
follies that are the lot of the poor creatures in the

world beyond—living out their few days in brutish
stupidity.   You are still young, but who knows ?
It means, my child, postponing a visit to a certain
old friend of ours—whose name is Death.'

She breathed the word as if in secret pleasure at
its sound.   Alice shuddered, and yet it gave her
fresh resolution.   She rose from her chair.

' I am young and stupid, I know, great-grandmama ; and I would do anything in the world not
to—not to hurt your feelings.   And of course, of
course I agree most people have a very hard time
and that most of us are not very bright-witted.   But
you said *death* ; and I think, if you will forgive me
saying so, I would rather I should have to die
when—just when, I mean, I *must* die.   You see, it
would be a very sorrowful thing for me if it came
after my mother had—if, I mean, she cannot share
the secret too ?   And even then. . . .   Why cannot
we all share it ?   I do see, indeed I do, there is
very little time in this world in which to grow wise.
But when you think of the men who have——'

' You are here, my child,' Miss Cheyney interrupted her, ' to answer questions—not to ask them.
I must not be fatigued.   Sleep is impossible then.
But surely you are old enough to know that there is
not one human being in a thousand, nay, not one in a
hundred thousand who has any hope of growing wise,
not if he lived till Doomsday.'

She crushed forward a little in her chair.   ' Supposing your refusal means that the secret will perish
with—with the possessor ?   Unless,' the voice sank
to a muttering, ' unless *you* consent to share it ?
Eh, what then ? '

Alice found herself staring at the old lady like a
bird at a serpent, and the only answer she could
manage was a violent shake of the head. ' Oh,' she
cried, suddenly bursting into tears, ' I simply can't
tell you how grateful I am for all your kindness, and
what a wretch I seem to myself to be saying this.
But please, Miss Cheyney, may I go now ? I feel
something dreadful might happen if I stay here a
minute longer.'

The old lady seemed to be struggling in her chair,
as if in the effort to rise out of it ; but her strength
failed her. She lifted her mittened hand into the
air.

' Begone at once, then,' she whispered, ' at once.
Even my patience is limited. And when the day
comes that will remind you of my kindness, may
you wish you had . . . Oh, oh ! . . .' The frail voice
rose shrill as a gnat's, then cracked. At sound of it
the old butler came hastening in at the further door ;
and Alice slipped out of the other.

Not until the house had vanished from sight behind
its groves of prodigious forest-trees did she slacken
her steps to recover her breath. She had run
wildly on, not daring to pause or glance back over
her shoulder, as if Fear itself with all the hosts of
nightmare were at her heels.

How she found her way to the gates she never
knew. On looking back, the remembrance of the
dense thickets, the soundless glens, tented-in by
trees, their budding branches stretched out into the
air like the arms of some gigantic stone image—all
this seemed to her like the scenery of an appalling
dream. Never before in her life had Alice been

Y

so pleased to see anybody as when she found herself
at last in the dusty hedgerowed lane beyond, looking
up into the purple face of the grumpy old cabman.

That evening her mother and she—seated in the
cosy red-curtained coffee-room of the ' Red Lion '—
actually sipped together a glass of the landlord's
old Madeira. Alice had never before kept any
secret from her mother. Yet though she was able
to tell her most of what had happened in her strange
afternoon adventure, she could not persuade herself
to breathe one word about the purpose which had
prompted Miss Cheyney to send her so unexpected
an invitation. Not then, nor ever afterwards.

' Do you really mean, my own dearest,' her
mother repeated once more, pressing her hand as they
sat in the chill spring night under the old oil lamp-
post awaiting their train in the little country railway
station ; ' do you mean she never gave you a single
ittle present ; never offered you *anything* out of all
those wonderful treasures in that dreadful old
house ? '

' She asked me, mother dear,' said Alice, turning
her face away towards the dark-mouthed tunnel
through which they would soon be venturing—' she
asked me if I would like to be as old as she was, and
honestly, I said I would much prefer to be just the
silly green creature I am, so long as I can be with
you.'

It was an odd thing to do—if the station-master
had been watching them—but however odd, it is
certainly true that at this moment mother and
daughter turned and flung their arms round each
other's necks and kissed each other as if they had

met again for the first time after an enormous journey.

Not that Alice had been quite accurate in saying that her godmother had made her no gift. For a day or two afterwards there came by post a package ; and enwrapped in its folds of old Chinese paper Alice found the very portrait she had seen on the wall on that already seemingly far-off day—the drawing, I mean, made by a pupil of the famous Hans Holbein, depicting her great-great-great-great-great-great-great-great-grandmother in the year 1564, when she was just turned seventeen.

MARIA-FLY

LITTLE Maria that morning—and this is a good many years ago now—was dressed in a black and white frock with a flounce to it. Her hair was tied back over her small ears with a white ribbon, and she was sitting in the drawing-room on a low arm-chair with a blue-cushioned seat; her stockinged legs dangling down in front of her. She was all by herself. She had wandered in there—nobody by; and after walking about for a little while looking at the things in the room, and sniffing at a bowl of red damask roses, she had sat down, looking so sleek and demure you might almost have supposed that company was present and that she was ' behaving.'

But she was not ; she was only thinking. It was a quiet morning. The room, with its two square-paned bow windows, was rather long. There was sunshine in it, and it was still, and though, as it appeared, there was no other living thing between its walls except herself, it seemed to be happy too. And Maria had begun to think—or rather not exactly to think and not exactly to dream, but (if that is possible) to do both together ; though she

343

could not have told anyone what she was thinking
and dreaming about.

She had had a bowl of bread and milk for breakfast,
half an apple, and two slices of bread and jam.   She
felt comfortable.   Her piano practice in the old
room by the nursery was over, and now she was
alone.   But she was alone more than usual.   It was
as if she were not only sitting there in her blue-
cushioned armchair with her legs dangling down, but
that she could see herself sitting there.   It startled
her a little when that notion occurred to her.   It was
almost as if at that moment she must have really
slipped into a dream.   And she glanced up quickly
with her rather round face and clear darting eyes to
make sure.   And on the white paint at the side of
the door, not very far away, she saw a fly.

It was just a fly.   But simply because at that
moment everything was so quiet in the world, and
because, may be, unlike the chairs and tables around
her, it was alive, Maria fixed her eyes on the fly.   It
was nevertheless a perfectly ordinary fly—a house-
fly.   It stood there alone on its six brushy legs and
clawed feet, their small, nimble pads adhering to the
white gloss of the paint.   But, though ordinary, it
was conspicuous—just in the same way as a man in
black clothes with immense boots and a high cap on
the enormous dazzling snow-slopes of a mountain is
conspicuous—and Maria seemed to be seeing the
fly much more clearly and minutely than you would
have supposed possible, considering the distance
between herself and it.

On the other hand, the fly was not standing there
doing nothing, as Maria was sitting there doing

nothing. It was not, for example, merely standing on the paint in *its* drawing-room and looking across at another fly infinitely tinier on the white paint of the minute door to that drawing-room. It was busy as flies usually are in the warm sunny months.

Maria had been up and had dressed herself hours and hours ago ; but flies seem to be dressing, or at least to be toileting and titivating themselves all the time when they are not prowling about on a table in search of food, or circling round, or sucking up water, or standing like mock flies asleep, or angling to and fro in the air under a chandelier or a fly-charm in one another's company.

Not that Maria was by any means fond of flies. She shooed them away with her spoon when they came buzzing about over her blancmange or red-currant-and-raspberry tart, or alighted on her bare arms, or walked rapidly about over her bedclothes. Once she had pulled off the wings of a fly, and had never forgotten how suffocatingly fusty and hot she had felt after doing so.

And if there was one thing Maria couldn't abide, it was a fly floating in her bath. It was extraordinary that though its carcase was such a minute thing you could at such a moment see absolutely nothing else. It was extraordinary that the whole of the water at such a moment seemed like fly-water

She would ask her nurse to take the ill-happed creature's corpse out of the bath and to put it on the window-sill in case it was not quite dead and might come-to again.

And if she remembered to look next morning, maybe it was not, or maybe it *was*, there still—just its body. She had more than once, too, heard the dismal languishing drone a fly utters when it has been decoyed into a web and sees the spider come sallying out of its round silken lair in the corner. It had filled her with horror and hatred and a miserable pity. Yet it had not made her any fonder of flies just for their own sakes alone. But then, one doesn't always feel exactly the same about anything. It depends on where you are, and what kind of mood you are in ; and where the other thing is, and what kind of mood *that* is in.

So it was this morning. For some reason, this particular fly was different ; and Maria sat watching it with the closest attention. It seemed to be that just as Maria herself was one particular little girl, so this was one particular fly. A fly by itself. A fly living its own one life ; confident, alert, alone in its own Fly World.

To judge from its solitude, and the easy careless busy way in which it was spending its time, it might be supposed indeed that it had the whole universe to itself. It might be supposed it was Sirius—and not another star in the sky. And after a while, so intent did Maria become that she seemed to be doing a great deal more than merely watching the fly. She became engrossed.

She was now stooping together in her chair almost as if she were a pin-cushion and her eyes were black-headed pins in it. She seemed almost to have *become* the fly—Maria-Fly. If it is possible, that is, she had become two things at once, or one thing at twice. It was an odd experience—and it lasted at least three minutes by the little gold clock, with the gilt goggling fish on either side its dial under the glass-case on the chimney-piece. Three minutes, that is, of ordinary clock time.

For when Maria herself came-to, it seemed she had been away for at least three centuries—as if, like the stranger in the rhyme, she had been with her candle all the way to Babylon ; ay, and back again : as if she had gone away Maria, come back Maria-Fly ; and now was just Maria again. But yet, when she came-to, everything was a little different.

She could not possibly have explained why, but she felt surprisingly gay and joyful. It was as if a voice, sweet and shrill as the angel Israfel's, had been singing in her mind from a very long way off. She looked about her in sheer astonishment. If anything, the things in the room were stiller than ever, and yet she would almost have supposed that up to a moment ago they had been alive and watching her, and were now merely pretending to be not-alive again.

She looked at the roses in the bowl : they were floating there filled with their fragrance and beauty as a dewdrop is with light. The fishes on either side the little clock seemed to be made of flames rather than gilded plaster. There was a patch of sunshine, too—just an oblong patch resting on the carpet and part of a chair. It seemed to be lovelier than words could tell and to be resting there as if in adoration of its own beauty. Maria saw all this with her young eyes, and could not realise what had happened to her. She was glad she was alone. She had never felt like it before. It was as if she had ceased to be herself altogether in her black and white

frock and had become just a tied-up parcel marked
' Pure Happiness,' with the date on it.

And as she gradually became aware how very still
the room was, almost stealthy—and all quiet things
of course seem in a way a little watchful—she felt
she must go out of it.   She felt she must go out of
it at once.   So she scrambled down off her chair.
On purpose, she didn't even glance again at her
friend the Fly.   She most particularly (though she
didn't know why) wished not to see it again.   So she
walked sidelong a little, her head turned to one side,
too, so that no part of her eye should see the fly again
even by accident.

She went out of the room, walked along down the
hall, and went down the rather dark side-stairs into
the kitchen.   There was a fire burning in the great
burnished range.   A green tree showed at the
window, and a glass jar half-full of beer and wasps
was twinkling on its sill.   Mrs. Poulton, the cook,
was rolling a piece of dough on her pastry or dough-
board, with an apron tied with all its tape round her
waist.   There was an immense flour dredger like a
pepper-pot beside the board, and a hare, its fur
soft as wool, cinnamon and snow-white, lay at the
further end of the table.   Its long white teeth
gleamed like ivory between its parted lips.

' Mrs. Poulton,' Maria said, ' I have seen a
fly.'

' Now, *have* you ? ' said the cook.   And the
' have ' was like a valley or a meadow that slopes
up and down with wild flowers all over it.   ' And
did the fly see you ? '

That hadn't occurred to Maria.   She frowned a

little. 'It's got lots of kind of eyes, you know,'
she said. 'But what I mean is, I *sawn* it.'

'And that was a queer thing, too,' said the cook,
deftly lifting up the dough and arranging its limp
folds over the fat dark sugary plums in the shallow
pie-dish, with an inverted egg-cup in the middle.
She gave a look at it ; and then took up her kitchen
knife and, deft as a barber, whipped the knife clean
round the edge of the dish to cut away what dough
hung over. 'Would you like a dolly, my dear ? '
she said.

'No, thank you,' said Maria, a little primly, not
wishing to have the subject changed. 'I have told
you about the fly,' she repeated, 'and you don't
seem to take a bit of notice of it.'

The cook lifted her doughy knife, turned her round
face and looked at the little girl. She had small
lively light blue eyes and the hair under her cap
was as fair and light in colour as new straw. It
was a plump face, and yet sharp. 'And what do
you mean by that, may I ask ? ' she said, eyeing
Maria.

'I mean,' said Maria stubbornly, 'I *sawn* a fly.
It was on the paint of the door of the droring-room,
and it was all by itself.'

'Whereabouts ? ' said Mrs. Poulton, trying to
think of something else to say.

'I said,' said Maria, 'on the door.'

'Yes ; but whereabouts on the door ? ' persisted
the cook.

'On the side where it's cut in and the other part
comes.'

'Oh, on the jamb,' said Mrs. Poulton.

'Jam!' said Maria. 'How could there be jam on the door?'

'Well, I'm not so sure about that, Miss Sticky-fingers,' said the cook. 'But by jamb I meant *door*-jamb, though it's spelt different—leastwise, I think so. And what was the fly doing?—nasty creatures.'

Maria looked at her. 'That's what everybody says,' she said. '*My* fly—wasn't doing anything.' This was not exactly the truth; and feeling a little uneasy about it, Maria remarked in a little voice, 'But I am going now, thank you.'

'That's right,' said the cook. 'And be sure and mind them steep stairs, my precious.'

Maria glanced at the wasps hovering over the bottle, she glanced at Mrs. Poulton, at the fire in the range, at the dish-covers on the walls—and then she went out of the door

She minded the steep kitchen stairs just as much as usual, though she was a little indignant after her talk with the cook. When she reached the top of them, she went on along the slippery hall, past the grandfather's clock, with the white moon's-face in the blue over its hands, past the table with the pink-flowering pelargonium on it, and climbed on up the wide shallow staircase, taking hold of the balusters one by one, but treading as near as possible in the middle of the soft rose-patterned stair carpet.

And when she got to the top she came to a room where she knew she would find a guest who was staying in the house. His name was Mr. Kittleson; he was a clergyman, and this Saturday morning he was writing his sermon for Sunday, and his text was

' Consider the lilies of the field. . . . They toil not
neither do they spin.'

After fumbling with the handle a little Maria
pushed the door open and looked in. And there sat
the old gentleman in a round leather chair, with his
silvery-grey beard spreading down over his chest,
his sermon-paper on the blotting book in front of
him, and a brass inkstand beyond that. His lips
were moving as he wrote. But on hearing the door
open he stayed his writing, and with stooping head
looked round over his gold spectacles at Maria.

' Well, well, my dear, this is a very pleasant
sight, and what can I do for you ? ' he said, being
one of those peculiar old gentlemen that don't mind
being interrupted even when they are writing
sermons.

' I,' said Maria, edging a little into the room, ' I
have just seen a fly ! It was standing all by itself
on the—the jamb of the door in the droring-room.'

' In the drawing-room ? Indeed ! ' said the old
gentleman, still peering over his gold spectacles.
' And a very fortunate fly it was, to be in your
company, my dear. And how very kind of you to
come and tell me.'

Maria was almost as little pleased by the old
gentleman's politeness as she had been with her talk
with the cook. ' Yes,' she said, ' but this was not a
norinary fly. It was all by itself, and I looked
at it.'

The old gentleman peeped down a little absently
at his clear sloping handwriting on the paper. ' Is
that *so* ? he said, ' but then, my dear little Maria,
no fly is really ordinary. They are remarkable

creatures if you look at them attentively. And
especially through a microscope. What does the
Book say : " fearfully and wonderfully made " ?
They have what is called a proboscis—trunks, you
know, just like elephants. And they can walk
upside down. Eh ? How about that ? '

At that moment, out of its shadowy lair a silvery
clothes'-moth came flitting across the sunlight over
his table. The old gentleman threw up his hands
at it, but it wavered, soared, and escaped out of
his clutches.

' Cook says flies are nasty creatures,' said Maria.

' Ah,' said the old clergyman, ' and I've no doubt
cook avoids them in our food. But they have their
ways, which may not please us, just as we have our
ways, which may not please somebody else. But
even a fly, my dear, enjoys its own small life and
does what it is intended to do in it. " Little busy,
thirsty fly," ' he began, but Maria, who was looking
at him as attentively as she had looked at the
insect itself (before, that is, it had actually become
a Maria-Fly), at once interrupted him. ' It's a
*beau*tiful rhyme,' she said nodding her head. ' I
know it very well, thank you. But that was all
I wanted to say. Just that I had sawn—seen it. I
don't think I could tell you anything else—so, I
mean, that it would be 'xplained to you.'

The old gentleman, pen in hand, continued to smile
at his visitor over his beard in the same bland cautious
way he always did, until she had slid round the door
out of his sight, and had firmly closed it after her.

On her way back along the corridor Maria passed
the door of the work-room ; it was ajar, and she

peeped in. Miss Salmon, in her black stuff dress, sat there beside a table on which stood a sewing-machine. At this moment she was at work with her needle. She always smelt fresh, but a little faint; though also of camphor. She had an immensely long white face—white forehead and chin—with rather protruding eyes and elbows; and she and Maria were old friends.

'And what can I do for you, Madam, this morning?' she cried in a deep voice like a man's.

'Well, I just looked in, Madam, to tell you I seen a Fly.'

'If you was to look through the eye of the smallest needle in that work-basket you would see the gates of Paradise,' said Miss Salmon, stitching away again with a click that sounded almost as loud as if a carpenter were at work in the room.

'Give it me,' said Maria.

'Ah ha!' cried Miss Salmon, 'such things need looking for.'

'Ah ha!' chirped Maria, 'and that means tidying all the basket up.'

'Nothing seek, nothing find,' cried Miss Salmon, 'as the cat said to the stickleback, which is far better than Latin, madam. And what, may I ask, was the name of Mr. Jasper Fly Esquire? If you would kindly ask the gentleman to step this way I will make him a paper house with bars to it, and we'll feed him on strawberries and cream.'

Maria's spirits seemed to sink into her shoes. 'It was not that kind of fly at all,' she said, 'and—and I don't wish to tell you the name, thank you very much.'

z

'*Good* morning,' said Miss Salmon lifting her needle and opening wide her eyes, ' and don't forget closing time's at seven.'

It was strange that Maria should feel so dismal at this turn of the conversation, considering that she and Miss Salmon were such very old friends and always had their little bit of fun together. Maria looked at her sitting bolt upright there in her high-collared black stuff dress, with her high head. ' *Good* morning,' she said politely.

' *Good* morning, madam,' said Miss Salmon.

And Maria withdrew.

Opposite the workroom there was a portrait hanging on the landing in a large gilt frame. Maria looked at the lady painted in it, in her queer clothes, with a dome of muslin draped on high over her head, and she said under her breath, though not out loud, ' 'Mm, *you* don't know I've seen a fly.' And then she ran off downstairs again and met her father at that moment issuing out of his den with the topmost joint of a fishing-rod in his hand. He had on his ugly brown suit and thick-soled brown shoes.

' Daddy,' she called at him, ' I've just been telling him I have seen a fly.'

' Oh, have you ? ' said he, ' you black-eyed young ragamuffin. And what business had you to be mousing into his room this time of morning, I should like to know ? And talking of flies, Miss Black-and-White, what would you recommend for this afternoon ? so as to make quite sure of a certain Mrs. Fat Trout I wot of ? '

' You see, Daddy,' said Maria stiffly, ' you always

turn things off like that. And it was something so
very special I wanted to tell you.'

'Now see here,' said her father, flicking with the
tip of his tapering rod-piece, 'what we'll do is this,
we will. You shall tell me all about that fly of yours
when I come into say good-night to-night. And
perhaps by then you will have seen lots of other
things. And you shall have a penny for everyone that
begins with a Q. There's plenty of flies,' he added.

'I don't think I shall *care* to see lots of other
things,' said Maria—' but I'll see.' And she walked
off, more sedately even than little old Queen Victoria,
into the garden.

Up till then it had been a morning like a blue-
framed looking-glass, but now a fleece of cloud was
spread over the immense sky. Far away in the
kitchen-garden she came across the gardener, Mr.
Pratt. With his striped cotton shirt-sleeves turned
up over his elbows, he was spraying a rose-tree on
which that day's sun even if it came out in full
splendour again would shine no more. Maria
watched him.

'What are you doing that for ? ' she said. 'Let
me ! '

'Steady, steady, my dear,' said Mr. Pratt—' you
can't manage the great thing all by yourself.' But
he put the syringe with a little drop of the liquid left
in its brass cylinder into her hands. 'Now, push ! '
he said, ' all your might.'

Maria pushed hard, till her knuckles on her fat
hands went white, and she was plum-red in the face.
But nothing came. So Mr. Pratt put his thick
brown hands over hers, clutched the tube, and they

pushed together. And an exquisite little puff of water jetted like a tiny cloud out of the nozzle.

' It came out then,' said Maria triumphantly ' I could do it if I tried really hard. What, please, are you doing it *for* ? '

' Ah,' said Mr. Pratt, ' them's secrets.'

' Ah,' said Maria imitating him, ' and I've got a secret, too.'

' What's that ? ' said the gardener.

She held up her finger at him ' I—have—just—seen—a—fly. It had wings like as you see oil on water, and a red face with straight silver eyes, and it wasn't buzzing or nothing, but it was scraping with its front legs over its wings, then rubbing them together like sticks, all round and round one another, like corkscrews. Then it took its head off and on, and then it began again—but I don't mean all that. I mean I sawn the fly—saw it, I mean.'

' Ah,' said Mr. Pratt, the perspiration glistening on his brown face, and his eyes at least two shades a paler blue than Mrs. Poulton's, as though the sun and the jealous skies had bleached most of the colour out of them. ' Ah,' he said. ' A fly, now ? And that's something to see too. But what about them pretty little Meadow Browns over there, and that Painted Lady—quiet, now, see—on that there mallow-bloom ! There's a beauty ! And look at all them yaller ragamuffins over the winter cabbage yonder. We won't get much greens Missie, if you can underconstumble, if *they* have their little way.'

Maria could perfectly well underconstumble. But she hated greens. She hated them as much as if she had eaten them on cold plates in another world. It

was odd too that nobody had the smallest notion of
what she wanted to say about the Fly. No one.
How stupid. But she looked at the Painted Lady
none the less. It was jimply perched on the pale
paper-like flower of the mallow, its ball-tipped
antennae sucking up its secret nectar for all the world
like the Queen of Hearts in her parlour with her slice
of bread and honey. And then the sunshine stole
out again into the heavens above them, and drew
itself like a pale golden veil over the shimmering
garden. The Painted Lady's wings, all ribbed and
dappled orange and black and white, trembled a
little in its gentle heat, as if with inexpressible
happiness and desire.

But though Maria admired the creature in its
flaunting beauty more than she could say, this was
not her Fly—this, at least, was no *Maria*-Fly. It
was merely a butterfly—lovely as light, lovely as a
coloured floating vapour, exquisitely stirring, its
bended legs clutching the gauzy platform beneath it
and supporting its lightly poised frail plumy body
on this swaying pedestal as if the world it knew were
solid as marble and without any change ; even
though it now appeared as gentle as a dream.

Maria was not even thinking as she watched the
butterfly, except that she was saying over to herself,
though not using any words, that she did not want
to go into the drawing-room any more just now ;
that she had no wish to see her fly again ; that she
didn't want ever to be grown-up ; that grown-ups
never could underconstumble in the very least what
you were really saying ; that if only they wouldn't
try to be smiling and patient as though the least

cold puff of breath might blow you away, you might prove you were grown-up too and much older than they—even though you had to eat greens and do what you were told and not interrupt old gentlemen writing sermons, and must wait for bed-time—*no*, she was not really thinking any of these things. But her small bosom rose and fell with a prolonged deep sigh as she once more glanced up at Mr Pratt.

He was hard at work again with his syringe, and now, because the sun was shining between herself and its watery vapour, it had formed a marvellous little rainbow in the air, almost circular, with the green in it fully as vivid as that of the myriad aphides clustering like animated beads round the stems of the rosebuds.

' I told you,' she quavered a little sorrowfully, though she was trying to speak as usual, ' I told you about something and you didn't take any notice.'

' Well, well, well,' said the gardener. But he hadn't time to finish his sentence before Maria was already stalking down the path, and in a moment had disappeared round the corner of the green-house.

And there, a moment or two afterwards, she happened to come across patient Job the gardener's boy. Job was an oaf to look at with his scrub of hair and his snub nose and silly mouth. He was little short of what the village people called a half-wit or natural. He laughed at whatever you said to him, even when you frowned double-daggers at him. But there was no gardener's boy like him ; the very roots of the flowers he handled seemed to want to net themselves about his clumsy fingers, and he was ' a fair magician ' with bees. Three little steel mole-

traps lay on the gravel beside him where he knelt,
and he was scouring flower pots with a scrubbing
brush, and as Maria appeared he looked up with a
face like a good-humoured pumpkin, and he grinned
at her with all his teeth.

' Marnin', missie,' he said.

' Good morning, Job,' said Martha. She stood
looking at him, looking at his tiny piglike eyes in
the great expanse of his good-humoured face, and
hesitated. Then she stooped a little and all but
whispered at him.

' Have you ever seen a fly ? '

' Oi, miss, seen a floi ? ' he replied, opening his
mouth. ' Oi, missie, oi've seed a floi.'

' But have you,' and Maria all but let all her
breath go—over just those first three words, ' But
have you, Job, ever seen the only teeny tiny fly
there ever was : *your* Fly ? '

Job scratched his head and looked so serious for
an instant that Maria feared he was going to burst
out crying. ' Oi, missie,' he suddenly shouted at
last with a great guffaw of laughter, ' that oi 'ave,
and avore I could catch un ee was gawn loike a
knoifejack clean down Red Lane ee wor. Oi and
ee *wor* a floi, ee wor.'

Maria burst out laughing : they laughed in
chorus ; and then she found tears were standing in
her eyes and she suddenly felt silent and mournful.
' And now,' she said, ' you had better get on with
your pots.'

She turned away, her small head filled as with a
tune ages old and as sorrowful as the sounds of
the tide on the unvisited shores of the ocean. There

was a little old earwiggy arbour not far away that
always smelt damp even after weeks of fine hot
weather—though then it smelt dry-damp.

Maria went into its shadow and stood there by
herself a moment. Why she had gone in she didn't
know. It was very still. But mustily, stuffily,
gloomily still—quite different from the sunny
coloured stillness of the drawing-room. There was
a wide droning in the air outside. Millions of minute
voices were sounding in concert like the twangling
of the strings of an enormous viol. A bird hopped
on to the roof of the arbour ; she could hear its claws
on the wood. Its impact dislodged a tiny clot of
dust. It fell into the yet finer dust at her feet. The
arbour's corners were festooned with cobwebs.

Maria gave yet another deep sigh, and then looked
up around her almost as if in hopes of somebody else
to whom she might tell her secret tale—about the
fly—about Maria-Fly. She paused—staring. And
then, as if at a signal, she hopped down suddenly
out of the arbour, almost as lightly as a thin-legged
bird herself, and was off flying over the emerald
green grass into the burning delightful sunshine
without in the least knowing why, or where to.

VISITORS

ONE of the very last things that Tom Nevis was to think about in this world was a sight he had seen when he was a child of about ten. Years and years were to pass by after that March morning; and at the last Tom was far away from home and England in the heat and glare of the tropics. Yet this one far-away memory floated up into his imagination to rest there in its peace and strangeness as serenely as a planet shining in its silver above the snows of remote hills. It had just stayed on in the quiet depths of his mind—like the small insects that may be seen imprisoned in lumps of amber, their wings still glistening ages after they were used in flitting hither thither in their world as it then was.

Most human beings have little experiences similar to Tom's. But they come more commonly to rather solitary people—people who enjoy being alone, and who have day-dreams. If they occur at other times, they are not so noticeable then because perhaps one is talking or laughing or busy, working away at what has to be done, or even reading or thinking. And then they may pass unnoticed.

But Tom had always been a funny solitary creature. Even as a child he enjoyed being alone. He would sit on a gate or a stile for an hour at a time just staring idly into a field, following with his eyes the shadows of the clouds as they swept silently over its greenness, or the wandering wind, now here, now there, stooping upon the taller weeds and grasses. It was a pleasure to him merely even to watch a cow browsing her way among the buttercups, swinging the tuft of her tail and occasionally rubbing her cinnamon-coloured shoulder with her soft nose. It seemed to Tom at such times—though he never actually put the feeling into words—almost as if the world were only in his mind ; almost as if it were the panorama of a dream.

So too Tom particularly enjoyed looking out of his window when the moon was shining. Not only in winter when there is snow on the ground, and clotting hoar-frost, but in May and summer too, the light the moon sheds in her quiet rests on the trees and the grass and the fields like a silver tissue. And she is for ever changing : now a crescent slenderly shining —a loop of silver or copper wire in the western after-glow of sunset ; and now a mere ghost of herself, lingering in the blue of morning like a lantern burning long after the party is over which it was meant to make gay.

Tom was more likely to be left alone than most boys, owing to a fall he had had when he was three. He had a nurse then, named Alice Jenkins. One morning she sat him up as usual close to the nursery table and his bowl of bread and milk ; and then she turned round an instant at the sound of something heard at the window. And he, in that instant, to see perhaps what she was looking at, had jumped up in his chair, the bar had slipped out, and he had fallen sprawling on to the floor.

The fall had injured his left arm. And try as the doctors might they had never been able to make it grow like his right arm. It was lean and shrunken and almost useless, and the fingers of the hand were drawn up a little so that it could be used only for simple easy things. He was very little good at games in consequence, and didn't see much of other boys of his own age. Alice had cried half the night after that miserable hour ; but the two of them loved each other the more dearly for it ever afterwards. Even now that she was married and kept a small greengrocer's shop in a neighbouring town, Tom went to see her whenever he could, and munched her apples and pears and talked about everything under the sun.

This accident had happened so long ago that he had almost forgotten he had ever had the full use of his left arm. He grew as much accustomed to it hanging limply to his shoulder as one may become accustomed to having a crooked nose or a squint in one's eyes. And though he realised that it kept him out of things like climbing trees or playing such games as other boys could do with ease, though it had made a kind of scare-crow of him, it was simply because of this that he was left more to himself and his own devices than most boys. And though he never confessed it to himself, and certainly not to anybody else, he immensely enjoyed being in his own company. It was not a bit—as it well might be—like being in an empty house, but rather in an enchanted one ; wherein you never knew what might not happen next, even though everything was still and quiet—the sun at the windows, the faint shadows in the corridors, the water in the green fishpond and the tangled branches in the orchard.

Tom, too, beside being for this reason rather odd in his body—small for his age, with narrow shoulders, a bony face, light grey-blue eyes and a stiff shock of light hair standing up on his high head—was also a little odd in mind. He was continually making up stories, even when there was no one to listen to them. For his black-eyebrowed elder sister very seldom had time to do so ; and the nurse he had after Alice was married had not much patience with such things. But he almost as much enjoyed telling them to himself. And when his sister Emily died he seemed to get into the habit of mooning and day-dreaming more than ever.

He had other queer little habits too. Whenever he went downstairs from his bedroom—unless he was in a violent hurry or his father had called him—he always sat down for a few moments on a narrow stair from which he looked out from a tall landing window over the garden. It seemed to him you could never tell what you *might* not see at such a moment ; though as a matter of fact he never saw anything there unusual : just the grass and the lawn and the currant-bushes and the monkey-puzzle ; perhaps a cat walking gingerly on its errand, and the usual thrushes and blackbirds, tits and robins, and the light of the sun on the red-brick wall.

Another fancy of his was, whenever he passed it,

to stoop down and peer through the keyhole of a cellar that spread out underneath the old Parsonage. He might just as well have looked up a chimney, for there was even less light to be seen through the keyhole. And nothing was stowed away in the cellar except a few old discarded pieces of furniture, some bottles of wine, empty hampers, an old broken rocking-horse and such things as that. None the less, whenever he passed that door, Tom almost invariably stooped on his knees, puckered up one eye and peered through its keyhole with the other, and smelt the fusty smell.

There was no end to his cranky comicalities. Long ago, for example, he had made a rule of always doing certain things on certain days. He cared no more for washing in those early days than most boys : but he always had a ' thorough good wash ' on Fridays; even though it was ' bath-night ' on Saturdays. He went certain walks on certain evenings, that is, evenings when it had been raining or maybe when some flower or tree was just out. And he always went to see his sister Emily's grave once a month.

She had died on the 12th of April ; and apart from her birthday, he always kept her month day— all the twelfths throughout the year. If he could, and if he had time, he would take a bunch of flowers along with him, choosing those which Emily had liked the best or those he liked the best, or both together. The Churchyard was not far away, as the crow flies, but it was yet another of his odd habits not to go there direct—as if that might be too easy— but to go round by a meadow path that was at least three-quarters of a mile further than the way by the village lane.

Except when he happened to be by himself at evenings just after the sun was set, Tom always felt more alone on these monthly journeys than at any other time. And for as long a time as he could spare he would sit on an old bench under the Churchyard yew. At first he had been exceedingly wretched and miserable on these visits. The whole Parsonage, his father and his sister and the maids— it was just as if a kind of thick cold mist had come over them all when Emily died. Everything that was familiar in the house had suddenly stood up strange and exclamatory, as if to remind them something was gone that would never come back again. And though none of the others, of course, really forgot what had happened, though he often actually noticed his father desisting from what he was just about to say simply because he could not bear the grief of mentioning Emily's name, as time went on, things began to be much again as ever.

In the early days Tom's black-haired elder sister, Esther, used to come with him to the Churchyard now and then ; but she soon had so many things to think about and to amuse herself with that there was very little time to spend with him. Besides, they agreed about nothing and spent most of the time arguing and wrangling. So for a good many months Tom had gone alone. He knew his own particular week-day walk to the Church as well as he knew his own clothes or anything else in the world. He never set out on it without wishing he could see his sister Emily again, and he never came home again to the

Parsonage without thinking to himself that it was better perhaps he could *not* bring her back. For he was somehow sure, wherever her body might be, that she herself was perfectly happy, and, as it were, always to be young. Now and then, indeed, it seemed as if some wraith of herself had actually whispered this into his ear as he sat on his bench looking out across the tombstones, and sometimes wondering how long it would be before he was dead too. But then Tom's little moperies came very near at times to being a little mad.

That was another odd thing about Tom. He enjoyed thinking and puzzling over everything that came into his head, whereas most people will not allow disagreeable thoughts to stay in their minds. They drive them out like mangey dogs or cats out of a garden, or wasps out of a sunny room. Tom thought of them, however, in the most practical way possible. He knew, for example, as much about grave-digging when he was ten as the old sexton could tell him at sixty. The thought of the bones beneath the turf did not frighten him a bit. Surely, he thought to himself, nothing could be as ugly as all that if it were just the truth. And if it was, why, then it *was*.

Not that he did not enjoy being alive in this world. He fairly ached sometimes with delight in it. He had talked to Alice about it, and to Emily too, sitting on a green bank in the sunshine or in the hayfields, or by the banks of their secret pond in the woods. He loved also to brood on what might happen to him in the future ; though he never had the faintest notion in those days that he was going to travel, that he was going to leave England when he was still a

young man, for good and all, and never come back.
He had no notion of that at all until there came a
talk one afternoon in her husband's shop with his
nurse Alice. After that he knew he had been born
to be a traveller in spite of his arm and his cranky
meagre body. And what led up to the talk was
what happened to him that March morning as he
came back from his customary visit to the churchyard.

A faint but bleak east-wind was blowing. Except
tor a light silvery ridge of cloud in the South the
sky was blue all over, and the sunlight was as bright
as if a huge crystal reflector behind it were casting
back its beams from the heavens upon the earth.
A few daffodils were out in the fields, and the
celandine with its shovel-shaped glossy leaves too ;
and the hedges were beginning to quicken, looking
from a distance as if a faint green mist hung over
them. The grass was already growing after its
winter's rest, and the birds of the countryside were
busy flying hither and thither as if time were something that melted in the sun. Instead of returning
from the Churchyard to the house by the way he had
come, Tom had turned in through a wicket gate into
a straggling wood of birch and hazel, and so came
out at the corner of a large meadow which lay over
against the Old Farm.

There had been heavy rains during the previous
week, and as Tom—absent-minded as ever—came
edging along the path of the meadow, he lifted his
eyes and was astonished to see a pool of water
in the green hollow of the meadow beneath him,
where none had lain before. Its waters were evi-

dently of the rains that had fallen in the past few days. They stretched there grey and sparkling, glassing the sky, and the budding trees which grew not far from their margin. And floating upon this new wild water he saw two strange birds. Never had he seen their like before, though he guessed they might be straying sea-birds. They were white as snow, and were disporting themselves gently in this chance pool, as if it were a haven of refuge or meeting-place which they had been seeking from the first moment they had come out of their shells.

Tom watched them, fixed motionless where he stood, afraid almost to blink lest he should disturb their happy play. But at last he took courage, and gradually, inch by inch, he approached stealthily nearer until at last he could see their very eyes shining in their heads, and the marvellous snow of their wings and their coral beaks reflected in the shallow wind-rippled pool. They appeared to be companions of all time. They preened their feathers, uttering faint cries as if of delight, as if they were telling secrets one to the other. And now and again they would desist from their preening and float there quietly together on the surface of the water, in the silvery sunshine. And still Tom continued to gaze at them with such greedy eagerness it was a marvel this alone did not scare the wild creatures away. It seemed to Tom as if he had been looking at them for ages and ages under the huge shallow bowl of the March sky. He dreaded every instant they would lift their wings and fly away. That would be as if something had gone out of his own inmost self.

He was whispering too under his breath, as if to persuade them to remain there always, and let there be no change. Indeed they might be human creatures, they floated there on the water so naturally and happily in their devotion to one another's company. And it seemed once more to Tom as if the whole world and his own small life had floated off into a dream, and that he had stood watching their movements and their beauty for as many centuries as the huge oak that towered above the Farm had stood with outflung boughs, bearing its flowers and its acorns from Spring on to Spring and from Autumn to Autumn until this very morning.

What was curious too, the two strange birds seemed at last to have no fear of his being there, even though the bright shallow basin of rain on which they rested in the meadow was not more than eleven paces wide. They eyed him indeed with a curious sharp brightness, almost as if they wished to be sharing their secret with him, one brought from the remote haunts from which they had set out overnight; as if this was the end of their journey. The drops they flung with their bills over their snowy plumage gleamed like little balls of changing silver or crystal, though not brighter than their eyes. The red of their webbed feet showed vividly beneath the grey clear water. And the faint soft cries uttered in their throats rather than with open bills, were not sweet or shrill as a nightingale or a linnet singing, but yet wonderfully gentle to listen to in its happiness.

And Tom's odd mind slipped once more into a deep day-dream as he stood there—in his buttoned-up jacket, with his cap over his short springy hair—in the light but bleak east-wind that swept out of the clouds across the meadow and the roof and chimneys of the old red-brick farm. . . . In the middle of that night he woke up : as suddenly almost as if a voice had called him. And the scene was still as sharp and fresh in his imagination as if he were looking at it again spread out in actuality in the morning light before his very eyes.

It was just like ridiculous Tom not to visit the meadow again for many days afterwards. Once or twice he actually set out in that direction, but turned off before the farmyard came into view. And when at last he did go back again, towards evening, the whole scene had changed. No longer was the wind from the East, but from the South. Lofty clouds towered up into the intense blue of the sky, like snow-topped mountains. The air was sweet with Spring. The tight dark buds had burst in the hedges into their first pale-green leaf ; thrushes were singing among the higher branches of the elms. But the pool of rainwater had sunk out of sight in its hollow, had been carried up by the wind and sun into the heavens, leaving only the greener and fresher grass behind it. The birds were flown.

One day in the following June, Tom went off to see his old nurse, Alice Hubbard. She had grown a good deal stouter after her marriage, and Tom sat with her in the cramped parlour behind the shop, looking out into the street across the bins of green peas and new potatoes, carrots and turnips, lettuces and mint, and cucumbers, the baskets of gooseberries and currants and strawberries and the first cherries. And while Alice was picking out for him a saucerfull of strawberries, he told her all about himself : what he had been doing and thinking, and about the new maid, and about the Parsonage. And she would say as she paused with finger and thumb over her basket, ' Lor, Master Tom ' ; or ' Did you ever, now, Master Tom ! ' or ' There now, Master Tom ! ' And all of a sudden the memory of the pool of water and the two strange birds flitted back into his mind and he fell silent. Alice put down before him the saucer of strawberries, with a little blue-and-white jug of cream, and she glanced a little curiously into his narrow, ugly face.

' And what might you be thinking of now ; I wonder ? ' she said.

An old woman in a black bonnet and shawl who had been peering about at the fruit from the pavement close to the window outside, at this moment came into the shop, and Alice went out to serve her with what she wanted. Tom watched the two of them ; watched the potatoes weighed and the sprig of mint thrown into the scale ; watched a huge dapple-grey cart-horse go by, dragging its cartload of bricks, with its snuff-coloured driver sitting on a sack on top. And then Alice had come back into the little parlour again, and he was telling her all about the birds and the pool.

' Lor now, that *was* queer, Master Tom,' said Alice. ' And where might you have been that morning ? '

And Tom told her he had been to the Churchyard.

' Now you know, my dear soul,' she said in a hushed voice as if somebody might be listening ; ' You know you didn't ought to go there too often.

It isn't good for you. You think too much already.
And Joe says—and you wouldn't believe how happy
I am, Master Tom, living here in this little shop,
though I never never forget the old Parsonage and
the kindness of your dear mother—but Joe he says
that one didn't ought to keep on thinking about
such things. Not keep on, he means. How would
the world go round, he says, if we was all of us up
in the clouds all day. It looks to me as if you were
more a bag of bones than ever, though p'raps you
have been growing—sprouting up a good deal.'

' But wasn't it funny about the birds ? ' said
Tom.

' Why,' said Alice, ' what was funny ? '

' Why,' said Tom, ' they weren't just ordinary
birds. I am not sure now they were even quite
live birds—real birds I mean, though they might
have come from the sea. And why didn't they fly
away when I got near ? They saw me right enough.
And why, do you think, do I keep on thinking
about them ? '

' Lor bless me,' said Alice. ' The questions he
asks ! And all them whys ! You ain't much
changed at that, Master Tom.'

' Yes, but why ? ' Tom persisted, spoon in hand,
looking up at her over his saucer of strawberries
and cream.

Alice stood on the other side of the table, resting
the knuckles of one hand upon it, and as she looked
out across the shop a vacancy came into her blue
eyes, just as if, like Tom himself, she too at times
fell into daydreams. ' Well, I suppose—I suppose,' she said at last in a low far-away voice, ' you

keep on thinking about them because you can't get them out of your head.'

' Oh that's all right,' said Tom a little impatiently ; ' but what I want to know is why they stay there ? '

' Well,' said Alice, ' some things do. I can see those birds meself. And of course they were real, Master Tom. Of course they were real. Or else '— she gave a little gentle laugh—' or else, why you and me would be just talking about ghost birds. What I mean is that it doesn't follow even if they *was* real that they didn't mean something else too. I don't mean exactly that such things do mean anything else, but only, so to speak, *seem* that they do. All depends, I suppose, in a manner of speaking, what they are to us, Master Tom. Bless me, when I stand here in the shop sometimes, looking out at the people in the street and seeing customers come in—even serving them, too—I sometimes wonder if the whole thing mayn't mean something else. How was I to know that I was ever going to get married to my Joe and keep a greengrocer's shop too, and yet, believe *me*, Master Tom, it seems just as ordinary and natural now as if I had been meant to do it from my very cradle.'

Tom looked at her curiously. ' Then what do you think the birds mean ? ' he repeated.

The soft lids with their light lashes closed down a little further over her blue eyes as Alice stood pondering over the same old question. ' Why,' she whispered almost as if she were talking in her sleep, ' if you ask me, it means that you are going to travel. That's what *I* think the birds mean. But then I couldn't say where.'

And suddenly she came back again, as it were—
came out of her momentary reverie or day-dream,
and looked sharply round at him as if he might be in
danger of something. She was frowning, as though
she were frightened. 'You know, Master Tom,' she
went on in a solemn voice, 'I can never never forgive
myself for that poor arm of yours. Why you might
by now. . . . But there! life *is* a mystery, isn't it?
I suppose in a sort of a way—though Joe would say
we oughtn't to brood on it—life itself is a kind of a
journey. That goes on too.'

'Goes on where?' said Tom.

'Ah, that we can't rightly say,' said Alice, smiling
at him. 'But I expect if them birds of yours could
find their way from over the sea, there is no particular reason why human beings should not find
theirs.'

'You mean Emily found hers?' said Tom.

Alice nodded two or three times. 'That I do,' she
said.

'Well, all I can say is,' said Tom, 'I wish they'd
come back, and the water too. They were more
—more—well, I don't know *what*, than anything I
have ever seen in the whole of my life.'

'And that's a long one too!' said Alice, smiling
at him again.

But it was not to be a very long one, after all; for
quite early in his twenties Tom had pushed on up
the gangway and into the bowels of the ship that
was to take him across the sea to that far-away
country from which he was never to come back.
And though green peas and mint and the last of the
cherries may not be quite such magical things in

the memory as the sight of two strange sea-birds disporting themselves in a pool of rainwater on a bleak silvery March morning far from their natural haunts, even they too none the less sometimes reminded Alice of that talk with Tom. Indeed she loved him dearly, for Tom was of course—and especially after his accident—a kind of foster son. And when she heard of his going abroad she remembered the birds too.

PRINTED IN GREAT BRITAIN
BY ROBERT MACLEHOSE AND CO. LTD.
THE UNIVERSITY PRESS, GLASGOW